STATE OF AFFAIRS

FIRST FAMILY SERIES, BOOK 1

MARIE FORCE

State of Affairs
First Family Series, Book 1
By: Marie Force

Published by HTJB, Inc.
Copyright 2021. HTJB, Inc.
Cover Design by Kristina Brinton
Cover photography by Regina Wamba
Models: Robert John and Ellie Dulac
Print Layout: E-book Formatting Fairies
ISBN: 978-1952793172

CHAPTER ONE

Afull minute after ending the bombshell call from the White House chief of staff, Nick Cappuano stared into the eyes of his wife, Samantha, looking to her for calm in the midst of calamity. However, he wasn't finding calm in her lovely blue eyes. Instead he saw the same panic he felt.

President David Nelson had been found dead in the White House residence.

Nick was going to be president of the United States of America.

The Secret Service was waiting to transport him and Sam to the White House so he could take the oath of office.

Five minutes ago, they'd been in bed, commiserating after eating too much at Thanksgiving dinner. And now... Now, he needed to breathe, to remain calm, to do what needed to be done for his family and his country. "Say something."

Sam licked her lips and looked up at him with eyes gone wild. "I... I don't know what to say."

"It's going to be okay. You and me... We've got this. There's nothing we can't handle."

She laughed, but it had a maniacal edge to it. "If you say so, Mr. President."

Mr. President.

She was the first to ever call him that, as it should be. She was the most important person in his life.

He held her precious face in his hands and gazed into her light-blue eyes. "Before we leave this room and step onto the biggest stage in the world, I want you to hear me when I tell you this won't change anything that matters. This—you and me and our family—will not change. I swear to you, Samantha."

She nodded and reached for him.

He took her into his arms and held on tight to the love of his life, determined to do whatever it took to reassure her even as he tried not to freak out himself. No one needed a president who was freaking out.

President.

This could not be happening. But it was. David Nelson was dead. Nick couldn't wrap his head around the last five minutes.

Still holding Sam, he said, "We need to get up, get dressed and make ourselves presentable for pictures that'll be in history books for the rest of time. But no pressure or anything."

Again, Sam's laughter had a hysterical edge. "I... We should tell people. Like Graham, Terry, Celia, my sisters... Your dad."

He shook his head. "They'll find out in the morning. For right now, we need to focus only on getting to the White House."

"We have to bring Scotty. He'd never forgive us if we didn't."

"Agreed. I'll go get him up and tell Elijah what's going on so he knows he's in charge of the Littles." Aubrey and Alden, the twins Sam and Nick had recently taken in after their parents were murdered, would be six on Saturday. Leaving them with their older brother, who was home from Princeton for the Thanksgiving holiday, was the right thing to do.

"Will we be allowed to come back for them?" Sam asked.

"Of course, or we'll have the Secret Service bring them to us. Try not to worry. We'll figure it out one step at a time."

Sam looked around at the bedroom that was their private sanctuary, their calm in the storm of their crazy lives. "We're going to have to *move.* This won't be our home anymore."

"This will *always* be our home. We can come back here anytime we want to." He pulled back to kiss her forehead and then her lips. "We have to go, Sam. Are you going to be able to do this?"

He watched as she took a deep breath and summoned the fortitude to take this formidable next step on their journey. "I'm about to prove to you that I meant it all the times I said there was nothing I wouldn't do for you."

Smiling, he said, "I love you more than anything. Don't ever forget that."

"Same."

They got out of bed, and he pulled on a T-shirt and pajama pants and grabbed the child monitor they kept in their bedroom to alert them if the twins woke up. When Nick opened the bedroom door to go wake Scotty, he found his lead agent, John Brantley Jr., waiting to speak to him.

"We're ready to transport you and Mrs. Cappuano to the White House, sir."

"We need a few minutes to pull ourselves together. I'm going to wake Scotty. He'll want to be there, and I need to tell Elijah what's happening."

"Yes, sir."

"We'll be quick." Nick went into Scotty's room and sat on the edge of the bed. "Scotty." He gave his son's shoulder a gentle shake. In the glow of the Capitals nightlight, he watched his son's eyes open.

"What's wrong?"

"President Nelson has died."

Scotty's eyes went wide as the implications hit him immediately. "*Holy crap.*"

"That's putting it mildly. The Secret Service is waiting to take Mom and me to the White House. Mom said you'd never forgive us if we didn't bring you with us."

"Hell yes, I want to be there."

"You have to hurry."

"Work clothes, I presume?"

Nick smiled and nodded at their code for the clothes Scotty wore when he accompanied Nick to official events—khaki pants, navy blazer, dress shirt and tie. Nick got up and headed for the door.

"Dad?"

He turned back to his son.

"Are you wigging out?"

"Trying not to."

"How about Mom?"

"Same."

"Are we bringing the Littles?"

"They're asleep, so we're going to have them stay here with Elijah for now. I think it would be confusing and upsetting for them until we have time to explain what's happening."

"That's a good call."

Nick smiled at his adorable son. "Glad you agree. I'm going to tell Elijah. Hurry up and get ready, okay?"

"I'm hurrying, and in case I forget to tell you later, I'm super proud of you, even if it's gonna be kinda weird at first."

Nick grinned. "Thanks, bud. That means the world to me. We'll get through it. Like I told Mom, nothing that really matters will change. As long as we're all together, we can handle whatever comes our way."

"I guess we're gonna find out if that's true. Thanks for getting me up. Mom was right—I never would've forgiven you if you hadn't."

"We had a feeling. You probably know this, but you can't say anything to anyone about this until the White House releases the news."

"I never would."

"Thanks. Be back in a few."

Nick went up to the third floor, where they'd made a bedroom for Elijah across the hall from the loft Nick had put together as a sanctuary for him and Sam to get away from it all. He knocked on Elijah's closed door.

"Come in."

Nick opened the door to find Elijah stretched out on the bed watching a movie on his laptop.

"What's up?" Elijah asked.

"I have to tell you something that you can't tell anyone. I need your word."

"You have it."

"President Nelson was found dead in the residence a short time ago. Sam, Scotty and I are headed to the White House so I can be sworn in."

"Holy. *Shit.*" Elijah sat up on the bed. "I, um... *Wow.*"

Nick handed the child monitor to Elijah. "We're going to leave the twins here with you for now. I think it would scare them if we woke them to take them with us."

"Yes, that's better. I'll talk to them when they get up, and then we can figure out what's next. But Jesus, Nick... I mean..."

"Believe me, I know. As I said to Sam and Scotty, nothing that matters will change. We're still a family. You and the twins are still our family, and we're going to stick together and get through this. I promise."

The young man nodded, but Nick saw the same wariness, fear and uncertainty they were all feeling.

"Try to get some sleep. It's going to be a crazy few days."

"Ah, yeah, sure," Elijah said, laughing. "Not seeing a lot of sleep in my future tonight."

"I don't want you to worry about anything."

"I'll try not to."

"We'll be in touch as soon as we can about what's going on."

"Okay."

Nick wasn't sure what else he could say to reassure him, so he left it at that and returned to his room, where Sam was emerging from the shower, wrapped in a towel.

"I'm hurrying."

"Thanks, love." Nick got in the shower and ran a razor over his face, being careful not to cut himself in his haste to get ready. His thoughts swirled a mile a minute, but he concentrated only on the task at hand. Shower, shave, get dressed, get in the car, go to the White House, take the oath. If he took this one minute and one step at a time, he could hold it together to do what needed to be done.

At least he hoped so.

∾

HOLY SHIT, HOLY SHIT, HOLY SHIT. THAT WAS THE ONLY THOUGHT IN Sam's head for the first ten minutes after The Call that changed their lives forever. Thankfully, she'd spent some time on her hair earlier in the day and needed only to give it a good brushing to make it presentable. After messing with it for a minute, she decided on a simple, elegant knot. Her hands trembled ever so slightly as she applied makeup and mascara. *Dear God...* Nick was going to be the *president.*

He'd only recently told the world of his decision not to run in the next election. Her relief had been overwhelming. She hadn't wanted him to be president, to be subjected to the scrutiny and stress that would come with the most important job in the world. She'd been thrilled to know he would become a private citizen again in three years, when his term as vice president ended and they got back to "normal," whatever that was anymore.

This couldn't be happening.

Except it was, and their lives were going to be turned upside down once again. She'd believed him when he'd said nothing that mattered would change. Their marriage was solid, and they were an awesome team.

But this...

She glanced in the mirror at him in the shower, seeing the tension in his shoulders that no one else would notice. But she saw it. She saw *him*, and as the dizzying array of implications settled on her, the weight of it threatened to crush her.

Yes, they'd known this was possible when Nick became vice president, but David Nelson had been a healthy man in his late sixties with decades left to live, or so they'd thought. She flattened her hands on the marble vanity and hung her head, trying to relieve the tension in her neck.

Nick had said nothing that mattered would change, but they both knew everything would.

The scrutiny, the security, the criticism, the *insanity...* Panic bubbled up inside her. What would she do? They'd make her give up her career as a homicide detective, the job that had defined her adult life. The realization filled her with a pervasive sadness that only compounded the grief she'd been living with since she lost her beloved dad just over a month ago. What she wouldn't give to talk this through with Skip Holland.

He'd tell her to toughen up and do for Nick what he'd always done for her—support her one thousand percent. Nick deserved nothing less from her and would get everything she had to give him, no matter what she had to sacrifice.

And then he was there, his hands on her shoulders, kneading the tension from her muscles. He kissed her neck and made her shiver. "Whatever you're thinking, just stop. It's you and me all the way, babe."

Sam turned in to his embrace and breathed in the fresh, clean scent of home, taking comfort in the familiar when everything had become uncertain in the span of one phone call.

"We really have to go," he said.

"I know." Sam gave herself another second to cling to life as she knew it before she reluctantly let him go, donned a robe and went across the hall to get dressed in the closet he'd had built for her. Thinking of photos that would last forever and in deference to the death of President Nelson, she chose a demure black dress and put on her diamond engagement ring and the diamond key necklace that'd been a wedding gift from Nick.

Taking a quick look in the full-length mirror on the back of the door, she decided she was presentable enough to be in photos that would be studied for generations to come. She stepped into the black Louboutins with the distinctive red soles that Nick had given her for Christmas last year, ran damp hands over her skirt to smooth the lines and tried not to think too far ahead of the next couple of hours.

She took a deep breath and released it slowly, determined to be there for him the way he always was for her. So much of their life together had been about her—her job, her family, her needs. This was about Nick, and she was determined to support him in every possible way as he took on the role that would define his life—and hers, whether she wanted that or not.

"You can do this," she told her reflection. "You can do it for him. You *will* do it for him."

A soft knock on the door sounded.

Sam opened the door to him dressed in a navy blue suit, a white dress shirt, a burgundy tie and an American flag pinned to his lapel. He looked handsome, sexy, competent and slightly petrified. The rest of the world would see the calm, cool, collected man he was under pressure. Only she would know how he really felt.

"You look beautiful," he said softly, aware of ears all around as the Secret Service hovered nearby.

"Funny, I was just thinking the same about you." Flattening her hands on his lapels, she looked up at him. "Is Scotty ready?"

He nodded.

"Are you?"

"As ready as I'll ever be."

She slid her hands down his arms and took hold of his hands, giving a gentle squeeze. "Then let's get going."

"Before we go, I just want to say... You certainly didn't sign on for this."

She went up on tiptoes to kiss him. "I signed on for *you*, come what may."

"But this..."

"This will turn out to be our greatest adventure yet." She wasn't sure she believed that herself, but she needed *him* to believe it. "I love you, and I'm right here with you. Always."

"That's all I need to know."

"Let's do this thing."

CHAPTER TWO

They met Scotty downstairs, donned their coats and followed the Secret Service agents out the door. Sam wasn't sure how Brant, Nick's lead agent, had gotten there so quickly after having been off on Thanksgiving Day. He'd probably known about Nelson's death before they had. Thinking about logistics was better than contemplating the myriad ways their lives were about to change forever. Her stomach ached the way it had years ago, when she'd been a stressed-out mess addicted to diet cola.

The limousine that usually transported Nelson was idling at the curb with a massive number of other vehicles lined up in front of and behind it. That ramped-up security presence served as further proof that everything had changed.

On the ramp that led out of their home to the sidewalk below, it occurred to her that they needed a Bible. "Nick," she said, "I should grab the Holland family Bible."

"That's a good idea."

He'd used the O'Connor family Bible to be sworn into the Senate and when he took the oath as vice president.

"Is it okay if I tell Celia what's going on?"

"Yes, but please ask her not to tell anyone until the news is announced."

"I will." Sam moved to the left, heading for her late father's home three doors down from theirs.

"Mrs. Cappuano," Brant said. "Where're you going?"

"To get our family Bible."

Brant nodded to one of the other agents, indicating that she should follow Sam.

Sam wanted to remind him that she wasn't officially under their protection, but she'd be fighting that battle in the days to come. She went up the ramp to Celia's front door and knocked. A few seconds later, the outside light came on as locks were disengaged.

Celia, who was wearing a robe, seemed surprised to see Sam there. "Come in." She opened the storm door. "What're you doing out so late? And why are you all made up?"

"I need to tell you something that you can't tell anyone else."

"All right..."

"President Nelson passed away."

Celia gasped. "What? When?"

"He was found dead a short time ago."

Her eyes went wide as the implications seemed to hit her all at once. "So that means... Dear God, Sam."

"Believe me, I know. I was hoping I could borrow the Holland family Bible."

"Of course. Do you know where it is?"

"The last time I saw it, it was on the bookshelf in Dad's room. Do you mind if I run up and see if I can find it?"

"My home is your home. You know that."

Sam kissed Celia on the cheek. "Thank you."

She ran up the stairs to the room that had been her dad's before he was shot on the job four years ago and left a quadriplegic. The last time she'd been in there, shortly after his death in October, she and her partner, Detective Freddie Cruz, had been looking for the messenger bag Skip had carried on the job. She hadn't been in there again since, and when she crossed the threshold and encountered the faint scent of the Polo cologne Skip used to wear, a million and one memories hit her in a tsunami of emotions.

Oh, how she missed him.

She found the Bible on the small bookshelf that also held numerous volumes about investigative techniques as well as fictional thrillers, held it to her chest and gave herself a second to wallow in the presence of Skip Holland in this place that had been his private sanctuary.

"Dad, if you can hear me, things are about to get crazy for me and Nick and the kids. Keep an eye on us, will you? Do whatever you can to keep him safe and give me a clue of how I'm supposed to deal with this. I'll take whatever you've got. I miss you every minute of every day, but never more so than right now."

Knowing Nick was waiting for her and time was of the essence, she left the room and went downstairs.

"I'm glad you found it," Celia said. "Please let me know what I can do for you, Nick or the kids. Anything you need, I'm right here."

Sam put down the Bible and hugged her. "I'm so scared." She could count on one hand the number of times she'd said those words out loud in her adult life. Sam wasn't known for being scared, but this...

"I'm sure you are," Celia said. "But if anyone can pull this off, you can. I have complete faith in you."

"Thank you. I needed that. I'll call you later."

"I'll be waiting to hear from you. I'll pray for you and Nick. Our country is lucky to have you both."

She retrieved the Bible. "Keep telling me that, okay?"

"Anytime you need to hear it."

"Love you."

"Love you too."

Sam went outside and down the ramp to the sidewalk, where the Secret Service agent waited for her. She hurried to the waiting limousine and got in the back seat next to Nick. Scotty sat across from them, his brows furrowed with the same anxiety she was feeling.

Nick reached for her hand. "I was just telling Scotty that the limo used to transport the president is known as The Beast."

"Why do they call it that?" Scotty asked.

"Because it's heavily armored and fortified against every form of threat, even a bomb."

"*Whoa.*" Scotty looked outside the window. "Is the motorcade way bigger than it was before?"

"Yep. The president gets a lot more security than anyone else."

"Does the Secret Service call it The Beast too?"

Nick shook his head. "They use the name Stagecoach for the president's car."

"Ah, okay."

"This car has a lot of the same survival features I had put into Mom's car when I had it tricked out for safety," Nick said. "I had it done at the same facility that produced this car. Like with hers, we could live for days inside this car if we ever had to."

"Let's hope we never have to." Sam couldn't bear to think of him being in that kind of danger. "You really should call your dad. He shouldn't hear this on the news."

"I was thinking that too." Nick retrieved his phone and placed the call to his dad, Leo, putting it on speaker so Sam and Scotty could hear.

"Hey," Leo said. "Didn't I just see you?"

"You did. I'm in the car with Sam and Scotty, and we have some news to share, but you have to keep it confidential."

"Okay... Is everything all right?"

"President Nelson passed away earlier tonight. We're on the way to the White House so I can be sworn in as president."

"Oh my *God,* Nicky. *Wow.* How do you feel?"

"Uh, can I get back to you on that?"

Leo laughed.

"I didn't want you to hear it on TV."

"Thank you for the call, and... I don't even know what to say, son."

"Right there with you. We're a little speechless ourselves."

"Do you know what happened to Nelson?"

"Not yet."

"If there's anything we can do, anything at all, just call."

"We will. Thanks, Dad."

"I'm so proud, Nicky. So very proud."

"Thank you. We'll be in touch when we can."

"Take care, son. You too, Sam and Scotty. We love you guys."

"Thanks, Leo," Sam said. "We love you too."

Nick ended the call and put his phone back in his pocket. On the short ride to Pennsylvania Avenue, he held on tight to Sam's hand.

The feel of his hand wrapped around hers calmed her as parts and pieces of his words from earlier echoed through her mind. *Nothing will change. The most important thing is us and our family. We can do anything if we do it together.*

One question burned at the tip of her tongue—*What about my job?*—but she knew this wasn't the time to ask. A minute at a time. That's how they had to approach this life-changing challenge, and when they got a minute to breathe, she'd address the issue with Nick. To her knowledge, no first lady in history had ever worked outside the White House while her husband was the president.

Her case was somewhat unique, however, as most first families relocated from outside the DC area. Sam's job was right in Washington, so no relocation was needed. For that reason, she held out hope that they could work something out to allow her to continue to do the job she loved. Nick had enough on his mind right now, and she wasn't about to add to his worries, but she had no doubt that the topic of her job would be an issue sooner rather than later.

Her phone rang with a call from Dani Carlucci, one of her third-shift detectives, reminding her that while her life was changing by the second, no one at work knew that. Sam showed Nick the caller ID on her phone. "You mind if I take this?"

"Of course. Go ahead."

"Hey. What's up?"

"Sorry to bother you on Thanksgiving, Lieutenant, but I thought you'd want to know that Gigi's in the hospital." Carlucci had recently told Sam she was concerned that her partner, Detective Giselle "Gigi" Dominguez, was in an unsafe relationship.

"What happened?"

"An altercation with the boyfriend."

"Oh God. Is she okay?"

"He tuned her up pretty good. The biggest concern at the moment is a concussion and possible injury to her spleen."

Sam closed her eyes and took a deep breath. "Is he in custody?"

"Not yet. We're looking for him." Carlucci sounded stressed and pissed. "I should've gotten involved."

"You tried, Dani. She told you she didn't want it."

"Still... I should've done it anyway. Sorry again for bothering you. I thought you'd want to know."

"I definitely want to know. Which hospital is she in?"

"GW."

"Listen, I'd come if I could, but I'm in the middle of something, and I can't get there right now." She glanced at Nick as his lips curved into a small smile at her massive understatement. "Please keep me posted, okay?"

"I will. Thanks, LT."

Long after the line went dead, Sam stared at the phone in her hand, torn between competing needs. At any other time, she'd already be on her way to GW to see what she could do to help her injured detective and to keep Gigi's partner from doing something stupid. But that wasn't possible right now.

"What's going on?" Nick asked.

"Gigi Dominguez's boyfriend beat her up. She's got a concussion and something with her spleen." Sam knew Nick would understand that she'd want to be with her officers at a time like this. So she acted quickly to keep him from thinking about anything other than the massive thing he was about to do. She flipped open her phone and called Gonzo.

The phone rang four times before he picked up. "Hey," he said. "What's up?"

Sam cringed over what she was about to ask of her sergeant on his wedding night, but he was second in command to Sam, and she wanted Dani to focus on her friend and partner rather than the effort to locate Gigi's boyfriend. Sam was also concerned about what Dani would do if she got her hands on the guy. "I need a huge favor."

"Okay..."

"Dominguez has been having some trouble with her boyfriend, and it exploded into something physical tonight. She's at GW with a concussion and other injuries. I can't go there for reasons you'll hear about very soon."

"Seriously, Sam?"

"Dead seriously. Carlucci is about to lose her shit because she knew something was brewing and didn't intervene. I'm worried about them both. I'd never ask this of you, especially tonight, if it wasn't urgent."

"I know," he said, sighing. "I'll get there as soon as I can."

"Thanks, Gonzo."

"You owe me big."

"Huge, and this won't ever be forgotten."

"Yeah, yeah."

"Keep me posted."

"Will do."

She closed the phone again, satisfied that she'd done what she could under the circumstances. Hauling Gonzo out of bed on his wedding night was a big ask, but he was the one she needed to handle this since she couldn't be there.

"I'm sorry you're not able to be with them right now," Nick said, sounding pained.

"It's fine. I'm where I need to be."

"Still..."

"It's okay." If she couldn't be there, Gonzo was the next best thing. He'd keep a lid on Carlucci and make sure others within the department were doing everything they could to apprehend the guy who'd hurt Dominguez.

This is how it'll be now, Sam thought, gazing out the window as the limo flew down deserted streets that would be packed with cars in just a few hours. *Nonstop competing demands.*

In a matter of minutes, they were pulling up to one of the White House entrances, where they were greeted by Nelson's chief of staff, Tom Hanigan, and Derek Kavanaugh, Nick's close friend and Nelson's deputy chief of staff.

What would happen to Derek and the rest of Nelson's staff now that he was gone? She remembered Nick saying after Senator John O'Connor died that the fortunes of political staffers rose and fell with their bosses. When John had been murdered, Nick had lost his best friend *and* his job as John's chief of staff.

Hanigan shook hands with Nick. "Thank you for coming."

"I'm very sorry for your loss."

Hanigan and Nelson had been old friends from South Dakota.

"Thank you. It's a shock, to say the least. I saw him two hours before the butler found him."

"Do you know what happened?" Nick asked.

Hanigan shook his head. "It wasn't immediately obvious to the medical staff, but there was no sign of foul play. They think whatever it was happened quickly."

"I'd ask how you're doing, but I can probably guess," Derek said to Sam as they followed Hanigan and Nick inside. Scotty brought up the rear as they marched into the White House so Nick could be sworn in as president.

Surreal.

Sam glanced at their close friend. "One minute, I was complaining about being too full from Thanksgiving, and the next..."

"I was playing a game with Maeve while my parents watched a movie when Tom called. I came right over when I heard what happened."

"Thanks for coming. It means a lot to us to have a friend here."

"It's so shocking. I saw Nelson yesterday."

"You never know what's coming."

"No, you don't," he said with a sigh, probably thinking of his late wife, Victoria, who'd been murdered almost two years ago.

Sam held out a hand to Scotty to bring him along with them as they were led deeper into the executive mansion that would be their home. It would probably be weeks before Sam wrapped her head around the events of this evening. How long, she wondered, would it take for the shock to subside and reality to set in?

She was due back to work in three days. Would they let her go? The possibility that they wouldn't was unthinkable.

One step at a time, she reminded herself. *One step at a time.*

They were taken to the East Room and offered refreshments.

"Nothing for me, thanks," Nick said, glancing to Sam and Scotty.

"Could I please have a Coke?" Scotty asked the tuxedo-clad butler.

"Absolutely."

"I'm Scotty Cappuano." He extended a hand to the older Black man. "It's nice to meet you."

Clearly delighted by the boy's manners, the man said, "I'm LeRoy Chastain, one of the White House butlers, and it's a pleasure to meet you too, young man."

"This is my mom, Sam."

LeRoy shook hands with her. "Pleasure to meet you, ma'am."

Sam wanted to tell him that he didn't have to call her ma'am, but she knew that would be pointless. "You as well, LeRoy."

"May I get you anything, ma'am?"

"I'm good, but thank you."

LeRoy nodded and went to get the drink for Scotty.

"Way to finagle another Coke," Sam said. "They'll be told to limit you to one per day."

"There has to be some benefit to being the first son. I mean, if a man has to live his life surrounded by Secret Service, he ought to be able to have a Coke at the end of a long day."

Derek choked back a laugh that he tried to cover with a cough.

"He's going to be on the Supreme Court someday," Sam said.

"If I can pass eighth-grade algebra, that is," Scotty said.

"We're waiting for Mrs. Nelson," Hanigan said. "She's en route from Pierre." The Nelsons had been living apart since Nelson's affair with a campaign staffer became public. "We thought it would be important for the optics to have her here when you take the oath. She's two hours out."

So they'd have to wait. *Great...* Sam was impatient at the best of times.

LeRoy returned with a tall, icy cola for Scotty as well as a pitcher of ice water with glasses and a tray of cheese, crackers, grapes and cookies.

Living at the White House might have a few perks after all.

"Thank you, LeRoy," Sam said.

"You're most welcome, ma'am. If there's anything at all we can do for you, please let us know. I'll be close by."

"That's very kind of you."

"We're here to serve you and your family."

They would have a *household staff*. Sam had no idea what to think about that. The very idea of it made her exquisitely uncomfortable as someone who'd grown up with a blue-collar work ethic and parents who'd made their daughters do chores and learn to take care of themselves.

Hanigan asked for a word with Derek, which gave Sam, Nick and Scotty a second to themselves.

Nick put his arm around her and kissed her temple. "How're you doing?"

"Just dandy. You?"

"Even dandier."

Scotty laughed. "You guys are so weird, even in the White House." He helped himself to another cheese and cracker as well as a handful of grapes. "It's pretty cool that we can get snacks and stuff anytime we want them."

"You're going to get your own snacks," Nick said, "and not become spoiled by the White House staff."

"Why do parents have to ruin everything fun?"

"That's our job," Sam said.

"What does this mean for our dog project?" Scotty asked. "My birthday and Christmas are coming up, and either would be the perfect opportunity to gift me with a dog. I checked Google on the way over here, and did you know that most presidents and their families have at *least* one dog? Many of them have two. We should try to keep up with tradition by getting two dogs. History will be watching."

"I can't with this kid," Sam said to Nick. "You're the one who found him and brought him home. Deal with him, will you?"

Nick and Scotty laughed.

"I know it's not the time or the place," Scotty said. "So don't mind me."

"It's still under advisement," Nick said. "We've got a few things to figure out first, and then we'll see what we can do, okay?"

"Okay." Scotty held up his hands. "Not trying to make it about me or anything."

"We appreciate the comic relief," Nick said.

Hanigan returned a few minutes later. "Mr. Vice President, if I might have a word."

"Duty calls," Nick said. "I'll be back. Don't go running for the exits when I'm not looking."

"We'll be here," Sam said.

"Counting on that." Nick left them with a smile as he went off with Hanigan to see to the fate of the free world.

"He's losing it, isn't he?" Scotty asked.

"He's always calm and cool under pressure, but he has to be having a meltdown on the inside. Anyone would be."

"Is it going to be a thing that he just told the world he doesn't want the job?"

"I suppose it probably will be." Sam was already exhausted from battles they hadn't even fought yet. "But if anyone can navigate something like this, Dad can. He's been working in this game his entire adult life. He knows what strings to pull and how to get things done."

"That's true. He'll figure out a way to spin it as a positive thing, even if he just said he didn't want it." Scotty gave her a wary look. "Are you losing it and pretending not to be?"

"What? Me, lose it? Nah."

"Right... What about your job?"

Leave it to him to home right in on her biggest concern, other than the loss of privacy, the scrutiny, the security... "I don't know, buddy. I just don't know."

"But you're going to fight to keep it, right?"

She looked at him, noting the wary expression on his sweet face. "Hell yes."

CHAPTER THREE

Hanigan escorted Nick to the West Wing and into the chief of staff's office, where Nelson's national security advisor Teresa Howard waited for them.

She stood to shake hands with Nick. "Mr. Vice President, you were briefed yesterday about the ongoing situation in Iran?"

"I was."

"Earlier today, I updated President Nelson on the latest developments." Teresa provided a detailed analysis of message traffic intercepted by U.S. intelligence agencies. "We believe they're planning to test a nuclear warhead in the next seven to ten days. President Nelson authorized Secretary of State Ruskin to leave tomorrow with orders to defuse the situation. We need to know if you wish to continue with that plan."

It's up to me, Nick thought, whether the U.S. secretary of State traveled to Iran on a mission to calm a potentially dangerous situation for the U.S. and the rest of the world. "What specifically did President Nelson instruct the secretary to do?"

Teresa went through the list of concerns and demands that the secretary would take with him.

"What about sanctions?" Nick asked.

"They're on the table if diplomacy fails," Teresa said.

Nick nodded. "Tell him to go ahead."

Hanigan picked up the phone to pass along Nick's order.

"If there's anything I can do to assist in the transition, I'm at your service, sir," Teresa said.

"Thank you, Teresa."

She shook his hand before she left the room.

It would also be up to him whether to retain Nelson's staff, cabinet and advisers or to bring in his own people. He'd give them the opportunity to resign if they wished to, and go forward from there. Nelson's team would be loyal to the late president, not him. He didn't want anyone working for him who didn't want to be there, or who'd be unable to transfer their loyalties to him.

When Hanigan hung up the phone, he said, "All set. Ruskin will leave as scheduled in the morning."

"I'd like to call Terry to notify him of what's happened." Nick referred to his chief of staff, Terry O'Connor. "Is there any reason why I shouldn't do that?"

"Not that I can think of, but of course please ask him to keep it under wraps until we've prepared the official statement for the media. Our primary goal is to get Mrs. Nelson here and swear you in. After that, we'll release the video of you taking the oath along with information about President Nelson's death. I don't have to tell you how important it is that this story gets released on our timeline and not someone else's. Thankfully, the press corps presence is light tonight with it being a holiday."

Nick certainly understood the importance of optics at a time like this. "I'd still like to call Terry and my communications director, Trevor Donnelly."

"Mr. Vice President, you're the boss. You can call anyone you want as long as you trust them to be discreet."

"I'd trust them both with my life."

"Please feel free to use my office."

"I'll go to my own, but thank you." Nick left Hanigan's office and encountered Brant outside, waiting for him as always. "Sorry to interrupt your holiday, Brant."

"No such thing as holidays in my line of work, sir."

Nick had grown to like the earnest young man charged with leading his detail and considered him a friend. "What a night."

"Indeed, sir."

They walked to the vice president's office together. He didn't feel right using the Oval Office until he'd taken the oath and the staff had the chance to remove President Nelson's personal effects.

"I'll be here for a few minutes before I rejoin Sam and Scotty in the East Room."

"Yes, sir."

Nick went into his office and closed the door. The first thing he did was reach for his cell phone to text Sam. *Be back in a few.*

We're fine, she replied. *Take your time.*

She was so calm. So unnaturally calm that it had to be shock. Her mind was probably racing the same way his was with details, scenarios and concerns. So many concerns.

He picked up the extension on his desk and put through the call to Terry, who answered on the second ring.

"Mr. Vice President." No matter how many times Nick told him to call him by his first name, Terry rarely did. "Hope you had a nice Thanksgiving."

"We did, until about an hour ago when Hanigan called to tell me President Nelson had passed away."

"*What?*"

Nick could almost hear Terry sitting up straighter and see the shock in his expression. "You heard that right."

"What happened?"

"No one knows yet, but Hanigan said there was no immediate sign of foul play. I assume there'll be an autopsy that'll hopefully provide some answers. Sam, Scotty and I are at the White House awaiting Mrs. Nelson's arrival from South Dakota before I take the oath."

"I'll be right there."

"Had a feeling you might say that. Needless to say—"

"I won't say a word, sir. To anyone."

"Thank you. Will you ask Trevor to come too?"

"I'll take care of that. Mr. Vice President... Nick..."

"I know. I'll see you soon?"

"On my way."

Nick was relieved to know his own people were coming to help guide him through these next few hours. With that detail taken care of, he was eager to get back to Sam and Scotty. He was on his way to the office door when a thought occurred to him that had him returning to his desk to place another call, this one to Sam's chief of staff, Lilia Van Nostrand. Since he didn't have her number, he asked the White House switchboard to put through the call for him.

"Mr. Vice President," Lilia said when she took the call. "Is everything all right?"

"I'm sorry to disturb you on a holiday, Lilia."

"It's no problem at all, sir."

"I'm also sorry to have to tell you that President Nelson died this evening."

"Oh my God. What happened?"

"We don't know yet. Mrs. Nelson is on her way from South Dakota, and when she gets here, I'll take the oath. I thought it might be helpful to Sam to have you here, if that's at all possible."

"I'll be there in thirty minutes."

"Thank you so much."

"Thank you for calling me, sir."

"If my friend is with you, please ask him to join you." Lilia was dating Nick's close friend Dr. Harry Flynn.

"I'll do that."

"I'll see you when you get here."

Nick felt a thousand times better knowing Sam's trusted aide would be there to see her through this challenging transition. Making sure she was cared for would be one of his top priorities over the coming days and weeks. She'd already had her world rocked recently when she lost her dad. Added to that, this new development might be enough to take her right over the edge.

She was on his mind as he left the office and went to rejoin her, determined to guide their family through these tumultuous days the best he could. They'd take their lead from him, and he would show them nothing but calm, cool collectedness, even as he quaked on the inside.

~

Mrs. Nelson arrived shortly after midnight in a Marine helicopter that landed on the South Lawn after having conveyed her from Joint Base Andrews in Maryland. Her daughters,

Amanda, Camille and Collette, accompanied her, all of them wearing expressions of shock and sorrow.

Sam and Nick were waiting for them as they came inside.

Nick went to Mrs. Nelson. "Please accept our heartfelt condolences."

Sam and Nick both hugged her.

Sam partook in the proceedings with a surreal feeling and sympathy for the late president's family. Derek had told her that the image of the late president's wife standing next to the new president would provide assurances to the country and the world that a smooth transition of power had occurred.

"Thank you," Gloria said, dabbing at her eyes with a tissue Collette handed her.

"We're sorry for the loss of your father," Nick said to her daughters.

"Do they know what happened?" Camille asked.

"I haven't heard anything yet," Nick said, "but due to national security concerns, there'll be an autopsy."

"Yes, we need to know," Gloria said. "The country needs to know."

"We're taking care of everything, ma'am," Hanigan said.

"Oh, Tom." Gloria hugged their old friend. "You must be heartbroken too."

"We all are, ma'am."

They were escorted by Hanigan, Derek and other staffers Sam didn't recognize back to the East Room, where Chief Justice Byron Riley waited for them. Also in the room were Terry O'Connor, Lilia Van Nostrand and her partner, Dr. Harry Flynn.

Sam was surprised to see her friend and aide and went to hug Lilia and Harry. "Thank you for being here."

"Your husband thought it might help," Lilia said.

"He's the best, and so are you."

"Everything will be okay."

Sam released the other woman, who had been such an asset to her as second lady. "Promise?"

"I promise."

"You got this, kid." Harry gave Sam a warm smile that

displayed his adorable dimples. "I know this isn't what you'd had planned, but you're going to be great. I know it."

Sam took a deep breath and let it out slowly, giving them a bug-eyed look that made them smile. They might've laughed if Mrs. Nelson and her daughters hadn't been there. It wouldn't do to show any sort of frivolity in the face of their tragic loss.

Nick held out a hand to her. "Samantha?"

For a second, she was frozen, unable to move or think or breathe out of sheer panic, the likes of which she hadn't felt in quite some time. But then his earnest hazel-eyed gaze collided with hers, calming and centering her the way no one else could. She went to him and took his hand.

The White House photographer arranged them the way he wanted them with Riley in the center, Sam holding the Bible for Nick with Scotty at her side. Gloria Nelson and her daughters were to their right. A camera crew recorded the event on behalf of the White House press corps. The footage of the swearing-in would be released along with the news of Nelson's death, all of it carefully choreographed.

"If you'd raise your right hand and repeat after me," Riley said. "I, Nicholas Domenic Cappuano, do solemnly swear that I will faithfully execute the Office of President of the United States and will, to the best of my ability, preserve, protect and defend the Constitution of the United States. So help me God."

After Nick had repeated the oath, Riley shook his hand and then Sam's and Scotty's. "Congratulations, Mr. President, Mrs. Cappuano, young Mr. Cappuano."

"Thank you for being here, Justice Riley," Nick said.

"My prayers and best wishes are with you and your family as you rise to this occasion, Mr. President," Riley said.

"Thank you so much."

After Riley left, Hanigan and Terry approached them.

"Is it okay to release the news, sir?" Hanigan asked.

Nick had agreed to the wording of the release before the swearing-in, but this would tell the rest of the world that the United States of America had a new president. "Yes, please go ahead." The release would mention that he'd be addressing the nation at eight p.m. Eastern Time. It would also report that he'd already been briefed on several pressing issues and had been given the preliminary information he needed as the new keeper of the nation's nuclear security codes.

"I'd like to get Sam and Scotty home to bed if there're no objections."

"We have one additional piece of business that can't wait until the morning," Hanigan said.

"We need about fifteen minutes. Would you like to send your family home, or have them wait?"

"We'll wait for you," Sam said to Nick. "Take your time."

"We'll get him right back to you," Hanigan said.

~

HANIGAN LED NICK AND TERRY TO THE WEST WING AND THE OVAL Office. A man in a military uniform followed them into the office carrying a large black bag that resembled an oversized briefcase.

The "nuclear football" was actually a metal briefcase inside a black leather "jacket" that served as a mobile command center to use in times of crisis when the president was away from regular communication centers, such as the White House Situation Room. In addition to nuclear-activation codes, the bag also contained the Black Book outlining options available to the president should retaliation be necessary, another book detailing classified site locations and a binder with Emergency Broadcast System information and procedures.

Nick had traveled with Nelson enough times to know the drill. The football would always be close at hand going forward. He hoped and prayed he'd never have to use it.

"Mr. President, I'm Lieutenant Commander Juan Rodriguez with the United States Navy. It's my honor to serve a rotation as one of the military aides in charge of overseeing your emergency satchel."

Nick, who was now the commander in chief, returned the other man's salute. "Thank you, Commander."

The phone call from Hanigan informing him of President Nelson's death had been surreal. Taking the oath of office had been even more so. But this—realizing he was commander in chief of the United States armed forces—made his change in status as real as it got.

After briefing him on what he needed to know about the nuclear codes, Hanigan, Derek and Lieutenant Commander Rodriguez accompanied him back to the East Room, where Sam and Scotty waited for him.

"We'll pick it up in the morning with next steps." Hanigan shook Nick's hand. "The usual protocol would be to put up you and your family at Blair House, but since you live locally and have established Secret Service protection there, the Secret Service has determined that you can remain in your own home until after the funeral. Mrs. Nelson will need some time to oversee the packing of their things."

"Of course," Nick said. "We want to be respectful of whatever she needs."

Nick felt a huge sense of relief at knowing they'd be able to stay at their house, at least for a few more days.

"I'd like to meet with the cabinet tomorrow if you can make that happen," Nick said to Tom and Terry.

"Yes, sir," Tom said.

"Let's bring Secretary of State Ruskin in by videoconference."

"I'll see to that."

"And please keep Terry in the loop on anything we need to know as we make the transition."

"Will do, Mr. President," Hanigan said. "We'll see you in the morning?"

"I'll be here."

Hanigan shook Nick's hand. "Excellent."

When the other man began to walk away, Nick said, "Tom."

He turned back, gray eyebrow raised. "Yes, sir?"

"I just wanted to say... I've been where you are right now. The chief of staff to a high-ranking official who died in office. Like you with President Nelson, John O'Connor was also my longtime friend. If there's anything I can do for you, please let me know."

Hanigan seemed momentarily stunned by Nick's kindness. In a cutthroat town like Washington, kindness was often in rare supply. "Thank you, sir. I appreciate that. I'll see you tomorrow."

Before they left with the Secret Service, Nick and Sam went to the Red Room to say good night to Gloria and her daughters.

"Please let us know how we can help with the funeral and anything else you might need," Nick said to her.

"Thank you, Mr. President."

"Call me Nick. Please."

Gloria's chin wobbled as she nodded. "Nick. And Sam, I'd be happy to show you around the residence and answer any questions you may have. Let's get that on the schedule in the next few days."

"That's very kind of you," Sam said. "Thank you."

"I was happy in this house for a long time," Gloria said wistfully. "I hope you will be too."

"We'll give it all we've got," Nick said.

"Don't give it everything," Gloria said. "We made that mistake and paid the price." She looked up at them with shattered eyes. "Don't let that happen to you too."

"Come on, Mom." Collette put her arm around her mother. "Let's get you up to bed."

"We'll see you tomorrow," Nick said. "If there's anything at all you and your family need, please don't hesitate to ask."

"Thank you so much, Nick," Gloria said.

Nick gestured for Scotty to come with them as he signaled to Brant that they were ready to go. They were escorted to the limo with the usual efficiency. Again, Nick sat next to Sam, while Scotty sat facing them.

"And with that, my dad became the most powerful man on earth," Scotty said, beaming. "So freaking *awesome.*"

"Glad you think so," Nick said dryly. "Let's hope you're still saying that when you're in high school being trailed by agents."

"They don't bother me. I barely notice them anymore."

"Until the first time you want to kiss a girl, and you've got agents watching," Sam said.

Scotty wrinkled his nose. "I'm not the one who does all the kissing around here."

"*Yet,*" Sam said. "Just you wait."

"Thanks for being there with me tonight, you guys," Nick said.

"Duh, where else would we be when you were being sworn in as the freaking *president*?" Scotty said.

"That's two freakings in two minutes," Sam said. "The swear jar will be expecting your contributions."

"That doesn't even count as a swear. If it did, you'd be broke."

"So that actually happened," Nick said on a long sigh as the rush of adrenaline seemed to leave him all at once.

Sam smiled and placed her hand on his leg. "How lucky am I to be sleeping with the president?"

"Gross," Scotty said.

"Nothing gross about it, my friend," Nick said.

Scotty put his hands over his ears and closed his eyes. "Get it all out of your system while the child isn't looking."

Nick took advantage of the opportunity to kiss his gorgeous wife. "Thanks for holding it together in there."

"Did I hold it together? Didn't feel that way to me."

"You did great."

"It was super sexy watching you give Hanigan orders," she said with a dramatic little shiver that made him laugh.

"I know we have a lot to talk about…"

"We'll do that tomorrow. Right now, you should just breathe."

Scotty, who'd become bored with hiding from the kissing, was looking at his phone. "You want to know what people are saying?"

"*No,*" Sam and Nick said together.

"I want him to sleep tonight," Sam said. "Let's worry about that in the morning too."

"Good plan," Nick said.

His insomnia was a bitch at the best of times. Nick wondered if he'd sleep at all over the next three years. *Ugh, three years… Don't think about it, or you'll never sleep again.*

They pulled up to their house on Ninth Street a few minutes later and were escorted up the ramp and inside. "The detail seems to have expanded," Nick said to Brant.

"Tripled, sir."

"Are you able to go home at some point?"

"Shortly, sir. I'll be back in the morning, and the director will want to meet with you in the next few days. They'll want to assign more senior agents to your details."

"Wait, what? So you won't be my lead agent anymore?"

"Probably not, sir."

"Yeah, that's not happening. I'll take care of it."

Brant cracked a rare smile. "If you say so, sir."

"I say so. I'll see you in the morning. Go home. Get some sleep."

"Yes, sir."

"So hot and commanding," Sam whispered, loving the way his face flushed with embarrassment.

"Hush and get your butt in bed. I'll be right there."

"Yes, sir, Mr. President."

His low growl had her laughing all the way up the stairs.

CHAPTER FOUR

After pouring himself a glass of bourbon, Nick went upstairs and saw that Scotty's door was open. When he stopped in the doorway, he found his son shirtless in the middle of the room, wearing a pair of Washington Federals pajama pants. For the first time, Nick noticed that Scotty's chest was filling out and taking on the contours of a young man. That was happening far too quickly. "You all set, bud?"

"I will be when I can find a T-shirt. I forgot to fold the laundry that Shelby left for me to do, so she took it back and hid it."

Nick made a mental note to compliment Shelby on the passive-aggressive parenting. "That's what you get for not doing what you're told."

"I know. I guess I'll have to freeze my balls off as a result."

"Your mother would tell you not to talk that way."

"I'm not saying it in front of her."

"I'll take mercy on you this one time and let you borrow one of my shirts. But next time Shelby tells you to fold your clothes and put them away, get it done, okay?"

"Yes, sir, Mr. President."

"Cut that bullshit right now."

"Swear jar!"

"You drive me to it. Be right back." Nick was endlessly amused by the smart, sassy boy he'd met two years ago at a state home for kids in Richmond. Bringing Scott Dunlap Cappuano into his and Sam's life was one of the best things he'd ever done. He found one of his favorite Harvard T-shirts and took it to Scotty. "This shirt is a precious relic, and I want it back—washed, dried and folded. You got me?"

"I got you. Thanks." Scotty put on the shirt, which was huge on him. "There's no way I'd ever get into Harvard, so stealing this shirt would make me look like a poser."

"Don't say that. You can still get into Harvard if you want it badly enough. When you walk into high school next fall, you start with a clean slate. The only thing that'll matter to Harvard or any other college is what you do during those four years. If you work really hard, anything is possible."

"Huh, well, it's good to know that eighth-grade algebra won't be held against me."

"Nope, but ninth-grade algebra will be."

"You had to go and kill my buzz. But," he said, visibly brightening, "don't schools like Harvard love to have presidents' kids go there because they get all the publicity? They'll probably let me in no matter how I do in ninth-grade algebra."

Nick rolled his eyes. "I've only been president for an hour, and you're already coattailing me."

"What does that mean? Coattailing?"

"When you grab hold of my coattails," Nick said, gesturing to the back of his suit coat, "and get ahead based on what I do."

"There has to be something in this for me," Scotty said with an impish grin. "If I gotta kiss girls in front of Secret Service agents, the least you can do is get me into Harvard."

Nick cracked up and then gave him a gentle bop on the head. "Go to bed and shut the light off. It's after midnight."

"Night, Dad. I mean, Mr. President. Sir."

"Shut it." He left Scotty laughing and nodded to Debra, Scotty's lead agent, who was positioned in the hallway.

"Congratulations, Mr. President."

"Thank you, Debra. I think…"

As she laughed, he went upstairs to check in with Eli.

"Just wanted to let you know we're back," Nick said.

"It all went well?"

"As well as possible, I suppose."

"I saw the video online. You guys looked great. Are you okay?"

"I'm still feeling shocked, but we'll figure it out. Everything okay here?"

"Yeah, I checked on the twins an hour ago. They're out cold."

"Then I guess we'll see you in the morning. Get some sleep."

"You too, Mr. President."

Nick smiled at the young man's cheeky grin. "Not you too."

"Sorry, I couldn't resist."

Amused by Eli, Nick went back downstairs and into his room, shut the door and leaned back against it.

"What's up?" Sam asked from bed.

"Everyone calling me Mr. President. It's very weird."

"It's only one word different from Mr. Vice President."

"And yet there's a world of difference between the two." Nick pushed off the door and went into the closet off the master bathroom to get undressed. As he hung up the suit he'd worn to be sworn in, it occurred to him that the suit would be featured someday at the Smithsonian, or within the walls of his own presidential library. Everything about him now belonged to the public, even his clothes. Well, almost everything... A few things were private and would remain that way, primarily the relationship he enjoyed with his wife.

He brushed his teeth and headed for bed, wearing only a pair of the same Washington Feds pajama pants that Scotty had. They'd been gifts to him and Scotty from Celia and Skip for Christmas last year.

"Both our phones are going nuts," Sam said of the phone he'd left on the dresser.

Nick went over to turn his off. "I guess the word is out."

"Gonzo texted to say, 'Holy fucking shit. I guess you did have something else to take care of tonight. Please tell Nick we said congratulations and... holy fucking shit.'"

Nick grunted out a laugh. "I guess that about sums it up."

"Do you want to turn on the TV?" she asked warily.

"Absolutely not."

"Good answer."

He reached for her, and she snuggled up to him, bringing the lavender and vanilla scents of home with her. She had the softest, silkiest skin and curves in all the best places. Her long toffee-colored hair tickled his nose until she looked up at him with light blue eyes full of questions and concerns about the momentous events of this evening.

"How're you doing, babe?" she asked.

"Um, fine. I guess. You?"

"Same. I guess."

Sam snorted out a laugh. "Hell of a first couple we're gonna be. We can't even figure out how we are."

"We're going to be an awesome first couple."

"You sound very sure about that."

"I am very sure about it. We'll give it all we've got, and that's all we can do."

"Well, I'm not going to give it all I have. I'll give it what I can. First and foremost is our marriage and our children and making sure they successfully adjust to this massive change in their lives. Second is my job. Third is being first lady."

Nick didn't say anything to that, mostly because he still hadn't figured out how it would be possible for her to continue to hunt down murderers while they served as president and first lady. The Secret Service would try to forbid it, and part of him hoped they did. He wanted her safe and protected from the crazies who'd try to get at him through her. But he also wanted her to be happy and was well aware that'd never be possible without the job she loved.

"You're not saying anything."

"I don't know what to say. Not yet, anyway."

"You could say, 'Of course those are your priorities, Samantha. Why would they have to change just because I got promoted?'"

"Promoted," he said with a chuckle. "Is that what we're calling it?"

She sat up and faced him with the covers wrapped around her. "That's what happened. You got promoted to a bigger job in the city where I happen to already work. We're only moving across town. Why should anything else have to change?"

He knew neither of them would sleep until they'd had this conversation. "Is that a rhetorical question?"

"It's not a rhetorical question, and you already know that. I'm going to need you to fight for me the same way you did when you became vice president."

"You know if I could do anything I wanted—"

"You can! You're the fucking president. You can do whatever you want."

"Within reason."

"Exactly! Don't tell me there's no way to make it work so I can keep my job while you're president. I refuse to hear that."

"Okay, then I won't tell you that. All I'll say is we're going to have to think it through and find a way to make it work for both of us."

"What does that even mean? Why does it have to work for you? You'd be the first one to say you're not running for anything. You're going to do these three years, finish Nelson's term and then figure out what's next. What do you care if they come at you about your wife working a job outside the White House?"

"I couldn't care less if anyone 'comes at me' about that. What I care about, more than just about anything, is your safety. This is a whole new ball game, Sam, and you know that as well as I do."

"So what're you saying?"

"That I need time to think and breathe and talk it through with my team and to figure out a plan that works for both of us. I'm not going to lie to you. It'll be an uphill battle. No one is going to approve of you keeping your current job while I'm president."

"Do you approve?" she asked in a small voice that was so not like her that it hurt him to hear it.

"I approve of you continuing to do what you love as long as you're safe. We're going to need to figure out what that entails."

"You mean Secret Service."

"Among other things."

"What other things?"

"I don't know yet!" He'd been president for ninety minutes, and they were already fighting.

"Here's what I know—I'm so happy for you to have this opportunity, even if I'm sad for the Nelsons that they had to lose their husband and father to make it happen. I wouldn't have wished for that in a million years, but here we are, and I was so proud tonight watching you take the oath. The American people are incredibly lucky to have you. They have no idea how lucky they are, but they're going to find out. I'm prepared to support you one thousand percent in this, even if it's not what I would've chosen for either of us. In return, I expect you to support me at the same level."

"I understand."

"Do you? Do you really?"

"I do, Samantha. After all this time, I certainly know what makes you happy, and I'll do everything I can to make sure you're happy."

"Everything in your *considerable power*?"

"Yes," he said with a sigh as he reached for her. "Come back. I don't want to fight. I hate fighting with you."

"I don't want to fight with you either. You know I don't."

"Then let's not do that, okay? Let's figure this out together. We're both going to have to compromise to make this work."

"I'm willing to compromise about everything except my job. That's nonnegotiable."

Nick wasn't sure how to respond to that. She might have to make some concessions to stay safe, but he wasn't going to be the one to tell her that. "It's going to take a minute for people to wrap their heads around the first lady having a job outside the White House."

"There's a first time for everything, and I'd love to make history by showing the world that a woman can support her husband *and* pursue an outside career at the same time."

"For the record, I have no issue with you working while you're first lady."

"Well, thank goodness for that."

"This is no time for sarcasm."

"It's always time for sarcasm."

"Your position has been duly noted, as has your sarcasm. I'll do everything I can for you, the way I always do."

"Why do I hear a 'but' in there?"

"Some of this might not be up to me, Sam. They're going to insist you have Secret Service, even if you're not required to have it."

"I might be willing to compromise—somewhat—on that if

necessary."

"Awww, look at you. My little girl is growing up."

She poked his ribs, which made him laugh. "It wasn't awful having them following me over the last week. If that's all it was, I could live with that. But I still get to drive myself."

He ran his hand up and down her arm. "We'll have a meeting and work out the details."

She released a deep breath and relaxed against him. "Thank you."

"Anything for you, babe."

"I feel like I dreamed this whole thing. Did you really just go to the White House to get sworn in as president?"

"I really did."

"Giving all-new meaning to Black Friday."

"Right?" he said, laughing. "What a fucking shit show. You know what the headlines will say tomorrow?"

"What?"

"Nelson dies, Cappuano sworn in to office he just said he didn't want."

"You said you didn't want to *run*, not that you didn't want to be president."

"They won't make that distinction. They'll make me out to be a reluctant president."

"You *are* a reluctant president."

"That'll make it harder for me to assert my authority. My political opponents will have a field day with my reluctance. They'll make it a nightmare for me from the get-go."

"Your party has control of both houses in Congress. It won't matter what they say or do."

"Maybe not, but it'll be ugly—and we only got control of the House because two congressmen resigned due to ethics violations."

"You can handle it. I have no doubt about that. You should govern like someone who has no plans to ever run for anything ever again. Like someone with no fucks to give for himself, but only for what he can do to make things better for others."

"The no-fucks-to-give president. I kind of like that."

Sam lifted herself up on an elbow so she could see him. "It's true, right? You haven't changed your mind about running in the next election just because Nelson died and you became president, have you?"

"No, I haven't, but if you think the pressure for me to run was intense when I was the VP, wait until you see what it'll be like when I'm the incumbent president." He cringed just thinking about it. "They won't take no for an answer."

"They'll have to if you refuse to run."

"I don't think it'll be as 'simple' as it was when I was VP, and you saw how that went."

"A lot can happen in three years."

"They'll be pressuring me right away about the next election, with the primary cycle starting in eighteen months."

"We don't have to think about that tonight. Did you take a melatonin?"

That was the only way he ever got any sleep. "I took two."

"Good. You need to close your eyes and clear your brain so you can sleep. You can pick it up in the morning and figure out what's next."

"Is that how you sleep during an investigation?"

"Yep." She kissed his chest and then moved farther down to kiss the muscles of his abdomen. He *loved* when she outlined his abs with her tongue. Burying his fingers in her silky hair, he sucked in a sharp deep breath when her chin brushed against the head of his suddenly hard cock. "You know what else helps?"

"Do tell."

"Showing is so much more fun than telling."

He closed his eyes and gave himself over to her care. "Couldn't agree more."

She took his cock into the heat of her mouth, making him gasp when she lashed him with her tongue.

His spine tingled, and goose bumps erupted on his skin as his cock nudged against her throat.

She released him slowly, going for maximum effect, and nearly succeeded in finishing him off.

He managed to hang on as she straddled him and took him into her body.

She was so fucking hot and sexy and perfect that he often

wondered what he'd done right in a previous life to deserve the love of such an amazing woman in this one. Especially now, when he'd once again turned their world upside down.

"Are you relaxing?" she asked as she moved with erotic precision.

"Not quite yet, but I'm getting there." Nick put his hands on her hips and then ran them up her sides to cup her breasts. She thought they were too big. He thought they were perfect. He'd never loved anyone the way he loved her, hadn't known it was possible to love someone so much until he loved her.

He put his arms around her and turned them so he was on top, looking down at her sweet face and the pale blue eyes that looked at him the way no one else ever had. "In case I forget to tell you, I'm sorry for everything that's going to happen over the next three years."

Sam laughed and curled her arms around his neck, sliding her fingers into his hair as he moved in her. "You're forgiven."

"You might want to wait to see how bad it gets before you forgive me."

"Three years out of a lifetime together is a blip in the grand scheme." As her legs curled around his back, he breathed in the vanilla-and-lavender scent that surrounded him in a cloud of comfort and desire and need so big, it could never be fully sated.

"Love you so much, Samantha. More than ever."

She clung to him as he drove them toward the finish line. "Love you just as much."

He smothered her cries with kisses that muffled his own groans of sublime pleasure. Careful not to crush her, he came down on top of her, both of them breathing hard.

"I've always wanted to bang a president."

Nick laughed so hard, he had tears in his eyes. "I hope it lived up to the hype."

"Way better than anything I ever could've hoped for."

"We aim to please."

"It's going to be okay, Nick. As long as we have this and each other, we'll be fine."

"Keep telling me that, will you?"

"Anytime you need to hear it."

CHAPTER FIVE

S am woke up alone in bed the next morning, and as she stretched, she wondered where Nick was and why she hadn't heard the twins. She'd no sooner had that thought than the events of the previous evening came rushing back in an overwhelming wave that stole her breath.

Her husband was the *president of the United States*.

She was the *first lady*.

They were the *first family*.

And today was the day their lives would change forever as the rest of the world woke up to the news. She wanted to put her head under the pillow, burrow in and not come out for three years. But since that wasn't possible, she reached for her phone to find three hundred and eighty-six text messages.

That was certainly a record.

From her sister Tracy: *Holy. Shit. Call me. OMG. CALL ME.*

From her sister Angela: *Whaaaaaaaat theeeeeeee fuckkkkkkkkk?!? Call me.*

From her partner, Freddie Cruz: *Um, ok. Holy crap. HOLY CRAP!*

From her boss, Captain Malone: *I'd say congratulations to you both, but I have no idea if I should say that. Lots to talk about when you get a chance. Proud to know you both. Rooting for you and wishing you all the best.*

From her colleague Dr. Lindsey McNamara, the District's chief medical examiner: *I'm in tears of sadness for the Nelsons and joy for you and Nick and the rest of us. Can't wait to see you and hear all about it. Love you both.*

From Darren Tabor, her reporter friend from the *Washington Star*: *If you're planning to give out any exclusives, you've got my number. Congrats!*

From Chief Farnsworth: *Marnie and I are so unreasonably proud. Your dad is dancing a jig in heaven. This country is lucky to have you both.*

The sweet message from her chief and Uncle Joe, along with the thought of her late father and his crazy dancing brought tears to her eyes.

From her friend Roni Connolly: *I'm so, so overwhelmed for you both. I can't imagine how you must be feeling. My new "shit friend" is the first lady! FLOTUS!*

Sam laughed at the message from Roni. When she'd befriended the woman who'd been recently widowed, she'd described herself as a shit friend because she had no time for anything other than her work and family. But she'd felt a connection with Roni and was pleased to call her a new friend.

From Shelby Faircloth Hill, their devoted assistant and friend: *I'm in tears. I don't even know what to say. I'm so damned proud of my sweet friends, our new POTUS and FLOTUS. If anyone can KILL this, you guys can. Tell me how I can help. I'm here for whatever you need. Assume the twins' party is still on for tomorrow? Your heads must be spinning. Let me know when you can. Love you guys so much! Avery and I are sending all the best.*

Sam responded to Shelby. *Thanks so much. We're spinning for sure. The party is still on. Trying to keep things as normal as we can for the kids for as long as we can. Making it up as we go. Going to need you more than ever, so don't go anywhere.*

Shelby wrote right back. *I'm here. Not going anywhere. Will take care of everything for the party. Don't worry about a thing. With all due respect to the Nelsons, I'm SO EXCITED. You're going to live in the WHITE HOUSE! Am I going to WORK in the WHITE HOUSE?!? What is happening?!?!*

LOL, Sam responded. *Stand down. We still live on Ninth Street until after the funeral. Mrs. Nelson needs time to pack, etc.*

Are they going to let you work?

Let them try to stop me.

Why did I know you'd say that??? GO, GIRL.

Gotta go see what's going on. Pray for me.

Already done. My phone is exploding with everyone I know reaching out to tell me my bosses are the new POTUS and FLOTUS. Like I didn't already know that. LOL

My phone is a mess.

I'll be there in a bit. Will do what I can to help!

Thanks, Tinker Bell. You're the best.

We got this! Xoxo

The last text was sent with pink fairy dust that made Sam laugh because it was so typical Shelby.

Sam scrolled through the sea of messages, looking for a new one from Gonzo, and finally found one from the night before. *Saw Carlucci and Dominguez, who's banged up pretty bad. Still looking for the SOB.*

That message was followed by a second one from this morning. *Are you freaking?!*

Trying not to.

How's that going?

Ummmmm…

He responded with laughing emojis. *What are they saying about your job?*

Haven't gotten there yet, but nothing will change as far as I'm concerned. I may need to rely on my SGT a little more than I have in the past…

I'm here. Ready to get back in the game and do whatever I can for you and the squad.

Thanks, Gonzo. That helps. How's married life treating you so far?

Fantastic.

Happy for you guys. Will be in touch.

Good luck with it all. Tell Nick, I mean, Mr. President, we're so proud of him.

Will do—and he'll want you to call him Nick.

After the hellish last year her dear friend had gone through after losing his partner to murder and then himself to a pain pill addiction, Sam was so happy to have her sergeant back to full health and ready to rejoin the squad. She'd missed her friend Tommy so much during his ordeal.

Sam got out of bed, took a shower and got dressed in leggings and a denim shirt, eager to spend a rare day off with her kids. Scotty was probably still asleep, but the twins would be up. Then she remembered they'd given the monitor to Elijah the night before, which was why she hadn't heard them. She went downstairs and found them in the kitchen with their brother, who was overseeing a breakfast of cereal and orange juice.

"Sam!" Aubrey jumped up and nearly spilled her cereal in her haste to run over to hug Sam.

She picked up the little girl and hugged her tight. "How's my favorite little girl today?"

"*So* good. Lijah says we can go to the zoo today. Do you want to go?"

Sam wanted to but wasn't sure she could. She needed to see Gigi at some point. "Let me see what's going on first." She returned Aubrey to her seat and kissed the top of Alden's head. "How's my favorite little boy today?"

"Good," Alden said around a mouthful of Apple Jacks.

The kids were always happiest when Elijah was home, and to his credit, he gave them his full attention when he was there. More than a month after the tragic loss of their parents, the twins were settling into their new normal, but Sam worried about how they'd take the news that they'd be moving—again.

"Where's Nick?" Sam asked.

"He left about an hour ago." Elijah handed her a folded piece of paper. "He asked me to give you this."

Didn't want to wake you when you rarely get to sleep in. Gone to "the office" for a few hours. Will be home as soon as I can. Let's do something with the kids later. Love you.

Sam folded the note and tucked it into her shirt pocket to add to her collection of keepsakes from him. "He'll be home a little later, so why don't you guys do the zoo this morning, and then we'll all do something later? Whatever you guys want."

"Should I wake up Scotty for the zoo?" Elijah asked.

"I think he'd want to go." Scotty was usually up for anything that involved Elijah and the twins.

"Are you... you know, doing okay?" Elijah asked, his expression troubled as he glanced at the morning editions of the *Post* and the *Star* that had banner headlines about the goings-on overnight. They must've had to move heaven and earth to get the news into the morning papers when it happened so late.

"Hanging in there."

Elijah sent the twins upstairs to brush their teeth and wash their faces. "I'll be up in a minute to help you figure out what to wear to the zoo."

They scampered off, leaving Sam alone with him. "Are *you* okay?" she asked.

"I was thinking... after you guys left last night... You're going to have so much to deal with. I'd totally understand if you wanted to make other plans for the kids."

"What? No way. That's not happening. We *love them*, Elijah. I promise they'll continue to be very well cared for no matter where we're living or what our jobs are."

"I'm not worried about that so much as the imposition on you and Nick with so many other demands on your time."

Forcing herself to stay calm, Sam poured a cup of coffee and sat at the table with him. "I know I speak for Nick when I tell you the twins, Scotty and you will be foremost on our minds as we make this transition. We're going to do everything we can to make this work for all of us. I promise you that. Not having them stay with us at the White House would never occur to any of us, Elijah. Nick would resign from office before he'd give them up voluntarily."

He seemed to sag somewhat, maybe with relief. "They're doing so well, better than I ever could've imagined after what they've been through."

"They're doing *great*. They still have their rough moments, for sure, but those seem to be less often than they were, and the therapist has been very good for them. She said they're opening up more than they were at first."

"Yes, I talked to her last week, and she said the same thing to me. She said they're doing as well as can be expected after such a trauma. It makes me sad to think they won't remember much about my dad and Cleo. They loved them so much." Elijah had been the result of his father's first marriage, and he'd been close to his father and stepmother, Cleo. He'd had a somewhat strained relationship with his own mother.

"They'll remember that, Elijah. They will."

"I hope so."

"Please don't ever worry about how they fit into our family. They *are* our family, and so are you. That's never going to change."

"Thank you," he said softly. "I have no idea what would've become of us if you guys hadn't stepped up for the kids the way you did."

"Me meeting them at the worst moment of their lives was fate. I believe that, and Nick does too. We love them, Elijah. We love you all."

Swallowing hard, he said, "We love you guys too." He stood and took the kids' bowls to the sink, washed them and left them drying on the rack. "I'd better go make sure they're not getting into mischief up there."

"If I had to guess, you'll find them bouncing on Scotty, trying to wake him up."

"Ah," he said, smiling. "Good to know. He's so great with them."

"He loves being a big brother and *having* a big brother."

"He's an awesome kid."

"So are you. You're doing an excellent job as the kids' guardian."

"Only because I have excellent help. You guys and Shelby, your whole family, your friends... Everyone has been so good to us."

"That's what family does for family. Shelby has already been in touch this morning, and the kids' party is still on for tomorrow. She's got everything covered."

"You all are the best. Thank you again."

"Don't worry about anything, okay?"

"I'll try not to. Now I'd better go save Scotty."

After he left the room, Sam had to take a couple of deep breaths to calm her racing heart. The thought of the twins being anywhere but with them was unthinkable. It had taken only a matter of days for them to become an essential part of their family.

Raised voices in the living room had Sam getting up to see

what was going on. Her sisters were standing in the doorway, arguing with Nate, one of the Secret Service agents.

"We're on the list!" Tracy said. "You're supposed to let us in."

"There's going to be a new list," Nate said. "I'm not authorized to let anyone in."

"It's okay, Nate. My sisters and Shelby should be on any authorized list."

Nate stepped aside to let them pass.

"I'm sorry about her," Angela said to Nate, gesturing to Tracy. "You're just doing your job."

"No problem, ma'am."

"I hate when they call me ma'am," Angela said. "It makes me feel nine hundred years old."

They came over to Sam and wrapped her up in a group hug.

"Let's go in the kitchen," Sam said.

They could speak in private there. The minute the kitchen door closed behind Tracy, the two of them were silent-screaming as they jumped up and down like idiots. Well, Tracy did most of the jumping. Since she was expecting her third child, Angela was in no condition to jump.

"Holy, holy, holy *shit*," Tracy said. "Tell us *everything*. Don't leave out a single detail."

Sam made another pot of coffee, poured some seltzer for Angela and then joined them at the table to tell them the whole story, from the second Nick got The Call last night, through the swearing-in to waking up this morning as the nation's new first lady.

"You looked so calm and composed in the pictures," Angela said. "You had to be melting down on the inside."

"I was pretty melty, but I held it together, thank God."

"Celia told us how you came to get the Bible," Tracy said. "It's so scary and exciting and freaking *huge* all at the same time."

"Yes, it is."

"What about your job?" Angela asked warily.

"I'm keeping it. I've already told Nick that's nonnegotiable."

"Um, how will that work exactly?" Tracy asked.

"We haven't figured out the details yet. It's all still very new, but

I've made my wishes clear. Nick said he'll do everything he can to make it happen for me."

"You'll be the only first lady to ever hold a job outside the White House," Tracy said.

"I might be the first, but I won't be the last. It's high time we had a first lady holding down a career in addition to being first lady."

"We completely agree," Angela said, "but you know lots of other people won't see it the way we do."

"I don't care how they see it. That's how it's going to be. The end. I'm not debating it."

The kids came into the kitchen with a grumpy Scotty, all of them dressed for an outing to the zoo. Scotty brightened when he saw Angela and Tracy.

"I guess this means you've heard the news," Scotty said.

"Uh, yeah, the whole world has heard the news, sport," Angela said.

Sam's stomach started to ache at the thought of her husband and their family being a news story around the world. She hated being the center of attention, but she probably ought to get over that now that she was half of the highest profile couple on the planet.

Scotty grabbed a granola bar, and the kids got ready to leave with the Secret Service for a trip to the zoo.

Sam excused herself from her sisters to follow them to the door, asking Scotty's lead agent, Debra, for a word. "I'm worried about them being bothered," Sam said.

"We're making arrangements to put space between them and the parties before and after them. We'll make sure no one bothers them."

"Thank you, Debra."

Sam hugged and kissed the kids and Scotty. "Elijah is in charge. Whatever he says goes."

"That's right," Elijah said. "I'm the boss of you."

She watched them go down the ramp and get into one of the ever-present black Secret Service SUVs, her anxiety spiking as she watched them go. Only because she trusted the Secret Service implicitly was she able to wave them off and return to the kitchen.

"Why do you look panicked?" Tracy asked.

"I worry about the kids and crackpots."

"They have the best security in the world with them at all times," Angela said.

"We're going to have to see about getting protection for Elijah when he goes back to school," she said. "He'll love that." She dropped her head into her hands. "So much to think and worry about."

"You'll figure it out," Angela said. "If anyone can handle this, you guys can."

"Thanks for the vote of confidence. Nick is worried about people making a thing of him becoming president right after he said he wasn't going to run."

Tracy bit her lip, which was a big "tell" for her.

"What?"

"They're already making a thing of it," she said, "but I think they'll get past it when he shows he's more than up to the job."

Sam's phone chimed with a text from Nick. *I'm calling you.* Her phone rang, and the caller ID reported the number as unavailable. "This is Nick. Sorry, but I have to take it."

"Go ahead," Angela said.

She decided at the last second to use one of her dad's favorite opening lines. "Kelly's Pool Hall. Eight Ball speaking. How may I help you?"

Chuckling, Nick said, "I'm looking for my wife. She's a hot blonde, about five-nine, curvy and sexy as all hell. Is she there?"

"She's flirting with a biker dude. You want me to get her?"

"Yeah, tell her that her husband loves her and needs her more than anything."

Swoon. "What's going on?"

"I have a favor to ask..."

"Another one? I just did you a rather big favor by becoming first lady. What more do you want?"

"Turns out that's just the start of what I'm going to need from you. Trevor and the communications team are strongly recommending we do a joint interview in the next few days with one of the networks. Would you be willing?"

"Is that another rhetorical question?"

"It's a yes-or-no question."

Sam propped her head on her upturned hand. "I suppose I could do it for you considering what you're going to do for me, *right*?"

"Right. We have a meeting Tuesday at two with the director of the Secret Service. Can you be here for that?"

"I'll see if I can fit it into my busy schedule."

"On Wednesday late afternoon, we'll be the first to greet the Nelson family at the Capitol where President Nelson will lie in state for twenty-four hours before the funeral on Thursday. Obviously, we're going to have to be there for all of that."

"I'll see about taking the time off."

"Thank you."

"Stop being so polite with me."

"How else should I be when I'm asking you to upend your entire life for me?"

"Be normal."

"I don't even remember what that is anymore."

"I'll do the interview and the funeral and anything else you need."

"And I'm working from my end to figure out what has to happen to get you back to work as soon as possible."

"Thank you."

"Quit being polite."

Sam laughed and immediately felt better. "Are you calling me from the Oval Office?"

"It just so happens that I am."

"I hope someone's getting pictures."

"One of the White House photographers has been here all morning recording history. I've got to run. I'm meeting with Nelson's cabinet in twenty minutes."

"Are you keeping them?"

"I'm giving them the choice to stay or go."

"Will they be loyal to you?"

"Maybe not at first, but they'll come around, or they won't be invited to stay. Terry was up all night reading about what Johnson did after Lincoln died, what Truman did after FDR died and what

Johnson did after Kennedy died. There's some precedent, and we're following it to a point."

"That's very interesting. Good luck with the cabinet."

"Thanks, babe. I have to renege on the plans for later. I hadn't had coffee yet when I wrote that note to you. I'm doing the address to the nation at eight p.m. It's critical I send the message that I'm in charge and taking care of business. I'll be home after that, but it'll be too late for the twins."

"They're having a blast with Elijah and Scotty. They went to the zoo just now. Don't worry about us. We'll be watching tonight."

"Love you."

"Love you too."

Sam ended the call and conveyed the gist to her sisters.

"You should go there," Tracy said. "After dinner with the kids. Go there and be with him before he gives that speech."

"She's right," Angela said. "He needs you."

"Okay, I will. You guys will keep telling me how to do this, right?"

"We've been telling you what to do all your life," Tracy said. "Why would we stop now?"

CHAPTER SIX

An hour later, Sam was ready to visit Gigi in the hospital. She went downstairs, put on her coat and headed out the door like it was any other day. However, the Secret Service agents standing on the ramp, wearing black from head to toe and toting machine guns, were a stark reminder that this day was like no other.

"Gentlemen," she said to agents she didn't recognize. "If you'll let me pass, I'll get out of your way."

"I'm afraid that's not possible, ma'am."

"Why not?"

"You're not to leave here without a detail, ma'am."

"And where did that order come from?"

"The top, ma'am. The very top."

Meaning Nick. Huh. That was surprising—and a little disappointing.

"I'd be happy to arrange transportation for you anywhere you wish to go, ma'am."

Sam realized she had two choices. The first would be to make a scene with the agents, who, as fellow law enforcement officers, were merely following orders. The second would be to allow them to do what they did and take it up with Nick later. She chose option B.

"Give us ten minutes, ma'am."

Sam went back in the house, stuffing the annoyance deep inside so no one would see how upset she was. Nick didn't need to hear through any grapevine that she was pissed. Not today, anyway. But they'd be discussing her desire to move freely as soon as possible.

Twelve minutes after the agent had asked for ten, Sam was about to go back outside when the door opened to Vernon and Jimmy. The two agents had recently been assigned to her after Nick's announcement that he didn't plan to run in the next election had led to an uptick in threats against him and their entire family.

"Gentlemen." Vernon was an older Black man with graying hair, his partner a baby-faced blond with an eagerness about him that annoyed her. "I'd rather hoped I'd seen the last of you."

"Likewise, ma'am," Vernon said with the cheeky sarcasm that had endeared him to her. She respected the hell out of anyone who could meet sarcasm with sarcasm. "Sadly for all of us, our time together is just beginning."

"We'll see about that."

"Indeed we will, ma'am. I understand you wish to go to the George Washington University Hospital?"

"I do. One of my detectives is a patient."

"We'd be pleased to get you there and back as safely as possible," Vernon said, signaling to Jimmy to do something.

Sam wasn't sure what the signal meant, but Jimmy clearly understood it.

"Right this way, ma'am." Jimmy smiled widely, as if this was the greatest day of his young life. It probably was. He was protecting the nation's first lady. He'd probably dine out on that for the rest of his days.

Sam got into the back of one of the black SUVs and put on her seat belt, determined to go with the flow and not to do anything to cause Nick any more grief than he was already contending with. If she raised hell with the agents, that would cause trouble for him that he didn't need. So she kept her mouth shut and did what she was told.

For once.

If there was one advantage to the Secret Service, it was that people got the fuck out of their way, which meant they arrived at their destination that much quicker. As someone who rarely had time to waste, there was something to be said for that kind of efficiency.

Jimmy opened the back door for her, and the two agents followed Sam into the hospital.

The young woman working the reception desk did a double take when she recognized Sam. "Mrs. Cappuano... Ma'am. It's such a pleasure to meet you."

"Thank you. I'm here to see a friend. Giselle Dominguez. Can you please tell me what room she's in?"

"Of course."

While Sam watched, the woman typed in Gigi's name, and if her eyes weren't deceiving her, the woman's hands trembled as she did so. *For fuck's sake.* It would never be "normal" to Sam to provoke that kind of reaction in people.

"She's in room 520. Take the elevators on your left to the fifth floor, and check in at the nurses' station."

"Thank you very much."

"If I may..."

Sam, who'd started toward the elevators, stopped and turned back.

"I'm sorry about what happened to President Nelson, but I'm very excited that your husband is president and that you're our new first lady."

"Thank you. I'll be sure to pass that along to Nick."

The woman nearly fainted when Sam said that. She quickly headed toward the elevators, aware of Vernon and Jimmy following her.

"Ma'am," Vernon said. "Let me go ahead."

Sam forced herself to stop and allow the agents to arrange things to their liking before she followed Vernon onto the elevator, gritting her teeth and biting her tongue the whole time. On the fifth floor, she inquired about Gigi and showed her badge.

"We know who you are." The nurse had short gray hair and wore glasses with gold frames. "Everyone knows who you are."

Her words had an edge to them that put Sam on guard. "That

doesn't mean I can't be polite and say please when I ask if I can see my detective."

"She won't be your detective for long."

Sam told herself she shouldn't engage, but damned if she could resist. "Why's that?"

"You aren't going to keep your job as first lady." She paused, took a closer look at Sam and probably saw bullish determination. "Are you?"

"That's the plan. If you don't mind, I need to see Detective Dominguez."

"Down the hall on the right."

Sam walked away, but could feel everyone looking at her as she headed toward Gigi's room, escorted by Vernon and Jimmy. Sometimes she wished people could just mind their own damned business, but she knew that was too much to ask, especially today when the world had woken to the news of a transfer of power in Washington. If she allowed herself to think about the implications of that seismic shift...

Nope. Not going there. Denial was her friend.

Outside of room 520, she glanced at Vernon. "You need to wait for me out here."

"One of us needs to check the room before you go in."

"That's not going to happen." The last thing Gigi needed was strange men in her room. "I'll be fine. Please wait for me here." Without giving them time to respond, Sam entered the darkened room, where Carlucci was standing guard over her partner's bed. Dani, who was tall, blonde and curvy, came over to Sam.

Sam hugged her. "I got here as soon as I could."

"You must be losing it. Both of you."

Sam waved her hand to send the message that she didn't want to talk about what was happening in her life. She wanted to talk about what was happening to Gigi. "How is she?"

"She had a rough night. She's in a lot of pain. The son of a bitch ruptured her spleen. She had surgery overnight."

"Jesus. Any sign of him?"

"Not yet. I want to be out there looking for him myself, but I don't want to leave her, especially with him in the wind."

"We can put people here to screen any visitors."

"It's okay. I'm in touch with Patrol and doing what I can from here. She doesn't want her family to know she's here, so I said I'd stay. I took leave."

Sam finally ventured a glance at Gigi and bit back a gasp at the sight of her bruised and bloody face. The petite, dark-haired woman looked extra tiny in the hospital bed. "Son of a bitch."

"I want to fucking murder him."

"Don't do that."

"I won't, but I want to."

"Right there with you. What do we know about him?"

"Ezra Smith. Gigi went to high school with him in Fairfax. They've been on again-off again for years, and when she tried to finally end it with him for good, he didn't take it well. That's what I told you about last week. They'd had a big verbal altercation that'd nearly gotten physical, but she felt confident that she'd made her point."

They already knew the guy had a sealed juvie record, but no record as an adult. Carlucci had investigated him on social media and picked up a vibe about him and past issues with other women, but had walked the fine line of giving Gigi a heads-up about that without tipping her hand that she'd been looking into him.

"Has she been awake?"

"Here and there. She's due for pain meds soon, so she'll probably be waking up. I haven't asked any questions yet..."

"I'll wait until she wakes up, and I'll ask so you don't have to."

"Thanks for coming, LT. It'll mean a lot to her, and it does to me too."

"I would've been here sooner, but it's been a weird day."

"I can't even imagine."

Thirty minutes later, Sam and Dani were standing at the bedside when Gigi's soft-brown eyes opened and immediately filled with tears when she saw Sam. "You didn't have to..."

"Hush, of course I did." Sam gently placed her hand on top of Gigi's. "I'm sorry this happened."

"My fault."

"In no way was this your fault."

"He'd changed into someone I barely recognize, but I kept letting him come back," she said as tears rolled down her face.

Dani gently dabbed at her partner's tears with a tissue. "Take it easy. It's not your fault. Caring about someone doesn't give him a right to do this to you."

"I never thought he would... He said he loved me."

"Can you give us any insight into where we might find him?"

Gigi closed her eyes and let out a deep sigh, wincing as she shifted to try to find a more comfortable position. "He has a group of friends he goes way back with. You could probably start there." As she recited the names, Dani wrote them down.

"Go call it in," Sam said to Dani. "Take a break."

"I'll be right back."

"I'll be here."

"She's upset," Gigi said after Dani left. "Blames herself."

"There's only one person to blame for this, and we'll make sure he pays for what he did to you."

New tears leaked out of the corners of Gigi's red-rimmed eyes. "I've known him all my life. We were in kindergarten together."

"Which is all the more reason why he never should've laid a hand on you."

Before Gigi could respond to that, the door opened, and Detective Cameron Green came in, looking as if he could kill someone. The blond detective, who was always dressed to perfection, looked like he'd thrown on clothes and run for the hospital the second he heard the news. He wore faded jeans and an old sweatshirt. His hair stood on end, and his jaw was covered in stubble. Sam had never seen him so undone.

"Gigi..." He stopped several feet short of the bed. "Son of a bitch."

She started to cry again, her chest heaving with sobs.

Cameron went to her, took her hand and gently brushed the hair back from her face. "We'll nail him for this."

Sam stood back to give him room, intrigued by the close bond between her two officers, a bond she hadn't noticed before now.

"What do we know?" Cameron asked Sam, his expression fierce and furious.

"Gigi gave us a list of his friends. Dani is calling that in."

"I'll go look for him myself," Cam said. "I'll find him."

"I don't think that's the best idea," Sam said.

He whirled to look at her. "Why not?"

"You seem to be... How shall I say... *Personally* involved?" She raised a brow in inquiry.

Cameron blinked, appearing confused for a second before his eyes widened and his mouth opened as if he was going to speak. But no words came out. And then he seemed to sag all of a sudden as some sort of truth settled on him. "Maybe."

The single word seemed to cost him something. As far as Sam knew, he'd been dating someone else for quite some time. Sam had met the woman a couple of times. "Let's leave it to the others, then." Her phone rang, and she stepped out of the room to take the call from Gonzo. "What's up?"

"Nothing yet. Dani called me with his list of friends, and I've sent McBride and O'Brien to Fairfax to track them down. We ran them all and found a couple of outstanding warrants we're going to use as leverage to get them to talk."

"That's something, anyway. Green is here. He's *extremely* upset."

"Really. Well, that's interesting."

"I thought the same thing, suggested as much to him, and it seemed to be the first time he entertained the idea of feelings beyond that of a colleague."

"Doesn't he have a girlfriend?"

"He does."

"Hmmm..."

"I suggested he might want to leave the vengeance to the rest of the team."

"Good call. Speaking of vengeance, Lenore Worthington is here looking for information about her son's case after the developments overnight."

Sam had promised to take a fresh look at her son's fifteen-year-old unsolved homicide. "Is she still there?"

"She is."

"Let me speak to her."

"Hang on."

Sam heard Gonzo speaking to someone in the seconds before Lenore came on the line.

"Lieutenant, I'd ask how your Thanksgiving was, but..."

Sam laughed. "It was pretty great until around nine o'clock."

"I know you must be reeling today and have so many other things on your mind. I didn't come here expecting to see you."

"I made you a promise that I fully intend to keep, Lenore. My plan is to continue my life as it was on Wednesday."

"Is that so? Well, that'd be quite something."

"No matter what happens, I promise I'll investigate Calvin's murder with fresh eyes and do everything I can to get you some long-overdue answers."

"Thank you," she said, sounding relieved. "That means so much to me."

"I also fully intend to remain engaged with the grief group." Along with the department's psychiatrist, Dr. Trulo, Sam had recently founded the support group for the victims of violent crime. Their first meeting had been a big success, and a second was planned for mid-December.

"I'll see you at the next meeting, if not before?"

"I'll be there."

"I know your participation meant so much to the other attendees, especially those who've just begun this journey," Sam said.

"It helps me to help them. Thank you for making that possible."

"I'll be in touch, okay?"

"Thank you, Sam, and if I may... God bless you and your husband as you begin this new adventure. I'll be cheering for you both."

"Thank you. That's very kind of you. Talk soon."

Lenore gave the phone back to Gonzo, and Sam heard her saying goodbye to him.

"Whatever you said made her very happy."

"I told her I fully intend to honor my promise to reopen Calvin's case."

"Let me know what I can do to help with that."

"I will. For now, let's find the guy who put our Gigi in the hospital."

"I'm on it."

CHAPTER SEVEN

Nick sat in the middle of the large conference table, surrounded by Nelson's cabinet and the media that lined the room and hung microphone poles over the table to record their every word. "We have the secretary of State?"

"Yes, sir." One of the aides clicked a remote to bring Secretary Ruskin onto a screen via secure transmission from his flight to Iran.

"Thank you for joining us, Mr. Secretary," Nick said. "I hope your trip has been uneventful thus far."

"So far so good. We're due to land in Tehran in two hours."

"Thank you for making the trip. And thank you all for being here today. I'd like to start with a moment of silence for President Nelson." The room went completely silent, and heads were bowed in contemplation. "May he rest in peace and may his memory be a blessing to all of us. I understand we're all in shock over the untimely loss of President Nelson. None of us planned to be here today to discuss continuity of government, especially me. As you know, I recently announced that I didn't intend to seek the party's nomination in the next election cycle. Less than a week later, I took the oath of office to become the nation's forty-seventh president. I'm the youngest president in history and only the ninth to come into office following the death of my predecessor. I can imagine any one of those things would give pause to those entrusted with serving in the president's cabinet. Taken together, they might bring about a crisis of confidence."

As he spoke, he was nearly blinded by flashes and almost drowned out by the machine-gun sound of camera shutters recording history.

"However, I wish to assure you that despite whatever shortcomings you may see in me, I intend to give this job everything I have for the next three years. I remain firm in my resolve to sit out the next election cycle, which means my focus will be exclusively on the well-being of the American people as well as the safety and security of our nation. That said, none of you are obligated to stay in your posts, if you do not wish to. I know President Nelson appreciated your loyalty, and I understand that loyalty may not extend to me. Obviously, I prefer to work with a cabinet that's loyal to me. I'll accept the resignations of anyone who wishes to leave with my gratitude for your service to your country. If you choose to stay, I hope you'll do so with an eye toward the future and not the past. I'm sure some of you must have questions and concerns. I'm happy to discuss anything that's on your mind."

He nodded to Trevor, who asked the media to clear the room now that they'd gotten their photos and footage.

After the journalists filed out, Nick waited to hear whether anyone had anything to say. For a long moment, there was only silence until Defense Secretary Tobias Jennings cleared his throat. "With all due respect, Mr. President, while your intentions may be pure, the reality is that there'll be questions about whether you're qualified to be president, or if you have the experience needed for the job."

"Understood." Nick kept his expression blank while he seethed on the inside. "However, in choosing me to be his vice president, I believe President Nelson had full faith in me to step in for him if the need arose, and as such, I'd hope the American people might be willing to give me a chance before they decide anything. I'll work just as hard for the people who don't support me as I will for those who do. I've devoted my entire adult life to public service, and I'm confident I have the experience needed to put together a dynamic team to serve the American people. But I can't do it alone, which is why I'm asking for your support."

"I have a question," Attorney General Reginald Cox said after more than an hour of questions from others. "Your wife... I assume she'll be leaving her position with the Metropolitan Police Department?"

"Actually, she intends to continue in her role."

That was met with shocked silence.

"I'll confess to finding that rather surprising," Cox said.

"We're meeting with the Secret Service on Tuesday to discuss the logistics. My goal is to make it possible for her to keep the job she loves while I'm in office. She's been very successful in navigating the demands of her job while serving as second lady, and I have every confidence she'll continue to do the same as first lady. I'd appreciate the opportunity to figure out a plan for her before it's made public that she intends to keep her job."

"I'm concerned about potential conflicts of interest," Cox said, "with your wife serving as a law enforcement officer while you're president."

"Since she works for the District of Columbia and not the federal government, I can't see where we have a problem."

"The FBI is currently investigating the Metropolitan Police Department, with the lieutenant playing a central role in the investigation."

"As I understand it, she's already been interviewed and fulfilled her obligations to the investigation."

Nick was thankful when Cox didn't engage any further, but the AG had raised valid concerns. Add them to the growing list of issues he'd need to address. "If there's nothing further, I want to thank you all again for coming in today. Terry and I look forward to hearing from each of you as to whether you intend to continue in your current role."

"Thank you, Mr. President," each of them said.

When he stood, everyone else did too. He left the room and walked with Terry back to the Oval Office.

"That went pretty well," Terry said.

"Do you think so? I detected an undercurrent of hostility."

"I don't know if I'd call it that. Probably more like uncertainty.

Everyone is still reeling from the news of Nelson's death. Let's give them a few days to get their heads around the change of command. I think most of them will stay and will serve you well. If they don't, we'll show them the door."

When they arrived in the lobby outside the Oval, Terry's father, retired Senator Graham O'Connor, was waiting for them. Graham jumped up to greet them. Nick could tell that his mentor and surrogate father was making an effort to be respectful in front of President Nelson's shocked staff. But the second the door to the Oval Office closed behind them, Graham let loose with a giddy-sounding laugh. "Hot *damn*, Mr. President!"

Nick laughed as he hugged the older man, who'd wanted Nick to be president much more than Nick himself ever had. "You finally got your wish."

"I did, but I'm heartbroken about David. Such shocking news." Graham had been close friends with the late president for decades. "Do they have any idea what happened?"

"I haven't heard. I hope we'll know more after the autopsy."

"I feel so sorry for Gloria," Graham said. "Things were so unsettled between them and now this. It must've been so hard for her to come back here under these circumstances."

"It was important that she be here to indicate a peaceful transfer of power," Nick said.

"Agreed. It was big of her to do it, though, after everything that happened between them. I almost died of shock myself when I saw the news this morning. What it must've been like to get that phone call..."

"I'll never forget it, that's for sure. I'm sorry I didn't call you myself last night, but everything happened so fast."

"Not to worry. Laine and I turned in early after a nice day with the family and woke up to the shocking news this morning. I couldn't wait to see you."

"I'm so glad you're here. And check out your son, the new White House chief of staff."

"I couldn't be prouder of you both. You're going to do a wonderful job."

"I'd like you to serve as a senior adviser."

Graham's expression registered genuine shock. "*Really?*"

"Yes, really," Nick said with a laugh. "That is if I can coax you out of retirement."

"Hell yes, but we'd better make it part-time, or Laine will divorce me."

"We can't have that, and I'll take whatever I can get."

"I'm so, so, *so* proud of you."

Nick hugged the man who meant so much to him. "This is all your fault."

Graham laughed as he patted Nick on the back. "I'll gladly take the blame, my friend."

"I'm sure you're very happy to have gotten your way, as usual."

"I am feeling rather smug today."

Nick took tremendous pleasure in the way Graham's smile made his eyes dance with unfettered glee. It'd been nearly two years since they lost Graham's son John, who'd been Nick's best friend since college. For a time, Nick had wondered if Graham would ever smile again. "What do you think John would have to say about this?"

"If you ask me, he's the one who made it happen," Graham said. "He's up there overseeing it all, and he loves seeing his brothers become the most powerful men in the world."

"I hope so." Nick never for one second forgot that he owed his career and position to the fact that his best friend had been murdered. What a strange and wild ride it'd been since the day he'd found John dead in his bed—and reconnected with Sam six years after their momentous first meeting.

"I can't believe we're standing in this office that now belongs to you," Graham said. "Of course, it'll need to be redecorated."

"Least of my concerns. We've got a speech to write and a secretary of State about to land in Iran."

"Before I let you get to it, I'm wondering what Sam will do," Graham said, his smile fading. "There's no way they're going to let her continue to run the streets hunting murderers."

"They're going to have to let her, because she fully intends to be business as usual."

"Nick... There's *no way*. If she's out working the streets, she'll be a hundred times more vulnerable than any other first lady has ever been. Every terrorist organization in the world will see her as an easy target."

Hearing that spelled out so bluntly was like a knife to the heart. "She'll have a detail."

"That won't be enough. You have to try to reason with her."

"You know my wife. You know *who she is,* and so do I."

"I do know, and she's brilliant at her job. Perhaps she could be convinced to put it on hold for a few years and go back to it after."

"I can't ask that of her. It would break her heart. I *won't* ask it of her. She married a senator. She sure as hell didn't sign on for this." He gestured to the Oval Office and everything it represented. "I can't ask her to be anything other than who and what she is, even if I'd prefer to keep her swaddled in bubble wrap so nothing can ever happen to her."

"I understand. I just think you need to prepare yourself for possible pushback from the intelligence and security sectors."

The thought of that fight made him weary, but he'd go to war for her if that's what it came to. As much as he'd prefer the bubble wrap, it would make her miserable.

"I won't take any more of your time, Mr. President. I'm only a phone call away if I can be of service."

Nick hugged him. "I'll be calling on you often."

"I'm at your service."

Terry walked his father out while Nick returned to the Resolute desk that'd been used by numerous presidents since the Queen of England had gifted it to President Rutherford B. Hayes in 1880. On the credenza behind the desk, he took note of the array of Nelson family photos. As he picked up a group photo of the Nelsons with their twelve grandchildren, he experienced a wave of sadness for the family's sudden loss.

The director of Oval Office Operations would be there shortly to begin the transition to making the office Nick's.

Earlier in the day, he'd received calls from the prime ministers of Canada, the United Kingdom and Israel, the president of Mexico, the chancellor of Germany and other world leaders, offering condolences for President Nelson and support for Nick as he assumed the presidency.

Tom Hanigan appeared in the doorway, carrying a box. "Sorry

for the interruption, Mr. President. I thought I'd help out by collecting some of President Nelson's things."

"Please come in. Do whatever you need to."

"Thank you, sir."

Nick returned the photo to the credenza and stood to give Tom access to the area.

"I met earlier with Terry and Trevor about the address to the nation tonight."

"Thank you for your help with that and everything else too."

Hanigan nodded. "People need the reassurance that it's business as usual during the transition. You'll need to get a press secretary soon. Trevor can handle it at first, but you'll want someone permanent. That's going to be critical. Among many other things."

This would be, Nick thought, as difficult a transition for Tom Hanigan as it would be for him. He recalled what it'd been like to be going a million miles an hour as chief of staff to a senator, only for everything to stop in a matter of minutes when John was murdered.

"My door is open to you and any suggestions you may have, Tom."

"You won't need me. You already have a great team. They'll take good care of you."

"Your input will always be welcome."

"Thank you, sir." Tom packed up the photos, fountain pen, mementos and the personal files, all of it fitting into a single box that would be saved for the eventual Nelson presidential library. "President Nelson didn't get a chance to leave the ceremonial letter to his successor, but if I had to guess, he would've told you to lead with your heart and take care of the people closest to you. He would've said he failed to protect the most important thing—his marriage. He was deeply regretful of the affair and the pain he caused Gloria and his children. He'd been very low since she moved home."

"There was no evidence he took his own life, was there?"

"No, but I wouldn't be surprised if we learned that was the case. He wasn't in a good place lately. It had really begun to sink in that he'd not only ruined his marriage but also his legacy. He would've advised you to be careful with both those things."

A few minutes later, Terry came in with the first cut of Nick's speech for that evening's address to the nation.

"I wish you and your family all the best," Hanigan said.

"Thank you, Tom," Nick said, shaking the other man's hand.

Tom picked up the box and headed out of the Oval Office, taking a last look back before leaving the room.

"I feel for him," Nick said to Terry.

"You've been right where he is."

"Yeah." Shaking off the painful memories of John's untimely death, Nick took the printout from Terry.

They spent the rest of the day refining the speech until Nick was satisfied with it. While they worked, one of the butlers was in and out, bringing sandwiches and drinks. He'd had some contact with the butlers and other household staff as vice president, but he already noticed a different level of attentiveness for the president.

"Thank you," Nick said when the man served a turkey club with fries for him and a cheeseburger for Terry.

"Pleasure, sir."

"I didn't catch your name."

"It's Anthony Jones, sir."

Nick stood to shake the man's hand. "Very nice to meet you."

"You as well, sir. Please let me know if I can get you anything else."

"Thanks very much." When he and Terry were alone, Nick said, "I could get used to this service."

"They'll take very good care of you and your family."

"I've never had people waiting on me before. It feels kind of weird."

"The White House residence staff is an incredible group of dedicated professionals. Many of them are the second and third generation of their families to work here. They take great pride in their work and in taking care of the first family."

"I'm still trying to believe this has actually happened," Nick said, taking in the Oval Office and all it signified. "What're we hearing from Ruskin?"

"Nothing yet."

"I hope he's able to get somewhere with the Iranians. I don't need an international incident on my first day in office."

"He has a good rapport with the Iranian president. Nelson was the one who was at odds with him. Ruskin has run interference from the beginning of the Nelson administration. He's the right guy to be there now."

"I hope so."

An hour later, a knock on the door preceded one of the receptionists. "Pardon the interruption, Mr. President, but the first lady is here to see you."

Surprised to hear that, Nick stood. "Please ask her to come in." When his people moved over from the vice president's office, they'd know to send Sam right in anytime she came by.

She came in wearing a pale peach silk blouse, black dress pants and heels. Spiral curls cascaded around her shoulders, and her pretty eyes looked at him with love and trepidation. Hopefully, the latter would recede once they settled into their new normal.

He went to kiss and hug her. "This is a very nice surprise."

"I'll be back after a while," Terry said. "We have an hour until the broadcast."

Nick kept his arms around Sam. "Thanks, Terry." Hugging Sam even tighter, he breathed in the scent of her hair. "I really needed this."

"I thought you might."

"How're the kids?"

"Everyone is fine. They had a great time at the zoo, and now they're playing Go Fish with Elijah."

"I wish I could've spent today at home with you guys."

"Soon enough, you'll be working from home. I talked to Lilia earlier, and she mentioned how most presidents say they get more family time living here than they did before."

"That's something to look forward to. What else did Lilia have to say?"

"That Mrs. Nelson invited me to afternoon tea and a tour of the residence on Sunday at two."

"Is that right? Are you going?"

"Of course I'm going. You don't say no to the first lady."

"*Former* first lady. You're the first lady now."

"Still trying to wrap my head around that." She snuggled into his embrace, wrapping her arms around him inside his suit coat. "Remember the night we got engaged in the Rose Garden?"

"How could I ever forget?"

"You said something then about promising me a rose garden."

"I always keep my promises."

Sam laughed. "This is one I sorta wish you hadn't kept."

"I know," he said with a sigh. "Sorry."

"Let's not do that. I was also thinking about what we talked about when we were first together, about what kind of people we were going to be—the kind who shrink from challenges or the kind who meet them head-on."

"We've had a lot of challenges in two years, more than some people have in a lifetime."

"And we've met every one of them head-on."

"It's a wonder we don't have chronic concussions."

Sam laughed. "We'll do the same with this one."

After they'd stood there, wrapped up in each other, for several minutes, Nick said, "You want to hear my speech?"

"I'd love to."

CHAPTER EIGHT

At exactly eight o'clock Eastern Time, Nick stared into the camera set up in front of the Resolute desk, tuned out the lights, the technicians, the staffers and even Sam, who stood off to his right, and focused on his message to the country on the teleprompter.

"My fellow Americans, I come before you tonight as your new president and ask for your patience, prayers and forbearance as I take on this challenge at a time of national mourning for a man twice elected president of this great nation. My wife, Samantha, and I extend our deepest condolences to Mrs. Nelson and the entire Nelson family, as well as President Nelson's cabinet, devoted staff, extended family and wide circle of friends both here in Washington and back home in South Dakota. President Nelson will long be remembered for his advocacy for the middle class and working Americans, his infrastructure program, his focus on the damaging effects of climate change, as well as caring for our veterans and the landmark immigration bill he championed along with my former boss, the late Senator John O'Connor. The sudden death of the president has left us all shocked and saddened, but as has been the case eight other times in our country's history, we have no choice but to move forward and to continue the work on behalf of the American people. Per the Constitution, I was sworn in overnight, and I'm honored to serve as your forty-seventh president, even if I'd never want to achieve the highest office in our land through a loss of this magnitude. President Nelson died far too young and was cheated of many years he should've had as your president and to later enjoy a well-earned retirement. I've ordered the flags lowered to half-staff for fourteen days in his honor, and we will pause as a nation this week to remember him. He will lie in state at the Capitol beginning Wednesday, and a state funeral will be held at the National Cathedral on Thursday. The federal government and schools in the capital region will be closed on Thursday in honor of President Nelson. Today I took the time to reflect on the other vice presidents who've assumed this office after the untimely death of their predecessor and to learn from their examples. I was struck by President Johnson's eloquent words after the tragic death of President Kennedy:

"'No words are sad enough to express our sense of loss,' he said. 'No words are strong enough to express our determination to continue the forward thrust of America that he began.' I feel that same sense of determination to continue the work begun by David Nelson and to represent the United States and her best interests at home and abroad.

"I've heard today from leaders around the world who extended their sympathies to the Nelson family and the American people. Each of them has pledged their support to me and my administration as we step forward to complete the work President Nelson began. I understand that many of you are concerned. Not only am I the nation's youngest president, but less than a week ago, I told you I wasn't planning to run in the next election. So, you may be wondering about whether you're stuck now with a reluctant president. Let me assure you, that is not the case. While it is true that I had chosen not to be away from my young family for months on end to campaign for the presidency, it is *not* true that I'm unwilling or unable to assume the duties of the office at this critical juncture in our history. I do so willingly, with an open heart and mind and a desire to serve you, my fellow Americans, to the best of my ability.

"Keeping our nation safe, secure and prosperous will be foremost on my agenda as I complete the remainder of President Nelson's term. It is a tremendous honor and the greatest privilege of my life to be your president. I will do everything in my power to be worthy of the trust and faith placed in me by President Nelson and the American people. May God bless and keep President Nelson and the Nelson family as well as our troops around the world, and may God continue to bless the United States of America."

When the cameraman signaled that the live feed had ended, Nick sat back in the chair and took a deep breath.

"You did *great*," Sam said.

Nick held out his hand to her, and she joined him behind the desk. "Thanks for being here."

"Well done, Mr. President," Terry said.

"Thank you and everyone who put that together. I think we struck the right note."

Nick had exactly thirty seconds to celebrate getting through his first address to the nation when Teresa appeared in the doorway to the Oval Office. "Mr. President, we need you in the Situation Room."

∾

WHEN IT BECAME CLEAR THAT WHATEVER CRISIS HAD TAKEN NICK TO the Situation Room wouldn't be resolved quickly, Sam went home alone. She caught the last half of the movie the four kids were watching and then helped to tuck in the twins, who were excited about their birthday party the next day. They requested stories from her, Elijah and Scotty before they settled into bed, an hour and a half later than usual.

"Hopefully, they'll sleep in tomorrow," Elijah said as he went downstairs with Sam and Scotty.

"They won't," Scotty said. "Whenever we let them stay up late, they seem to wake up even earlier the next day."

"Awesome," Elijah said, grinning. "Let's watch the playback." They had recorded Nick's speech to watch after the twins went to bed.

Sam poured a glass of wine and sat with the boys on the sofa, feeling strangely detached as she watched her husband—the president of the United States—address the nation.

"He sounds really good," Elijah said. "Very presidential."

"He does," Scotty agreed, sounding proud and excited. "What do you think, Mom?"

"He did a wonderful job. His primary goal was to soothe and reassure the citizens that they're in good hands."

"When will he be home?" Scotty asked.

"I don't know. Something came up right when he finished."

"It was weird not seeing him at all today."

"That won't happen when we live at the White House," Sam said, even as a feeling of dread settled in her belly. God, they had to *move*. Even if they were just moving across town, the thought of it was so exhausting.

"Do you know when that will be?" Elijah asked.

"Not yet, but I figure in the next week or so."

"Wow."

"You just never know what's going to happen next," Scotty said. "First the twins came to live with us, and then Gramps died, and now this." He turned his head so he could look at Sam. "Mrs. Littlefield called today and so did Tony." For Elijah's sake, he added, "That's my former guardian and my biological father."

"What did they have to say?" Sam asked.

"Mrs. Littlefield said she can't wait to visit me at the White House, and Tony said he thinks it's so cool. He's happy for us."

"That's nice of them."

"Are you okay with it?" Scotty asked, sounding hesitant.

"I'm very proud of Dad."

"But?"

"No buts. I'm determined to support him every way I can."

"Are you bummed that we have to move?"

"Kind of, but at least it's just across town. We can come back here anytime we want to."

"It'll be weird not to live here anymore."

"It's temporary," Sam said, uncertain of who she was trying to convince—him or herself. "Three years."

"Please," Scotty said disdainfully. "It'll be seven. He'll run for reelection and win in a landslide. You saw how bummed people were when he said he wasn't going to run."

Sam couldn't begin to think about anything beyond him

completing the last three years of Nelson's term. She'd learned to compartmentalize things that were too big for her brain to handle, and this certainly counted. "He's not deciding anything right away. He has enough to contend with as it is without worrying about the next election cycle."

"Tell me you understand that regardless of what he just said about not running, they won't let him bow out, not as the incumbent," Scotty said, his gaze earnest and intense.

"As I've asked many times before—whose idea was it to send you to school?"

"Definitely not mine," he said, as he usually did.

"I hear what you're saying, but I can't think about that tonight." Not when Nick had been at the White House for more than fourteen hours—on his first day as president.

Eli was scrolling through his phone. "Twitter liked what he had to say. For the most part."

"What does that mean?" Sam asked, even though she didn't really want to know.

"There're detractors, of course. Always will be."

"They make me nervous," Sam said. "That people will hate him simply because of the office he holds. They won't even give him a chance because he's from an opposing party or has ideas they don't agree with."

"That goes with the territory in politics," Scotty said. "You'll never please everyone, no matter how hard you try."

Sam put her arm around him and kissed the top of his head. "You're very wise, Scott Cappuano."

"Did Dad say what took him to the Situation Room?"

"He didn't. That's where the secret stuff happens."

"I hope it's nothing big."

"Me too."

~

SAM WAS DEAD ASLEEP WHEN SOMETHING WOKE HER. THE CLOCK read three ten. She realized what had woken her was Nick getting into bed. Turning, she curled up to him. "So late."

"Sorry to wake you."

"I tried to wait for you. Is everything okay?"

"Nope. Not at all okay."

"Can you talk about it?"

"I'm not supposed to."

"Can we make a deal on day one—or I guess it's day two now?"

"What kind of deal?"

"The kind where you can tell me anything, and it'll never be repeated to anyone even under threat of torture."

"Jesus, Sam. Don't put that horror in my mind when I've got plenty of others already there." He ran his fingers through her hair the way he often did, but every muscle in his body felt tense. "I'll take your deal, and I'll tell you the secretary of State and his detail have been detained by the Iranians."

"Detained. What does that mean?"

"Not allowed to leave." He slumped back against the pillows. "The Air Force pilots were told to take off, but they refused to leave without the secretary and his detail, so now the plane, with two dozen military flight crew, civilian support staff and traveling press corps, is surrounded by Iranian forces, and we've got ourselves a full-fledged international incident."

Sam's mouth had gone dry as her anxiety spiked into the red zone with every word he said. Just over twenty-four hours ago, this would've been Nelson's problem. Now it was Nick's. "What are your advisers saying?"

"The chairman of the Joint Chiefs thinks it's a test to see what I'll do. They say Nelson's death created an opportunity."

"What're you doing?"

"We're meeting at seven to go over the options the others are preparing for me overnight. Everyone is involved, from intelligence to military to allies. I may have to send in special forces, which could lead to war if it goes badly. Of course, them detaining our secretary of State is an act of war in itself, but the goal is to not let it blow up into an actual war."

"Good God. On day one."

"Right? Good times."

"Are you panicking?"

"Trying not to. That won't help anything."

"You can panic with me."

"Thanks, babe. I was going to stay in the Oval, but they said I should go home and sleep while I could. It's apt to be a tense few days. I'll probably miss the twins' party, and that bums me out big-time."

"Don't do that to yourself. They'll have a wonderful time, and we'll tell them you got called into work. They'll understand."

"I want to be with them for their party."

"They'll know that, Nick. We'll make sure of it."

"Why exactly is it that so many people want this job, anyway?"

"Um, if I had to guess, they get off on the idea of being the most powerful person on earth."

"I don't feel very powerful right now with my secretary of State and six Secret Service agents being held hostage by a hostile government."

"You're surrounded by the top minds in the world. They'll tell you what to do."

"I'm surrounded by Nelson's people with no idea whether they're loyal to me, or if they think—like the vast majority of Americans probably do—that they're stuck with a young, inexperienced president who doesn't actually want the job."

"Don't do that. Don't anticipate trouble. If you step up and do the job and handle the crises, they'll see you're more than capable. You're just going to have to show them, one day at a time." She kissed his cheek and got out of bed. "Don't go anywhere."

"Where're you going?"

She went into the bathroom, got a melatonin from his medicine cabinet and returned to bed to give it to him along with the glass of water from her bedside table. Since he had to be back at the White House by seven, she only gave him one. "Take it. You're going to have to sleep to survive this job."

He took the pill, downed it with a swallow of water and handed the glass back to her. "Not sure how I'll ever sleep again."

"You will. Not every day will feel as crazy as the first one did."

"It'd better not, or I might flee the country."

"You'd never do that."

"No, but I wish I could."

"If you did, you'd never forgive yourself for running away."

"I wouldn't."

"Come here." Sam held out her arms to him, and he rested his head on her chest. She ran her fingers through his hair, wishing there was something she could say or do to soothe him. Since there wasn't anything she or anyone could do to ease his burden, she could only love him as fiercely as she ever had while he made this transition and took on the awesome responsibility that came with his new office.

She caressed his back with her other hand, keeping up both until she felt him start to relax as his breathing deepened. If she had to stay up all night rubbing his back, she'd do it if it meant he got some much-needed sleep.

While she waited to be certain he was asleep, she forced her mind to think of anything other than the secretary of State being detained by the Iranians. It was still surreal that something of that magnitude was her husband's problem. *But it's not yours*, she told herself. In an effort to get her mind off Nick's problems so she might sleep too, she thought about Gigi and the way Cameron Green had looked when he came into her hospital room earlier.

Cam and Gigi weren't a pairing she would've considered had she not witnessed a spark of something urgent coming from him when he saw Gigi in that hospital bed. What Sam had noticed went far beyond one colleague's concern for another. She picked through memories of the two of them at work, looking for clues that simply didn't exist.

If something had happened between them, it had occurred outside of work. Both were consummate professionals, so she wasn't worried about their ability to handle a romantic entanglement on the job. It was just odd that he and Gigi had been dating other people, and yet, Sam had witnessed his intense reaction to seeing Gigi injured earlier. Was the attraction—or whatever it was—mutual?

Under normal circumstances, Sam wouldn't give a potential attraction between two of her detectives even ten minutes of her attention until it affected her. Since nothing about her current circumstances could be considered "normal," she was almost relieved to have something to think about other than Nick being president, the Iranians, the location of the man who'd hurt Gigi and her promise to Lenore Worthington to reopen her son's case.

Other than that, Mrs. Lincoln…

She was used to her plate being full to overflowing, but lately, it had been nothing short of ridiculous, beginning with the home invasion that had left the twins orphaned, her father's death and the subsequent closing of his four-year-old case, the murder of President Nelson's former mistress and the ensuing scandal, the murder of the woman who'd defrauded her friends and family, the starting of Sam's grief group at work… It'd been a lot, but then again, it was always a lot in her line of work.

How in the world would she handle her caseload on top of being first lady while also raising three children? Granted, she had lots of help with her three "jobs," but would she be able to do any of them well if she was juggling all of them? Probably not, which made her feel sad and overwhelmed.

The press would be watching her, critiquing her, criticizing her for not being a conventional first lady. With so much weighing on her mind, she wouldn't have thought she'd sleep, but she must have, because she woke with an awful crick in her neck when Nick's alarm went off at six.

He raised his head off her chest and looked up at her with those hazel eyes that slayed her every time he looked at her with so much love. "You have the magic touch, babe. On the way home, I thought there was no way I'd sleep."

Sam sat up while carefully trying to move her head, but her neck wasn't having it.

"Why are you crooked?"

"Slept funny on my neck, and now it won't move."

"Oh damn. Want me to massage it?"

"You need to get going to rescue the secretary of State."

"I have time." He arranged himself in front of her. "Where does it hurt?"

She pointed to the lower left side of her neck, and he focused his attentions there.

"How's that feel?"

"Good."

He kept it up until she could move without pain and then rested his forehead on her shoulder.

Sam curled her hand around his neck. "When I first started on the job, my dad told me that no matter what happened, I should follow my gut and my heart and always try to do the right thing. That's all you can do, Nick. It's all any of us can do."

"Thank you for that," he said, kissing her. "A little Skip Holland was just what I needed today."

"He's available to both of us anytime we need him. I know exactly what he'd say about any situation." She caressed his face and looked into his eyes. "He'd be as proud of you as I am."

"That's good to know. I guess I'm off to see what fresh hell awaits me today."

"That expression is trademarked, but in deference to current events, I'll allow you to use it as you see fit."

"Gee, thanks. I think for the next three years, my fresh hell is going to top your fresh hell, and that's saying something."

Sam laughed and gave him another kiss before he got out of bed. "You win."

"I usually like to win, but in this case, not so much." He headed for the shower while Sam made the mistake of using his phone to scroll through the morning headlines, which were full of news about the situation in Iran as well as all kinds of speculation involving her husband and family. She quickly put the phone down, determined to avoid the news so she could focus on the twins and their birthday party.

Nick came out of the master bathroom fifteen minutes later, wearing a navy suit, a white dress shirt and a blue-and-white-striped tie.

Sam had gotten up and put on a robe. She went to him, slid her arms around his waist under his suit coat and gave him a hug, while breathing in the fresh, clean scent of home. "Good luck today. I'll be thinking of you and the secretary of State and hoping for a quick, peaceful solution."

"From your lips to God's ears."

"Follow your heart and your gut. Your heart is the best heart I know. It'll never steer you wrong."

"Thanks, babe. Tell the kids..." His grimace said it all.

Sam went up on tiptoes to kiss him. "I'll tell them. They'll be fine. They're going to have a wonderful day."

"Save me some cake."

"I will."

"When we get a break in the action, we need to talk to the twins about the upcoming move. Probably before Eli goes back to school."

"We'll do that tonight or tomorrow morning. I agree he needs to be there to reassure them."

Sam walked him downstairs, where Brant and the rest of his much-larger detail waited for him. "Do you ever take a day off?" she asked Brant.

"I almost had a full day off on Thanksgiving, ma'am. Are you ready to go, Mr. President?"

Nick cast a longing eye toward the dining room, where Shelby had been making preparations for the party all week. "I'm ready," he said to Brant.

"Have a good day, love," Sam said.

"You too." He gave her another quick kiss and was out the door. God only knew when she'd see him again.

CHAPTER NINE

Nick hadn't been gone even a minute, and Sam was already lonely for him and worried about what he'd have to contend with over the course of the day. When he'd agreed to be Nelson's new vice president, neither of them could've imagined a day like this one, when he would be heading to the White House, as president, to negotiate the release of the secretary of State from Iranian detention. It sounded more like a plot out of a spy movie than real life.

Sam went to the kitchen to brew coffee and check the to-do list Shelby had left for her when she insisted on helping with the party. Before kids, Sam would've been inclined to delegate the whole thing, but now she wanted to be as involved as she could be and was determined to make sure the twins had the best possible day on this, their first birthday without their beloved parents.

She spent the next hour and a half assembling thirty goody bags from the items Shelby had ordered. They'd invited all the twins' classmates as well as several of their former neighborhood friends—and their parents—all of whom had been vetted by the Secret Service weeks ago.

Of course, both parents in each family had RSVP'd to attend a birthday party at the vice president's home. How excited they must be to tell their friends they were now going to a birthday party at the home of the *president*. The thought of having sixty strangers in her house, all of them gawking at the new first lady, was enough to give her hives. Thankfully, they'd also invited their personal friends and family, who'd hopefully provide a buffer to the gawkers.

Shelby came in a few minutes later, carrying her son, Noah, and followed by her husband, Avery, who was hauling multiple containers. "You can put that in the dining room," Shelby told Avery, already in party-planning-general mode.

Sam had learned to stay out of Shelby's way when she was in general mode. She held up her hands to take Noah, and Shelby gratefully transferred him to Auntie Sam, as Shelby referred to her.

"He suddenly weighs a ton," Shelby said, shaking out her arms as she followed Avery to the dining room.

As Sam ran her lips over the soft silk of the baby's blond hair, an irrational yearning overtook her. It'd been a while since that particular yearning had shown up to remind her of the fertility issues that had plagued her adult life. What in the name of all that was holy would she ever do with an infant in the midst of the madness that was their life? Especially now, when everything had changed. But the yearning was there just the same, impossible to ignore as she snuggled the sweet-smelling baby.

Avery came back to the kitchen. He was tall and handsome, with golden-brown hair and eyes and cheekbones to die for. "How're you holding up?" he asked in the honeyed accent of South Carolina.

"We're doing just great, especially since the Iranians decided to detain the secretary of State."

"What the hell is that about?"

"Great question, Agent Hill. We believe it may be to test the mettle of the new president, or some such thing."

"By risking war?"

"Let's hope it doesn't come to that."

"How is Nick? I mean... Jesus, Sam. You guys must be reeling."

"It's been an interesting couple of days."

Avery snorted out a laugh at what had to be the understatement of the decade. "Listen, before Shelby comes back, she's been really tired lately. This pregnancy is kicking her ass, though she'd never say so. Keep an eye on her today?"

"I will. Thanks for sharing her with me. I couldn't survive without her."

"Me either."

His heartfelt statement was a testament to how far they'd come from the days when the FBI agent had convinced himself he was in love with Sam. They'd traveled a million miles from that unfortunate situation. He was now happily married to Shelby, and they were expecting their second child.

"I'll take him," he said of Noah. "We'll be back for the party."

Sam reluctantly turned the baby over to his daddy.

"We need to talk on Monday."

"What about?"

"I don't want to disrupt your weekend."

Sam laughed. "My husband became president of United States this weekend. There's nothing you can say that'll disrupt my weekend any more than that already has."

"It's about the investigation, which I probably shouldn't even talk to you about since your husband's Justice department oversees my agency." The FBI had been brought in to investigate the Metropolitan Police Department after a series of high-profile officer arrests. Those arrests included the deputy chief, who'd been charged with withholding vital information pertaining to the shooting of Sam's father.

"What about it?"

"You sure you want to do this now?"

"No time like the present."

"And we're acknowledging the potential conflict of interest here?"

"Duly noted."

Avery shifted his weight to better accommodate the baby. "Someone mentioned we need to take a closer look at what went down with the Johnson case."

"Someone mentioned that, did they?" Sam made an effort to hide the blast of rage she felt at knowing one of her colleagues was trying to drag that painful incident into the FBI's probe of the MPD. Two years ago, a child was killed in a shootout after she gave the order to raid a crack house. She'd been haunted by that child's death ever since. "I'm sure it was one of my good friends. Was it Ramsey? Or maybe Offenbach. He's still pissed at me for outing his affair. Apparently, the mother of his five children doesn't want to be married to him anymore, and it's my fault because I'm the one who figured out that he wasn't where he was supposed to be."

"I'm just saying it came up in the context of black marks on the department."

"An internal investigation has already determined Quentin Johnson was killed because his deadbeat father took him to that crack house, not because I ordered our people to invade it. He shot at us. We shot back. His son was killed."

"I understand this is a sore subject—"

"Do you? When was the last time you gave an order that got a kid killed? I spent months undercover with the Johnsons, and never once did I see either of them do anything to endanger Quentin. Why in the world would he be at that house late at night when he'd never been there before?"

Sometimes when she closed her eyes at night, she could still hear Marquis Johnson's anguished screams following his son's death. "Are we really going to revisit that case? I'd imagine that after recent events, the department has much bigger problems than a crack house shooting from two years ago, especially when everyone involved was already found to not be at fault."

"I'm not planning to revisit it," Avery said. "I just wanted to give you a heads-up that it's been mentioned."

"Noted. I'll be disappointed if that case gets relitigated in the media. The first time was more than enough for me."

"We're getting a lot of press inquiries about the investigation, but we're stonewalling them for now. Our job is to provide a report to the U.S. Attorney at the end of this, and I've got no intention of mentioning the Johnson investigation in that report."

"Thank you for the heads-up. It's appreciated, even if it doesn't seem so."

Shelby came back into the kitchen, carrying a plastic bag full of plates and other paper products.

"I'll get out of your hair, ladies. Call me if you need me to grab anything on the way back, and don't overdo it, Mrs. Hill." He kissed his wife and held the baby so she could kiss him.

"You boys have fun at the park," Shelby said, "and try to make sure he gets a nap, or he'll be a bear at the party."

"Will do."

"What can I do?" Sam asked Shelby.

"Start unwrapping the plates and napkins while I finish the goody bags."

"I finished the goody bags."

"Um, no, you started them."

"What's the secret?"

"To what?" Shelby asked.

"To knowing how to do all this stuff."

"You know how to do stuff that I'll never know anything about. You have your gifts, and I have mine. You don't need to worry about knowing how to do any of this, because you have me, and I've got you covered."

"You'll never know how thankful I am to have you, Tinker Bell. Especially on days like today. You're going to come to the White House with us, aren't you?"

"Of course I am. I can't let you make a hot mess of it."

Sam cracked up laughing. "I don't want you to overdo it today. Tell me what to do, and I'll do it."

"Sounds like a plan. I took the liberty of consulting with Lilia about how best to deal with the curious parents, and she suggested we draft something to hand each of them as they arrive. I wanted to run it by you to make sure you approve."

Sam took the sheet of paper that Shelby handed her.

THANK YOU SO MUCH FOR ATTENDING ALDEN AND AUBREY'S BIRTHDAY party! We hope you and your children have a wonderful time. We ask that you please keep the focus on our birthday boy and girl and refrain from asking President or Mrs. Cappuano to pose for photos or provide autographs. We sincerely appreciate the friendship and support provided to Alden and Aubrey during this difficult time in their lives, and we thank you for joining us today.

Sincerely,

Nick and Sam Cappuano

"THAT'S PERFECT," SAM SAID. "DO WE NEED TO RUN IT BY NICK'S people?"

"Lilia was going to take care of that and call me if there're any concerns."

"Thank you so much for thinking of that. I'll admit I was feeling freaked out about sixty strangers coming to my house on this of all weekends."

"I figured you would be, so I also texted your friends, including Freddie and Elin, Gonzo and Christina, Harry and Lilia, Jeannie and Michael, the O'Connors, Celia, your mom, your sisters and Nick's dad, to put them on notice that we need them to help run interference with the other guests."

"That's very good thinking too."

"Is Nick going to make the party?"

"Probably not. The Iranians have messed up his plans for the weekend."

"I saw that on the news this morning. What could they possibly be hoping to achieve?"

"I don't know, but I hope they can resolve it soon."

~

THE NEWS FROM IRAN WAS GRIM. ACCORDING TO NICK'S ADVISERS, the Iranians hadn't responded to a request for information about the well-being of the secretary and his detail. The secretary's plane was still surrounded by Iranian forces, with more than two dozen Americans on board.

"According to the Air Force, they have six days' worth of food and water," Terry reported during the day's first meeting in the Situation Room, "but the bathroom situation will become a concern sooner rather than later if they can't get it pumped."

Nick took calls of concern and offers of support from U.S. allies, all of whom were equally anxious to see the situation resolved peacefully.

Over the next few hours, Nick received briefings from

intelligence and military officials that made him increasingly more nervous about what the Iranians' end game might be.

"Are they hoping we'll send in U.S. forces?" he asked the chairman of the Joint Chiefs of Staff.

"We believe so, sir," Army General Michael Wilson said.

Nick expelled a long deep breath. "I'd like to see my options by the end of the day. We can't let this go on indefinitely."

"If I may, sir," Jennings, the Defense secretary said, "I prefer to see us discussing sanctions before we talk about sending in troops."

"Everything is on the table," Nick said, "up to and including sending in special forces if it comes to that." He'd instructed the Treasury and Commerce secretaries to work on a list of economic sanctions designed to cause the utmost pain to the Iranian economy. However, those sanctions would mostly hurt regular people in Iran who'd had nothing to do with detaining the United States' top diplomat. There were no good solutions to a problem like this, which of course the Iranians had known when they took the bold action of detaining the secretary in the first place.

Nick returned to the Oval Office and placed a call to Secretary Ruskin's wife, Marilyn.

"Mr. President," she said, "thank you so much for calling."

"I'm so sorry for the need to call to reassure you that we're doing everything we can to ensure the safe return of your husband and the others involved in this incident."

"I appreciate that," she said, sounding tearful. "Marty would want you focused on the agents and the others on the plane ahead of him."

"We're focused on bringing all of them home safely. I'll make sure you're kept informed of what's going on."

"Thank you again for calling, Mr. President. It means a lot to my family and me."

"We'll be in touch."

He made calls to the distraught families of everyone else involved in the incident, did his best to reassure them and was emotionally drained by the time he was finished. A quick check of his watch indicated it was nearly party time at home, where he longed to be.

Terry came into the office. "Did you finish the calls?"

"Yes, and you'd never believe how much fun that was."

"I can only imagine."

"I want to call Sam. Am I allowed to use my phone?"

"I have a new, secure BlackBerry for you."

"Ugh, back to the BlackBerry, huh?"

"Afraid so. It's that or nothing, my friend. They're going to want Sam to have one too."

Nick cracked up laughing. "Good luck with that. If the phone doesn't slap shut, she doesn't want it."

"It's one of the few things they'll probably insist on, since she'll be talking frequently to you."

"We'll make it work." Somehow. Maybe she could use a secure phone for anything to do with him and her duties as first lady, and her regular phone for work and personal contacts. Using the new BlackBerry, he made the call to Sam's cell phone, hoping she'd take the call from a number that would show up on caller ID as unavailable.

It rang four times before she answered with a breathless hello.

"Hey, it's me."

"Hey! How's it going?"

He was so damn glad to hear her voice. No one had ever been able to calm him with just a few words the way she could. "It's going. Tense. How are things there?"

"The six-year-old excitement is off the charts. Eli predicted the twins are going to spontaneously combust before the day is over."

Nick chuckled as he imagined the scene and desperately wished he were there to see it. Missing something like the twins' birthday party was exactly why he'd made the decision to sit out the next election cycle. He didn't want to miss anything with them or Scotty, who'd be playing high school hockey by this time next year. "Did you tell them how sorry I am to miss it?"

"I did, and they understand. I told them you'd celebrate with them when you got home."

"It makes me sick to miss it."

"There'll be so many other years, Nick. Try not to let it upset you."

"I'm trying." He fiddled with a pen while he talked to her. "I'm worried about the other parents hassling you for pictures and shit."

"Shelby and Lilia already thought of that. Lilia prepared something to hand out to each of the parents as they come in. Lilia cleared it with Trevor and Terry."

"I'm glad they've got that covered," he said, relieved to know she wouldn't be bothered in her own home because of his job.

"Vernon and Jimmy told me they plan to stay close today too, and I'll be surrounded by friends and family. Try not to worry. Just do what you need to do there so you can get home to us."

"That's the only place I want to be. I hope you know that."

"I do know that, and one of the benefits of living at the White House is if something like this happens again next year, you can pop into the party and then go right back to work."

"That's true." He sat up straighter as an idea took hold. "Take lots of photos and videos for me."

"Will do. We miss you and we love you."

"Love you too, babe."

He ended the call and bellowed for Terry and Brant.

They came in together.

"You rang, sir?" Terry asked, eyebrow raised.

"I want you to take me home for thirty minutes." He checked his watch. "I'll be back in plenty of time for the five o'clock briefing." He was the fucking president and could do whatever the hell he wanted, and what he wanted more than anything—other than for the fucking Iranians to let his secretary of State leave the country—was to be home with his family for the kids' birthday party.

"Yes, sir," Brant said. "We'll make that happen."

CHAPTER TEN

This had to be what it was like to be trapped in elementary school hell, Sam thought, giving thanks to the teachers who spent their days with excited, loud, screeching children and put up with their annoying parents. Shelby, being Shelby, had donned a pink fairy godmother costume and was leading the kids through crafts and games and snacks. Not surprisingly, they hung on her every word.

Sam had sat with Alden and Aubrey to make masks of glitter and sequins that they were now wearing as they played a competitive game of musical chairs.

Despite the written order to leave her the fuck alone, the parents were still all over her, killing her with kindness, probably in hope of securing an invitation to the White House.

Freddie approached her as she spoke with six other mothers, who were peppering her with questions about Nick, her job, their plans, how they felt about moving to the White House. "Sorry to interrupt, Lieutenant. But could I have a moment of your time?"

"Who's this cutie?" one of the perky blonde mommies asked, taking a lustful look at Sam's handsome partner.

"This is my partner, Detective Freddie Cruz. He's happily married—as are you."

The other woman blushed. "I'm never too married to appreciate a handsome man."

Sam linked her arm with Freddie's, wondering if he could sense her desperation. "Excuse us." Under her breath, she said, "Get me out of here."

He led her into the kitchen.

Sam went straight for the liquor cabinet, poured vodka on the rocks and downed it quickly—probably a little *too* quickly.

"Have another one," Freddie said. "So you won't give in to the urge to actually throat-punch someone."

Sam poured another drink, but sipped this one. "Thanks for the rescue."

"Anytime." He grabbed a cola from the fridge and popped it open. "How're you holding up?"

"Just dandy. I've got sixty-something strangers in my house one day after my husband unexpectedly became president. Meanwhile, he's at the White House trying to negotiate the release of his secretary of State, who's been 'detained' by the Iranians. Other than that, all good in the hood."

Freddie made a visible effort not to laugh.

She took another sip from her glass. "Hold it in, or I might throat-punch *you*."

"What're they saying about work?"

"I have no idea. I told Nick that I plan to be business as usual, and I expect him to make that happen."

"And he was cool with that?"

"I guess. I made myself very clear."

"There's a lot of talk in the media about how we've never had a first lady who chose to keep a job outside the White House."

"It's probably high time we did, wouldn't you say?"

"I would, and lots of others are saying that too."

"That's good to know." She took another sip of her drink before dumping the rest down the drain so she wouldn't be tempted to guzzle it all. "I need to get back to the twins."

"I'll stay close to keep the parents away from you."

"Thank you. In case I forget to tell you, you're the best."

"I gotcha covered."

Tracy poked her head into the kitchen. "Ah, Sam, you're going to want to come here."

Sam gave Freddie a *what the hell is this?* look and left the kitchen in time to see Brant come into the house ahead of Nick. A buzz of excitement went through the room when the guests saw him.

Nick spotted Sam and went right to her, putting his arm around her and kissing her forehead. "I heard there's a party here and didn't want to miss it."

"I thought you couldn't get away."

"So did I until I realized if there's any benefit to being president, it's that I should be able to decide what I do and when I do it."

"Good thinking, Lincoln."

"Actually, it's Cappuano, with two p's."

Sam smiled up at him, wishing she could kiss him the way she wanted to, but with scores of strangers watching them, she resisted the urge and led him to the dining room, where the kids were playing pin the tail on the donkey.

Alden and Aubrey let out cries of happiness when they saw Nick, leaving their friends and the game to come hug him.

He squatted to their level and hugged them both at once.

Seeing him with them made Sam forget all about her earlier aggravations so she could focus on him and their family.

They sang "Happy Birthday," helped the twins cut the cake, took pictures with them, Scotty and Elijah, and supervised the opening of an enormous number of presents that would have to be moved to their new home. Goody bags were distributed as school friends began to leave with their starstruck parents until they were finally down to their own family and close friends.

"What an awesome party, Shelby," Sam said. "Thank you so much." She led a round of applause for their Tinker Bell, the maker of magic.

Shelby bowed dramatically and straightened the crown on her head that had gotten crooked during the course of the afternoon.

"Come get off your feet," Sam said to her, gesturing to the sofa. "We'll clean up."

"Don't mind if I do. The old gray mare ain't what she used to be."

"Who do you think you are, calling my beautiful wife an old gray mare?" Avery asked as he put an arm around her.

She reached for Noah, who was on Avery's lap, and snuggled him into her embrace.

"I hate to say I have to go," Nick said, "but I have to go."

"What're you hearing from Iran?" Harry asked him.

"Nothing," Nick said, seeming disheartened. "I'm due to hear my options at five, and I expect them to be unsettling."

"I don't envy you that," Harry said, grimacing.

"Why do people want this job so badly?" Nick asked, forcing a smile for the sake of their friends.

Sam could see he was deeply troubled and stressed, as anyone would be with so much at stake in this situation.

He went to say goodbye to the kids, who were sitting in the middle of their own personal toy store while Scotty and Elijah helped them with packaging and setup. "I'm so glad you guys had such a fun day. Make sure you say thank you to Shelby."

"Thank you, Shelby!" they said together.

"You're welcome, my loves."

Nick said his goodbyes to their friends and family, all of whom had congratulated him and given him their best wishes. The support of those closest to them was good for him as he stepped into this difficult role.

Sam walked Nick to the door. "I'm so glad you got to be here."

"Me too. They're so damn cute."

"They sure are."

At the doorway, Nate, the Secret Service agent on duty, stepped outside to give them a minute of privacy.

"Are you doing okay?" she asked.

"Taking it a minute at a time. Big meeting at five. After that, I should know more."

"Good luck. We're all praying for a peaceful resolution."

"Thanks," he said, kissing her. "I'll be home as soon as I can."

"We'll be here. Do you think I should talk to the Littles about the move while I've got the chance with Eli here?"

"I hate to say you probably should, because I really wanted to be here for that. But I think it's more important that *he's* here to reassure them."

"Don't worry about it. Eli, Scotty and I will take care of it. You take care of you." She kissed him again. "We love you."

"Love you too."

And then he was out the door, surrounded by Secret Service agents.

"The poor guy has the weight of the world on his shoulders," Graham O'Connor said.

Sam turned to him. "It would've been more than enough without the situation in Iran."

"Indeed," Graham said. "Take comfort in knowing he's surrounded by great people who will help him figure out what to do. I'm going to the White House myself after this, and I'll stay for as long as he needs me."

"That'll mean a lot to him, Graham. Thank you for that."

"Try not to worry too much. He's one of the smartest guys I've ever known, and I have full faith in his ability to navigate everything that'll come his way."

Sam had no doubt that Nick had all the intelligence and political savvy needed to be a successful president, but she couldn't help but wonder about the toll his new job would take on their marriage and family.

Lilia came over to talk to her, holding her smart phone. "Mrs. Nelson's chief of staff wants to confirm your appointment for afternoon tea and a tour of the residence tomorrow at two."

"I'll be there." After Lilia confirmed the appointment and ended the call, Sam said, "What do I wear to meet with the first lady?"

"Don't you mean the *former* first lady? Since, of course, you're now the first lady."

Sam scowled at her. "I keep forgetting that."

Lilia laughed. "I'm sure you have a nice dress and a pair of heels you can wear. There'll be photos, so you'll want to do your hair and makeup."

"I'll see what I can do to not look too feral."

"You're going to have a lot of wardrobe demands. We should introduce you to some stylists and designers who can provide you with what you need. That'll take some of the guesswork out of it."

"That's the one part of this whole thing that sounds fun to me —clothes and shoes."

"If you give me some idea of what you'd like, I'll make some calls."

"I'll think about that."

"You also need to think about who you'd like to serve as your social secretary."

Sam recoiled. "I need a *social secretary*?"

"I'm afraid so." Lilia glanced over at Shelby. "I think you have someone very close to you who'd do a marvelous job."

"I... uh... Maybe."

Lilia squeezed her arm. "Try not to worry about anything. We'll walk you through it and make sure you shine. I do have one other thing for you to think about."

"What's that?"

"Andrea has informed me that she's getting married in the spring and planning to move back to Boston with her future husband after the first of the year."

Sam was almost ashamed to admit that she barely knew the woman who'd been her communications director and spokesperson during her tenure as second lady. "That's good news, I suppose."

"She and Brad are very happy. They've been together since their freshman year of college."

"Very nice."

"So we need a new communications director and spokesperson. Before I tap into my professional network, I wanted to ask if you have anyone you might wish to ask."

Sam immediately thought of her new friend Roni Connolly, an obituary writer at the *Washington Star*. "I actually do have someone I'd like to talk to about it, if that's okay."

"Of course. You're the boss, ma'am."

"Don't call me ma'am."

"Yes, ma'am."

"Are you ladies bickering?" Dr. Harry Flynn asked as he put his arm around Lilia.

Sam raised a brow. "Us? Bicker?"

Harry laughed. "What am I saying? You two would have no reason to bicker. You're going to be the most malleable, mild-mannered first lady in history. Lilia will have no problem managing you."

Sam scowled at him as Lilia hooted with laughter. "None of that is funny."

"Oh, yes," Harry said, flashing his dimpled smile. "It's all funny."

~

AN HOUR LATER, AFTER EVERYONE HAD LEFT, SAM HUNG OUT WITH Eli, Scotty and two happy, tired six-year-olds, who were still playing with their new toys. She realized there'd never be a better time to talk to the kids while Eli was still home. She'd given Eli and Scotty a heads-up about talking to them while the kids ate pizza for dinner.

"Hey, guys," she said to Alden and Aubrey. "Can you come sit with me for a minute?"

The kids got up and ran over to her, launching themselves at her with sugar-fueled excitement. She hated that she had to tell them something that might take some of the shine off their perfect day.

"Did you guys have fun today?" she asked when she had her arms full of the blond children who'd captured her heart from the first second she met them.

They nodded.

"It was so much fun," Aubrey said. "Thank you for the party."

"You're welcome, sweetheart. I wanted to talk to you about something that happened the other night. It's nothing bad, so don't worry. But on Thanksgiving, after you guys went to bed, Nick got a phone call from the White House. You remember he works there, right?"

"He's the vice president," Alden said.

"That's right. Do you know what one of the most important jobs the vice president has is?"

They shook their heads.

"If something happens to the president, the vice president has to be ready to become the president. And the other night, when the

White House called, they told Nick that President Nelson had died." They'd been advised when the twins lost their parents to use words they'd understand. *Died* versus *passed away*, for example.

"Like Mommy and Daddy?" Alden asked.

"Yes, honey."

"Is he in heaven with them?"

"I'm sure he is. But the thing is, because President Nelson died, Nick had to become the new president." She watched them carefully, noting the way their little eyebrows furrowed as they tried to make sense of what she was telling them. "Do you know where the president lives?"

"At the White House!" Alden said.

"That's right, and so that means Nick will have to live there."

"Won't he be lonely?" Aubrey asked.

She was the sweetest, most compassionate child.

"Not if we're there with him," Sam said. "That's what I wanted to tell you. We're going to move to the White House to live there with him for the next three years."

Alden bit his lip as he thought about that. "So we won't live here anymore?"

"This will always be our home, but we're going to stay at the White House most of the time. It'll be like when you go to a hotel, but you still have your house at home."

"Can we come home to sleep at night?" Alden asked.

"No, honey, we'll sleep at the White House. You'll have your bed and all your toys and clothes right there with you. And most important, you'll have us—me and Nick and Scotty and Eli when he's home from school. He'll have his own room at the White House just like he does here."

Aubrey's chin wobbled, and her eyes filled with tears.

"We don't want you guys to worry about anything," Elijah said. "Sam and Nick and Scotty will be with you every day, and I'll come home on weekends whenever I can. The most important things aren't going to change."

"I don't want to move," Aubrey said.

"I know you don't, honey." Sam hugged her close. "I don't either, but we don't want Nick to be lonely at the White House by himself."

"You know what's really cool about the White House?" Scotty asked.

Alden perked up. "What?"

"We'll have a pool, a bowling alley and our own movie theater!"

Alden's eyes widened. "No way."

"Yes way," Scotty said. "We're going to have *so much fun.*"

Aubrey reached for Elijah, who took her from Sam.

"Everything is going to be just fine," Elijah assured his siblings. "I promise."

They spent another half hour talking about the White House and answering the kids' questions about living there. Finally, Sam told them it was time for baths and bedtime. They went more easily than usual because they were tired after their big day. She, Eli and Scotty tucked them in, and Eli read them a birthday book he'd bought for them that had their names as part of the story.

After the story, Sam and Scotty gave the three of them a few minutes alone.

In the hallway, Scotty said, "I guess that went pretty well."

Amused as always by him, she said, "I think so. I feel for them. They just got comfortable here, and now we're going to disrupt them again."

"They'll be okay as long as we're all there with them. That's what'll matter most."

She hooked an arm around him and kissed the top of his head. "You were great. Telling them about the fun stuff was brilliant."

"That's the stuff that matters to kids, along with the people they love being there with them."

Elijah came out of the bedroom a few minutes later, looking a little undone.

Sam experienced a maternal wave of love for the young man who'd become such a big part of their lives along with his siblings. She went to him and hugged him. "They're going to be fine. Try not to worry. We'll take good care of them."

He returned her embrace, seeming to need it as much as she did, and then pulled back to run a hand through his dark hair, something she'd noticed he did when he was stressed. "I'll come home every weekend until they get settled into a new routine."

"I don't want you to worry either. They'll be fine. We'll make sure of it."

The boys went downstairs to play video games while she went into her room to text Nick. *Talked to the Littles. It went pretty well. A few chin wobbles and lots of questions, but Scotty was awesome and told them about the pool, bowling alley and movie theater, and that made it much more exciting. He was brilliant. And so was Eli.*

He wrote back thirty minutes later. *Glad to hear it went well. Scotty to the rescue. I'm not surprised that he knew what would make them feel better. Sorry I couldn't be there to help.*

Don't worry. It's all good. We told them we can't let you be lonely at the White House, and they definitely don't want that.

Love those Littles so much. Wish I was there with you guys.

We'll be here when you get home. Xo

CHAPTER ELEVEN

Much later, long after she and the boys had gone to bed, Sam was struggling to sleep without Nick. Her phone rang with a call from Gonzo that had her sitting up in bed.

"Hey, what's up?"

"We found Gigi's ex."

"That's good news."

"Yeah, not so much. He's holding her mother, sister and two nephews hostage in the mother's house in Fairfax."

Sam's heart sank. "Seriously?"

"Dead seriously. We talked to a bunch of his friends, all of whom mentioned he's been increasingly erratic and unstable lately. And the kicker is, he wants to talk to you."

"*To me?* What the hell do I have to do with anything?"

"I have no idea, but the Fairfax County SWAT captain asked me to get you here ASAP. Can you do it?"

"I'm on my way." Sam ended the call, got out of bed, crossed the hallway to the room that served as her closet and put on jeans, a sweater and running shoes. She would miss the amazing closet Nick had built for her. What kind of closets would they have at the White House? Ugh, she couldn't think about that right now.

Back in the bedroom, she unlocked her bedside table drawer and retrieved her service weapon, sliding it into the holster on her hip. She went up to give Elijah the monitor for the twins.

"I don't know how long I'll be," she said.

"No worries. I'll listen for them, but they're probably out cold after the amazing day they had. Thank you again for that."

"It was entirely my pleasure and all thanks to Shelby. I'll text you when I'm back."

"Okay."

She went back downstairs, knocked on Scotty's door and poked her head in. "I have to go out for work. Eli is here if you need anything."

"I'm fine. Just watching the end of the Caps game."

"I'll see you in the morning."

"Are you allowed to just leave?"

"I guess we're gonna find out." She dared anyone to try to stop her. The lives of Gigi's loved ones were on the line, and if her presence would help to save them, she was going.

Downstairs, she encountered Nate still at the door. "Good evening, Mrs. Cappuano. May I help you with something?"

"No, thanks, I'm all set. If you could just let me out, I'd appreciate it."

"I'm, ah, under orders..."

"So am I. Please step aside."

After a long moment of staring at each other, neither of them blinking, he finally did as she'd directed. Sam made haste down the ramp and was in her car and pulling away in a matter of seconds. She headed for the checkpoint and didn't slow down as she zoomed through the exit lane.

She let out a happy laugh as she made her escape and headed for the 14th Street Bridge and Northern Virginia. Maybe there'd be hell to pay with Nick and the Secret Service, but she was determined to keep her life as close to what it had looked like on Wednesday as she possibly could. With that in mind, she turned on her emergency lights and pressed the accelerator almost to the floor. Her phone rang with a call from Captain Malone that she took on the Bluetooth. "Hey."

"You heard about Dominguez's family?"

"I did, and I'm on my way."

"Oh, good. We were worried the Secret Service might try to stop you from leaving."

"They tried and failed." Sam couldn't think about how pissed Nick would be that she'd left without a detail. She'd contend with the fallout after she'd done what she could to stop Dominguez's nightmare from compounding exponentially. "What're you hearing from the scene?"

"Fairfax County SWAT is in place and prepared to go in, but they want you to try first. Ezra specifically asked to speak to you."

"Any idea why?"

"The thinking is that he's well aware of who you are as Gigi's boss and now the first lady. He's wanting attention from a high-profile officer."

"Well, we'll give it to him and hopefully talk him into letting his hostages go." A memory of being held hostage herself, first by Clarence Reese and then by Lieutenant Stahl, made her break into a cold sweat. Reese had shot himself only feet away from her after a standoff in which she'd nearly talked him into handing over the gun before SWAT burst into the diner where she was being held. The situation with Stahl had been a lot worse for her, but she didn't have the bandwidth to revisit that awful day.

Hostage situations were the worst, and she prayed for Gigi's sake—and that of her family members—that they'd be able to peacefully resolve this one. Sam's cell phone rang with a call from Nick.

"Hey, I know you're pissed, but I got a life-or-death call—not my life or death—that I'll tell you about later. Everything is fine, but I have to go."

"This isn't cool, Samantha."

"I know. I'm sorry. I'll call you as soon as I can."

"See that you do."

When he ended the call without telling her he loved her or to be careful, her anxiety spiked the way it did anytime they were at odds. As she pulled onto the street where Gigi's mother lived, Sam had to stay focused on the task at hand before she dealt with the consequences waiting for her at home.

The street was full of public safety vehicles with red and blue lights flashing. She parked and pressed the button on the door to open the trunk. After retrieving her bulletproof vest, she donned it as she walked toward the epicenter of the activity.

Gonzo saw her coming and waved her over to where he was consulting with Fairfax County SWAT team members.

"Lieutenant Holland, this is Captain Bruce," Gonzo said, "and Lieutenant Dorsey, the hostage negotiator."

"Good to meet you both." Sam sensed instant hostility from both men. Awesome. She could never understand why some officers hated her on sight, when they'd never even met her. Apparently, her reputation preceded her.

"Glad you could make it, Lieutenant," Dorsey said. "We've been talking to the suspect, and he's very interested in speaking to you personally."

"I heard. Let's get me in there."

"So you're just going to walk in there, no big deal?" Bruce asked.

Sam gave him a perplexed look. "He wants to talk to me. I want to get my detective's family members out of there. So yeah, I'm going to walk in there, no big deal. Is that a problem?"

"Not for me," Bruce said.

"Captain, why don't you just say what's on your mind so we can get back to doing our jobs here?"

"I'm just wondering what business the first lady has at a crime scene and how much of a clusterfuck it's gonna be for me if the first lady gets herself killed on my watch."

Sam bit back the bitchy reply that burned on the tip of her tongue, which would've been something like, *Mind your own fucking business.* Instead, she said, "Right now, I'm not the first lady. I'm a police commander intent on saving the lives of one of my detectives' family members. If you're done wasting time, I'm ready to get to it."

Gonzo grunted under his breath, which meant he was trying not to laugh.

Giving Sam an openly hostile look, Bruce said, "Fine. Get him on the phone, then."

Dorsey made the call. "Ezra, I have Lieutenant Holland here, and she'd like to talk to you." He handed the phone to Sam.

"Hey, Ezra. This is Sam Holland. I heard you wanted to talk to me."

"Why do you go by Holland when you're married to the president?"

That was his first question? "I'm Holland on the job. You wanted to talk to me. What can I do for you?"

"I want you to help me."

"With what?"

"I need you to talk to Gigi. She respects the hell out of you, and if you tell her she needs to listen to me, she'll do it."

"I'm afraid I can't recommend she do that while you're holding her family and she's in the hospital with injuries you inflicted."

"That wasn't my fault! She wouldn't listen to me. I tried to tell her..." A muffled sound that might've been a sob came through the phone. "I love her so much."

"If that's the case, why did you hurt her?"

"I didn't mean to. I was so scared she would leave me. She stopped taking my calls and wouldn't answer my texts. I didn't know what to do."

"Ezra, you have to know if you hurt her family, you'll never see her again. Tell me you understand that."

"I don't want to hurt them."

"Then let them go. They haven't done anything to deserve being put in this position. Please let them go."

"I can't do that. If they're here with me, then Gigi will have to talk to me."

"She's in the hospital, Ezra. They had to do surgery to remove her spleen because it ruptured after you punched her in the stomach. Did you know she had surgery?"

"No," he said, sniffling. "I love her so much. I just wish she'd listen to me."

"What else can I do to help you? Besides bring her here. If I got her on the phone, would you let her family go?"

"I... I don't know."

"I'd need some assurances before I reach out to her. I'll ask you again... If I promise to get Gigi on the phone, will you release her family members?"

"If I agree, you're not going to fuck me over, are you?"

"I give you my word that if you release them, I'll get Gigi on the phone for you. But I'm not going to wait all night, Ezra. You either take the deal, or you don't."

"I... I really want to talk to Gigi."

"Then let them go, and I'll get her on the phone." While she waited to see what he would do, Sam used her own phone to call Dani.

"Hey," Dani said.

"Are you aware of what's going on at the Dominguez home in Fairfax?"

"What? No..."

"Ezra has taken Gigi's mother, sister and nephews hostage."

"Oh my God."

"I'm there now, and I've got him on another line. I think he'll let them go if he can talk to Gigi. Are you still at the hospital?"

"Yes, I'm with her."

"I'm afraid you'll have to tell her what's going on and ask her if she's able to do this."

"Hang on."

In the background, Sam could hear the rumble of voices and the moan of agony from Gigi when Dani told her what was happening with her family.

"She'll do it," Dani said. "Patch the call through to my phone."

"Stand by." Sam ended that call and returned to the call with Ezra. "Gigi is willing to talk to you, Ezra, but only if you release her family members first." While she waited for him to reply, she watched the house so intently that she barely blinked. *Please*, she thought. *Please, let them go.*

"Ezra, are you there?"

"I'm here. How do I know you aren't going to fuck me over?"

"Because I gave you my word. Are you willing to give me yours? Will you release Gigi's family?"

"I... Okay."

Sam released the deep breath she'd been holding and turned to Dorsey. "Can you conference someone in on your phone?"

He took the phone from her. "What's the number?"

Sam found Dani's number in her contacts and recited it. "Don't put it through yet." She took back the phone from Dorsey. "Ezra, we're ready to get Gigi on this call. All you have to do to talk to her is let them go. Just send them out. She's waiting to talk to you."

"She really is? You're not just saying that?"

"I swear on the lives of my husband and children that she'll talk to you after you release her family members. I can't think of any other guarantee I can give you that would mean more to me than that."

After a long moment of silence, a flurry of activity in the doorway preceded two women and two young boys emerging from the house.

"Hold your fire," Sam called to the line of officers who had guns trained on the house.

Fairfax County police officers rushed forward to meet them, guiding them toward the driveway and away from the activity on the lawn.

"Put through the conference call," she said to Dorsey.

When he hesitated, she gave him a withering look. "Do it!"

He made the call to Dani's phone.

She answered on the first ring.

"Ezra," Sam said, "Gigi is on the line."

"Ezra," Gigi said, her voice soft.

"Gigi," he said, "I'm so sorry I hurt you." He was almost inaudible over the sound of his sobs. "I love you so much. I never meant for any of this to happen."

"You need to get some help."

"I need *you*."

"I can't do this anymore, Ezra."

"No, don't say that. You don't mean that."

Captain Bruce, back from checking on the former hostages, leaned across Dorsey to speak to Sam. "How long is this going to go on?"

Sam held up a finger to hopefully shut him up. Gigi knew what needed to be done, and Sam wanted to give her the chance to talk him out before SWAT went in after him.

"Ezra, I want you to do something for me," Gigi said.

"Anything. I'll do anything for you."

"I want you to surrender to the police and let them help you. Will you do that for me?"

"I can't do that. They'll lock me up, and I'll never see you again."

"You'll see me again, but only if you do the right thing. Put down your weapon, raise your hands over your head and walk out of there. No one will hurt you if you do the right thing. Will you do that for me, Ezra? Please?"

"I'll really see you again if I do that?"

"You will. I promise."

"Gigi..."

"It'll be okay. You just have to do what I said."

Gigi's voice had become softer as she got tired. Sam hoped Ezra would surrender sooner rather than later.

"I have to go now," Gigi said. "The doctor is here, and he wants to talk to me."

"Gigi, don't go."

"I have to, and you do too. You need to surrender, Ezra. Please do that for me."

"Gigi..." Ezra broke down into sobs that Gigi didn't hear because she'd ended the call. She'd done what she could.

"Ezra," Sam said. "You got to talk to Gigi like you wanted. Now you need to leave your weapon in the house and come out with your hands above your head, like Gigi said. No one wants to hurt you. Come out, and we'll make sure you get the help you need."

"You'll throw me in jail."

"We'll get you help and figure out what you need."

"I don't believe you. You're Gigi's friend."

"I've kept my word to you so far. Why would I start lying to you now?" Her cell phone was ringing relentlessly, but Sam ignored it to stay focused on Ezra and bringing this unfortunate incident to a successful conclusion. Success in this case meant no one got hurt. "Ezra, are you there?"

"I'm here."

"Come on out, and let's figure this out together."

"You're the new first lady. What do you care about me?"

"I'm still a lieutenant with the Metro PD, and I will be until I retire. I care about you and about Gigi. You've been important to her for a long time, so that means you're important to me too."

A sob came through the line. "I love her so much."

"I know, Ezra. She knows that too. She knows this isn't you and that what happened to her isn't you."

"It's not me. I'd never hurt her. I'd die before I hurt her."

"She doesn't want you to die, Ezra. That wouldn't help her."

"I want to die because I hurt her."

Captain Bruce leaned in to whisper to Sam, "You've got thirty seconds. I'm sending my people in whether you're done chatting or not."

She again held up her hand to hold him off. "Ezra, are you coming out?"

Bruce scowled at her.

Sam didn't care if he was pissed. She cared about getting Ezra out of there safely so Gigi wouldn't have to live with his death on her conscience for the rest of her life. None of this was her fault, but she knew Gigi, and despite what Ezra had done, Sam was certain her detective would never get over it if this incident ended with his death.

They waited another ten minutes in tense silence.

Sam knew Bruce and his team wouldn't wait forever for Ezra to come out on his own. She was about to ask him again if he'd come out when the front door opened, and he appeared with his hands raised above his head. "Hold your fire," she said, in case anyone decided to get trigger happy.

Sam stepped around the barrier the police had erected.

"Lieutenant!" Bruce said. "Come back."

Since he wasn't her commander, she ignored him and walked toward the sidewalk, wanting Ezra to see her there waiting for him. Maybe if she was in the middle of things, none of the other cops would be tempted to shoot. She kept her hands in front of her so he could see she wasn't pointing a weapon at him. As she got closer to the house, his gaze locked in on her.

He took a step out of the house.

"I'm here, Ezra. It's okay to come out. Just keep your hands where we can see them."

He was crying uncontrollably as he came toward her. Right away, Sam could see he was an exceptionally handsome young man with dark hair and eyes, a chiseled jaw and muscular build.

Sam held out a hand to him, and when he was close enough, he took hold of her hand.

"I'm sorry," he said, shaking with sobs. "I'm so sorry."

"I know, Ezra." She signaled to Captain Bruce. "The captain is going to cuff you and take you into custody. I'm going to keep in touch and make sure you're given a full mental health evaluation and that you have legal representation. All right?"

He nodded.

Bruce and Dorsey approached them. Dorsey recited the Miranda rights and cuffed Ezra.

"It's going to be okay, Ezra," Sam said. "Do you have an attorney I can call for you?"

Shaking his head, he said, "No."

"I've got someone I can call. His name is Devon Sinclair. Wait for him to get there before you talk to anyone. I'll check on you tomorrow."

"Thank you. I... Please tell Gigi... Tell her I love her, and I'm sorry. I'm so sorry."

"I'll tell her."

A uniformed officer led him toward a patrol car.

"That was well done, Lieutenant," Bruce said, sounding somewhat begrudging.

"You'll make sure he gets the consult, right? By all accounts, his recent behavior is wildly out of character."

"I'll take care of it."

Sam extended her hand. "Thank you."

He shook her hand. "You're really going to keep the job?"

"That's the plan."

"Well, I wish you luck with that."

"Do you really?"

He laughed. "Yes, I do. I have four daughters. It'd be nice for them to see you hold on to your career while serving as first lady too."

"In that case, thank you for the good wishes."

"I was sorry to hear about your dad's passing. I knew him years ago when we were both in Patrol. And I was also sorry to hear where the investigation led."

"Thank you, Captain. I'm going to go call my detective and let her know we were able to resolve this peacefully."

"Here's my card if you need anything."

Sam took it from him. "Thanks." As she walked away, she placed a call to Dani.

"What's happening?" Dani asked, sounding stressed.

"He's surrendered to Fairfax County police. The captain in charge promised a full psych eval."

"I guess that's good news."

"Best possible outcome, all things considered. How's Gigi?"

"Better since she could talk to her mom and sister."

"Let her know Ezra said how sorry he is that all of this happened and he loves her very much. It was important to him that I tell her that, so I'm keeping my promise."

"I'll let her know."

"You should go home and get some rest, Dani."

"That's the plan. Green is coming back in an hour and planning to stay with her."

"What's up there?"

"I'm not really sure, to be honest. He's been here all day and seems... How shall I say it? *Devoted.*"

"I picked up on that vibe earlier. Doesn't he have a girlfriend?"

"Far as I know."

"Very interesting."

"Indeed."

"I know I speak for Gigi when I tell you how much we appreciate you being personally involved in this."

"Of course I am. She's one of mine, and so are you."

"Thank you."

"I'll be by to see Gigi tomorrow."

"See you then."

Sam ended that call and checked her phone to see she had ten missed calls from an unavailable number. Crap. She took a minute to check on Gigi's mother, sister and nephews, who were being checked out by EMS.

"Thank you so much, Lieutenant," Mrs. Dominguez said, her face awash in tears. "My Gigi... She speaks so highly of you."

"I'm so glad you and your family are safe."

CHAPTER TWELVE

The minute she was able to, Sam called Nick. It rang a bunch of times before his voice mail picked up. She ended that call and tried Terry.

He answered on the third ring. "Sam, er, Mrs. Cappuano."

"Sam is fine. Is Nick there?"

"Hang on."

"Samantha."

"I tried to call your phone, but it went to voice mail."

"Because I'm not allowed to use that phone anymore. It's not secure."

"Oh. Sorry."

"What's going on?"

"I got called into a situation with Gigi's ex in Fairfax. He took her mother, sister and nephews hostage. I didn't have time to wait for a detail. Thankfully, I was able to talk him out with no one getting hurt."

When he had nothing to say to that, Sam realized he was seriously pissed, which had a twinge of anxiety zinging through her. She hated when he was upset with her, but she wasn't about to apologize for doing her job and saving lives in the process.

"How are things there?" she asked.

"Tense. I'm waiting for a call from the Iranian president, and we're hearing that someone from the party posted a photo of me there with the kids. From what I hear, Twitter is on fire about me having time for birthday parties when the secretary of State is being held hostage by the Iranians, with the hashtag illegitimatePOTUS trending."

She leaned against her car and expelled a deep breath. "Shit. I'm sorry. One of those fucking idiot parents must've posted it."

"And took great pleasure in doing it."

"I knew we should've confiscated their phones, but everyone said they'd want pictures of their kids, so I was overruled."

"Next time, we will, or they don't get in."

"I'm sorry that happened and that you were worried about me."

"We need to talk."

Her stomach began to ache at the way he said that. "Okay..."

"I have to go. They've got the Iranian president on the line."

"When will I see you?"

"No idea. I'll call you when I can."

The line went dead before she could reply. Again, he hadn't said goodbye or told her he loved her or asked her to be careful. "Shit, fuck, damn, hell."

Gonzo approached her. "That was exceptionally well done, Sam."

"Thanks, but apparently, I'm in big trouble for leaving without a detail." Knowing Nick was pissed with her ruined the high that came from successfully resolving the hostage situation. "Go on home to your wife and do the paperwork tomorrow."

He flashed her a dirty grin. "Don't mind if I do."

Sam got back in her car and took a call from Captain Malone on Bluetooth.

"What's going on in Fairfax?"

Sam updated him on the resolution of the situation with Ezra Smith.

"Well, that's a relief. Your husband is looking for you."

"I got that memo. I just talked to him."

"He's very upset that you left home without a detail."

"I didn't have time for them to figure that out when I had Gigi's ex holding her family hostage. This is exactly why I can't be expected to have a detail when I'm working. Who has the *time* for it?"

"He told me there's a meeting to discuss your work situation on Tuesday. I heard something else that'll interest you."

"What's that?"

"The mayor called the chief to request a meeting with you."

"What? With me? What the hell does she want?"

"She wouldn't say. Just asked him to make you available to her in the next couple of days."

"Like I don't have enough going on."

"She said she understands you're very busy, but she'd like to see you nonetheless, and since you technically work for the woman, I'd see to that sooner rather than later. I emailed you the info about who you need to call to set it up."

"I'll get right on that," Sam said, her tone dripping with sarcasm.

"See that you do. The chief wants her taken care of so she's not up in his grill."

"I hear you. I'll do it, even if I don't want to."

"Such is life, Lieutenant. Full of things we don't want to do but *have* to do."

"You're actually telling me that after what's just happened to me?"

His ringing laughter pissed her off even more than she already was. Why in the hell was the mayor asking for a meeting with her? "The mayor isn't going to ask for my badge, is she? Because she'll have to fight me for it."

"I don't think that's it. She was vague with the chief, but she didn't say anything about asking for your badge or you no longer working for the District."

"She'd better not say anything like that." The very thought of it was enough to make Sam sick. "I'm coming in on Monday, and I'm reopening Calvin Worthington's case. I have a Secret Service meeting at La Casa Blanca on Tuesday and the funeral for Nelson on Thursday. Other than that, I'll be at work. I'll take annual leave for the funeral and the meeting and anything else that comes up respective to the new situation."

"Do what you need to do, Lieutenant. I'm fairly confident we owe you thousands of hours in overtime that you'll never get paid for."

"Tens of thousands."

"We're going to need to work out some sort of formal arrangement that allows you to successfully juggle your various duties in a way that works for everyone."

"*Ugh.* That is my word of the day. I've said it a hundred times today."

"One hell of a holiday weekend, huh?"

"You said it, Captain."

"Make sure you file a report on what went down in Fairfax."

"I'll get right on that too." She hated doing reports almost as much as she hated being the subject of meetings at City Hall and the White House. "Talk to you Monday, if not before."

"I'll look forward to that."

Sam laughed as she slapped the phone closed. Would they require her to have a different phone too? Crap, she hoped not. Her phone rang again with a call from her partner. "What's up?"

"That's what I was going to ask you. Everyone is looking for you."

"So I heard. I just helped to defuse a hostage situation in Fairfax. Gigi's ex took her mother, sister and nephews hostage. He asked for me, so I went. I guess that's now a federal offense."

"I think it's more that you went without a detail."

"I didn't want to wait for them! People's lives were at stake, lives that matter a great deal to one of my detectives. Would you want me to dick around if your family was being held?"

"No, I wouldn't."

"There you have it. I did my job, and now everyone's in my face about it."

"Including your husband?"

"Beginning with him."

"What'd he say?"

"That we need to talk. Nothing good ever comes from an appointment to *talk*."

"I think you guys will figure this out. It might take some time, but you'll get there. Concessions will need to be made on both sides. You're going to have to compromise, Sam."

"I'm willing to compromise, but how far will I have to go?"

"You're going to have to let them protect you."

"I don't care about that, but I'm not going to wait around for them when there're lives at stake. That's my line in the sand."

"I understand that, but you're going to have to make them understand too. And you're going to have to do it in a way that wins them over to your way of thinking."

"Are you saying I have to charm them?"

"Um, well... Charm isn't exactly your strong suit."

"Exactly! So how am I supposed to do that?"

"Talk to them about what the job means to you, how you serve the people by protecting them, by locking up murderers. Nick knows, but the others don't. Make them see why this matters to you and to others."

"You're right. He's right. Everyone is right. That's the problem. I know it's dangerous for me to be without protection."

"You'd be one hell of a prize for anyone trying to get the president's attention. He's never been shy about what you mean to him."

"I know," she said, sighing. "Someone at the party posted a picture of him there, and now it's trending on Twitter that he's got time to attend a birthday party when the Iranians are holding the secretary of State hostage."

"Come on," Freddie said. "You're kidding."

"Nope. It was one of those fucking parents. Next time, we're banning phones and hiring a photographer to take pictures for everyone."

"You'll have a White House photographer at your disposal."

"Huh, well, that's one perk."

"Dude, you're going to have *butlers*."

"Not sure how I feel about people waiting on me. Makes my blue collar feel kinda tight."

Freddie cracked up. "I'm sure you'll get used to it, and remember, the job of the butlers is to serve the first family. You have to let them do their jobs, and you have to be gracious about it."

"So I have to be charming *and* gracious?"

"I'm afraid so, and for what it's worth, I think you're going to be a fantastic, beloved first lady."

"I wouldn't go that far."

"I'm not changing my mind about that. People already love you guys, and they're only going to love you more when they really get to know you."

"I guess we'll see. On Monday, we're reopening Calvin Worthington's case, so come in ready to dig deep. I promised Lenore we'd get justice for her son, and I fully intend to honor that promise."

"I'll be there, and I'll be there for you and Nick through all of this. I'm so incredibly proud of you guys. My friends, the first couple. It's unreal."

"Thank you," she said, touched by his emotional outpouring, "but if you break into 'Kumbaya,' I'm going to throat-punch you the next time I see you."

"Haha, I wouldn't offend you by singing. Call me if you need anything before Monday."

"Dive into the Worthington files. I emailed you a copy of everything I have."

"I saw that earlier, and I'm going to give it some time tomorrow."

"Thanks. We're going to get this done for Lenore. She's waited long enough for justice for her son."

"Completely agree. I'm on it."

"Hey, one more thing. Will you call Devon Sinclair and ask him to check on Ezra Smith in Fairfax County?"

"Gigi's ex?"

"Yeah."

"Uh, why are we helping him get a lawyer after what he did to her?"

"Because from all accounts, his recent behavior has been out of character. I think he needs a mental health eval, and for Gigi's sake, I want to make sure he's represented. I thought of Devon after we saw him recently." Devon had played into an earlier case involving his late uncle, Julian Sinclair, who'd been nominated to the Supreme Court before his murder.

"All right. I'll find his number and give him a call."

"Tell him it's me asking."

"Will do."

"Thanks. I'll see you Monday, if not before."

"Are you still on call for any homicides?"

"You bet your ass I am."

"That's okay. Elin likes my ass. Not willing to risk it."

"Shut up and go away."

He hung up laughing, pleased with himself and his stupid joke.

"Insubordinate fool," she muttered as she crossed the 14th Street Bridge that took her from Northern Virginia back into the District where she belonged. The thought had her longing for her dad, who always hated to leave the District for any reason. "Ah, Skippy. Where are you when I need you? Nick is the freaking *president*. Can you even believe it? I can't wrap my head around everything that's happened in the last forty-eight hours." Her eyes filled with tears that she couldn't give in to. If she started crying, she might never stop. "I sure do miss you, Dad. I could use your calm voice right now, telling me how to handle this unexpected detour. You'd know just what I should do."

In a spontaneous moment, Sam decided to take the exit to her favorite place in the capital city. She parallel parked on 23rd Street, found an MPD ball cap in her trunk and tugged it down over her eyes in the hope that she wouldn't be recognized. She jogged toward the Lincoln Memorial, which had always been the place she'd been drawn to when life became too much for her. On the white marble steps, she nodded to the guard on duty, who didn't seem to realize he was greeting the new first lady.

She landed on her preferred side of the monument that paid tribute to the Gettysburg Address and slid down the wall to sit on the cold marble floor. Just that quickly, she felt a sense of peace come over her as she took the first deep breath she'd been able to manage since Nick got The Call, as it would forever be known.

Looking up at Mr. Lincoln, she wondered what he'd have to say about the new president. Would he approve of Nick Cappuano from Lowell, Massachusetts? Though they were of different political parties, Sam had to believe that Lincoln would recognize the fundamental honor and decency that Nick brought to everything he did.

"I don't want to be first lady, Abe," she whispered. "I really, *really* don't. But I love him so much. So, so much. There's nothing I wouldn't do for him. Even this." She wiped tears from her face that made her angry. Under normal circumstances, she wasn't a weepy kind of woman, but the sheer magnitude of what'd happened had her emotions all over the place as she tried to accommodate this massive change in their lives.

They'd have to move. Granted, it would only be across town, but it might as well be overseas for the changes that move would bring. They'd be in the glare of the most relentless spotlight on earth, their every word and action critiqued by people who'd never meet them or really know them. Their already high profile would become even more so, which spiked anxiety the likes of which she hadn't felt this acutely since Stahl wrapped her in razor wire and threatened to set her on fire.

And then she was laughing at the sheer madness of comparing being first lady to being wrapped in razor wire. That was worse. For sure. But this...

It was a lot on top of a lot, and it would take a minute to figure out how she was supposed to react, to behave, to go forward from here. Her phone rang, and she checked the caller ID to make sure it wasn't Eli or Scotty looking for her. She decided to take the call from her new friend Roni Connolly.

"Hey."

"I was planning the voice mail I was going to leave. I didn't expect you to actually answer."

"Well, here I am." She'd met Roni after her young husband, Patrick, was killed by a stray bullet.

"How are you?" Roni asked.

"Is that a rhetorical question?"

Roni laughed. "It wasn't supposed to be."

"I'm currently sitting at my favorite place in the District, staring up at Lincoln and asking him how in the hell I'm supposed to do this."

"Are you there by yourself?"

"Yep."

"How'd you pull that off?"

"I walked out of my house to deal with a hostage situation that involved the family of one of my detectives."

"Is the family okay?"

"They are now."

"Cripes, your life is too crazy."

"And getting more so by the minute."

"Can I do anything for you as your newest friend?"

Sam smiled. She liked this woman—a lot—and that was saying something, since she usually hated people. "Actually, there is something you can do for me if you're so inclined."

"Whatever you need. Just name it."

That made Sam laugh again. "You ought to wait to hear what it is before you say that."

"You don't scare me. Other things do, but you don't."

"Clearly, I'm doing something wrong with you if that's the case."

"Whatever," Roni said sarcastically, which only made Sam like her more. Sarcasm was one of her favorite features in a potential friend. "Bring it on."

"I'm in need of a first lady communications director and press secretary and wondered if you might want the job." After a long moment of complete silence, Sam said, "Hello? Roni? Are you there?"

"I'm here."

"Have I finally found a way to render you speechless?"

"I think maybe you have."

Sam cracked up. "Oh, come on. You're not going to roll over that easily, are you?"

"Uh, well... You're not serious about this, are you?"

"I am. The woman I had as second lady is getting married and leaving town. When they told me I'd need a new one, I immediately thought of you."

"I'm an obituary writer, Sam. Not a press secretary."

"I assume you went to school for the job you currently hold?"

"I went to journalism school at the University of Virginia."

"There you go. You're qualified."

"No, I'm not!"

"You have the most important qualification as far as I'm concerned."

"I can't wait to hear this."

"I assume that as my newest friend—and the first friend I've bothered to make in a while—you'd be somewhat loyal to me, my husband, our family."

"I would be. Of course I would, but I don't know anything about being a press secretary."

"And I know nothing about being first lady. Maybe we could figure it out together?"

"You need to think about this."

"I have. I want you. Any questions?"

"For God's sake, Sam. You need someone who knows what they're doing, who isn't a red-hot emotional-widow mess. You need—"

"I need *you*, Roni. I need my friend to do this for me and to have my back. Can you do that?"

"You're really serious about this?" she asked, her voice higher than Sam had ever heard it.

"Dead serious."

A long sigh came from Roni.

"Do you want some time to think about it?" Sam asked.

"No, I don't want time to think about it."

Sam's heart sank at the possibility of having to hire a stranger for the critical role of speaking for her. She could ask Darren Tabor, who also worked for the *Star*, but she suspected he wouldn't want to change sides. He was a reporter through and through. "It's okay. I understand."

"What do you understand?"

"That you don't want to do it. I know you've got a lot going on and that you're grieving. It's a big ask and probably insensitive of me to even propose this to you, but I told you I'd be a shit friend." Sam stopped talking when she realized Roni was laughing. "What's so funny?"

"You are. I never said I didn't want to do it. I just said I didn't need time to think about saying yes."

"You're saying *yes*?"

"That's what I just said. But I'm warning you I'm apt to be a shit press secretary."

"I'm a shit friend, so we're good."

"I may be a shit press secretary, but I'll always be your friend and will protect you with everything I've got."

"You're hired."

Roni's giddy laughter filled Sam with an unreasonable feeling of joy. Sam hoped the new job might provide a distraction that would help Roni adjust to her new normal. "I seriously can't believe you asked me."

"Believe it. Other than your professional skills, you have the most important quality."

"I'm almost afraid to ask what that is..."

"I actually *like* you. Do you *know* how rare that is?"

Roni laughed some more. "Gee, I'm so honored."

"You should be. Ask anyone, it's a rare, rare thing for me to admit to actually liking someone."

"When do I start?"

"Andrea is here until the end of the year, so after the holidays?"

"That sounds good. I probably ought to give the *Star* some notice."

"If you need more time than that, my chief of staff, Lilia, can handle things for a while, I suppose. She's awesome. You'll like her."

"That makes two people you actually like. Be careful, you might get a reputation for being a nice person who likes people."

"Shut your filthy mouth."

Roni was laughing so hard, she couldn't speak for a second. "In case I forget to say so, thank you for this. It may turn out to be just what I need."

"You say that now. Talk to me in a couple of months when you're ready to have me murdered."

"Nah, I wouldn't do that to you."

Sam cringed when she realized what she'd said. "Jeez, Roni. I'm sorry. That was incredibly insensitive."

"Stop. I didn't even think of Patrick when you said that."

"Still... I shouldn't have gone there."

"Please don't walk on eggshells around me. I'm tougher than I look."

"I already know that. Why do you think I asked you to run interference for me with the press? Because I know you can handle it."

"Means a lot to me. I won't let you down."

"I know you won't, but if I let you down, I want you to say so, you hear me?"

"Yes, ma'am."

"And don't call me ma'am."

"Got it, sir."

Sam was looking forward to working with Roni, even if she wasn't looking forward to being first lady. Having Roni and Lilia and the rest of her second lady staff helping her would make it a little more bearable. That was for sure. "Well, I suppose I ought to get my frozen ass home before they send out a search party."

"Probably a good idea."

"Let me know when you're thinking you'd like to start, and I'll put Lilia in touch with you to handle the details."

"I will, and thank you again, Sam. You'll never know what this means to me."

"Means a lot to me that you said yes when you had every good reason to say no."

"Funny, I couldn't think of a single one. Talk soon."

CHAPTER THIRTEEN

Sam closed her phone and had to smile when she thought about Roni and the way she'd reacted to being asked to join Sam's team. She was one hundred percent sure that Roni would do a brilliant job.

Since her ass was, in fact, frozen, Sam pushed herself to her feet and stretched out the stiffness that came from sitting on cold marble. She looked up at Honest Abe. "Keep an eye on things in the White House for me, will you?"

A good talk with Abe usually made her feel better. And while she was still deeply unsettled, the time with Abe and the chat with Roni had helped. When she went down the marble steps, the same guard nodded to her, but this time, he did a double take when he seemed to recognize her.

Sam put her index finger over her lips. "Shhh," she said without slowing. She hoped it wouldn't be all over social media that she'd spent time at the Lincoln Memorial. It would suck if she couldn't visit Abe when she needed to.

The guard made a show of pretending to zip his lips, and Sam found another person to like.

"Best of luck to you and your husband," he said. "We're pulling for you."

"Thank you so much."

Her phone rang as she walked to her car, and when she

checked the caller ID, she saw the word *Dispatch* on the screen. Just seeing that word gave her a kick of adrenaline. "Holland."

"Lieutenant, I wasn't sure if we're still supposed to call you for every potential homicide."

"Why wouldn't you?"

"Oh, um, well…"

Not wanting to talk to the dispatcher about becoming first lady, she said, "What've you got?"

"A report of a bleeding, unresponsive man on Rhode Island Avenue." The dispatcher gave Sam the exact address.

"Is he unresponsive or dead?"

"The woman who called it in said she believes he's dead."

"Was she with him?"

"No, she found him when she was walking her dog."

"Got it. Please call Detective Cruz and Sergeant Gonzales and ask them to meet me."

"Yes, ma'am."

"And let all the dispatchers know I'm to be called for any suspected homicide. Got it?"

"Yes, ma'am."

"Thank you." Sam ended the call and jogged to her car, eager to get to the scene as quickly as possible. In the back of her mind was the nagging concern that maybe she shouldn't go, but she refused to think about that. If she gave in on the second day, she'd spend the next three years caving. No, like she had since the day she joined the police force fourteen years ago, Sam was going to do her job and hope for the best.

∿

NICK FUMED WHILE HE WAITED FOR HIS CALL WITH THE IRANIAN president to resume after the president had been temporarily "called away." His ire was directed at the Iranian president, at David Nelson for dying, at the parent who posted the photo of him at the birthday party and at Sam for going rogue at the worst possible time. His entire body was rigid with tension that made his muscles tight and his jaw ache from clenching.

"Did I really get put on hold?" Nick asked Terry and Teresa, both of whom sat across the table in the Situation Room. Earlier, Nick had been briefed on a wide range of military options available to rescue the secretary of State and his delegation. None of them were things he wanted to be thinking about on his second day in office—or ever, for that matter.

"It looks that way," Terry said.

Nick hung up the phone. "This is kind of crazy, right? Who puts the president of the United States on hold?"

"Apparently, the president of Iran does," the chairman of the Joint Chiefs said.

"Call him back," Nick said. "Tell him he's down to ten minutes if he wishes to avoid military action. Enough dicking around. He needs to let Ruskin and the others leave, or we're going in after them."

It took a few minutes, but they got President Rajavi back on the phone with the message that President Cappuano was running short on patience.

"My apologies for the interruption, Mr. President." Rajavi spoke in perfect British English. Before their call, Nick had read briefing documents about the president that had included information about his tenure at Oxford as a graduate student. "One of my aides had additional information that I wanted to gather before we continued."

"I want to know when my secretary of State will be permitted to leave Tehran. Any other information you might have is irrelevant."

"I understand your concerns, Mr. President."

"Do you? I've just been briefed by my military leaders on the staggering array of options available to the United States should you fail to immediately release Secretary Ruskin and his security detail."

"I assure you that the secretary and his detail are being well cared for at a five-star hotel with deluxe accommodations."

"I don't *care* about where they're staying! They came to meet with you in the hope that we might de-escalate the tensions between our two countries and convince you to cease the testing of your nuclear arsenal. Instead, you've only made things worse by detaining him without even telling us the purpose of the detention. And let me assure you, he's there against his will despite your five-star accommodations. You have until midnight Eastern Time to release him and allow his plane to depart, or we'll take action."

"After our meetings, we invited the secretary to extend his stay so we could demonstrate that our hospitality is second to none. Your secretary was more than happy to avail himself of our resort and spa. I believe you'll find the photographs we sent quite illuminating."

Nick looked to Teresa, his brow raised.

She got busy on her laptop, turning it a minute later to show photographs of a smiling Ruskin in a swimsuit and sitting by a pool, drink in hand, surrounded by attractive, topless women.

Nick pressed the mute button. "What the hell am I seeing?"

The question was met with shocked silence.

He pressed the button to unmute the call. "I'd like to speak to the secretary."

"I'm afraid that's not possible. He's currently having a massage."

Nick was quite certain his head was going to explode. "Get him out of the massage and put him on the phone. *Now.*"

"Please hold."

"He put me on fucking hold again. What is this? A test to see if the new American president is trigger happy?"

The secretary of Defense stared at the images on the laptop, his mouth partially open in stunned disbelief. "I... I don't know, sir."

Nick waited impatiently for the secretary of State to come on the line, which took ten excruciating minutes.

"Mr. President."

"Secretary Ruskin, what's the meaning of these photos we're seeing?"

"Staged."

Nick had no idea what to believe. "Are you free to leave the country?"

"I believe I am now, but I wasn't previously."

"Get on the plane and get out of there right now."

"Yes, sir."

"I'd like to speak to the president again."

"Hold on, sir."

Nick listened as the phone was transferred from one man to the other.

"Mr. President."

"I have no idea what kind of game you're playing, but hear this. I'm not playing. Unless you want to face new sanctions and potential military action, you'll immediately allow the secretary of State and the others to leave Iran and you'll stop your nuclear testing. Do I make myself clear?"

"Abundantly. However, you should know that the secretary was always free to leave. It was his choice to stay."

Nick would deal with that possibility when Ruskin and the others were safely on their way home. "I'll be waiting to hear that their plane is in the air." He pressed the button to end the call. "*What the fuck is this?*"

"I have no idea, sir," the Defense secretary said.

"We're working intelligence channels to get more of a handle on what took place," Teresa said. "I've also reached out to the Secret Service director about debriefing the secretary's security detail upon their return."

"I want to know exactly what happened," Nick said. If this was some sort of lapse on Ruskin's part, Nick would see to it that he was prosecuted.

"Yes, sir," the others said.

They'd come to the brink of war while the secretary of State was cavorting with topless women? He wasn't sure he believed the man when he'd said the photos were staged. Ruskin wouldn't have been Nick's first, or even his hundredth, choice to be secretary of State. Ruskin had a swagger to him that was off-putting to Nick. His ego was as big as the ten-gallon hat he wore every chance he got. In Nick's opinion, Ruskin lacked the gravitas to properly represent the United States as its top diplomat.

They waited another tense hour before they received word that the secretary's plane was in the air.

"I prepared a statement for you to make to the media," Trevor said, handing it to Nick, who quickly skimmed it.

"Let's do it."

Trevor made a call and asked someone to put the statement on the teleprompter.

Nick walked with his team to the press briefing room, where the White House press corps awaited an update, even though it was after two on a Sunday morning during a holiday weekend. The tensions in Iran, the sudden death of a president and adjusting to a new administration had all hands on deck.

That was another reason why the idea of running for president and holding the office hadn't appealed to him. He wanted to be home with his family, not about to brief the media at the White House on the Sunday morning after Thanksgiving.

When he walked in, everyone stood, and the room went quiet.

"I have a statement I'd like to share, and then I'll take a few questions. At just after one thirty a.m. Eastern Time, we received word that the plane carrying Secretary of State Ruskin and his entourage departed Tehran, and the plane has now cleared Iranian air space. I've been in touch with Iranian President Rajavi, who has characterized the incident as a 'misunderstanding.' Needless to say, we're eager to debrief the secretary, as well as the others who were with him, about exactly what transpired. Until we're able to do that, we're not going to speculate on what occurred or make any statements about what, if any, consequences will be considered. At this moment, I'm relieved that our fellow Americans are safely on their way home, and I appreciate the cooperation of President Rajavi in bringing this incident to a safe, successful conclusion. I'll take a few questions."

The room erupted into calls of "Mr. President." He chose the longtime White House reporter from NBC News. "Peter."

"Mr. President, did President Rajavi give you any indication that the Iranians were attempting to provoke some sort of military or diplomatic response?"

"Our main focus at this time is getting the secretary and the others safely home. As soon as we know more about what happened, we'll brief you further."

He answered a number of similar questions from other

network and newspaper reporters, who were looking for details he simply didn't have. Then he called on a reporter he didn't recognize, who was seated in the back of the room.

"Mr. President, can you please tell us more about the party you attended earlier today in the midst of this crisis with Iran?"

"I'd be happy to tell you that I returned to my home for thirty minutes between meetings so I could see my six-year-old twins on their birthday."

"Do you think that was the right message to send to the American people who were worried about the situation in Iran?"

"I wasn't sending a message to the American people. I was sending a message to my children that their birthday is important to me. At no time was I out of touch with my advisers, and as we weren't expecting an update from the Iranians until hours later, I took advantage of the break in the action to tend to my family."

"Isn't it true that the children in question aren't *technically* your children?"

The question enraged him, as it had when it was raised in the past. "I think most Americans are able to understand that the concept of 'family' has many different meanings to many different people. That's all for now. We'll provide an update after Secretary Ruskin and the others are back in the country."

He left the podium and walked out of the room, his entire body vibrating with rage over the outrageous questions. "Let's figure out who posted the photo. I'm going to enforce that NDA."

"Yes, sir," Trevor said. "We'll get right on that."

"Brant, I want to go home."

"Yes, sir."

Nick had had more than enough of this day.

～

ON THE WAY TO RHODE ISLAND AVENUE, SAM CAUGHT NICK'S PRESS conference, which had been carried live on the radio. While she was relieved to hear that the secretary and the other Americans were on their way home, she was furious with the questions he'd been asked about the twins. Why did people have to be so insensitive about what constituted a family?

Families came in all shapes and sizes. Working to bring attention to the many issues involved with infertility, adoption, surrogacy, foster care and other associated subjects would be a focus for Sam as first lady. She hadn't asked for the massive platform that came with her new role, but now that she had it, she would use it to call for sensitivity and empathy and to celebrate the American family in all its many forms.

She would also continue to advocate for law enforcement concerns, including racial justice, as well as advocating for spinal cord injury research in honor of her father and learning disabilities related to her lifelong struggle with dyslexia. If there was anything good about Nick being president and her being first lady, it was the opportunity to shine a light on issues that mattered to them.

On Rhode Island Avenue, she spotted the emergency vehicles, parked a block from them and jogged toward the scene, ducking under yellow crime scene tape that surrounded the body of a man on the sidewalk. Upon a quick glance, she noted the man was young, Black and lying in a pool of blood coming from a chest wound.

"What do we know?" Sam asked the Patrol officers at the scene.

"We received a 911 call about a body on the sidewalk, and when we got here a minute ago, this is what we found. We checked for a pulse but couldn't find one."

Sam squatted for a better look at the young man and the wound that'd ended his life. "Have you gotten an ID?"

"We only touched him to check for a pulse, but didn't want to go any further until you arrived."

"Any witnesses?"

"Not that we've found yet."

"You've called the medical examiner?"

"Yes, ma'am."

"Any sign of the weapon that caused the wound?"

"Not, but we haven't looked yet. We only got here two minutes before you did."

Sam pulled gloves from her coat pocket and checked for herself to make sure the man had no pulse. A faint sound in the alley to her left caught her attention. Sam moved quickly to investigate, withdrawing her weapon from the holster on her hip and holding it in front of her while signaling to the other officers to back her up as she crept toward the sound. "Flashlight?"

One of them illuminated the alley, where a naked young Black woman watched them with big, haunted eyes. She had abrasions and cuts all over her and was bleeding from her face or neck. Sam rushed to her side, trying to determine where the blood was coming from. "Call for a bus and get me something to cover her with."

A bloody knife was on the ground next to her.

"Are you cut?"

Wincing, she turned her head so Sam could see a wound in her neck.

Sam immediately put pressure on it to stop the blood gushing from it. The other woman cried out in pain. "Sorry. I know it hurts. What's your name?"

"Shanice Williams."

"Hang in there for another minute, Shanice. Help is on the way."

"What've we got?" Freddie asked when he joined her with a sheet they used to cover the young woman.

"Two vics, one probably DOA." She nodded to the knife. "Bag that and then see if he's got ID on him."

Freddie stored the knife in an evidence bag and then went back to the male victim to find his wallet. He opened it, found the man's driver's license and took a photo of it. "Eduardo Carter, age twenty-three."

"Such a waste."

EMTs arrived a minute later and worked feverishly to stabilize the woman and prepare her for transport.

To Freddie and Gonzo, who'd also joined them, Sam said, "Let's start a canvass of the area and see if anyone saw or heard anything. Find out if we've got cameras nearby, and get me that footage. Get Crime Scene here to do a full analysis."

They left the alley to see to her orders while Sam stayed with the young woman until she was loaded into the back of the ambulance.

"Where're you taking her?" Sam asked the EMTs.

"GW Trauma."

"Is she going to make it?"

"She's stable even though she lost a lot of blood."

Since she was stable, Sam would talk to Shanice in the morning, after she'd been treated for her injuries. Sam joined Cruz and Gonzo to knock on neighborhood doors, looking for witnesses, but they couldn't find anyone who'd admit to having seen anything. After an hour of working both sides of the avenue and putting up with shocked people who recognized her, she checked in with Lieutenant Haggerty, the Crime Scene Unit commander.

"We're not finding much of anything," Haggerty said. "I sent the knife to the lab for analysis."

"Keep me posted on what the lab has to say."

"Will do."

They waited until Dr. Byron Tomlinson, one of the deputy medical examiners, arrived on the scene with his team.

Byron squatted to take a closer look at Eduardo's wound. "Fancy meeting you here," he said to Sam.

"What's that mean?"

"Didn't think we'd be seeing you out here anymore."

"You thought wrong."

"I see that. No detail?" he asked, looking around for Secret Service agents.

"Just do your job, Byron, so I can do mine, okay?"

"Yes, ma'am."

"And don't call me that."

He chuckled at her testy tone even as he moved forward with his exam of the victim. "Looks like one stab wound straight to the heart. No defensive wounds to his hands," Byron said as he placed bags on them to preserve evidence. Byron and his colleagues transferred the young man's body to a gurney and loaded it into the back of their truck. "I'll shoot you a report the minute I have it."

"Thanks."

"Sorry to poke the bear."

"No worries." It wouldn't be the first or last time she'd have to deal with colleagues who had questions about her new role—

and Nick's. "Let's go notify the family," she said to Freddie and Gonzo.

"We can do it if you want to go home," Freddie said.

"I'm not going home until the work is done." Notifying the family members of murder victims was the worst part of the job, and she wasn't about to delegate it to her subordinates so she could go home to fight with her husband.

CHAPTER FOURTEEN

S am, Freddie and Gonzo took her car to a Dupont Park address in the District's Southeast quadrant.

"One of you do a run on Carter," Sam said.

"I'm on it," Gonzo said.

"I heard they released the secretary of State," Freddie said, glancing at her from the passenger seat.

"I heard that too," Sam said.

"Nick sounded pissed in his press conference," Gonzo said. "Have you talked to him about it?"

"Not yet." She wondered if he was still at the White House or had gone home. Anxiety chased through her when she thought about the reckoning she faced when she saw him.

They arrived at the address listed on Carter's license, a standalone single-family home off Minnesota Avenue.

"I used to spend a lot of time in this neighborhood," Gonzo said. "I played frisbee football in the park and hung out with some guys who lived a few blocks from here."

"This was a rough part of town when I was growing up, but it's gotten really nice," Sam said, her heart aching when she took in the well-kept two-story home. Was she going to have to tell parents their son was dead? Or had Carter lived in this house with a partner? Either way, it would suck.

"Long list of priors for Carter—mostly misdemeanor drug stuff until recently, when he was charged with felony assault of his mother over a year ago."

"Where does that case stand?"

"He was out on bail awaiting trial."

"Let's get this over with. Cruz, come with me. Gonzo, wait on the sidewalk so we don't overwhelm them."

"Got it," Gonzo said.

Ever since she and Freddie had been shot at through a closed door, Sam had been a lot more cautious about approaching doors on the job. She rang the doorbell, which she could hardly hear from outside. "Now that's how a doorbell ought to sound." They encountered far too many that sounded like air raid sirens that would scare the shit out of her if she had to live in those houses.

As they waited for someone to answer the door, it occurred to her that living in the White House might be scarier than living in a house with an obnoxious doorbell. She made a fist, banged on the door and heard the distinctive sound of a weapon engaging.

Freddie heard it too.

They both reached for their weapons.

"Who's there?" a man asked.

They held up their badges to the peephole. "Metro PD."

"What do you want?"

"To speak to you about Eduardo Carter."

"He doesn't live here."

"Are you his family?"

"Not anymore."

"Sir, would you please open the door? We're not here to cause you any trouble."

"If you're here about that punk, you're causing me trouble."

"Please put down your weapon and open the door."

"Not until you do."

Sam nodded to Freddie, and they both lowered their weapons.

A series of locks disengaged, and a Black man in his mid to late forties opened the door. He stood in the doorway, making it clear they weren't welcome in his home. "What's he done now?"

"Are you his father?"

"Unfortunately."

Sam glanced at Freddie before forcing herself to say the words.

"I'm sorry to say your son was found dead on Rhode Island Avenue a short time ago."

The man's expression never changed. "Is that all?"

"Can you tell us anything about his associates or activities?"

He huffed out a laugh. "No, I can't, because I threw him out of here after he beat up his mother when she wouldn't give him money for drugs. This after we each worked three jobs to pay for his *four* trips to rehab. We haven't had any contact with him in more than a year."

"Is your wife at home?"

"She's asleep, and I'm not waking her up to talk about him."

"I'm sorry to have to ask if you know where he was living."

"I have no idea."

"How about any known associates?"

"No clue. He moved on from the kids he grew up with. They dropped him when he became a criminal to support his drug habit."

Sam realized they weren't going to get anything useful from him. She handed him her card. "If you think of anything we should know, please call me. My cell number is on there."

"Aren't you the new first lady?"

"I am."

"And you're still a cop?"

"That's right."

She could feel the disapproval coming from him, but didn't care enough to ask him what the problem was. As they returned to the car, Sam hated having to turn her back on him and his gun. Her anxiety spiked into the red zone.

"What now?" Freddie asked.

"In the morning, I'll call my parole officer friend Brendan Sullivan to see what I can find out about Carter and where he was living." Sullivan had been her ex-husband Peter's PO and had been helpful to her in the past. "We'll pick it up at zero eight hundred. I can give it half a day before I have a thing... at the White House." Speaking of anxiety.

Freddie's lips quivered.

"If you laugh, I'll stab you with the rustiest steak knife I can find."

"I'm not laughing."

Sam gave him her foulest look. "Get in the car, and I'll drop your asses at the Metro."

"Don't lump my ass in with his," Gonzo said. "I'm not the one laughing."

It was so good to have him back with them after months of rehab. Hearing what Eduardo Carter's family had been through with an addict son made her doubly grateful that Gonzo had kicked his addiction to painkillers.

"What'd he say about Carter?" Gonzo asked when they were in the car.

"They were estranged since he beat up his mother when she wouldn't give him drug money."

"Aw, geez," he said with a sigh. "I feel so sorry for people who lose their kids to drugs. I met a lot of those kids in rehab. My biggest fear as a father is that Alex will get into that shit."

"You won't let that happen." Sam glanced in the rearview mirror so she could see him. "You know what to look for and will be vigilant."

"I guess so."

Sam dropped them off at L'Enfant Plaza. "See you in the morning."

"See you then."

She watched as the two men took off jogging toward the Metro that would deliver them back to their cars and then merged into light traffic to drive the short distance to Capitol Hill, wondering what level of shit storm awaited her at home. At the checkpoint, she was dumbstruck by the massive security presence that was easily five times what they'd had when Nick was vice president. Agents dressed in riot gear and carrying machine guns worked the perimeter of the checkpoint, where she was normally waved through. Not this time, which meant Nick was home.

Sam stopped the car and lowered the window.

"Oh, Mrs. Cappuano." Sam didn't recognize the female agent who had a machine gun strapped across her chest. "My apologies. Please go ahead."

"Thank you."

Sam drove through and parked in her assigned spot, taking

note of the agents on both sides of Ninth Street and the line of black SUVs parked in the middle of the street. The Beast was parked in the middle of the line of vehicles. The neighbors probably couldn't wait for them to move to the White House so they could have their street back.

She was about to get out of her car when an agent materialized to open the door for her. Biting her tongue against the impulse to tell them she could open her own damned door, she started to nod to the agent and then realized he was Vernon.

"Oh, hey," she said.

"Ma'am."

Did she know him well enough to deduce he was pissed after he said a single word to her? "How are you?"

"The person I'm assigned to slipped her detail and took off unprotected, but otherwise, everything is just great."

Yep, definitely pissed. "Sorry. I got called into work."

"So I heard. Are you working tomorrow?"

"I am. I caught a homicide tonight and have to be at HQ at eight."

"We'll be ready to accompany you." Vernon escorted Sam up the ramp to the front door that was monitored by Nate, one of her favorite agents.

"Good evening, Mrs. Cappuano," Nate said.

"Hi, Nate. Thanks for letting me into the doghouse."

Nate smiled, but he didn't reply.

She took off her coat and hung it in the closet so Nick would have one less reason to be angry with her. If she'd lived by herself, she would've flung it over the sofa. Why hang it up when she was going to need it again in the morning?

Brant came out of the room the Secret Service used as an office and nodded to her. "Ma'am."

"I have a question."

"Yes, ma'am?"

She'd told him not to call her that, but hadn't gotten anywhere with the handsome, earnest agent. "Is my Secret Service name still Fuzz?"

"No, ma'am. You're FLOTUS now, and the president is POTUS."

"Well, there's one thing to celebrate about our change in status." She hesitated before she said, "Can I ask you something else?"

"Of course."

"Is everyone pissed with me, or does it just seem that way?"

"I think 'concerned' is a better word."

"I'm sorry I concerned you all. I heard we're meeting Tuesday to figure this stuff out."

"Yes, ma'am."

"Have a good night, Brant."

"You do the same, ma'am."

Sam went upstairs and looked in on Scotty, who was asleep with the lights and TV still on. She shut them off and tugged the comforter over him before taking advantage of the opportunity to run her fingers through his soft dark hair. Their little boy was becoming a young man too quickly. She bent to kiss his forehead and then went across the hall to check on the twins, who were curled up together as usual.

As she kissed them both, she experienced the kind of wild love she'd only ever felt for Nick and Scotty. She didn't care who said otherwise. These kids were *hers*—hers and Nick's and Scotty's. Let anyone say otherwise. They knew the truth. Outside their room, she nodded to Darcy, an agent who'd been with them for a while.

She went into her closet, closed the door and took a deep breath as she changed into pajama pants and a T-shirt. When she was as ready as she'd ever be to deal with Nick's wrath, she crossed the hall and went into their bedroom.

Nick was sitting up in bed, shirtless, a massive document on his lap.

Sam closed the door and stopped for a good look at her handsome, sexy husband.

"Whatcha staring at?" he asked without glancing up from what he was doing.

"The sexiest president I've ever seen."

"Personally, I think Millard Fillmore was way sexier."

Sam snorted out a laugh as the anxiety she'd been carrying for hours drained out of her in a single instant. That kind of anxiety belonged in her first marriage. Not this one. This one was as close to perfect as she'd ever hoped to achieve in this lifetime, and with one comment, he'd let her know that while he might be upset with what she'd done, he still loved her. That was one thing she could always count on, no matter what. "Fillmore had nothing on Cappuano with two p's."

After locking her weapon and cuffs into her bedside table, she went into the bathroom to brush her teeth and hair. Then she smoothed on the vanilla-and-lavender lotion he loved so much. Even though she was relieved to realize they weren't going to fight, she was under no illusions that she'd get away with what she'd done tonight. They were going to talk about it, and she was going to have to make some concessions. Just how many remained to be seen.

Sam went back to the bedroom and got into bed. "I heard the secretary is on the way home."

"Yeah."

She looked over at him. "How'd that go?"

"I'm not really sure," he said, filling her in on how the incident had concluded.

"Holy shit. What do you think happened?"

"I wish I knew. Ruskin says it was a setup, but we have intelligence that suggests he might've gone along with it. We'll know more when we can debrief him and the detail that traveled with him. Either way, it's a huge relief that they're safe and coming home. At least we won't be going to war on my third day in office. I'd call that a win."

Sam laughed at the sheer lunacy of that understatement. "Thank God it didn't come to that."

"You said it."

"What's that you've got there?" she asked of the book on his lap.

"Briefings about other nightmares that await me."

"In other words, some light bedtime reading?"

"Exactly."

And it was the last thing he needed. "Why don't you put it down for now so you'll have a prayer of sleeping tonight?"

"Not sure I'll sleep again until I'm out of office, but I've certainly had enough of this day." He closed the book and dropped it to the floor. It landed with a loud crash that made them both laugh.

"That's a whole lot of nightmare right there," Sam said.

"Sure is."

Sam held her arms out to him. "Come here."

"Don't mind if I do."

He snuggled up to her, placing his head on her chest and putting his arm around her.

Sam ran her fingers through his hair and caressed his back.

"In case I forget to tell you, this is the best minute of my entire day."

"Mine too."

"Where'd you go tonight?"

"Gigi's ex held her mother, sister and nephews hostage in Fairfax. He wanted to talk to me, so I went. I was able to talk him out, thankfully."

"Jeez, what was he thinking?"

"No idea, but hopefully, he'll get some help. From what Dani said, he seems to have suffered some sort of breakdown and has been acting differently for a while now. He really hurt Gigi, so I'm just glad he's safely out of her life. For now, anyway. And get this... Cameron Green has been glued to Gigi's side all day."

"That's interesting. I thought he had a girlfriend."

"Apparently, he does. No one's really sure what's going on there." She continued to play with his hair. "Are we going to talk about how you're mad with me?"

"I'm not mad."

"Really?"

"Really. I'm afraid."

Ugh, Sam thought. *That's worse.* "I'm sorry I did that to you, but when I heard Gigi's family was in danger and there was something I could do, I had to go. And I couldn't wait around for the Secret Service to figure out a plan. Every second was important."

He raised his head so he could look at her with those potent hazel eyes. "I want you to know I truly understand how important it was that you got there as fast as you possibly could to save the lives of Gigi's family members. And I seriously respect that you're capable of handling something like that. I'm in awe of what you do every day and how much it matters to people."

"You were already going to get lucky tonight," she said, dramatically fanning her face. "But now you might get birthday- or anniversary-level lucky."

His laughter lit up his entire face as he moved to kiss her. He leaned his forehead against hers. "Here's our problem, though. You're extremely vulnerable in the field without added security."

"But—"

He kissed her again. "No buts. You are *vulnerable*, Samantha. We didn't plan this, but here we are, and we have to figure it out. I know it's not what you signed on for, but it's our reality. And my reality is that I can't do this job if I have to worry about one of this country's many enemies deciding to make a point by kidnapping or murdering my wife. You're vulnerable simply because of the office I hold. You were when I was VP, but it's ten million times more so now."

Sighing, she said, "I know."

"I want you to think about how you'd feel if the shoe were on the other foot."

"What do you mean?"

"If you held a job that by its very nature endangered my life, what would you want for me?"

"I'd want you to have an army around you."

"Exactly. And here's my bottom line... If you can't handle having at least a small army around you, I can't do this job. I *won't* do this job."

"What do you mean?"

"I'd give up the job if it came to that, but the one thing I won't do is hold the office if I can't be absolutely certain you're safe."

"I get it. I really do, and I want you to be the best president we've ever had because I truly believe you will be. But we have to figure out something that makes it so I can leave on a moment's notice like I had to do tonight. I'll agree with having a detail as long as they can be nimble and are *only* there for worst-case scenario. They're not to intervene in police matters even if they see me about to get hurt. I need to be able to do my job without worrying about them getting in the way."

"If I pledge to work with the Secret Service to make that happen, will you promise me you'll never again leave this house without a detail?"

This was a moment of truth. If she made that promise, she'd have to keep it. She took a deep breath and let it out. "I promise."

CHAPTER FIFTEEN

"Thank you." He kissed her, lingering for a second before he broke the kiss and moved to kiss her neck. "I know it's so much to ask."

Sam tipped her head to give him better access. "It's really not. You've got enough to worry about. I don't need to be making it worse for you."

"I'll still worry about you, even if you're surrounded by an army."

She wrapped her arms around him, breathing in the fresh, clean scent of home, the scent of her love.

"I have a present for you," he said.

"Really?"

"Don't get too excited. It's not a sparkly present." He reached for his bedside table, and when he opened his hand, a black object sat on his palm.

"What is that?"

"Your very own secure BlackBerry so you can call or text me anytime you want without either of us having to worry about security breaches."

"So, um, I have to carry that with me?"

"Only if you want to be able to talk to me when we're apart. It's fully charged and programmed, so you only have to push two buttons to call me."

"What two buttons?"

"Six nine."

Sam cracked up laughing. "Did you pick those numbers?"

"So what if I did? We've gotta laugh in the midst of all this nonsense, right?"

"That's not very presidential of you."

"I knew it would make you laugh and take some of the sting out of having to carry a second phone."

"I don't have to use it for other stuff, do I?"

"Nope. As long as you're not talking to or about me on your other phone, you're allowed to still use it. I actually went to bat for you on that. They wanted you to be all BlackBerry, all the time, and I told them that wouldn't be possible unless they have a flip version that you can slap closed."

"You get me."

"I love you." He moved the hand containing the BlackBerry toward her until she had no choice but to take it from him. "When that phone rings, it's me. Will you take my calls?"

"Always."

"Likewise, love. Unless I absolutely can't."

"Same."

"I plugged in the charger next to the other one on your bedside table."

"Aren't you Mr. Efficient?"

"That's Mr. President to you, ma'am."

Sam laughed as she put the BlackBerry on the table. Everything in her resisted carrying a second phone, but if it meant she'd have a bat line straight to him, she'd do it. "I knew you'd make me call you that."

Nick yawned and reached for her, bringing her back into his embrace. "You only have to call me that in bed."

"Haha. Dream on."

"Do you have to work tomorrow?"

"I do. We caught a new case tonight. I already told Vernon that I have to be at HQ at eight."

"That's good. Now about that birthday-level treatment I was promised..."

"Speaking of your birthday—and Scotty's—what do you want

to do?" He'd be thirty-eight in December, and Scotty would be fourteen next week.

"I don't care as long as we spend the day with the kids."

"We can make that happen. We also need to be thinking about visiting the shelter to find a dog for our boy."

"Or we can ask the shelters to come to us with some options."

"That's risky. He'll want them all. He won't be able to send them back—and neither will we."

"True. Let's look online and narrow it down after we move."

"Don't remind me that we have to move."

"Okay, I won't." He kissed down her neck and along her collarbone, pushing her T-shirt out of the way as he went. "You're way too overdressed for a birthday-level treatment."

"I figured I was in big trouble, so I dressed accordingly."

"I'll admit I was upset—seriously upset—that you were off the grid, but after hearing where you were and why, and I... I can't be upset with you for being who you are and doing what you do." With his chin propped on her chest, he gazed at her. "I know exactly who I married, Samantha, and I hate how my career has impacted yours."

"It hasn't. Not really."

"Yes, it really has. You're recognized everywhere you go, and I know you hate that. My higher profile has raised yours, which makes an already dangerous job that much more so."

"It's no big deal."

"It's a huge big deal and a massive safety issue that we have no choice but to address."

"It'll be fine. We'll figure it out, the way we always do. And for what it's worth, I can't tell you how much I appreciate the way we *deal* with this shit when it comes up. In my past life, I would've been in for days or even weeks of passive-aggressive silence while I was punished for the transgression of the moment."

"That's no way to run a marriage."

"Believe me, I know. That was awful, and this... This is magic."

He pushed up her T-shirt and helped to ease it over her head. "Mmm, so sexy."

Sam crossed her arms over breasts.

He moved her arms aside to kiss and caress her breasts before he finally sucked her nipple into the heat of his mouth while running his tongue over it. The sensations zinged through her body, gathering in a tight throb of need between her legs. "Nick," she said, gasping and squirming beneath him.

"Not so fast, my love. First, you're going to take your punishment for making me suffer."

"Wha... What? *Punishment?*"

"You heard me."

She sagged into the mattress. "I thought you wanted birthday-level treatment."

"We'll get there. Eventually."

Resigned to being tortured in the best way possible, she grasped handfuls of the sheet and held on for dear life. When her husband set his mind to sensual torture, there was no point in fighting him.

~

NICK BREATHED A SIGH OF RELIEF THAT THEY'D GOTTEN THROUGH that conversation without a big fight. He'd been spoiling for one when he got home and discovered she was still out there somewhere, unprotected and vulnerable to those who'd harm her just because she was married to him. Between his worries about her and the baffling incident with Ruskin, he'd been wound up tighter than he'd been in a long time.

Until she walked into the room, safe, sexy and perfectly imperfect. Just that quickly, the fight had gone out of him, replaced by gratitude for her safety. This time. He was under no illusions that they'd completely solved the problem, but he took her at her word when she promised to allow a detail going forward.

He never wanted to treat her the way her first husband had, but he couldn't back down when it came to her safety. However, he didn't need to think about any of that now that she was naked and soft and sexy as she tried to move him along. Always impatient, his Samantha. The more she tried to rush him, the more inclined he was to slow down. He placed kisses on her abdomen, smiling when goose bumps erupted on her skin.

He loved the way she gasped and struggled against the arm he had across her hips, holding her down so she couldn't get away as he moved down to prop her legs on his shoulders.

"Nick."

"Shhh."

"Come on..."

She was so easily annoyed, not that he minded that. All her rough edges made her who she was, and he loved everything about her.

He ran his tongue over her most sensitive flesh, making her tremble in response as he sucked on her clit and drove his fingers into her. She came hard. He gave her no time to recover before he took her up again, letting her linger this time right at the precipice. Then he backed off, withdrew completely and kissed her inner thigh.

"You're being so mean," she said, her breathing choppy.

"How so?" He had to fight the urge to laugh at her incensed tone. "By my count, you owe me one."

"You know what you're doing—and you're doing it on purpose."

"Yes, I am, so be quiet and take it like the badass boss you are."

"Revenge is a bitch, and so am I."

"You don't scare me."

"Now you're just pissing me off."

"Just now I am? I need to work on my technique."

Her low growl made him laugh. Since her eyes were closed, that was the perfect time to bite down on her nipple as he pushed his fingers into her again, curling them to hit the magic spot that made her crazy every time. He had her on the verge of another climax when he stopped again.

"I hate you."

"No, you don't."

"Yes, I really do."

"Well, we can't have that." Nick moved to align his cock and pushed into her in one deep thrust that triggered her release.

She actually scratched his back in the throes of passion, and he loved it.

"No more," she said when she'd recovered enough to speak.

"Yes more."

She shook her head.

He kissed her until her arms encircled his neck and her legs curled around his hips. That's when he knew he had her. He gave it to her hard and fast, the way she liked it best, until they were both coming, clinging to each other in a moment of unity that made him forget everything that wasn't her, them and the perfection they found together.

"I hope you're not still expecting birthday-level service after that. I'm wrecked."

"Then my work here is finished."

"I've been thoroughly punished with three orgasms. That's not exactly a deterrent to future bad behavior."

"Hmm, I'll have to work on my punishment technique going forward."

"If your technique was any better, I'd be dead."

"You're not allowed to die. That's the point I've been trying to make."

"Your point is very well made. And what you said... About how I'd feel if the very nature of my job endangered your life..."

He raised his head from her shoulder and found light blue eyes looking at him with so much love. She was everything to him. Every. Single. Thing. A life without her wouldn't be worth living, thus his desperate desire to ensure her safety.

"I couldn't bear that. So I want you to know, I get it. I always did, but now I really do. I get it. I want you to be president and to continue to make us all so proud, and I don't want to do anything to ruin that for you. I really don't."

"I know that, babe. And I don't want to do anything to ruin your job for you either. That's the last thing I want. I know how important it is to you."

"Before I had you, it was everything to me. That wasn't really healthy, but it's such a big part of who I am. I'd be lost without it."

"As awful and upsetting and terrifying as it can be sometimes, I know how much you love it."

"I do love it. I love the challenge of the cases, the people I work with—most of them, anyway—the satisfaction of getting justice for the loved ones of victims. I love it all."

"I'm going to fight as hard as I can to make sure you get to keep doing what you love. I'll take every political hit I have to in order to make that happen for you."

She tightened her arms around him and bit back a yawn. "I love you so much for that. More than you'll ever know. You get me."

"I speak Samantha fluently, and I swear to you I'll never ask you to be anyone other than who you are, no matter what happens on this crazy ride we're on."

"Thank you."

Nick silently vowed to do whatever it took to keep that promise no matter what it might cost him in the court of public opinion.

~

BEFORE SHE LEFT THE HOUSE THE NEXT MORNING, SAM KNOCKED ON Elijah's door.

"Come in."

"Sorry to wake you, but I wanted to say goodbye before I go to work."

"I thought you were off this weekend."

"So did I. We caught a homicide last night, and I'm going to give it a few hours before my meeting with Mrs. Nelson."

"Going to check out the new crib, huh?"

Sam laughed. "Something like that."

"I wanted to thank you again for the incredible party for the kids. They absolutely loved it."

"That was all Shelby."

"It was all of you, and they know it. I'm really sorry that one of the dick parents released that photo and caused problems for Nick."

"Don't worry about that. He doesn't care what anyone says. He was right where he wanted to be while also juggling an international crisis. You said you'd come home every weekend for a while, but I really don't think you need to. Focus on school, and we'll take good care of the twins."

"Are you sure?"

"Positive. We'll call you in if they're having trouble adjusting, but I think they'll be fine."

"If you're sure."

"I am. We'll see you in a few weeks for Christmas?"

"I'll be here. Or I guess I should say I'll see you across town."

"There'll always be a room for you at our home."

"That means so much to me, especially now with everything you guys have got going on. My mom is making noise about me coming to visit her, but I told her I want to be with the kids, so she has to come to me if she wants to see me." Before their murders, he'd lived with his father and stepmother, Cleo, when he wasn't away at school.

"We'll make her feel welcome too."

"That's awesome. Thanks. She'll shit her pants when I invite her to the White House."

Sam laughed.

"Nick told me I've got to have a detail going forward." His expression told her what he thought of that. "Just what every college student wants."

"Every homicide detective too. It sucks, but I'm trying to tell myself it beats the alternative. People know you're part of our family now, so that makes you vulnerable, as Nick would say."

"That's what he told me. I'm willing to do it if it gives him peace of mind, but..."

"I know. Trust me. I get it."

"I guess that's the price we pay for having our own bowling alley."

Laughing, Sam said, "Exactly. I hear we'll have butlers too."

"Well, that won't suck."

"From what I'm told, it's quite lovely. I guess we'll find out soon enough." Sam checked her watch and saw that she had twenty minutes before she was due to meet Freddie and Gonzo at HQ. "I'd better hit it. Let us know if you need anything at school. We're here for you."

He got out of bed to hug her. "Thank you, Sam. You guys are the best."

"We love you. Be safe."

"You too."

Sam went down the stairs and found Vernon and Jimmy

waiting for her by the door. "Morning," she said to them and the new agent working the door. "I'll be ready in a minute."

She went into the kitchen, brewed coffee to go and grabbed a protein bar to hold her over until she had time to eat a real meal. Juggling her mug and coat, she met the agents at the door.

"I'm going to MPD headquarters."

"We'll be right behind you," Vernon said.

"Thank you." She could tell she'd taken the agents by surprise by thanking them. That wouldn't do. When they were on the sidewalk and out of the earshot of the others, she said, "Listen, I know I'm a total pain in the ass, which some would say is part of my charm. But as a fellow law enforcement officer, I want you to know I respect the role you guys play in keeping me and my family safe. I'll do my best to cooperate with you going forward."

"And we'll do our best to let you do your job without interference," Vernon said. "We respect the fact that you're staying on the job when you certainly don't need to."

"I do, though. It's in my blood, you know?"

"I get it," Vernon said. "My father and grandfather were federal agents."

"That's really cool. Thanks for telling me that. Well, I guess I'd better get to it."

CHAPTER SIXTEEN

S am got into the black BMW that used to belong to Nick. He'd made it so she could live for days inside that car if it ever came to that, which was probably the only reason the Secret Service was allowing her to drive herself without objection. When she'd cleared the checkpoint, she put through a call to Brendan Sullivan.

He answered on the third ring. "Is this the first lady or Lieutenant Holland?"

"Both, I guess."

"Congratulations. I think?"

Sam laughed. "Still not quite sure. I'm sorry to bother you on a Sunday morning, but a parolee landed in the morgue last night, and I'm looking for some info."

"Name?"

"Eduardo Carter."

His deep sigh came through loud and clear. "Why am I not surprised? He's been in and out of trouble for years."

"Can you tell me where he lived? We went by his parents' home last night and didn't get very far with the father."

"The parents washed their hands of him after he beat up his mother. They stuck with him a lot longer than I would have. He put them through hell." She heard rustling in the background. "Let me log in to my work computer to find an address for him."

"Shoot it to my email, along with any known associates and a rundown on what I need to know about him?"

"Will do."

"Thanks, Brendan."

"You got it. Best of luck to you and your husband."

"Thanks. We appreciate the good wishes." She flipped the phone closed and headed for HQ. On the way, she put through a call to Dr. Anderson, a friend at GW Hospital.

"Are you seriously calling me, or is this a butt dial?"

"My butt's not that talented."

"Don't you have a new job?"

"Nope. I still have the same old lousy one, and that's why I'm calling."

"You're really still doing your job?"

"I really am."

"Wow. I wondered what you were going to do."

"Now you know. I'm looking for info about Shanice Williams, who was brought in by EMS last night. She had a stab wound to the neck. I need to speak to her this morning and was hoping you could help me get around the privacy stuff and tell me where I might find her."

"Hang on."

She heard him typing on a computer.

"She's in the ICU."

"Am I allowed to see her there?"

"Let me know when you're coming, and I'll see what I can do."

"Thanks, Doc."

"Haven't seen you in a while. You must be due for some sort of disaster by now."

"Shut your mouth!"

He hung up laughing.

Sam ended the call. "Cheeky bastard." Despite her overall disdain for people in general, she'd made some good friends through her job, and they often came in handy. She drove through quiet Sunday morning streets and was at HQ twelve minutes later. For once, the place wasn't surrounded by media trucks, as the press probably didn't expect her to be there on a Sunday.

Their absence made it possible for her to enter the building through the main entrance, which was a rare treat. Usually, she had to sneak in through the morgue to avoid reporters holding out hope that she'd one day comment on her husband, his public persona, their personal lives, etc. The only thing she was ever willing to comment on—and *willing* was a stretch—was her cases. Otherwise, they could kiss her ass. She'd never give them anything about Nick, no matter how many times they asked.

The first person she encountered was the one she least expected to see there on a Sunday—Chief Farnsworth.

"Fancy meeting you here," she said. "No church this morning?" For as long as she'd known him—and she'd known him all her life —he'd never missed weekly Mass.

"We went last night. I prayed for you and your husband as you begin this challenging new journey."

"Thank you," she said softly. "We need all the prayers we can get."

"You're going to be a terrific first couple. I have no doubt about it."

"He'll be a great president. I have no doubt about that. The jury's still out on the first lady, however. I hear she's a ball-busting cop who's refusing to give up her day job."

Smiling, he said, "She's the best ball-busting cop on this force, and I, for one, am very relieved that she's stubbornly clinging to her day job. She makes me look good on the regular."

"She does what she can for the people. Are we done speaking of her in the third person?"

"We can be. How are you?"

"I'm strangely okay. Talk to me when I have to move, which I hear is happening as soon as later this week. Did you know they come in, pack up all your crap for you and then unpack it there?"

"Is that right? Well, I suppose it's the least they can do with the way you're turning your lives upside down in service to the country."

"Yes, that's true. So what're you doing here?"

"I have a meeting with Agent Hill about the investigation later this morning, and no, I don't have anything new to report. In addition to that, the mayor has been blowing up my phone wanting to talk to me—and to you."

"I heard about that. What's she want with me?"

"She's on her way over here, so you can find out for yourself."

Sam grimaced. "Like, *now*?"

He checked his watch. "Any minute now. She was coming to talk to me, but she'll be thrilled to hear that you're here too."

"I'm only here because I caught a new case last night. I've got real work to do."

"The mayor wants to talk to you. That's your job at the moment."

She scowled at him. "I never should've come here today."

"Hindsight is twenty-twenty, Lieutenant."

"You don't have to appear to enjoy this so much. Am I in some kind of trouble that I'm unaware of?"

"Not that I've been told. I believe she's interested in offering you a promotion."

That surprised the hell out of her. "What kind of promotion?"

"The deputy chief position is currently open."

"Shut up." She'd no sooner said the words than she remembered who she was speaking to. "Sir."

Farnsworth laughed. "Don't kill the messenger."

"She is not going to offer me that."

"What if she does?"

"I, uh... I've got nothing on that. The thought never occurred to me."

"I think you need to formulate some thoughts on it in the next..." He checked his watch again. "Ten minutes or so."

"You can't be serious."

"I'm serious, and I think she is too."

"Can she just do that?" Sam's voice sounded high and squeaky, even to her. "Jump me over two ranks and put me in a job like that?"

"She can do what she wants. She's the mayor, and from what I hear, she likes you a lot. Admires your career, your moxie, your success at closing the toughest of cases. And she likes that you're a woman. She says we're long overdue for a woman in the department's top leadership, and I agree with her."

"I completely agree too, but if she does this, she'll set me up for a nightmare with the people I jumped over to get there."

"Which I mentioned to her when the idea was first proposed to me."

"How long ago did that happen?"

"Last Wednesday."

"So, before Nick became president." It was, in a way, a relief to know that his promotion hadn't led to talk of hers.

"It's got nothing to do with him and everything to do with you."

"And you think this is a good idea?"

"I think it's an intriguing idea. She's been under fire for the lack of women in command within city departments, and I believe she sees you as a potential high-profile appointment that she could refer to when she's criticized for her record with elevating women. If I had to guess, that is. And that would explain why she's in such an all-fired rush to make this happen."

"There's no way I could do this, Chief. I'd be vilified by every officer in this department who will once again say I got there on my back, because of who my father is, because I've known you all my life, because I'm an attention-seeking whore. You name it, they'll say it. They even say I sleep with *you*! My freaking *uncle*."

His bark of laughter made her smile. She loved him so much and always had. Somehow they'd managed to navigate the tricky nature of their longtime personal relationship in the context of their professional duties. Not that it hadn't been without its challenges. Chief among them—no pun intended—was the low-level talk about them having an inappropriate relationship. Disgusting.

"We both know how you got where you are in this department, so don't let baseless gossip get to you."

"I have a feeling the gossip is only going to get worse." She made a face that had him laughing again. "Let me get my team started before the mayor gets here."

"You've got five minutes. Meet us in my office."

"I'm never coming here on a Sunday again." She stalked off toward her pit, trying not to think about the latest earth-shattering development that'd been tossed her way.

Deputy chief.

Just that quickly, she had tears in her eyes as she longed for her father. He'd know how she should respond to this news. While she had no intention whatsoever of taking the job, she had to be careful in how she declined the mayor's offer. The woman was, after all, the boss of them all, and it wouldn't do to laugh in her face when she made a genuine offer.

Thank God the chief had given her a heads-up, or she might've been tempted to laugh in the moment. The very idea of it was preposterous. She'd been a lieutenant for only two years and wasn't even eligible yet to sit for the captain's exam, not that she had any desire to be a captain, either. No, the only job in the department she wanted was the one she already had.

Freddie, Gonzo and Jeannie were in the pit when she walked in.

"Heard we caught a new one," Jeannie said. "Figured I might be able to help."

"Happy to have you, but I can't authorize overtime on this one. Not yet, anyway. I can shave some hours off the regular week for all of you, though."

"That's fine," she said. "Michael left for a conference this morning, so I wasn't doing anything."

"Let me check my email to see if Brendan Sullivan came through." She used up two of the five minutes the chief had given her to unlock her office and boot up her computer. Another minute passed while her antiquated printer spit out the three pages of info Brendan had sent. "I bet the printer at the White House doesn't take that long," she muttered, taking the pages to the conference room and handing them to Freddie. "I need to do something with the chief. I'll be back in a few."

"What's up with the chief?" Gonzo asked.

"Nothing important." Under no circumstances would she accept that kind of promotion. Not like this. "I'll be back ASAP. Get me some threads to pull."

"On it," Freddie said.

Sam left them to do what she wanted to be doing herself and made her way to the chief's suite. Normally, his assistant, Helen, would be standing guard, but even the faithful Helen got a day off every now and then. Through the door, which was cracked open, she could hear the chief speaking to the mayor. She took a deep breath to calm nerves that were suddenly on full alert and knocked on the door.

The mayor, a Black woman named Monique Brewster, stood to welcome Sam with a warm smile and a handshake. Sam had long admired the woman who'd risen through the ranks on the city council to become the city's first Black female mayor three years ago at the age of forty-two. Since then, Sam had found her to be tough but mostly fair. The only thing she'd disagreed with her on was her criticism of the chief when things happened that were in no way his fault—such as his former deputy chief sitting on evidence in her father's shooting *for four fucking years*, or Lieutenant Stahl wrapping Sam in razor wire and threatening to set her on fire. Again, not the chief's fault.

"I'm so glad to have the chance to sit down with you," Brewster said, "but I'm surprised you have the time to be here this weekend."

"I'm here because I'm the Homicide commander, and we caught a new case last night."

"I meant that you have better things to be doing."

Wondering if she was being tested in some way, Sam glanced at the chief.

"What you need to understand about the lieutenant, Madam Mayor, is that there's nothing more important to her—other than her husband and children, of course—than her duties to the department, her squad and the victims they serve."

Sam couldn't have said it better herself.

"Even being first lady?"

The chief cleared his throat, which meant he was trying not to laugh. "Especially that."

Sam pointed to the chief with her thumb. "What he said, not that I'd want that to become public. It's important to me to support my husband in his new role, but I have no intention of completely changing my life to accommodate his job."

Was it her imagination, or did the mayor seem to be looking at her with new respect?

"Well, that works out rather nicely considering the reason I wanted to meet with you."

Sam thought about stopping her, of telling her she already

knew and wasn't interested, but decided to wait her out and let her make the offer before she declined it.

"As you know, we have an opening for a deputy chief, and as you also may know, I've told Chief Farnsworth that the MPD is long overdue to see a woman as one of the department's top commanders. With that in mind, I'd like to offer the job to you as one of the top-ranking women in the department."

While Sam's first inclination was to say *thanks, but no, thanks* and then ask if she could get back to work, she took a second to come up with a diplomatic response that would be more advantageous to her career in the long term. "Thank you for thinking of me," she said after a long pause. "As you know, the position is particularly meaningful to me because my father was the deputy chief when he was shot on the job."

"I do know that, and may I please extend my sympathies again on his passing? I had the chance to work with him many times over the years and always found him to be a delightful, engaged public servant."

"He was, for sure, and we appreciated the flowers you sent to the funeral home."

"I'm also extremely sorry for the role my colleague—and yours —played in his death. I continue to be horrified by what was uncovered after he died." Longtime City Councilman Roy Gallagher was one of three defendants facing murder charges in the wake of Skip Holland's death. The MPD's former deputy chief, Paul Conklin, was locked up on related charges after sitting on evidence that could've broken the case years earlier.

"That's something we have in common," Sam said. "It also means a lot to me that you thought of me for the job, but I'm unable to accept your kind offer."

"Because of your new duties as first lady," she said. "I actually thought you might snap it up as it would allow you to take on more of an administrative role at a time when you'll be juggling multiple priorities."

The chief coughed, and Sam had to force herself not to look at him or risk the two of them devolving into uncontrollable laughter.

"I can see how that would seem to make sense. However, if I may speak frankly..."

"Please," the mayor said. "Of course you may."

"I'd rather be strung upside down by my toes than have an administrative job."

The chief could no longer cover his laughter with coughing. He cracked up. "Welcome to the species known as Lieutenant Holland, Your Honor. She's a little feral and uncivilized, but we love her anyway."

Sam rolled her eyes at him. "He's known me too long."

"And she's always been this way."

"Which is another reason why I have to decline your generous offer. As much as I'd love to see a woman in the deputy chief's office, it can't be me. I have a hard enough time navigating the old boys' club around here because of my last name and the fact that people think the only reason I've gotten to where I am is because of my name and my father and the fact that the chief is my beloved adopted uncle. If you move me up two levels to deputy chief, I won't have the respect of the people I command. I think the chief would agree that's an essential element to being successful in his job and the deputy's job."

"Lieutenant Holland is right about the pecking order around here, and you're right, Your Honor, that she'd be a marvelous deputy chief—if she earned it the usual way. She's also right that she'd hate the job. When she became the lieutenant in charge of the Homicide division, she made a comment I've never forgotten."

Sam was trying to remember what she'd said to him in the midst of attaining her most cherished goal.

"She said she'd reached the pinnacle by getting the only command-level job she'd ever want within the department. Not only is she happy as the Homicide commander, I think you'd agree she's also extremely effective in that role."

"I completely agree, and I hear what you're both saying," the mayor said. "However, I'd still like you to think about it for a day or two before you decide."

Again, Sam looked to the chief.

"She's not going to change her mind, Monique," he said in the kind, conciliatory tone that made him such a great chief.

Not that she was biased. Much.

"Well, I'll confess to being disappointed, as I'd hoped you'd want the job as much as I want you in it, but if that's not the case, I'm certainly not going to force the point."

Sam expelled a deep breath. "Thank you so much again for thinking of me. I'm honored to have been considered. And now I need to get back to work, since I've got a deadline today. I'm meeting with Mrs. Nelson at two for afternoon tea and a tour of the residence."

The chief ran a hand over his mouth.

"If you laugh, I'll never forgive you. Sir."

"I'm just trying to picture you at afternoon tea."

"I'll make sure there are pictures for you to laugh at later."

"I'll look forward to that."

To the mayor, Sam said, "If I could ask one favor…"

"Of course."

"Please don't let it get out that you were considering me for deputy chief. I've got enough on my plate without having to deal with the media storm that would bring."

"I understand, and no one will hear it from me or my office. I wish you and your husband all the best."

Sam shook her hand. "Thank you, ma'am. I appreciate that."

The second the mayor released her hand, Sam scooted out of the chief's office with all due haste, feeling as if she'd just dodged a bullet as lethal as any of the actual bullets she'd faced on the job. Being stuck in an office job was her idea of hell, and for a second there, she'd feared the mayor might order her to take the job because of her desire to see a woman in the role.

What would she have done then? She shuddered at the thought of it. Thank goodness it hadn't come to that.

CHAPTER SEVENTEEN

Still reeling from meeting with the mayor, Sam joined her team in the conference room where they were working on a fresh murder board. To the far left side was a photo of a smiling, cocky-looking Eduardo Carter, probably taken from his social media, and another photo from the morgue. The detectives had begun to list the information they had on him and the various connections to others.

"What've we got?" she asked.

"Numerous domestic calls for the girlfriend, Shanice Williams. Apparently, he'd been escalating lately."

"We need to talk to her," Sam said. "She'll help us determine where we go from here."

"Your thinking matches ours," Jeannie said.

"Cruz, you're with me." To Jeannie and Gonzo, she said, "Give it another two hours working the computers. Shoot me anything you have before you go."

"Will do," Gonzo said.

"It's weird to walk out the main door," Freddie said as he donned one of his ever-present trench coats and chased after her while stuffing a pack of powdered doughnuts into his face. His words were muffled by doughnuts.

"You gotta love a Sunday. Never occurred to the media that I'd be working today."

"They probably don't believe you're going to keep your job. That's still the plan, right?"

"I'm here, aren't I?"

"Yeah, but I guess I'm wondering if someone's going to pull the rug out from under you."

"The only one who could do that is Nick, and he's not going to."

"You're sure about that?"

Sam smiled as she thought of their conversation the night before. "Positive. Don't worry about it. We're going to work it out." She nodded to Vernon and Jimmy, who were leaning against their SUV and snapped to attention when they saw her coming. "I'll have a detail going forward. That's his line in the sand."

"I suppose that's not the worst thing that could happen. They're going to let you drive yourself?"

"They haven't said anything about not letting me do that. I was thinking earlier that it's probably because Nick turned my car into a mini Beast that's as safe as the president's limo."

"True." After fastening his seat belt, Freddie said, "What'd the chief want?"

"If I tell you, you have to promise me you won't tell another living soul."

"Promise."

"Even Elin."

"Even Elin."

Sam pulled out of the parking lot and headed for GW Hospital. "We met with the mayor. She offered me a promotion."

Freddie looked over at her. "What kind of promotion?"

"The deputy chief kind."

"*Seriously?*"

"Yep."

"What'd you say?"

"Thank you, but no, thank you."

"Whoa. You said no to the mayor."

"I did."

"How'd she take that?"

"She was disappointed. She wants a woman in the top ranks, and she'd made up her mind it was going to be me. Thankfully, the chief and I were able to convince her that I'd be the worst possible person to put in that position."

"No kidding."

"It's okay for me to say that about myself, but you can't."

"My apologies," he said on a low laugh.

"I also pointed out to her that my life wouldn't be worth living within the department if she bumped me up two ranks, especially since people already think I'm where I am because of my last name, not to mention it happening right as Nick becomes president. It's the last freaking thing in the world I'd want or need."

"It would be cool to have your dad's old job, though."

"That's the only part of it that would've been cool. The rest would suck. I'd be off the streets, pushing paper, dealing with City Hall and even more department bullshit than I have to contend with now. Ugh, no, thanks."

"What'd the chief have to say about it?"

"He agreed that my 'talents,' such as they are, are more useful in Homicide."

"That's a fact."

"Not to mention I'd die sitting in an office all day."

"That's also a fact."

"I just hate the feeling that I'm fighting on all fronts for my right to do what I do. It's exhausting."

"You're blazing a new trail as the first president's wife to hold a job outside the White House."

"I want to live in a world where that's not big news."

"It'll be awesome for you to continue on the job while also using your enormous platform to advance the issues that matter to you."

"That's the plan."

"It's easier for you to do this because you're not moving to a new city the way most of them do. So it makes sense that you're the right one to lead this new movement of modern first ladies—and maybe even first gentlemen, eventually—pursuing their own careers while their husbands—or wives—are in office."

"I'd be all for leading that movement. Where is it written that the wife has to give up her entire life to support her man?"

"It's not written anywhere. It's tradition."

"Well, fuck tradition."

"Do me a favor and keep that thought between us."

"Duh. I'm not about to say that to anyone else. But I do intend to live that as my mantra for the next three years."

"Looking forward to watching that show." He finished the first pack of doughnuts, chased them with a bottle of chocolate milk and opened a second package.

"You're revolting."

He burped loudly. "Huh? What'd I do?"

"Your diet is disgusting."

"Don't be a jealous cow. You'd be face-first in the doughnuts if you could eat anything you wanted."

"No, I wouldn't."

"Liar."

"Pig."

"Jealous cow."

That, right there, was what she needed when everything around her was spinning out of control. She needed him, her beloved partner and the little brother of her heart, to keep things "normal" with the friendly bickering that made up their days together. She also needed a body in the morgue and threads to pull to keep things normal, and since she had both, today was looking up.

After parking at GW Hospital, she put through a call to Dr. Anderson. "We're here."

"Come in through the ER. I'll meet you."

"Be right there."

As they got out of the car and headed for the ER entrance, Sam was thankful to have a friend on the inside who could help her navigate the privacy maze that made it difficult to get to patients.

Sam was aware of Vernon and Jimmy following her, but she ignored them and put her focus on the case at hand. The high she got from doing this job couldn't be achieved by anything else, except maybe the high that came from loving and being loved by her husband. She needed the job the way she needed oxygen. It fed her soul to chase justice on behalf of those who needed it most.

When she walked into the busy Emergency Department

waiting room, the entire place went silent as people stared at her with unbridled disbelief. As step one of her fuck-tradition campaign, she had to pretend to be unbothered by the attention. She showed her gold badge to the receptionist, who gawked right along with everyone else.

"Lieutenant Holland to see Dr. Anderson. He's expecting me."

"I... um..."

Before the receptionist could wet herself, Anderson came out from the back and waved at Sam and Freddie to follow him.

"I come with an entourage now," she said, gesturing at the agents who were hot on her heels.

"Come on back." Anderson led them to a bank of elevators at the far end of the Emergency area. "I confirmed she's still in the ICU. Second floor."

"Thanks, Doc. Appreciate the assist."

"Whatever I can do to make your life easier, Lieutenant."

"Why can't everyone cooperate with me that way, Detective Cruz?"

"Am I required to answer that question?" Freddie asked.

Anderson cracked up laughing.

She pushed the up arrow to summon the elevator. "Don't laugh at his impertinence. It only encourages him."

"We should talk sometime, Detective," Anderson said to Freddie. "I bet we could share some good stories."

She stepped into the elevator. "He won't be doing that because he's very busy working for me. Thanks for paving the way for me here."

"Always a pleasure to be of assistance, Lieutenant."

As the doors started to close, she waggled her fingers at the good doctor.

"You ruin all my fun," Freddie said.

"That's my other goal in life."

On the second floor, Sam turned to Vernon and Jimmy. "Can you please wait for us here?" she asked, gesturing to the waiting room.

"Yes, ma'am."

"Thank you."

Sam went to the nurses' station, showed her badge and asked

for Shanice. "I understand this isn't the best possible time, but we're investigating a homicide, and we very much need to speak to her."

"Let me check with her doctor. One minute, please."

Sam gave the nurse credit for doing her job and not acting the fool at having the first lady turn up at her workplace. Perhaps over time, as people became accustomed to her continuing to do her job the way she always had, there'd be more like her and fewer like the one downstairs.

"What if we can't talk to her?" Freddie asked quietly so they wouldn't be overheard.

"We'll find some of her people and see what they can tell us."

The nurse returned seven minutes later. Sam knew that because she passed the time by watching the big black-and-white wall clock. "Right this way."

Sam gave Freddie a pleased look as they followed the nurse to a room with glass walls. Inside the room, the relentless beeping of the machines attached to Shanice rattled Sam's nerves. She had no idea how medical professionals could stand to listen to that all day long. The beeping would drive her mad.

Shanice watched them with big, frightened brown eyes.

Sam noted that the wound on her neck was covered with thick bandages. She showed Shanice her badge. "I'm Lieutenant Holland. I was there last night."

Shanice licked dry lips. "I remember."

"Can you tell us what happened?"

"Eddie... His friends... They came to our apartment and wanted him to go with them." She took a couple of deep breaths.

"What's the address of your place?"

Shanice recited the address. Sam realized it was near the house where Clarence Reese had killed his family two years ago in Southeast.

"Let's request a warrant and get Crime Scene there," Sam said.

Freddie got busy on his phone, seeing to her orders.

The nurse held a straw to Shanice's lips so she could take a sip of water.

"He didn't want to go. They... One of them pulled a gun and pointed it at me. He... he told me to take off my clothes. Eddie, he told them to fuck off and leave me out of it. One of them grabbed me and ripped off my clothes." Tears rolled down her face. "They made him watch while they took turns with me." Her chest seized with sobs that made her wince in pain.

"Shh." The nurse gently wiped away the young woman's tears. "Take it easy."

"How many men were there?" Sam asked.

"Five," Shanice said softly.

"Was a rape kit performed?" Sam asked the nurse as she boiled with rage over what those men had done to this young woman.

"Yes."

"We'll need to get that to our lab." She glanced at Freddie, silently giving him the order to see to that. To Shanice, she said, "Did you know these men?"

"One of them. Kelvin Evans. I didn't know the others."

Freddie would text the name to Gonzo.

"Can you describe them? Any distinguishing features would help."

Shanice gave them descriptions of each of the men, her voice catching repeatedly as she was forced to recall the horror of the attack.

Freddie typed on his phone, capturing the information she was providing.

"What happened next?"

"They forced us out of the apartment and made us get in a car. One of them held a knife to my neck to keep me quiet."

So that was how she'd gotten cut.

"While we were in the car, one of them stabbed Eddie, and then they pushed us out of the car."

"Could you identify the one who stabbed him if you had to?"

"No, I couldn't tell who it was. They were in the front seat. I was in the back."

"Were they arguing with him before they stabbed him?"

"No, they just did it and tossed us out of the car."

"How did the knife end up with you?"

"I pulled it out of his chest before I went to hide. I was afraid they'd come back, so I took it for protection."

"Do you know anything at all about why they'd do this to Eddie and to you?"

"He owed them money."

"How much?"

"More than twenty-five thousand." She licked her lips and took a deep breath. "He lied to them. He told them he had the money, but he didn't. When Kelvin figured that out, he got really, really mad." Her hands shook violently, so she clasped them together over her lap.

The nurse eyed the beeping monitors. "We need to wrap this up."

"Why did he owe them the money?"

"They'd given him drugs to sell for them, and he was supposed to get them at least twenty-five, but he'd gotten half that."

"Is there anything else you can tell us that might help us find the men who hurt you and killed Eddie?"

"No, but I'm so afraid of them. If they find out I talked to you, they'll kill me."

"We won't let that happen."

Freddie left the room to see to getting Patrol officers there to guard her.

"We're going to put a couple of officers outside your room, and when you're released, we'll provide protective custody. They're not going to hurt you again. Is there anyone else we should contact about Eddie's death?"

"Just his parents, but they don't talk to him."

"They already know."

"There isn't anyone else. It's just been the two of us for a long time."

"What about your family?"

Her eyes closed for a second. "We're not in touch."

"You must have a friend or someone we could call for you."

When Sam looked at the nurse, she shrugged, as if she'd maybe tried and failed to get that info.

"I used to have friends, but not so much now. Eddie and I... It was just us."

"Is that the way Eddie wanted it?" Sam asked, working a hunch after hearing there'd been multiple domestic calls to their place.

"He... he said we were better off going it alone."

So he'd isolated her from her family and friends, which was typical abuser behavior.

"Can I tell you something as a mom myself?"

"I guess."

"If one of my kids was out there somewhere in need of help, I'd want her to call me no matter how long it'd been since we'd talked. It wouldn't matter to me."

"I... I guess you could call my mom." Her chest heaved with a sob. "I'd really like to see her."

Sam pulled the notebook from her back pocket. "What's her number?"

The young woman recited the number.

"What's her name?"

"Brandy Wilson."

"I'll call her for you."

"You can tell her it's okay if she doesn't want to come. It's been a while..."

"I'll tell her." She rested a hand on Shanice's arm. "Try not to worry. We're going to help you."

"Thank you. I can't believe the first lady herself is going to help me."

"Right now, I'm not the first lady. I'm a cop and a mom and a friend, okay?"

Shanice bit her lip and nodded, wincing and blinking back new tears.

"I'll check on you later."

CHAPTER EIGHTEEN

S am left the room and went to the ICU waiting room, which was blessedly empty other than Vernon, Jimmy and Freddie, who was on his phone. She placed the call to Shanice's mother.

The call went to voice mail. "Ms. Wilson, this is Lieutenant Sam Holland with the Metro Police Department. I'm calling about your daughter. Shanice is currently admitted to GW Hospital and gave me your number. She wanted me to tell you that it's okay if you don't want to come, but she'd like to see you." Sam left her number so the woman could call her back and then slapped the phone closed. If she didn't hear from her, she'd try calling again shortly.

"I asked Captain Malone to get the warrant, put Crime Scene on notice that we'll need them at the apartment and made arrangements to get the rape kit to the lab," Freddie said. "I also passed along Shanice's descriptions of the men to Gonzo."

"Excellent. Thank you."

"What's next?"

"What do we know about Kelvin Evans?"

"I'm waiting for Gonzo to get me the lowdown on him."

Sam's cell rang, and she took the call, recognizing the number as the one she'd just called. "Lieutenant Holland."

"This is Shanice's mother. I... I got your message. What happened to her?"

"She was assaulted by several men."

The woman's moan came through the phone. "Because of that asshole Eddie?"

"It was related."

"Of course it was. I've been trying to get her to leave that monster for years. I hope he's locked up."

"He was killed in the incident."

"Good. He doesn't deserve to live in a world with civilized people. He's the reason none of us has seen her in more than a year."

"I'm sorry for what you've been through. Are you able to be with her in the hospital?"

"Did she really ask for me?"

"She gave me your number."

She released a deep sigh. "I'll be there shortly. Thank you for calling me."

"Of course. No problem."

"I've been waiting for this call for a long time while praying it wouldn't be the worst possible news."

"It's going to take a while, but she'll get through this."

"I really hope so."

They said their goodbyes, and Sam slapped her phone closed, feeling satisfied that she'd made a difference for one family that day, which was one of the many reasons she loved this job so much.

"Gonzo emailed me Evans's sheet. It's long and ugly." Freddie handed his phone to her. "He's been in and out of trouble for most of his life. Mostly in."

Sam scanned the lengthy sheet that included burglaries, drug charges and assaults. "How is this guy still on the streets?"

"That's a very good question."

She handed the phone back to him and checked the clock to make sure she still had plenty of time before her meeting with Mrs. Nelson. "Let's look in on Gigi and then go pick him up. Tell Gonzo to meet us there with backup in thirty minutes."

Gigi was asleep when they dropped by her room, so Sam left a note that they'd been there and were hoping she felt better. *I'll check in later*, she added before signing her name and Freddie's.

Back in the car, Freddie put the Anacostia address for Kelvin into the maps app on his phone, which gave them the fastest route.

"That's pretty cool."

"What is?"

"The way the phone gives you the fastest way to get there."

"You too could have this technology if you upgraded from the flip."

"Shut your filthy mouth. Me and my flip are ride or die."

Thanks to her peripheral vision, she caught him rolling his eyes. "They'll probably make you have a BlackBerry now that Nick is president."

"That may or may not have already happened."

"Really?" he said, laughing. "I would've liked to have seen that conversation."

"We were naked in bed. Still wish you were there?"

"Ew."

"Thankfully, I only have to use it when I talk to him." She patted her coat pocket where the direct line to her beloved resided. "It's fine."

He dropped the visor and opened the mirror. "You're being very mature about all of this."

"I expect you to be on my side at all times."

Laughing, he said, "I am on your side, but I'm still allowed to find all of this funny. I bet the BlackBerry also has high-tech GPS locators so you can't go missing."

Sam wasn't sure how she felt about being tracked by Big Brother. "I'm so torn between being crazy proud of him and incredibly annoyed by all the ways this is going to fuck up my life." The minute she shared that thought, she felt guilty for saying it out loud. "Never mind. Forget I said that."

"It's okay, Sam. You know you can share your true feelings with me, and it'll never go any further."

"It can't. Not even to Elin."

"It won't. I promise. No matter what happens over these next few years, I want you to know you can talk to me about it, and I'll always be happy to listen and talk you down from the cliff."

"Thanks. That means a lot. I don't want you to think I'm complaining. I'm not. Well, not really…"

He laughed. "I don't blame you. Most first ladies have a year and a half to prepare for the possibility that their spouse might win the presidency and force them into the brightest spotlight on earth. You had like an hour to prepare for that. I don't blame you at all for being totally wigged out by it."

"I'm trying not to be, but I do feel like I've been tipped upside down and flung into something so much bigger than I can wrap my head around. My husband is the freaking *president* of the United States. Like, what the actual fuck?"

"I can only imagine what that's like. I can barely wrap my head around the fact that my good friend is the president and you're the first lady. Everyone I've ever known in my entire life has reached out to me in the last few days to say 'holy crap.' They all want to know about you guys and whether you're going to keep working and a million other things."

"Ugh, I hate that people want the dirt on us. That makes me feel like I'm going to break out in hives or something."

"Don't do that. You have that network interview tomorrow night, right?"

"Jesus H. Christ. I forgot about that."

"What've I asked you about taking the Lord's name in vain?"

"It's a *network interview*, Frederico! When the hell else should I take the Lord's name in vain?"

"How about never? That would work for me. And don't call me Frederico. You know I hate that too. Only my mother gets away with calling me that—and she's busy losing it about Nick being president. She said she can't believe *people we know* are going to live in the White House."

"We'll have your folks over as soon as we can."

"She'd lose her mind. Seriously."

"We'll make that happen. We may as well take full advantage of the coolness of living there while it lasts, right?"

"We can have some epic parties—and from what I've read, there're enough bedrooms for everyone to sleep over. I call the Lincoln Bedroom."

"We'll make that happen too."

"That'd be so freaking cool. I'd live off that for the rest of my life."

"Maybe it won't totally suck."

"No, it will, but there'll be good times too. Just keep the people you care about most close by to help you keep things real. Speaking of that, I actually had an idea for you."

"What's that?"

"In the past, there have been cases of grandparents moving into the White House with the families so they can be there for the children when the first couple has to travel and stuff."

"Okay..."

"You ought to ask Celia to move in with you guys so she can do that for your kids. It'd be good for her to have something new to do now that your dad has passed away, and it would give you guys peace of mind when you can't be with the kids."

"That's a really great idea."

"I get full credit."

Sam laughed. "I'm happy to give you full credit for a truly brilliant idea. One of my biggest concerns is how I'll ever juggle it all. It was tough enough when I was the second lady, but now it just seems so overwhelming. Keeping my job is critical to me, but the reality is I've been very uncertain how I can do both jobs and be a good mother to three kids. Having Celia there would be such a tremendous help."

"You're a wonderful mother to those kids, Sam. They love you so much."

"I'm an okay mother. I spend less time with them than I should."

"All working mothers say that. Anyone who has a full-time job feels guilty for the time they spend away from their kids. You're no different that way."

"I suppose. I think all the time about how great of a mom Cleo was to Alden and Aubrey. She was the mom with the glue gun who was always doing something amazing with them. I consider it a good day if everyone is fed and bathed."

That made him laugh—hard.

"I'm serious!"

"I know. That's why it's funny. So when I was a kid, maybe seven or eight, I overheard my mom telling my grandmother that she felt like she was doing an awful job being a single mom to me.

That was back when my mom was working two jobs after my dad left, and I spent more time with my grandmother than I did with her. My mom was saying how I was going to grow up thinking my grandmother was my actual mother."

"Oh, damn. What did your grandmother say to that?"

"She said, 'That boy knows exactly who his mother is, and he adores you. He'll remember how hard you worked to provide for him and how he had everything he needed—food, clothing, a roof over his head and all the love in your heart. He's not keeping score about how much time he spends with you. Only you're doing that.'"

"That's lovely, Freddie. Thank you for sharing that with me."

"What my grandmother said is true. I do look back and remember how hard my mom worked so I could have the right clothes and play Little League and be in Cub Scouts and learn to ice skate. She made all that possible for me. Were there times when I wished she didn't have to work so much? Sure, but that's not the thing I remember most about my childhood. I remember laughing with her—a lot. I remember going to church with her and out to eat with her and my grandparents on Sundays and sleepovers with my cousins and how she somehow made it to just about everything that happened at school. I remember most of all how much she loved me. Almost too much, as you know."

"She's a great mom, even now. She loves you more than anything."

"Which can be a little suffocating at times. Like when she decided she hated Elin for me and set out to make my life a living hell."

"Fortunately, she came around to realizing you had to make your own decision about who you love."

"And now they're friends. Who'd a thunk it, right? Bottom line —your kids will remember how much you love them. They'll remember the amazing adventure of living in the White House, and they'll be so proud of what you and Nick will accomplish together."

"Thank you for this. I truly needed to hear it."

"Glad I could help."

"You did."

"I'm on Team Sam and Nick. Whatever you need, you let me know, and I'll do what I can."

"That means a lot. I'm sure you'll end up shouldering more than your share of the paperwork and bullshit going forward."

"I'll trade you that for a night or two in the Lincoln Bedroom."

"You've got yourself a deal, my friend."

They arrived at the Anacostia neighborhood a few minutes later and saw two Patrol cars and Gonzo's car parked a block away from Evans's home.

Sam slid into a space behind Gonzo.

She and Freddie donned bulletproof vests and joined him and the other officers on the sidewalk.

"I put two people on the back door and the other two with us," Gonzo said.

"Sounds good," Sam said. "Let's do it."

When the two Patrol officers radioed to let them know they were in position behind the row of townhouses, Sam led the way to the front door and rang the bell. After a minute without a response, she pounded on the door with a closed fist. "MPD. Open up."

Inside, she heard locks disengaging and reached for her weapon.

The door opened, and a frightened young woman appeared.

"We're looking for Kelvin Evans," Sam said, showing her badge and weapon.

"H-he's n-not here." She flinched as if in pain, which tipped Sam off that he was probably holding a gun on her.

"Can you step outside, please?"

The woman's eyes shifted to the left as her entire body trembled.

With her free hand, Sam pulled the storm door open. "Put your hands up and step outside the door. *Now.*"

The woman took a step forward and then another. Once she crossed the threshold, she sprinted forward like a threatened jackrabbit. Knowing one of the Patrol officers would deal with her, Sam kicked the door hard and heard a gasp from the man hiding behind it when it hit him. "Put down your weapon and come out with your hands up, Kelvin."

While she waited for him to comply with her order, her heart beat fast, and adrenaline zipped through her system the way it always did when shit got real on the job. She took perverse pleasure from getting scumbags off the streets, especially one who'd done what this guy had to Shanice.

"I want a deal," he said.

"No deal until you come out here with your hands up."

"I know stuff. You guys need me."

"You'll have your chance to negotiate once you come out. Until then, no deal. You've got one minute to come out on your own, or we're coming in." She counted down in her head. "Thirty seconds."

The sound of a gun landing on the floor had her expelling the breath she'd been holding.

"Let me see your hands."

His hands came around the edge of the door.

"Move nice and slowly."

Kelvin came around the door, keeping his hands up, and walked toward them. He was about thirty years old, Black, handsome enough to be a model and heavily tattooed. But his eyes were hard with outrage and hatred.

When she lowered her gun, grabbed her cuffs and reached out to him, he suddenly threw an elbow that hit her square in the face, sending her flying backward off the stoop and into bushes made of sharp-ass sticks. While she recovered her senses, Freddie and the two Patrol officers tackled Kelvin and had him cuffed in the time it took Sam to crawl out of the bushes.

Freddie came rushing over to give her a hand up. "You're bleeding like crazy."

When he pulled on her hand, she cried out in pain. Her palms were bloody from trying to stop her fall into the holly bush.

Sam wiped her face, and her hand came away covered in blood. *Great.* As always, the perps had perfect timing, seeming to know when she had something important to do. That was when they took their best shots at her face.

Vernon and Jimmy were watching the goings-on with concerned expressions, but she appreciated that per her request, they hadn't come running to her rescue.

"You, um, might need some stitches."

Stitches meant needles, and she didn't do needles.

"You need to hit the ER to be sure."

"I don't have time for this today."

"I'm sure they'll get you right in. Ask the agents to drive you while I take Evans to HQ."

Resigned to seeking medical attention, she handed over her keys to him. "See what you guys can get out of him. We need to find his accomplices before they take off."

"Will do. No one is doing arraignments until tomorrow anyway, and he won't get bail with murder and felony assault charges looming. So you have time to go to the ER and find some makeup to cover the carnage." He checked his watch. "You have three hours until your meeting with Mrs. Nelson."

Sam groaned when she thought of showing up at the White House looking as if she'd lost a boxing match. "Take care of the girlfriend too. We need to find out what she knows."

"I'm on it. Go take care of yourself. I'll check in later."

Sam was infuriated to have to leave the case to others at this critical juncture, but if the pain radiating from her face and hands was any indication, Freddie might be right about her needing stitches. She stomped down the stairs to the sidewalk, where Vernon met her, holding a wad of gauze that he handed to her.

"Thank you. Would you mind giving me a lift back to GW?"

"It'd be a pleasure, ma'am."

"Stop being nice to me. It's irritating."

"Yes, ma'am." He held the back door for her and then handed her an ice pack.

"You're a regular Boy Scout, aren't you?"

His lips quivered with the start of a smile. "I read up on you before I took this assignment. I learned that having a first aid kit handy would be useful."

"That's very funny. Ha. Ha."

Laughing, he closed the door.

Sam pressed the ice pack to her throbbing cheek and used the gauze to mop up some of the blood pouring from her hands as she realized she needed to call Nick to let him know she was injured. Again. Ignoring the pain coming from her hands, she fished the

BlackBerry from her coat pocket and tried to remember how to use it. Oh, right. Press 69. He was a comedian.

He answered on the third ring. "Samantha? What's up?"

"Everything is fine, but I wanted to tell you I took an elbow to the face, and I'm on my way to GW to get it checked because Freddie said I might need stitches because I also fell into a holly bush."

"Oh no, babe. That's my favorite face in the whole wide world."

She smiled and then winced from the pain of the movement. "The worst part is that I'm going to have to meet with Mrs. Nelson looking like I just stepped out of a boxing ring. There won't be pictures, will there?"

"Uhh, well..."

Sam moaned.

"We have the network interview tomorrow too, don't forget."

She wanted to scream with frustration. "I'm going to need Tracy's theater makeup again."

"You want me to call her?"

"Nah, that's okay. I'll do it. What are you up to?"

"We just saw Elijah off, and the Littles are sad, so Scotty and I are keeping them busy while I wait for Terry to get here. We're going to meet about potential VP candidates."

"I'll be home as soon as I can. Vernon and Jimmy are taking me to GW, and I'm going to call my buddy Dr. Anderson to let him know he can punch my frequent-flier card again. He'll get me in and out."

"It's nice to have friends in high places."

"I have a friend in the highest of high places," she said suggestively. "He's actually more like a fuck buddy."

He snorted with indignant laughter. "You'll pay for that later."

"Can't wait."

"You're really all right?"

"I'm fine, but my hands and face hurt like a bitch. Why do they always have to go for the face?"

"I hope you arrested his ass and tossed him in the can."

"It's hot when you talk like a cop."

"I mean it! He hurt you. What else did he do?"

"Participated in a gang rape and murder."

"Ugh, I'm sorry I asked. Let me know when you're on your way home."

"I will. Tell the kids I look scary."

"They won't care. Love you."

"Love you too."

She ended the call and put her throbbing head back for a minute, looking for relief from the pain. Then she remembered she needed to contact Tracy. Hopefully, she still had that theater makeup she'd used in the past to help Sam cover the carnage of the job. She used her flip phone to put through the call to her eldest sister.

"Madam First Lady, how nice to hear from you!"

"Shut your face with that shit."

"Ah, I see your change in status hasn't sweetened you up any."

"It's made me meaner than ever."

"Dear God."

"I have a situation I could use your help with."

"What's that?"

"I took an elbow to the face three hours before I have to meet with Mrs. Nelson—with photos—and one day before a network interview. I need that stage makeup you used on me the last time this happened."

"I've gotcha covered. Text me when you're on the way home."

"I will."

"You're okay?"

"I will be, but my face and hands are a mess..."

"Ouch."

"Hurts like a mofo."

"I'll get you fixed up for your meeting with Mrs. Nelson. And can I add that I cannot believe you're going to the White House to get the 411 on how to be first lady?"

"Neither can I." A thought occurred to her, one she should've had before now. "You want to come with me?"

"*What?* Shut up!"

"I mean it. You and Ang should come. They didn't say I had to come alone. If she wants one-on-one, I'll meet alone with her while you guys check out my new digs. What do you say?"

"Holy crap, Sam. My roots are popping. I can't go to the White House with roots."

"Yes, you can. Put your hair up in a clip. That hides everything. I want you guys to come with me. Call Ang and meet me at the house in an hour or so. Okay?"

"This is crazy," Tracy said, giggling like a girl. "I can't believe you're going to *live* at the freaking White House."

"Well, believe it, and we're going to have all the fun while we're there." If they had to make this huge life change, they might as well enjoy it as much as they possibly could.

Sam ended the call and held the phone to her chest, overwhelmed by her sister's excitement. Tracy and Angela had been her touchstones all her life, and having them by her side for this latest adventure would make it bearable. She was glad she'd thought to invite them to come with her today, even if she should've had the idea sooner. Maybe it was better this way, since now they wouldn't have time to melt down about it.

She dashed off a quick text to Lilia to let her know her sisters were coming to her meeting with Mrs. Nelson.

Lilia wrote right back. *No problem. I'll let her team know.*

Thanks. You'll be there too, right?

Wouldn't miss it.

Sam felt better knowing the incredibly competent Lilia would be there to smooth the way for her.

As they got closer to GW, she called Dr. Anderson.

"Didn't I just see you?"

"Funniest thing happened after I left you."

"What's that?"

"I took an elbow to the face and messed up my hands, and my buddy Cruz thinks I might need a stitch. Any chance you can get me in and out of there quickly? I have a meeting in two and a half hours with Mrs. Nelson that I can't be late for."

"This will require two punches on your frequent-flier card."

"Everyone is a comedian today."

Laughing, he said, "How far out are you?"

"Five minutes."

"Come to the ambulance bay. I'll meet you there."

"Thanks, Doc."

"Anything for you, FLOTUS."

"Don't call me that, or I'll stab you."

"You need me too much to stab me."

Sam let him have the last word, closed her phone and her eyes and tried not to think about how the throbbing in her face was getting worse rather than better.

CHAPTER NINETEEN

"Was that Mom?" Scotty asked Nick after he got off the phone. They were on the sofa, watching football while the Littles played with their toys on the floor in front of them. They'd cried when Elijah left and had been subdued for the last hour or so.

"It was."

"Is she hurt again?"

"Yep. Took an elbow to the face while arresting a bad guy."

"Ouch."

"She's worried about looking like she just got out of a boxing ring when she sees Mrs. Nelson later."

Scotty tried not to laugh but failed. "I know it's not funny, but of course this happened when she's going to be in pictures."

"And on TV."

"That too. I can't believe everything that's happened this weekend. Thanks again, you know, for taking me with you for the swearing-in and making me part of it."

"Of course you're part of it. You're part of us."

"Thanks for that too. When I think about how much my life has changed in the last two years…"

"Right there with you, pal. On this day two years ago, I was still John's chief of staff. I probably played basketball at the gym with my friends and went out for beers and nachos afterward. And then

I went home by myself to prepare for work the next day. That was my life. And now..."

"Now you're president and have a family that keeps you from going out for beer and nachos with the boys."

"I got to do that for a lot of years. This is way better. Except for the being-president part, of course."

"I think you're going to end up liking being president."

"Is that right?"

"Uh-huh. You're the most powerful guy on the planet. That's super cool."

"Ah, but as Spider-Man's Uncle Ben would say, with great power comes great responsibility."

"Spider-Man's uncle was right."

"Spider-Man was John's favorite. He was always quoting him and his uncle."

"It must be weird to think that if your friend hadn't died, none of this would've happened."

"It's very weird. Who knows if I ever would've seen Mom again, even though I wished for years after we first met to see her, and I never would've met you. There'd be no family or presidency."

"One event led to all of that."

"And another event led us to Elijah and the twins. You ever hear the expression about life turning on a dime?"

"I think so, but I'm not sure what it means."

"When a car is super maneuverable, they say it turns on a dime. The same is true for life. One big or small event can change everything."

"Like you coming for a tour at the home in Richmond changed my life."

"And mine, and Mom's."

He gestured to the twins, who were playing with their Little People village that Nick and Scotty had helped them set up after Elijah left. It included several new pieces from their birthday party. The volume of the TV made it so they couldn't hear what Nick and Scotty were saying. "Do you think they're really okay?"

"They will be. In time. According to the therapist, they're doing as well as can be expected under the circumstances. Having Elijah here for almost a week was like old times to them, so it's natural for them to be sad about him leaving."

"They were so happy yesterday at their party. I was hoping that would last awhile longer."

"They'll bounce back. Eli will FaceTime with them tonight, which will help."

"I just feel really sorry for what they're going through," Scotty said.

"I'm sure it's brought back some memories for you too."

He shrugged. "A few. I understand how they feel. I wish there was more we could do to make them feel better."

"All we can do is love them. That's what they need most right now."

"I love them so much. They've only been with us a month, and they already feel like my brother and sister. Eli too."

"I know what you mean, buddy. It didn't take long for them to become part of us."

"It took, like, an hour."

Nick laughed. "It's because they're so damned cute and sweet." He glanced at his adorable, thoughtful, sensitive son. "You've been so great with them. We're so thankful for that."

"You don't have to thank me for helping with them."

"I know I don't have to, but I want to anyway. And I also want you to know that I'm sorry you're going to be stalked by Secret Service agents while you're in high school. I'm really sorry about that."

"It's fine. I've gotten used to them. I mean it when I say I barely notice them anymore."

Nick laughed. "Sure, you don't."

"It's hard to believe that this time next week, we'll be living in the White House."

"I know." Nick took a look around at the place that had become the first real "home" he'd ever had, a thought he shared with his son.

"A big part of me doesn't want to move," Scotty said, "even if I know it'll be cool to live in the White House."

"All of me doesn't want to move. I hate moving, even when other people come in and do all the work for us. But we need to remember that home is the people we're with. It's not a building. As long as we're all together, we'll be home wherever we are."

"I guess. I'll miss this place, though. We became a family here."

"I'll miss it too, but we can come back here anytime we want. This will always be our home."

"That makes me feel a little better about moving."

"I want you to spend some time today deciding what you want to take and what can stay here. We don't need to take every single thing we own."

"Mom said moving is a good chance to get rid of crap."

"Mom is right, as usual."

The agent working the front door let Terry in a few minutes later.

"Duty calls," Nick said to Scotty. "We need to find a vice president."

"I was thinking about that. You ought to have a woman. It's time for that, don't you think?"

Amused, Nick said, "Long overdue. Your thinking matches mine. I asked Terry to come up with a list of five or six women who'd be outstanding candidates."

"That's cool."

"I'm glad you think so. Keep an eye on the Littles and let me know if you need me. I'll be in the dining room."

"Okay."

"And get your homework done."

"Was that really necessary?"

He ruffled Scotty's hair, earning a playful scowl from the boy. God, he loved that kid and had from the first minute he met him that fateful day in Richmond when he'd been campaigning for the Senate seat he'd inherited from John. That seemed like a lifetime ago in light of everything that'd happened since then.

"Mr. President," Terry said. "How are you this morning?"

"I'm fine, Terry, and you know that because you've already talked to me three times today. And you can cut out the Mr. President stuff when it's just us."

Terry smiled. "Yes, sir."

"I asked Derek to join us for this. He's got the inside scoop on everyone who's anyone."

"Good call."

"He'll be here shortly. In the meantime, what's the latest on Ruskin? There was no mention of him in this morning's intelligence briefing."

"We're still working on putting together what actually took place," Terry said. "We have a team meeting the plane at Andrews. They'll be taken to a secure location for the night and brought to the White House to be debriefed in the morning. We'll get Ruskin in to see you as soon as we have all the info you need."

"Thank you for handling that, Terry."

"That's my job, sir. Next up is vice presidential vetting." Terry put five eight-by-ten photos on the table in front of Nick, all women he recognized. The first was Evelyn Hodges, the Transportation secretary, followed by Michaela Johnson, a congresswoman from Maryland; Inez Cortez, the governor of New Mexico; Jessica Sanford, the senior senator from Illinois; and Gretchen Henderson, a well-respected political operative who'd done an outstanding job of turning out the young adult vote in the last presidential election.

"The Nelson team thoroughly vetted Johnson, Hodges and Cortez when he was considering them before his first election. He ended up going with the safe choice in Gooding and then with you because he wanted your approval ratings to transfer over to him. We all know how that worked out." Nick had only become *more* popular as vice president, which had annoyed Nelson—and his murdering son, Christopher.

"So we'd only need to vet Sanford and Henderson, then?"

"Right. I've got people working on both right now, with orders to keep it low-key. We don't want to tip our hand in any direction until we have a front-runner."

"Johnson would be my first choice. I'd love to have the first woman and first Black vice president."

"And she'd be an excellent choice, but I'm actually more interested in Henderson myself."

"How come?"

"Roll with me here. Your youthfulness is going to be a big part of what your administration is remembered for, and the way I see it, we have an enormous opportunity to engage young people in government service, voting, activism, etc. That plays nicely with the work you've already been doing in engaging kids and young people in government. That's why I think Henderson is the ideal choice."

Nick picked up the photo of the dark-haired, dark-eyed beauty who was a Rhodes scholar, a fellow Harvard graduate and a former Miss New Jersey. "I don't know much about her beyond her successful get-out-the-vote work in the last two presidential elections."

"She's a go-getter," Terry said. "Her story isn't all that different from yours. She was raised in public housing in Newark, won an academic scholarship to Harvard. She's worked for a number of New Jersey governors and members of Congress and is very well regarded by everyone who knows her."

Nick was aware that whoever he chose to be his vice president would also be the party's heir apparent, like he'd been as vice president. He was also painfully aware that this first major decision as president would be thoroughly dissected, which further amplified the need to get it right.

Derek joined them a few minutes later. "Sorry I'm late. My parents came to stay with Maeve for a few hours, and they got caught in football traffic."

Washington's football team had a home game that afternoon.

"No worries," Nick said. "We were just talking about Gretchen Henderson. Any thoughts?"

"I like her, but her personal life has been messy."

"How so?" Nick asked. "We don't have any formal vetting on her yet."

"She's been divorced twice. The second divorce was ugly, from what I heard, with restraining orders filed on both sides."

Nick winced. "Both sides, huh?"

"I don't know all the details," Derek said, "but we'll need to take a deeper dive before we seriously consider her. Or, I should say, before *you* seriously consider her."

Nick glanced at Terry, who smiled and nodded, agreeing with him that this was the perfect time to tell Derek they hoped to retain him in their administration. "I was hoping you'd consider sticking around."

"Oh," Derek said. "Really?"

"Of course," Nick said, laughing. "You can't be all that surprised that I want you on my team."

"I didn't want to assume anything."

"I'd love for you to stay as deputy chief of staff, continuing your role as our liaison to Congress," Nick said. "If you're willing, that is."

"I'd be honored." Derek paused before he added, "Mr. President, sir."

"Terry, what's the rule on the Mr. President and sir stuff?"

"None of that shit when we're alone," Terry said.

Derek laughed. "Got it. And thank you. I have to confess, I've been reeling a bit since I got the word about Nelson's passing and realized I was out of a job."

He'd become a single father to his daughter, Maeve, after his wife, Victoria, was murdered almost two years ago. "I'd considered you for loftier posts, but I had a feeling you'd rather stick with the routine that allows you to be home for dinner with Maeve most nights."

"You figured right. Thank you again for asking me."

"Since I'm inheriting Nelson's cabinet, I need all the friends around me that I can get. I was thinking about asking Christina to come back as press secretary." His longtime friend and aide had married Sam's colleague Tommy Gonzales on Thanksgiving. "What do you think?"

"I'm not sure she'd want the full-time gig, not to mention the stress, especially after what she and Tommy have been through lately," Terry said.

"I've considered that, and I won't be surprised if she declines. But I do plan to ask her. A few roles that require my own people, and that's definitely one of them." No way would he trust Nelson's communications people to speak for him. "Trevor will be the communications director. I've already discussed Christina with him, and he's all for it. We'll see what she has to say about it. In the meantime, let's get the vetting on the last two VP candidates and start meeting with them this week."

They were still working their way through Terry's agenda of items that needed Nick's immediate attention when he heard Sam talking to the kids in the family room. "Excuse me for just a minute."

He went to see how bad the damage to the face of his beloved was and had to bite back a gasp when he saw her. Her cheek was going to be badly bruised, and both hands were wrapped in gauze. "Aw, babe."

"I told you it was no big deal," she said, wincing when she tried to smile.

"Did you need stitches?"

"Thankfully, no, but getting the crap cleaned out of the cuts on my hands was all kinds of fun, let me tell you."

"How did you hurt your hands?"

"Breaking my fall into a holly bush."

He gently kissed the backs of her hands. "Ouch. You want to reschedule with Mrs. Nelson?"

"No way. I can do it. Tracy is coming to make me presentable."

"Babe..."

"I'm fine. I'm going up to wash off the blood. I'll be ready by the time Tracy gets here. I invited her and Ang to come with me, and yes, I asked Lilia to let Mrs. Nelson's team know I'm bringing my sisters." She glanced at the kids, all of whom were playing with the toys on the floor. "Scotty says they seem better than they were right after Eli left."

"They're hanging in there. I've been with Terry and Derek for the last hour, with Scotty under orders to come get me if needed." He kissed her forehead. "Go take your shower." He waited until she was all the way upstairs before he went to find Vernon, who was outside the front door with Jimmy. The two of them and the other agents they were with snapped to attention when he appeared at the doorway.

"Mr. President," Vernon said. "May we help you with something?"

"I was wondering if I could have a word, Vernon."

"Of course, sir." He stepped inside the house and followed Nick to the kitchen, the one place on the first floor where they could speak privately.

"Can I get you anything?" Nick asked as he poured himself a cup of coffee.

"No, thank you, sir."

"I was just wondering if you had to get involved at the incident earlier."

"No, sir. Your wife and her team had the situation well in hand. The perp got off a lucky elbow, which is how she got hurt. We did give her a lift to the ER, but otherwise, we weren't needed."

"Well, I guess that's good."

"If I may, sir..."

"Please, speak freely."

"Your wife is very good at what she does."

"Yes, I know."

"It'd be a shame if she had to stop doing her job."

"That's not going to happen."

"Good to know."

"If there's nothing else, I should get back to work."

"One other thing." Nick hesitated before he said, "Please don't let anything happen to her. She's everything to me."

"I'll do everything in my power to keep her safe. You have my word on that. But we're trying to stay out of her way when she's working."

"I understand you're walking a fine line there."

"Indeed, sir."

"Thank you, Vernon."

"My pleasure, sir."

Alone in the kitchen, his mind swirling with worries about the many ways his job made his beloved wife unsafe, Nick wished he could go back in time to the day President Nelson asked him to replace the ailing Vice President Gooding. If he'd known then what he knew now, the answer would've been an unequivocal no.

CHAPTER TWENTY

Sam showered, brushed her hair with hands that hurt like hell and made herself as presentable as possible. Now it was down to Tracy and her theater makeup to finish the job.

"I'll try not to hurt you," Tracy said as she came at Sam with a triangle-shaped sponge dipped in stage makeup.

Despite Tracy's best efforts to be gentle, it was agonizing to have anything touch her face. "This could've only happened to me."

"You do have a propensity for spectacular injuries at the worst possible time." Tracy worked with intense concentration that would've made Sam giggle if it didn't hurt so much to laugh.

"You look really nice."

Her sister, who'd battled weight challenges since giving birth to the youngest of her three children, was wearing a black wrap dress with a jaunty cranberry-colored jacket and matching jewelry. "I did what I could on short notice."

"You did good."

"A little more warning before you take me to the White House next time, huh?"

"I'll do what I can."

"Ang is so excited I think she peed herself."

"Don't make me laugh."

"It's not funny," Ang said when she came into the room. "I did actually pee myself, but that happens a lot these days with baby number three ruining what's left of my bladder."

"TMI," Sam said, quelling the envy that erupted inside her every time she was reminded that each of her sisters had no problem getting pregnant or staying pregnant—three times each —while she'd never been able to do it once. The envy wasn't as fierce as it'd been before Scotty, the twins and Elijah had come into their lives, but it was still there, reminding her of the most vexing challenge of her adult life.

"It's gotten so bad that Spence is calling me Leaky—and I'm only in the fourth month. Looking forward to what's ahead."

"Now that's funny," Tracy said.

Angela moved so she was on Sam's right side. When she wasn't pregnant, she was whip thin, which irritated her sisters endlessly. Pregnancy made her even prettier than she already was, infusing her cheeks with a glow. Sam had always thought Angela was the stunner of the three of them. Nick said he disagreed, but he had to say that. "It doesn't look that bad," Angela said of Sam's face.

"No need to lie. I can see it's awful."

"It's way better than it was," Tracy said. "Take a look."

Sam finally ventured a glance at the mirror and was astounded to realize Tracy was right. "I'm in awe of you and your ability with makeup."

"We just need some eye makeup and lipstick to finish you off."

"Let me do her eyes," Ang said. "I watched this cool video on YouTube last night, and I want to try it on her."

"Nothing crazy," Sam said. "I'm going to a meeting at the White House."

"I gotcha covered. Don't worry."

"I found big flesh-colored bandages we can use on your hands," Angela said. "No one will even know you're injured."

Thirty minutes later, the three of them trooped downstairs, ready to kick ass and take names at the White House. With all her heart, Sam wished her dad could be there to see them off. He'd be busting his buttons with pride for his three daughters.

Sam wore a black and red floral dress with a black jacket and her prized Louboutins. Being first lady would probably mean more cool shoes, which was the one thing about the gig that truly made her happy.

She was also wearing her gorgeous engagement ring, which she never wore to work, and the diamond key necklace. Despite the carnage on her face, she felt as prepared as one could be to visit the now-former first lady at the White House to learn what she needed to know to succeed in the role herself. The sheer lunacy of it made her laugh despite the pain that caused her. She carried a large black purse that contained a gift she planned to leave for her husband in his new office.

Nick came out of the dining room when he heard them come down and let out a low whistle. "Three hot mamas going to the White House, and wow, Tracy, that makeup is incredible. You look great, Sam."

"Hopefully, I won't embarrass us too badly," she said, grimacing.

"You'll be awesome." He kissed her forehead. "I can't wait to hear all about it."

Sam took a minute to sit with the kids, who were snuggled up to Scotty watching a Minions movie for the nine-hundredth time. "When I get home, we'll make some pizza and play Candy Land, okay?"

Aubrey smiled and nodded. "Okay, Sam. How does your face feel?"

"It still hurts, but it's better than it was." That wasn't true, but she didn't want the little girl to worry about her. She leaned in to kiss her, her brother and Scotty.

"Good luck at the White House, Mom," Scotty said. "Pick out the coolest room for me."

"Will do, pal."

Vernon and Jimmy led them to a black SUV and waited for them to be settled before closing the door.

"This is so freaking *cool*," Tracy said.

"I'm glad you think so."

"Come on, Sam," Angela said. "Even you have to agree that living in the White House is going to be an amazing experience for all of you—and the rest of us who get to visit you there."

"It will be. I have no doubt about that. It's just the intense scrutiny and attention and safety concerns that make me anxious. So many people are pissed about the way Nick became president. They think he's too young. They think he doesn't want the job because he basically said that a week ago. The whole world is talking about my husband and my family, and today, the mayor asked me if I'd like to be the department's new deputy chief."

"*Seriously?*" Tracy asked with a high screech to her voice. "And you're just telling us this now?"

"Relax. I said no."

"Why?" Angela asked.

"Because! I don't want that job. I want the one I already have, and besides, it's bad enough that I have to hear all the time that I'm only where I am because of *who* I am, that my father and uncle and all their buddies are the only reason I've been successful. The last freaking thing I need is to be promoted two ranks the same week my husband gets the ultimate promotion. I'd never hear the end of that, which is why you guys can't breathe a word of this to anyone, even Spencer and Mike."

"We never would," Tracy said. "What did the mayor say?"

"That she was disappointed, but said she understood how I felt. Thank God Uncle Joe was there to assure her there was no chance I'd change my mind."

"Still, it's kinda cool to be asked, right?" Ang asked.

"I guess. I mean, it's not lost on me that it'd be awesome to have the job Dad once had, but I love what I do. I can't imagine being stuck in an office all day pushing paper and dealing with City Hall and the union." She shuddered. "I'd go mad."

"And your talents would be wasted," Tracy said.

"That too. I'm really only good at one thing, and I need to stay in my lane."

"You're good at lots of things," Angela said.

"Name something else," Sam said, giving her a withering look that wasn't as withering as it would've been if her face hadn't been killing her.

"You're a great mom."

"No, I'm an adequate mom. Look at what my kids are doing today while I'm off working and meeting with the former first lady."

"Your kids had a very big day yesterday," Tracy reminded her. "They're probably exhausted from all the fun they had."

"Thanks to Shelby," Sam said.

"Thanks to you, Nick *and* Shelby," Angela said. "You need to lighten up. They're all doing great, and that's because they know how loved they are."

"I hope they know that. So, hey, Freddie had a big idea I wanted to run by you guys."

"What's that?" Tracy asked.

"He thinks we ought to ask Celia to move to the White House with us so she can be there for the kids when we can't be."

"I *love* that idea," Ang said. "She's been so down since Dad died. That would give her a wonderful new adventure and a change of scenery. She told me the other day how hard it is to be at the house without him there with her."

Sam was sad to hear that. "You think she'd want to do it?"

"I think she'd love it," Tracy said. "You should ask her."

"I haven't really talked to Nick about it yet."

"He'll love it," Ang said. "Of course he will. It's a great idea."

"I'm glad you guys think so."

When the Secret Service was driving, it took less than five minutes to drive from Ninth Street to Pennsylvania Avenue. As they pulled through the gates, Sam began to feel like she was hyperventilating, even though she'd been there many times before. Everything was different now. This was their house, on loan from the people, for the next three years. The enormity of it all seemed to swoop down on her in the seconds before the car door opened.

"Breathe, Sam," Tracy said softly. "Just breathe."

She was so glad her sisters were with her as they made their way inside, where Lilia was waiting to greet them.

"I heard you got hurt," Lilia said, eyeing Sam's face and bandaged hands. "Are you all right?"

"I will be. No big deal."

"Mrs. Nelson asked me to bring you to the residence for tea and a tour. Right this way." She led them down red-carpeted hallways, past portraits of former presidents and gorgeous antiques. "Tomorrow, the volunteers will begin decorating for Christmas. Next year, you'll get to choose the theme."

"That doesn't sound at all overwhelming," Sam said.

"We'll help you," Angela said. "We'll help you with everything."

Sam smiled at her sister. "Thank you. I need all the help I can get."

"We're here to make you look good," Lilia said.

"On days like today, that can be one hell of a job," Tracy said.

The four of them shared a laugh as Lilia ushered them into an elevator that took them to the second-floor residence, where Gloria Nelson met them. She wore a red pantsuit with a black-and-red floral blouse and black heels.

"We look like we called each other to coordinate our colors," Gloria said as she greeted Sam with a smile and a hug.

"That's funny," Sam said, touched by Gloria's warmth.

"I heard you were injured earlier. Are you all right?"

"Other than my banged-up face and hands, I'm fine."

"Ouch."

Aware of a photographer documenting the moment, Sam stepped back, but kept a light hold on Gloria's hands, ignoring the pain radiating from hers. "How are you holding up?"

"Oh, you know... Good moments and bad moments. It's helped to have the family here with me. I've sent them down to the bowling alley so we can have a few minutes to ourselves."

"I'd like to introduce you to my sisters, Tracy Hogan and Angela Radcliffe. Ladies, this is Gloria Nelson."

"It's so lovely to meet you both," Gloria said as she shook their hands. "I'm so glad you could join us today."

"Thank you for having us," Angela said, seeming starstruck.

Gloria had had the same impact on Sam the first time they'd met at John O'Connor's funeral. She was an impressive, accomplished woman in her own right, and Sam had always admired her, never more so than how she'd handled the scandal that followed her husband's affair.

"We're very sorry for your loss," Tracy said.

"Thank you. The outpouring of love and support has just been overwhelming. Despite everything, people still loved David." She led them into a beautifully appointed sitting room with red walls, high ceilings, elaborate moldings and priceless artwork. Sam had been in that room once before, when she and Nick met with President and Mrs. Nelson after their son Christopher targeted them and was charged with murdering Sam's ex-husband. It was there that the Nelsons had assured them they'd known nothing of their son's schemes until the rest of the world found out. "Please, have a seat and make yourselves comfortable. Lilia, you're welcome to join us."

Sam waved for her to come in.

"Thank you, ma'am," Lilia said, sitting across from Sam.

As usual, Gloria looked as if she'd just stepped out of a beauty salon, with every one of her blonde hairs perfectly coiffed and her makeup flawless. Sam felt like an impostor sitting in Gloria's presence as the nation's new first lady.

An older Black man in a tuxedo uniform appeared, rolling a cart with a silver tea service and a wide assortment of pastries that made Sam's mouth water, reminding her she hadn't eaten anything but the granola bar hours earlier.

"Roland Daniels, I'd like you to meet Mrs. Cappuano and her sisters, Mrs. Hogan and Mrs. Radcliffe. I believe you know Mrs. Cappuano's chief of staff, Lilia Van Nostrand."

"A pleasure to meet you all," Roland said. "We look forward to welcoming your family, ma'am."

"Thank you, Roland," Sam said. "It's wonderful to meet you too."

"Roland has been here for six administrations, counting your husband's," Gloria said. "And his father was here for twenty-eight years before that."

"That's amazing," Sam said. "Thank you for your service."

"It's been an honor and a privilege, ma'am."

He poured tea for each of them and offered them plates and pastries.

"I can already see that living here isn't going to be good for my waistline," Sam said as she took a raspberry tart and a lemon danish. Just to be polite, or so she told herself. Whatever.

"You'll have your very own pastry chefs," Gloria said.

Sam groaned with pleasure when she took a bite of the tart. "This won't be good at all."

The others laughed, which went a long way to making her feel more relaxed.

"I'll be sure to let the pastry chefs know that Mrs. Cappuano has a sweet tooth," Roland said.

"She has a sweet tooth, a pizza tooth, a chips-and-salsa tooth," Tracy said, using her fingers to count. "She really has *all* the teeth."

"You be quiet," Sam said teasingly. "We don't need them to know all my faults on the first day."

"We're here to fill you in, Roland," Angela said with a wink.

Amused, he said, "That's good to know, ma'am. Please let us know if you need anything further."

"The staff is *amazing*," Gloria said after Roland left the room. "You'll be pampered to within an inch of your life. They work so hard to make your lives easier."

"I have to confess that the idea of having people wait on us is going to take some getting used to."

"I felt the same way you did when I first arrived. I was accustomed to taking care of myself and my own family, but Mrs. Harrigan told me something I've never forgotten," she said, referring to her predecessor. "She said this is their life's work, to take care of the presidents' families. We have to honor and respect that and allow them to care for us the way they've been trained to do."

"That's a lovely way of putting it," Sam said.

"They're here for you. If you don't need them, they don't have jobs."

"She needs them," Tracy said. "You have no idea how much she needs them."

"Whose idea was it to bring my sisters?" Sam asked.

Gloria laughed. "Leave it to your sisters to tell it like it is."

"For sure. I do need all the help I can get, if I'm being honest."

"I heard you intend to keep your job, and if I may say, I think that's marvelous."

"I'm glad you think so. It makes me antsy to know the eyes of the world will be on me, my husband, our family, even more so than they were when he was VP."

Gloria stirred some honey into her tea. "The one word of advice I'll give you is to stay true to what matters most to you— your husband, your marriage, your children, your work. David and I... We got caught up in the madness and paid a terrible price for that. I don't want to see that happen to you."

Sam swallowed hard at the thought of anything coming between her and Nick the way another woman had with the Nelsons.

"Anyway," Gloria said, making an attempt to rally. "Have you given any thought to who you might like to have as your social secretary? I know Cornelia would be happy to stay on, but I'm sure you have your own people to draw from."

"I do have someone in mind," Sam said. "I haven't yet spoken to her about it, but we'd appreciate Cornelia's help during the transition." The Nelson administration's social secretary was a Washington institution and would be invaluable to Shelby, if she agreed to come on board. That was a big *if* for Shelby, who had a soon-to-be one-year-old son and another baby on the way.

"I'll make sure Cornelia is available as long as needed. The one thing to keep in mind about being first lady is there's no guidebook to follow, which is a good and bad thing. Each of us makes it up as we go along, which in some ways gives us tremendous power to carve our own paths. Jacqueline Kennedy famously disliked the title of first lady. She said, 'It sounds like a saddle horse. I felt as if I'd just turned into a piece of public property.' In many ways, she was right about that. You do become public property, but it's up to you to decide how much or how little you choose to give."

"I appreciate knowing that," Sam said. "I'll confess that while I'm indeed determined to keep my job, I'm also intimidated by the idea of being a mother and first lady at the same time."

"You'll have lots of wonderful help. Rely heavily on the people whose jobs it is to make it easier for you. Now, enough talk of business. Let me show you around your new home."

CHAPTER TWENTY-ONE

S am, Tracy, Angela and Lilia followed Gloria to the hallway. "First, some stats. The White House is an eighteen-acre property, and the mansion has one hundred thirty-two rooms, thirty-five bathrooms, twenty-eight fireplaces, eight staircases, three elevators and two hidden mezzanine levels that make for six floors tucked inside a building that has the appearance of three floors from the outside."

"Am I required to know all that?" Sam asked, at once impressed and horrified.

Gloria laughed and squeezed her arm. "I'll make sure you get a cheat sheet."

"That'd be appreciated."

"You'll give the tour often enough that you'll have it all memorized in no time."

Sam wasn't so sure, but she kept the thought to herself.

"The White House is beautifully run by ninety-six full-time and two hundred fifty part-time staff of dedicated ushers, butlers, housekeepers, photographers, florists, chefs, carpenters, plumbers, electricians, gardeners, calligraphers, engineers, maids and doormen, all of them overseen by the chief usher, whom you'll meet shortly."

"Holy moly," Sam said, her mind spinning. "In all my years of living a few blocks from here, I've never given much thought to what goes into running this place."

"You'll find the staff is a well-oiled machine made up of wonderful people, many of them like Roland, the second or third generation of their family to work here. Many will become lifelong friends to your family." She gestured to a small kitchen. "This is the family kitchen Jacqueline Kennedy had installed so the family could cook for themselves if they so desired. She also established this dining room on the residence level and is largely credited with making the residence feel more like a home. The old family dining room is tucked in next to the State Dining Room downstairs. There are sixteen rooms and six bathrooms on this floor as well as twenty rooms and nine more bathrooms on the third floor, all of which are for your use, along with a wet bar and second kitchen on the third floor."

"After hearing that, Sam, aren't you glad the residence comes with a staff?" Angela asked.

"For sure," Sam said. "All the houses I've ever lived in could fit into the two floors we'll live in here."

"People are always amazed by how much bigger the White House is than it appears from the outside. I should warn you that you'll receive a grocery bill at the end of every month, to cover your family's needs as well as any personal entertaining you may do."

"That's good to know."

"People don't realize that the first family pays for their own food." As Gloria opened a door, Sam was aware of the photographer following them to document the moment for history. "This will be your bedroom."

Sam stepped into the spacious room that included a huge four-poster bed, a sitting area and a fireplace. "This is beautiful."

"You'll be welcome to redecorate the residence to your taste. The chief usher will help you with that as well as redecorating the Oval Office in conjunction with the director of Oval Office Operations."

Sam gulped at the thought of redecorating. That was so not her thing. "Nick is better at that stuff than I am. Since he won't have anything better to do, I'll put him in charge of that."

The others laughed as Gloria showed them bedrooms that would work for Scotty, Eli and the twins and then led them to another room at the end of the hallway. "This is the famous Lincoln Bedroom, which was actually President Lincoln's office when he was president. Presidents have lived in the White House through moments of great personal celebration, including the weddings of children, and great tragedy, such as when the Lincolns lost their son Willie to typhoid fever at the age of eleven. He died in that very bed, although it wasn't in this room at that time."

"That's so sad," Tracy said.

"It's believed that he—and his brother, who survived—contracted typhoid from the contaminated water in the White House," Gloria said.

"Oh God, that's awful," Sam said.

"Things have come a long way since then." Gloria showed them the famous Truman Balcony before leading them to another flight of stairs. "I want you to see the solarium on the third floor."

As they followed her up the stairs, Sam thought about the house parties they could host for family and friends with all those bedrooms and bathrooms and a wonderful staff to handle the cooking.

"This is one of my favorite rooms in the house," Gloria said of the solarium that boasted a sweeping view of Washington. "It has an amazing history—it was FDR's favorite place to take a lunch break. President Eisenhower liked to have barbecues on the parapet. It also served as Caroline Kennedy's preschool and the Bush twins' high school hangout. We had some of our best times as a family here."

"This is incredible." Angela moved to the wall of windows to take in the view. "I had no idea this was even here."

"It's a hidden gem." Gloria cast a wistful glance around the room, probably thinking of happier times. "We'll take the elevator down to the main floor."

Over the next half hour, they toured the public spaces, which included the Red, Green and Blue Rooms, the East Room and the State Dining Room. Then they went down another floor, where Sam met chefs, florists, calligraphers and other staffers whose names flew by in a whirlwind. Gloria knew every one of them by name and asked after their families and parents. She was obviously well loved by the staff, some of whom were emotional as they expressed their condolences to her.

Sam couldn't help but wonder what the staff would think of her. It was probably better not to speculate about that. Their tour ended in the office of the chief usher, Gideon Lawson, a handsome man of about forty-five years old, who stood to greet her with a warm handshake.

"Gideon is basically the general manager of the entire White House," Gloria said.

"It's a pleasure to meet you, ma'am." He had short-cropped light blond hair and kind brown eyes that twinkled when he smiled.

"Gideon will be your very best friend in this place," Gloria said. "He knows everything about everything and can get anything done on a moment's notice. He's your go-to guy for all things White House."

"You flatter me, ma'am," Gideon said with obvious affection for the outgoing first lady.

"I'll try not to make your life too difficult," Sam said.

"Nonsense," Gideon said. "My job is to make your life as easy as possible."

"She's a handful," Tracy said bluntly. "You'll have your job cut out for you."

Gideon laughed. "Thank you for the warning, ma'am, but I've heard only good things about your sister and brother-in-law." To Sam, he said, "My staff and I are ready to welcome your family to the White House. It'll be the first time in many years that we've had young children in residence. Everyone is looking forward to that."

"The kids are excited about the bowling alley, the pool and the movie theater," Sam said.

"We'll make sure all three are ready for them. Your husband has already spoken with us about procuring a play set for the South Lawn for the little ones."

Touched to hear that, Sam said, "Why am I not surprised? He thinks of everything."

"We'll be reaching out this week to finalize the plans for your move." Gideon handed her his business card and a file folder. "That's a copy of the in-depth questionnaire we ask all incoming families to complete so we can have what you need ready for you. It covers everything from your preferred shampoo to food choices and sizes for new bowling shoes for each family member. The sooner we can get that information, the faster we can get busy preparing for your arrival."

"I'll get it right back to you," Sam said, handing it to Tracy.

"She means that one of us will get it back to you," Tracy said.

Gideon laughed. "Whatever works for you works for us. We'd also love to have a collection of family photos we can use to decorate the residence."

"We can take care of that too," Angela said.

He handed business cards to Tracy and Angela. "In the meantime, we're at your service. Please feel free to call me with any questions or concerns you may have."

"Thank you, Gideon," Sam said. "I look forward to working with you."

"Likewise, ma'am. Say the word, and I'll have staff assigned to packing up your current home to prepare for the move."

"I can do that? Just say the word and make that happen?"

"Yes, ma'am. You're the first lady. We work for you."

"Let me speak to Nick... er, the president, about that and get back to you tomorrow."

"I'll look forward to hearing from you."

Gideon escorted them to yet another room on the main floor. "This is called the Vermeil Room, or the gold room." He gestured for them to go into the room where Gloria waited for them.

A staffer materialized with a gift bag that she gave to Gloria. "Thank you, Ariana." Gloria handed the bag to Sam. "This is for you. I've included some of my favorite books about the White House as well as a guestbook. You'll have a lot of visitors while you're here. You'll want to record them all for history."

"Thank you so much for the gifts, the generosity, the information and, most of all, for the gracious example you've set for me and everyone who will follow us both," Sam said. "I appreciate your willingness to help me during this difficult time for you and your family."

"It's been a pleasure to have you and to get to know you and your husband over the last year. My door is always open to you and the president if I can be of service to you. I included my contact information in the bag."

"Thank you, Mrs. Nelson."

"Please, call me Gloria. We're members of a very small club, and we have to stick together."

Sam hugged her. "I too will wish for all the best for you and your family."

"I'll pray for your every success."

"Before we go, I wondered if I might leave a gift for Nick in his new office."

"I can help with that," Gideon said. "Right this way."

"Thank you again," Sam said to Gloria before she, her sisters and Lilia followed Gideon to the West Wing. She realized she was taking the route Nick would travel each day to go to work.

"Nick is lucky he gets to walk to work," Angela said, echoing Sam's thoughts.

"I was just thinking the same thing."

"Previous presidents have referred to it as 'living above the store,'" Gideon said. "Many presidents would tell you that working and living in the White House is good for families that are accustomed to spending a lot of time apart during campaigns or when separated by other offices."

"We haven't spent much time apart," Sam said, "but I can definitely see the benefit of living above the store."

"I believe you'll find your husband will be more readily available to his family than he was as vice president," Gideon said.

That might be true, Sam thought, *but will I be less available to them?* Ugh, that would suck.

When they walked into the West Wing, Sam noted it was more subdued than it had been when she'd visited in the past, probably due to the president's death and the transition currently under way. Plus, it was Sunday on a holiday weekend.

Even the desks outside the president's office were vacant.

"What happens to all the people who worked for President Nelson?"

"A few will remain to work with President Cappuano, but most of them will be looking for new positions," Gideon said. To the Secret Service agent positioned outside the Oval Office, Gideon said, "Mrs. Cappuano would like to leave a gift for her husband in his office."

The agent nodded and opened the door for Sam. "I'll be right out," she said to her sisters, wanting to take this mission on her own. Inside the Oval Office, Sam noticed that President Nelson's personal effects had already been removed to make way for the new president and his belongings.

Sam went around the Resolute desk, which she'd once done a report about in a high school history class, never dreaming that her husband might one day be the temporary custodian of the desk, the office and the people's house. She sat in his seat and took in the majesty of the most powerful office in the world, letting it settle on her that this was really Nick's office and their home for the next three years. Would they be here longer than that? If someone asked him that today, he'd say no way. In a year or two, he might feel differently, and she was prepared to support him, no matter which path he took.

She withdrew the silver-framed photo they'd taken on Thanksgiving with Scotty, Elijah and the twins, the first photo of them as a family, which she'd asked Tracy to have printed and framed for her so it could be the first photo to grace President Cappuano's desk. She placed the photo on the desktop and then opened a drawer to find a piece of paper. The only paper in the drawer had the Office of the President of the United States of America embossed in gold at the top along with the presidential seal.

Hoping he wouldn't mind if she borrowed a piece, she grabbed a pen from her bag and wrote him a note.

Dear Nick, We love you so much and we're so, so proud of you. Love, Sam, Scotty, Elijah, Alden and Aubrey.

On a second sheet of paper, she wrote, *Sam loves Nick*, and drew a heart around the words. She folded it in half and tucked it into the top drawer. Then, since there was nothing else she could mess with on the pristine desktop, she got busy moving around the few other things he'd already put in the drawers, making sure he'd know she'd been there. She smiled as she imagined him discovering her handiwork. She'd messed with all his previous desks, so she had to keep the tradition alive.

It was important, she knew, to keep it real between them going forward and to take Mrs. Nelson's wise advice not to get so caught up in their new roles that they lost track of what was truly important. She also couldn't wait to tell him they had plenty of bedrooms to use as a makeshift loft in their new home.

After taking another long look around the room that would be Nick's office for the next three years, Sam went to rejoin her sisters in the reception area. To Vernon, she said, "Would it be possible to make a stop on the way home?"

"Of course, ma'am. Just let us know where you'd like to go."

"Let me check to see if she's home." Sam sent a text to Shelby. *Could I stop by for a minute to talk to you about something?*

Oh lord, I'm a mess and so is my house.

Stop it. We both know your definition of mess and mine are two very different things.

Haha. We're here. Come on by.

Will be there in a few.

Sam gave Shelby's address in Adams Morgan to Vernon. "It's the home of FBI Special Agent-in-Charge Avery Hill," Sam told him.

"That's good to know, ma'am. Thank you."

Sam hugged Lilia. "Thanks for coming in to be here with me for this."

"It was a pleasure. I hope you enjoyed the tour."

"I'm dazzled and overwhelmed."

"Don't be. You've got this. *We've* got this."

"I'm a thousand times more confident that's true because you're here to make it so. If I forget to say so later, thank you for what you're going to do for me over the next three years."

"I'm honored to serve you and your family." She leaned in to whisper, "Are you going to ask Shelby to be your social secretary?"

"How'd you guess?"

"She'd be perfect."

"She would indeed. It's just a matter of whether she wants the job when she's going to be juggling two little ones before much longer."

"If anyone can find a way to make that work, she can."

"I'm glad you agree. I'll let you know what she says. Now go home to your handsome doctor and give him my love."

Lilia blushed at the mention of Harry. "I'll do that."

Sam followed Tracy and Angela into the black SUV and buckled in for the short ride to Shelby's.

"That was one of the most incredible things I've ever done," Angela said. "Thank you for asking us to come with you."

"I agree," Tracy said. "It was awesome."

"Thank you for coming. I want you guys to be by my side through all of this."

"Where else would we be?" Tracy asked.

Sam was saved from having to give an emotional response to her sisters' outpouring when her phone rang with a call from Freddie.

"Hey," she said. "What's up?"

"I was expecting to have to leave a message."

"Sorry to disappoint you. You've got me in the flesh."

"Ew. Anyway, I wanted to let you know that one of Gonzo's informants led us to Evans's known associates. We've rounded them up and have them all in custody. We have Byron Tomlinson lined up to get DNA from all of them."

"That's great work, you guys," Sam said, wishing she could've been there with them.

"Another very interesting thing is that one of them was at Ballou High School with Calvin Worthington."

Sam nearly stopped breathing when she heard that. "Is that right?"

"I recognized his name from a search I did of kids he went to school with who were in trouble before or after Calvin was killed."

"That's good thinking and very interesting indeed," Sam said. "In the morning, let's dig into that and see if he knew Calvin. Good work, Cruz. And tell Gonzo I said the same to him."

"Will do. We're waiting until they're processed, and then we're punching out for the day."

"See you in the morning."

"Later."

She closed her phone with a satisfying slap. "That's the best news I've had all day. We've got all five of the men who gang-raped a woman last night and murdered her boyfriend."

"Jeez," Angela said on a low whisper.

Sam glanced at Tracy, regretting the way she'd dropped that bomb in the middle of their good time. "I'm sorry, Trace. I wasn't thinking." Just over a year ago, Tracy's daughter Brooke had been the victim of a similar attack.

"It's okay," Tracy said with a small smile. "She's doing great now, and that's what matters."

"These things are so routine to me that I almost become numb to them," Sam said. "I'm sorry to be insensitive."

"Don't worry about it, Sam. Really. I know it's your job to deal with stuff like that all the time, and I often wonder how you can stand it."

"The numbness helps, but it also makes me a clod at times."

"Let it go. I totally understand. Really, I do."

They pulled up to Shelby and Avery's townhouse a few minutes later. "Come with me," Sam said.

CHAPTER TWENTY-TWO

The sisters went up the stairs to the door, where Avery waited to let them in.

"I come bearing friends," Sam said.

"I see that. Welcome, ladies. This is the first time we've ever had a first lady visit us," Avery said with a devilish twinkle in his eye. "We're honored."

"Shut it." She'd last been there for Shelby and Avery's surprise wedding on Shelby's forty-fourth birthday. "Sorry to drop in on you guys this way, but I need a word with my favorite personal assistant."

"She's in the family room with Noah." He pointed the way. "Make yourselves at home, and if possible, Sam, I could use a minute with you before you go."

"Sure." Sam wondered if he had new information about Nick's mother. She'd asked him if the FBI could take a below-the-radar look at the woman who'd brought nothing but hell and heartache to Nick since the day he was born. Nicoletta had been worse than ever since Nick became vice president, using his standing to boost her own like the grifter she was. Sam shuddered to think about the damage her mother-in-law could do now that Nick was president.

She followed her sisters into Shelby's family room. "Don't get up," she said when Shelby made a move to stand.

"I want to hug my friend the first lady."

"Your friend will come to you." Sam dropped to her knees and bent to hug Shelby and kiss Noah. As usual, Shelby was dressed from head to toe in pink, including sweats and a plaid flannel shirt that was tight against her blossoming pregnancy belly.

"Sorry about the mess."

"I don't see any mess. I see a little boy having fun with his mommy and his toys."

"He loves his toys. How are my other favorite kids today? Still living off the sugar high?"

"They're taking it easy, but enjoying playing with all their new stuff. Thank you again for the most magnificent party ever."

"It was fun, until one of the jackass parents posted a picture. Next time, we're banning their phones and hiring a photographer."

"We can rely on the White House photographer next year."

"I told Avery I want him to find and arrest whoever posted that picture."

"I want that too, but it might not be the best thing for the kids at school."

"Makes me so bloody mad that people would betray your privacy that way."

"It just proves that as popular as Nick is, he still has his detractors."

"It's disgusting, especially after you welcomed them into your home. We'll figure out who it was and make sure they're never invited again."

"I'm a little turned on by this vindictive side of my Tinker Bell," Sam said with a teasing grin.

"She's fierce when anyone messes with her loved ones," Avery said.

"That's right. Don't mess with my people."

"We're honored to be among your loved ones, and we're hoping you'll still love us when you hear what I've come to ask you."

Shelby cast a wary glance at her and then expanded it to include Avery, Tracy and Angela. "I'm almost afraid to ask…"

"I, well, I guess it's *we* need a social secretary at the White House, and we want you." Sam hadn't gotten a chance to ask Nick first, but she had no doubt he'd fully support her choice of Shelby for the pivotal role. They needed someone who understood protocol and official Washington, and Shelby was a true insider.

She stared at Sam with what appeared to be shock.

"Hello? Earth to Shelby?"

"Did she really just ask me that?" Shelby said to Tracy and Angela.

"She did," Ang said, "and we all agree you'd be the best at it."

"Uh, I have no idea what to say."

"*Please*, Shelby? You know how much I need you for this and to keep me straight as first lady. As social secretary, you'd be an official adviser to the president. You've been preparing for this role all your life."

To Sam's great dismay, Shelby began to cry. She looked to Avery for insight.

"Don't fret," he said in his sweet South Carolinian accent. "She cries over everything these days. Last night, it was an ice-cream commercial, and don't even get me started on what happens when those ASPCA commercials come on with the sad, shivering dogs. She's given them half our net worth since she got pregnant."

That made Sam feel a little better, but she wouldn't be happy until Shelby stopped crying.

"I'm sorry." Shelby wiped away tears. "You took me by surprise. For a minute there, I thought you were asking me to be the social secretary at the White House."

Sam nudged her shoulder. "You heard me right."

"Oh, Sam. How could I ever take on something like that with two little ones underfoot?"

"I've given that some thought since the idea first occurred to me, and what if we were able to make it so you worked mostly from home, coming in only when needed?"

Shelby rolled her lip between her teeth as she gave that some thought. "That might work, but what about your kids? I'm hopelessly devoted to them, and I couldn't imagine not seeing them every day."

"They're equally devoted to you. We can finagle the details so it works for all of us. We have a million rooms in the residence. Why couldn't one of them be used as a nursery for your kids for when you're working? The bottom line is we need you, Shelby. We'll take you any way we can get you. I'd love for you to be the social secretary because I truly feel you've been preparing for that role all your life. But if it's not going to work for you, we'll keep things the way they are now and go forward. Take some time to think about it. Talk it over with Avery, and let me know what you decide. No pressure and no tears."

Shelby laughed even as new tears spilled down her face. "You've honored me beyond all comprehension by even asking me."

"You're fully aware that I can't do this without you, I hope," Sam said.

"The thought did occur to me."

Everyone laughed, and Sam felt better about upsetting her dear friend.

"We won't take any more of your precious time off. It was important to me that I ask you in person."

With Sam's help, Shelby managed to stand and hug her. "Thank you for thinking of me for this. The people who've done the job before me are some of my biggest heroes and heroines. Letitia Baldridge," she said with a shiver. "The master class."

Sam had no idea who that was.

"Tish Baldridge was Jackie Kennedy's social secretary. She more or less invented the modern role."

"See? You already know more about it than I do."

"Noah knows more about it than you do," Tracy said, cracking up the others.

"That's absolutely true," Sam said. "These things are in his DNA."

"Our people didn't get that DNA," Tracy said bluntly.

Sam laughed. "Which is why I need my Tinker Bell."

"I'm going to think long and hard about this," Shelby said, "and if we can find a way to make it work, I'm all yours."

Sam hugged her. "No matter what you decide, we love you. You and yours will always be family to us."

Shelby sniffled. "Same to you."

"I need a minute with Avery, and then we can head home," Sam said to her sisters.

"We're with you, sis," Angela said. "Take your time."

Avery led Sam into his study, which had floor-to-ceiling bookshelves and dark wood furniture. A fire simmering in the fireplace gave the room a cozy vibe. "What a great room this is."

"Thanks."

"Have you read all those books?"

"Most of them."

"Of course you have." Sam took a seat on the leather sofa while he took a chair across from her. "What's going on?"

"We're continuing the investigation into the MPD, and we've picked up a rumbling that I wanted to run by you."

"What's that?" she asked, her stomach feeling weightless, the way it did when things went sideways.

"Does the name Hector Reese ring a bell?"

She licked lips suddenly gone dry. "What about him?"

"Word on the street is that you tuned him up pretty good when he was in custody. Is that true?"

Sam forced herself not to blink or give away how rattled she was to have this blast from the past land in her lap. "It is."

"Can you give me some context?"

Her brain wanted to shut down and run away from memories she'd much sooner forget. "Hector's brother, Clarence, murdered his wife and children. It was one of the worst scenes any of us has ever worked. It was the same day I took the lieutenant's oath and Nick became a senator. New Year's Eve, almost two years ago. Clarence was in the wind for days. He came back to the house at one point and shot Freddie."

When she suddenly began to feel overly warm, she took off the coat she'd left on for what she'd thought would be a quick visit.

"While we were working the scene, we found newspaper clippings about my father's shooting that made it even more urgent that we find Clarence. He came back to the house a second time, this time with his brother, who we were able to arrest even as Clarence got away again." This was where the story got dicey for her. "I'll confess to desperately wanting to find the man who'd shot Freddie and to know who was collecting those clips. It'd been two years since my dad was shot, and we hadn't had so much as a thread to pull."

She swallowed hard and forced herself to finish the story. "I asked to have him brought to an interrogation room, and I went at him hard, trying to get him to tell me what he knew about where his brother might be. I crossed several lines during that interrogation."

"I was told you beat the hell out of him while he was cuffed. Is that true?"

Sam had regretted her actions that day ever since. "It's true. I'm not proud of it, but I don't deny it happened."

"Who else knows about it?"

"Do I need legal representation, Agent Hill?" Over the years of their tumultuous professional and personal relationship, Sam had begun to consider him a friend at some point. In this moment, she wasn't sure if he was a friend or adversary.

"Not at this time. This is between you and me for now."

"For now. What does that mean?"

"I'm collecting information that may or may not be relevant to our investigation."

"I made a mistake, but I was running on emotion after my partner was shot and possibly finding a lead in my dad's case."

"Do you have a sense of why Hector Reese didn't file a complaint?"

"Perhaps it was because his brother later forced his way into my car, kidnapped me and held me hostage, demanding we return the ten thousand dollars in cash that we'd recovered from the house. As you may recall, Clarence took his life when he was standing right next to me, which was actually devastating for me because I'd talked him into letting me help him before the SWAT team burst in."

"This helps to give me some perspective."

"What'll you do with this info?"

"I honestly don't know yet."

"Will you give me a heads-up if you're coming for me?"

"If I can."

That was, Sam knew, the best he could do. "Was that all you wanted to talk about?"

"I wanted to also tell you that we're continuing to dig into your mother-in-law, and we're finding some interesting things. I'm not yet ready to talk about it, but as you know, where there's smoke, there's often fire."

"Why am I not surprised?"

"She's a piece of work."

"You have no idea." She put her coat back on. "I need to get going."

"Before you do, thank you for asking Shelby to be your social secretary. I know it means the world to her that you asked."

"There was no one else in the world I would've asked. And I know it's a big ask at this moment in your lives."

"We'll find a way to make it happen if it's what she wants."

He walked her out to rejoin her sisters. They said goodbye to Shelby and Noah, and as they headed home in the Secret Service SUV, Sam couldn't help but wonder if a mistake she'd made two years ago was going to come back to haunt her.

~

ON MONDAY MORNING, NICK ARRIVED AT THE OVAL OFFICE to discover that his lovely wife had been there. He grinned as he read her note and viewed the beautiful photo of the family they'd created together. Knowing his wife, she'd been up to other mischief, so he wasn't surprised to find that the items he'd placed in the drawers had been "reorganized." He found the second note she'd left and sighed with pleasure at knowing he was loved by the most extraordinary woman.

He was asking a lot of her. He knew that. And yet, she'd stepped up to the challenge with admirable fortitude. Last night, he'd found her in bed, reading one of the books Mrs. Nelson had given her.

"Did you know," she'd asked, reading from *Inside the White House: Stories From the World's Most Famous Residence*, "that the president is all at once the ceremonial head of government, leader of a political party, administrator of the nation's laws and domestic affairs, director of foreign policy and commander in chief of the armed forces?"

"Is that right?" he'd asked, amused by her as always. "I didn't realize that."

"That's a big-ass job, Nicholas."

"Yes, Samantha, so I've heard."

"You know what's seriously hot?"

"What's that?"

"You all the time, but even more so as the ceremonial head of government, leader of a political party, administrator of the nation's laws and domestic affairs, director of foreign policy and commander in chief of the armed forces." She'd shivered dramatically. "Way sexier than seersucker."

Nick laughed to himself as he recalled finding her reading *Congress for Dummies* way back when he was first in the Senate and she'd wanted to better understand his job. She'd been particularly intrigued by the Senate tradition of Seersucker Thursday. How far they'd come from those early days in the Senate when he'd been under the impression that he'd reached the pinnacle of his career.

Terry knocked before he entered the Oval Office. "Mr. President, we're ready for you in the Situation Room."

Nick walked with Terry to the most secure room in the White House, where the national security team waited to brief him on the incident in Iran with Ruskin.

"Mr. President," Teresa said, "per the reports you were provided with at your morning briefing, we've met with Secretary Ruskin and the security team that accompanied him. We've received two very different stories. According to Secretary Ruskin, he was told the talks with President Rajavi would continue at the resort. Once there, he claims he was denied outside communication. He believes he was tricked into the photos that were taken."

"He seemed awfully happy for a man who'd been kidnapped, tricked and misled," Nick said.

"That was our impression as well, sir. The security team told an entirely different story. The lead agent indicated that Ruskin was offered a weekend of debauchery, and he willingly accepted the invitation."

"Why were we unable to reach the security detail during the hours in question?" Nick asked.

"They were put up in rooms at the resort that they believe were in some sort of blackout zone that made it impossible to use any of their communication devices."

Nick took in the information and looked for the truth in the various versions. "Who do you believe?"

"The agents," Teresa said without hesitation. "It seems Ruskin suffered a breach of judgment, perhaps in part because of the changing of the guard here and his belief that he wouldn't be held accountable. One of the agents overheard him saying you don't 'have the stones' to discipline him."

"Well, that was a significant error on his part." Nick glanced at Terry. "Please ask the secretary to come in."

"Yes, sir."

"Give him thirty minutes to get here."

"Yes, sir."

They left the Situation Room to return to the Oval Office, where Nick met privately with Terry.

"What's your plan, sir?"

"I'll request his resignation in exchange for not asking the Justice Department to investigate and potentially charge him."

"That was going to be my recommendation."

Having to fire the secretary of State on his fourth day in office wasn't Nick's idea of a good time, but it had to be done.

"I've also heard officially from the secretaries of the Treasury, Homeland Security and Education that they're not planning to stay on. Each will be submitting their resignations in the coming days."

"We'll need to name acting secretaries until permanent appointees can be confirmed."

"I'll work on that."

"Trevor and the communications team would like a bit of time this afternoon to prepare you and Mrs. Cappuano for the interview tonight."

"I can't guarantee she'll be available for that."

"It's highly recommended, sir. That interview will set the tone for your entire administration."

"I'll see what I can do to get her here early, but that's the best I can do." After Terry left the office, Nick called Sam's secure phone.

"Mr. President. What can I do for you?"

Her voice was enough to send a shiver of desire down his spine. Any time away from her was time he wished he was spending with her. It had been that way from the day they reconnected nearly two years ago. Even before that, he'd longed for her after having spent one night with her six years before they found each other again.

"Nick?"

"I'm here. How's your day going?"

"Not bad so far. I'm about to sit down with my squad. I've got about two minutes."

"I wondered if you could be here around five to prep for the interview tonight."

"Oh, um..."

"Did you forget about the interview?"

"Of course not."

"Are you lying to me?"

"Would I do that?"

He laughed at the way she said that. "Never."

"I'll be there."

"Thank you. For this, for the photo of our beautiful family, for rearranging my desk and a million other things you don't want to do that I'm going to ask of you over the next few years."

"There's nothing you can ask of me that'll be too much."

Touched by her unwavering support, he said, "Yes, there is, and I'm sure it won't be long before I cross the line. You just have to tell me when that happens."

"You'll be the first to know. There's one thing you need to remember above all else."

"What's that?"

"I love you more than anything, and there's nowhere I'd rather be than wherever you are, even if you're in the freaking Oval Office."

"Thank you, babe. I love you too. More than you'll ever know."

"Can't wait to see you at five."

"See you then. In the meantime, be safe out there."

"I always am."

CHAPTER TWENTY-THREE

Nick ended the call with a big smile on his face. Only she could've made him forget, even for a few minutes, about the crisis looming with the secretary of State. That crisis was front and center twenty minutes later when Ruskin came in, disheveled and clearly irritated at being summoned. He was in his mid-sixties, with gray hair that could use a combing. He wore jeans and a navy V-neck sweater over a dress shirt. Clearly, he hadn't expected to be summoned to the White House, which was surprising.

"Pardon my appearance, Mr. President, but I wasn't prepared to be ordered to the White House and given a time limit after having only returned home early this morning. This is all highly irregular."

Nick stood and went around the Resolute desk to stand face-to-face with the secretary. "Do you want to know what I find highly irregular?"

"What's that, sir?"

"This nation's top diplomat allowing himself to be put in a highly compromising position while representing the United States in vitally important meetings with one of our most challenging adversaries. You've embarrassed yourself and this country."

"See here," Ruskin huffed indignantly as he prepared to go on a tirade.

"Stop right there. I've been fully briefed, and I'm well aware of what actually happened. I have no choice but to ask for your resignation."

"And if I refuse?"

"I'll inform the American people what you were really doing while two dozen of their fellow citizens were being held against their will by the Iranians. Do you have any idea what you put them and their families through? I know, because I was talking to their families while we tried to ascertain what was happening. At the same time, I was meeting with the Joint Chiefs about our military options." Nick produced the printouts of the photos he'd requested for this meeting. "Meanwhile, this is what you were doing." He held up the photo of Ruskin in the middle of a group of topless women, a drink in hand and a big smile on his face.

Ruskin stared at the photo, seeming momentarily speechless.

"Is it possible you weren't expecting them to blackmail you in some way? Because a freaking Cub Scout could've seen that coming."

"I..."

"I'll expect your resignation by five p.m."

"What'll become of those photos?"

"I don't know. I'm not the one who took them."

Ruskin clearly didn't like hearing that Nick had no plans to try to protect him from scandal. Why should he after Ruskin nearly caused a war with his stupidity? "How will my resignation be explained to the media?"

"That a number of President Nelson's cabinet secretaries, including the secretary of State, have chosen not to retain their positions in the new administration."

Ruskin's sneer turned his face ugly. "I'm sure you're feeling all hopped up on the power of your new office, Mr. President, but I'm afraid you're rather naïve about the way things work in this town."

"I'd rather be naïve than cynical, and after fifteen years of working in government, I'm confident that I know how things work. You've wasted enough of my time and the resources of the federal government. This meeting is over. I'll look forward to receiving your resignation letter."

Nick held Ruskin's glare for a long moment before the

secretary spun around and stormed out of the office. "Well, that went well."

Terry came in a few minutes later. "How'd it go?"

"Apparently, I'm naïve and don't understand how things work in this town."

"I hope you told him you're fully aware of how things work, and by now he ought to be too."

"I told him he has until five to submit his resignation. I told him we'll include him in the group of secretaries who've tendered their resignations."

"I'm already working on replacements for all of them. We have Senator Sanford coming in." Terry checked his watch. "In ten minutes. After that, we're meeting with the economic and budget team and later with the congressional leadership."

"This place is a nonstop good time."

"You already knew that, sir."

"Give me a minute to review the vetting on Sanford before she gets here."

"Yes, sir. I'll be back with her when she arrives."

He sat behind the Resolute desk to go through the files he'd been given about Sanford and Henderson. The other potential candidates on their list had indicated they weren't interested in the position for a variety of reasons, such as family concerns and hesitation about round-the-clock security, which had narrowed their field to two.

Sanford's illustrious career began as a prosecutor in Chicago, followed by two terms as attorney general of the State of Illinois before she ran for the Senate ten years ago. She was an influential member of the Armed Services and Foreign Relations committees, and her knowledge in both areas would be useful to him.

His party held a slim majority in the Senate, which made him somewhat reluctant to tap that body to fill the vice president opening and risk losing a seat. Which was why he was leaning more toward Gretchen Henderson, who didn't currently hold office. She would be the far less complicated choice, not to mention she was a firebrand, popular within the party and had a bright future. The one drawback, other than the messy personal life Derek had mentioned, was that she was only five years older than him, which would make her the second-youngest vice president—after him. However, he planned to meet with both women before he decided anything for certain.

Terry returned a few minutes later, escorting Senator Sanford into the Oval Office.

Nick stood, buttoned his suit coat and went around the desk to greet her with a handshake. She was tall, with short brown hair and green eyes that were complemented by the dark green jacket she wore over black pants. "Welcome, Senator."

"Thank you for having me, Mr. President."

As she stepped forward to shake his hand, he caught a whiff of her perfume and had to stop himself from recoiling from Chanel No. 5, the scent his mother wore.

"Ah, please." He desperately tried to recover from the visceral reaction he always had to that scent. "Have a seat."

"Thank you, sir."

One of the White House butlers came in with a tea service. He poured coffee for Nick and tea for the senator.

The White House photographer was also in the room, subtly capturing the meeting for history. Nick wanted to tell them all never mind. Though it was completely unfair to her, the scent was so triggering to him that he wasn't sure he could bear to be around it every day. But since he couldn't discuss that with her, he went through the motions of polite small talk as they enjoyed their beverages and the pastries the butler had brought.

"I was flattered to hear you wished to meet with me so soon, Mr. President," Sanford said. "You must have so much on your plate."

"I do, and at the top of my to-do list is naming a vice president."

"Oh, I see," Sanford said, smiling. "Does this mean I'm on your short list?"

"You are. If you wish to be, that is."

"Again, you flatter me."

"Having recently served in the position myself, it's important to me that the candidates fully understand the pros and cons of the job." He gave her a high-level view of his perspective on being VP, having been the most recent one to hold the position, and answered a number of questions she had about how he would want to work with his vice president.

"As a senator, you're able to move about somewhat freely, which would change as vice president. I'm not going to sugarcoat it, Senator. Being surrounded by Secret Service takes some getting used to."

"I'm sure it does. Let me make this easy for you, sir. I'd be delighted to be chosen and would fully commit to supporting you and your agenda to the best of my ability."

"That's nice to hear. Thank you. And your family would be willing to accept the presence of the Secret Service?"

"I believe they would be in order for me to accept this incredible opportunity."

They made small talk for a few more minutes before Nick stood, signaling the meeting was over. He shook hands with the senator, let her know they'd be in touch to discuss further vetting and waited for Terry to escort her from the room.

Then he went straight to the restroom located off the Oval Office to wash his hands and rid himself of the horrible scent. Here he was, president of the United States, and that particular scent still took him right back to being a young child who refused to bathe for days after a rare visit from his mother left her scent on him. He was disgusted with himself for being so wrecked and with his mother for the emotional damage she'd done to him with her callous disregard.

When he returned to the Oval Office, Terry was waiting for him. "Did something happen, sir?"

Because he couldn't very well confess to taking an immediate dislike to the senator because she smelled like his mother, Nick said, "I didn't really feel a connection to her."

Terry eyed him with curiosity. He knew Nick well enough to know he rarely met anyone he couldn't connect with in some way or another.

"What's next?" Nick asked.

"The economic and budget team is waiting in the Cabinet Room when you're ready."

What did it say about him that an economic and budget

meeting sounded better than staying in the room where the horrid scent remained?

~

SAM MADE IT TO THE WHITE HOUSE AT FIVE AFTER FIVE, WHICH SHE considered a win. Anything less than thirty minutes late was a win in her book. She'd run home to change into the one black pantsuit she owned, as well as a hot-pink silk blouse. Running short on time, she'd done what she could with her hair and the makeup Tracy had left for her to cover the colorful bruise on her face, all the while ignoring the pervasive pain coming from her hands. Even though she was probably presentable for TV, she still felt thrown together and scattered. Hopefully, there'd be someone at the White House to help pull her together before the interview.

Lilia was waiting for her when she came in through the East Wing entrance, startled to realize that at some point over the last year, being in this hallowed place had become somewhat routine to her. That was probably a good thing since it was about to also be home.

"Welcome, ma'am." Lilia wore a sharp black suit with white trim, a crisp white blouse and her famous pearls. Every one of her dark hairs was smoothed into the adorable bob that framed her pretty face.

"How do you always look so put together? What's the secret to that?"

"Ah, well... I don't know."

"Yes, you do, and I need to know. I love clothes and shoes and accessories, but I suck at pulling off the effortless class that you do so well."

"You look lovely."

"I look okay. *You* look lovely. Maybe you could do the interview with Nick?"

Lilia laughed. "I think we'd have a little trouble getting away with that. But you'll be glad to know that as first lady, you have access to your own hair-and-makeup team."

"No way." As they talked, they walked toward the West Wing through red-carpeted hallways full of artwork that told the

American story, from the Revolutionary War to Reconstruction to the moon landing.

"Way. I took the liberty of scheduling them ahead of the interview in case you were interested in their assistance."

"Hell yes, I'm interested."

Laughing, Lilia said, "I had a feeling you might be. The president is waiting for you in the Oval Office. When you're ready, the communications team will help prep you for the interview, which is set to film in the East Room at six thirty."

Sam rubbed her abdomen. "My stomach hurts."

"Can I get you something for that?"

"Only if you can get me out of this national interview about my husband becoming president and me becoming first lady."

"I wish I could, but alas, my superpowers don't extend to rewriting history."

"Why did I have a feeling you were going to say that?"

In the reception area outside the Oval, they were waved in by a woman Sam recognized from Nick's tenure as vice president.

"Nice to see you, Mrs. Cappuano," she said.

"You as well," Sam said.

"Jennifer," Lilia said under her breath.

"I love you."

As they stepped into the Oval Office, Sam stopped short at the sight of her handsome husband sitting behind the Resolute desk. Her husband, her Nick, was the *president of the United States*. How long would it take until this was no longer surreal? A while longer, apparently.

"Are you all right?" Lilia asked.

"Yes, but this is just... *wow*."

"I can only imagine."

Nick looked up, saw her there and smiled as he got up to greet her, and just that simply, he was back to being her husband again and not the leader of the free world.

"I'll give you two a minute before your meeting with the communications team," Lilia said.

"Can you sit in on the meeting?" Sam asked her.

"Of course. I'll be back in a few." Lilia closed the door behind her as she left the Oval.

"You look gorgeous, babe." Nick leaned in to kiss her. "I thought Brooke wouldn't let you wear pink?"

Her niece had a thing about any woman over the age of four wearing pink, something Brooke frequently debated with Shelby, the queen of all things pink.

"Shelby gave it to me last Christmas, and I thought it worked for the occasion, so I made a rare exception. I fully expect to hear from Brooke about my lapse."

"For what it's worth, I love that color on you."

She slid an arm around him. "It's worth a lot."

They sat together on one of the sofas in the center of the room. "I heard we have to redecorate this room," Sam said.

"I met with the director of Oval Office Operations earlier today and gave her some guidance."

"I can't believe there's an actual *director* for Oval Office Operations?"

"I know."

"What did you decide to do?"

"In an effort to send the message of bipartisan cooperation, I'm using the carpet from Ronald Reagan's office and the curtains from George H.W. Bush's office, along with photos of FDR, JFK, Lincoln and John McCain. I requested sculpture busts of Harriet Tubman, Martin Luther King Jr. and Susan B. Anthony."

"I love that lineup and that you included a suffragist."

"Just over one hundred years ago, women finally earned the right to vote, and this month, we may see the first female vice president."

"Oh, Nick, really? That'd be amazing."

"That's the plan. We have two left on the short list, though one..." He shook his head as he frowned. "I don't think she'll work out."

"Why?" she asked, picking up on a bigger story just from the way his body language changed so profoundly.

"You'll think it's ridiculous. Hell, I think it is."

"Tell me anyway."

"She wears Chanel No. 5."

Sam winced, immediately understanding his point. "That's not ridiculous. That's self-preservation. If you really liked her, I'm sure there's something that can be done, like telling her you're allergic to perfume or something."

"That's true. I suppose I could do that if she's the top contender at the end of the process. I really did like her, and it wouldn't be fair to disqualify her because of something that's not her fault."

"If there's anything I can do to make this easier on you, I'm your girl."

With his arm around her, he leaned his forehead against hers. "My very best girl."

They were still there, lost in a stolen moment to themselves, when a knock on the door had them moving apart.

"Come in," Nick called. "Someone must've given them a heads-up that you were in here, and they know better than to barge in when you're here."

Sam laughed at that. "Probably so."

Trevor came in with several other people, including Christina Billings, or Christina Gonzales now.

"Did I tell you Christina agreed to be my press secretary?" Nick asked.

"You didn't. Congratulations, Christina."

"Thank you. I think. I'm still trying to wrap my head around the last few days, as I'm sure you are as well."

"The head spins," Sam said as the others took seats on the sofas and the chairs. "What'll you do with Alex?"

"He's back with Angela as of tomorrow," Christina said of her and Gonzo's son. "Thank goodness she was able to take him."

"I'm sure she's thrilled," Sam said. "She's missed him."

"All right, everyone," Trevor said, his curly hair out of control as usual. After he introduced the communications team to Sam, he said, "Let's get to work preparing for the interview. The number one question we've received from the media since you were sworn in is about you being the youngest president in history."

"It's incredible to me that with all the problems this country has, that's their top question," Nick said.

"We agree, but you need to be prepared to answer questions about your qualifications and experience."

"Is it okay to remind them that I was chosen by the president with the full understanding that if I was called to step in for him, I'd be the youngest president in history?"

Trevor looked to the others for consensus.

"I don't see a problem with that," Christina said. "It's the truth. Nelson put his faith in you when he asked you to replace Gooding. The people who twice elected Nelson should have some faith in him, that he knew what he was doing."

"I'm not afraid to remind people of that if need be," Nick said, even though he was fully aware that the primary reason Nelson had chosen him was to benefit from the popularity Nick had enjoyed as a senator.

"The other most pressing question we're receiving," Trevor said with a nervous glance toward Sam, "is about Mrs. Cappuano continuing her role as a lieutenant with the Metro PD."

"Are they for or against it?" Sam asked.

"Pretty evenly split," Trevor replied. "Women are, in general, far more supportive than men."

"Why doesn't that surprise me?" Sam asked, feeling irked. "They think I ought to be barefoot and pregnant in the kitchen. Is there anyone left out there that doesn't know that the pregnant part is a problem for me?"

"We don't care what other people think," Nick said. "What matters is what *we* think, and *we* think you're an amazing detective doing the job you were born to do."

How did he do that? How did he take her from steaming mad to swooning with a couple of perfect words? She relaxed against him, and he squeezed her shoulder, fully aware of his superpowers where she was concerned.

"What else should we be prepared for, Trevor?" Nick asked.

"Lots of questions about Ruskin and what happened in Iran."

"I'll take care of that." To Terry, Nick said, "Did we receive the secretary's letter?"

"We did."

"Excellent. I'll announce his resignation during the interview. That'll give them a sound bite to promote it."

The staff filed out a few minutes later, and Lilia took Sam to the in-house salon to have her hair and makeup done for the interview.

"I could seriously get used to this," Sam said to Davida, the hairstylist.

"We're here for you, ma'am, so take full advantage of us."

Another woman named Kendra did Sam's nails, while Davida gave her a blow-dry that left her hair looking sleek and shiny.

"Why does it never look like that when I do it?"

"Everyone says that," Davida said, laughing.

The makeup artist, Ginger, was equally talented, and by the time they were finished with her, Sam felt as ready for prime time as she'd ever be.

CHAPTER TWENTY-FOUR

Peter Wagner, a TV personality known for his interviews of famous and infamous people, had scored the coveted interview with the new first couple. Nick told Sam they'd chosen Wagner because they knew he'd be thorough and ask the questions most people had about their new first couple, but he wouldn't come at them with his claws out.

Nick met Sam in the Blue Room, which had been transformed into a TV studio with lights, cameras and wires running across the carpeting.

"Whoa," Nick said. "You look gorgeous. Your hair is so..."

"Brushed?"

He laughed. "I was going to say shiny and smooth."

"Thanks to our new in-house salon. Don't get used to it. When we're back to normal, my hair will be too."

"You know I think you're gorgeous all the time." He gave her an ass grab that no one else could see, to make his point.

They were shown to side-by-side plush blue chairs.

Nick started to sit next to her but stopped short. "These chairs won't do. Can we get something like a love seat?"

"Yes, sir, Mr. President," one of the White House staffers said.

"I'd like to sit next to my wife, not separate from her."

Sam smiled at him. Could he be any more adorable?

"I couldn't hold your hand in those chairs."

She reached out a hand to him, and he took it, giving it a careful squeeze in light of her injuries. "You're giving away all our secrets, love."

"They'll find out soon enough."

Standing in the middle of the beautiful, historic room, surrounded by strangers, there was only him, only them.

A love seat was brought in from another room and positioned where the TV producer wanted it. Then they were wired with microphones.

Nick scowled at the young man who attached the microphone to Sam's lapel.

"Stop that," she whispered. "He's just doing his job."

"He needs to keep his hands off my wife."

Sam rolled her eyes at him.

Wagner came in, looking ridiculous in his pancake makeup.

Apparently, Nick didn't need that. He was perfect just the way he was. His olive-toned skin was made for prime time.

Wagner shook hands with both of them. "Mr. President, Mrs. Cappuano, thank you so much for doing this. I'm honored to be your first interview in your new roles."

Sam had been prepared to automatically dislike him, but he didn't seem totally awful. She set a low bar for the media, and most of them lived up to her expectations, with few exceptions, such as her friend Darren. Not that she'd ever let him know she considered him a friend.

When the cameras were rolling, Wagner recited a prepared opening. "I'm honored tonight to have landed the most-sought-after interview in the world this week, with America's new first couple, President Nick Cappuano and First Lady Samantha Cappuano. We're so honored to have you here with us tonight."

"Thank you for having us," Nick said, gracious as always.

"The first thing I want to talk about is the question that's on everyone's mind. What was it like for you to get that call from the White House on Thanksgiving night?"

"Needless to say, it was shocking on a number of levels. Separate of what it meant for us and our family, we were saddened by the president's death. I'd been with him the day before, and he was fine. President Nelson was still a relatively young man, and his premature death is a tragedy for his family and our country."

"Indeed, it is. Has there been any more information about what might've happened to him?"

"We learned today that President Nelson died of a pulmonary embolism. Mrs. Nelson will release further details when she feels ready."

"It's no secret that you've had your challenges with President Nelson and his son Christopher, who's in prison awaiting trial after targeting you both and murdering Mrs. Cappuano's ex-husband, Peter Gibson. How does your history with the Nelson family color your impressions of the events of the last few days?"

Jeez, Sam thought. *What're we supposed to say to that?*

"It doesn't really. President and Mrs. Nelson assured us that they had no knowledge of what Christopher did, and we believed them. As parents ourselves, we felt their anguish over what happened and weren't interested in doing anything that would make that worse for them."

Leave it to Nick to know just how to handle a question like that.

"Mrs. Cappuano, you recently led the investigation into the murder of President Nelson's mistress, Tara Weber. Was that investigation made more difficult by the stakes involved for your husband?"

Yes, she wanted to say, but didn't. "Every homicide investigation is complicated for different reasons. There was an intense level of interest in that one due to the president's previous involvement with the victim, and of course there was a back-burner concern for how it might impact Nick and our family if the president had chosen to resign or had been forced to do so. At the time, though, one hundred percent of my focus was on getting justice for the victim, her newborn son and the rest of her family."

"During that investigation, it was learned that Mrs. Nelson had secretly undergone treatment for ovarian cancer at the same time the president was engaging in an affair with a campaign staffer. Two questions—one, did you know at the time that she was ill, and how did you feel when you heard about the timing of the affair?"

Yeah, that one is all Nick's.

"We did know that Mrs. Nelson had been ill, and like many others, we felt compassion for her at that difficult time. And like most Americans, we have the utmost respect and admiration for Gloria Nelson. She's been nothing but welcoming and gracious to us while seeing her family through the shocking loss of her husband and their father and grandfather."

"Mr. President, just over a week ago, you released a statement indicating you didn't plan to run in the next election. I'm sure you can understand the concerns of the American people about the possibility that they now have a reluctant president. How would you address those concerns?"

"As I said in my remarks Friday night, when I accepted President Nelson's invitation to become his new vice president, I did so with the full understanding and appreciation for the fact that I might have to step up should the need arise. After receiving the news about President Nelson's death, I took the oath of office with the intention of giving the job and the American people my very best effort for the remainder of President Nelson's term. I never said I didn't want to be president. I said I didn't wish to spend the better part of eighteen months away from my young family campaigning for the job."

"Will you run for reelection in the next cycle?"

"While everything in our lives has changed in the last few days, the one thing that hasn't changed is we still have a young family. The thought of months away from my wife and children isn't at all appealing to me. But I'm not thinking about campaigns or elections at the moment. I'm entirely focused on completing the transition to a new administration, with an eye on critical national security and defense matters, as well as continuing the work President Nelson began in the areas of infrastructure, immigration, economic policy and finance, while helping my family to make a smooth transition to our new home."

"Mrs. Cappuano, you're a lieutenant with the Metropolitan Police Department in Washington, DC, and the American people are interested in your intentions as first lady regarding your current position."

"My intention is to keep my current position and continue my career during my tenure as first lady."

"I can't help but wonder how that's possible with the public nature of your position."

"I'll go to work the same way I did as second lady, and I'll do the job the taxpayers in the District pay me to do."

"From a security perspective—"

"I'll be accompanied by a Secret Service detail while on the job."

"Which was not the case when you were second lady, correct?"

"That's correct." Sam refused to give him any more than she absolutely had to.

"Mr. President, how do you feel about your wife being the first first lady to work outside the White House?"

"I'm extremely proud of the work Sam does to get justice for murder victims and their families, and I love that she'll make history this way."

"Are you concerned about your wife's safety on the job, Mr. President?"

Sam held back a groan. *For fuck's sake.*

"I'm always concerned about her when she's working, but she's a highly trained police officer surrounded by other highly trained officers. It would never occur to me to ask her to give up the work that means so much to her and many others."

Sam squeezed his hand and smiled. "It's easy to see why I love him so much."

Nick's face flushed with a hint of color that only she would notice.

She loved to fluster him because it so rarely happened, except with her.

"Mr. President, you're the youngest president in American history. Do you feel that comes with a certain level of pressure to prove yourself?"

"Not particularly. I'll be thirty-eight in a few weeks, so I'm not exactly a child. I've spent my entire adult life—more than fifteen years—working in the highest levels of the legislative and executive branches. I'd contend that my time working for Congress and my understanding of the intricacies of getting things done in this town will be extremely beneficial to my administration and what we're hoping to accomplish for the American people."

"You were criticized for leaving the White House in the midst of the standoff with Iran to attend your children's birthday party. What do you say to that?"

"I was exactly where I needed to be that day. I'd been at the White House for fourteen hours on Friday and since early in the morning on Saturday and was waiting for the next briefing on the situation in Iran, which wasn't due until five o'clock. While I waited, I went home to see the children at their party. At no time was I out of touch with my national security team or the rest of the group that was working feverishly to bring the matter in Iran to a successful conclusion."

"I assume you've met with Secretary Ruskin since his return from Iran?"

"I have, and he's resigned his post as of five o'clock today."

Wagner clearly wasn't expecting that scoop.

"He's one of several of President Nelson's secretaries who've chosen not to remain in their posts in my administration. We'll be vetting replacements for each of them in the next few weeks."

"Is Secretary Ruskin's resignation tied to the events in Iran?"

"You'd need to speak to him about that."

"The Iranian regime has referred to the incident as a misunderstanding. Would you call it that?"

"My team is doing an in-depth review of the events that took place from the time the secretary and his entourage landed in Tehran until the moment of their departure. When we know more, we'll report our findings to the American people and the international community. I was relieved that we were able to get the secretary and the others home safely without further escalation of tensions. Several of our international allies were critical in helping us to bring the matter to a peaceful conclusion."

Sam was so damned proud of him that she could bust from trying to contain it. The American people hadn't known how lucky they were to have him, but they'd certainly know it after this interview.

"Can you tell us who you're considering to fill the vice president opening?"

"We have a number of qualified candidates we're considering and will have more information about that in the next week or two."

"We're hearing you're considering a woman for the position. Is that true?"

"It is. I think we're long overdue to see women at the highest levels of our government. If I'm remembered for nothing else, I'd like it to be that my administration was one of the more inclusive and diverse in history."

Wagner asked several questions about Nick's domestic and international agendas and plans, as well as when he thought he might take his first foreign trip.

"We're still working on the schedule for the next few months, but as soon as we know more, we'll be sure to make our agenda and schedule public."

"During your tenure as vice president, you were an advocate for bringing awareness of public service careers to schoolchildren. Do you plan to continue that effort now that you're president?"

"Absolutely. I think it's critically important to the future of our country for children and young people to see a place for them in government. Our country relies on career civil servants to execute tens of thousands of programs and policies that have a direct impact on the daily lives of our citizens. We need smart, thoughtful people to serve in our armed forces and to work on the many challenges facing our country and the world, as well as to manage national security challenges, especially those in the increasingly complex area of cybersecurity. The next generation of diplomats and Peace Corps volunteers are in high school now, and I think it's essential for them to be aware of the many opportunities they have to serve their country."

"Does that include your hopes for your own children?"

"I hope they'll do whatever it is that calls to them, the same way Sam and I have. Right now, our thirteen-year-old son Scotty's most pressing goal is to bring a four-legged friend into our family as soon as possible."

"And what do you say to that, Mr. President?"

"We're looking forward to visiting one of the local shelters before too much longer so Scotty can pick out a friend to live with us at the White House. But don't tell him we said that."

"Your secret is safe with me. However, as a father myself, let me warn you that you'll be pressed to deliver on that the minute this interview goes live."

Sam and Nick laughed.

"We're ready for that," Nick said.

"Your family lives locally and remained in your Capitol Hill area home during your tenure as vice president due to the proximity to Mrs. Cappuano's disabled father. Do you have an idea of when you may move to the White House?"

"Sam and I will accompany President and Mrs. Nelson, as well as the Nelson family, home to Pierre on *Air Force One* on Thursday after the funeral."

It was news to Sam that she'd be making a trip to South Dakota...

"We'll move into the White House after that, but we aren't exactly sure when yet. The Secret Service is eager to get us settled here, so probably sooner rather than later."

"Mrs. Cappuano, you recently lost your father, retired Metro PD Deputy Chief Skip Holland."

Sam was immediately on guard against wherever he was going with that line of questioning. "That's right."

"What do you think he'd say about his daughter and son-in-law becoming the nation's first couple?"

"Oh, well, I think he'd be thrilled. He loved Nick very much, thought of him as a son and was delighted when he became vice president. I'm just sorry he can't be part of it. As a proud DC native, he would've loved visiting us here."

"He's part of it," Nick said, glancing at her with warmth in his eyes . "He's always with us, and we both carry his words of wisdom with us as we move through the challenges we confront on a daily basis. He's very much a touchstone to our entire family."

Damn if he didn't nearly move her to tears with those words.

"I want to thank you again for sitting down with us tonight for your first network interview since becoming president and first lady. I know I speak for so many when I wish you Godspeed and good luck. Your success is our success, and we'll be rooting for you."

"Thank you, Peter," Nick said. "We appreciate that very much."

"And we're out," the producer said.

"That was wonderful, Mr. President, Mrs. Cappuano." Wagner shook both their hands, and Sam tried not to wince from the pain that caused her. "I'm deeply honored to be your first interview."

"Thank you for having us," Nick said. The minute the TV people were out of earshot, he said to Sam, "Let's get the hell out of here. I want to see my kids."

"I'm with you, Mr. President."

CHAPTER TWENTY-FIVE

Because Sam had ridden home with Nick in The Beast the night before, Vernon and Jimmy drove her to the White House to pick up her car the next morning. She'd helped Nick get the kids up and ready for school and had breakfast with them before leaving the house and was trying not to think about how "off" the twins had been since she'd broken the news to them about the impending move. She planned to check in with their therapist to figure out how they could support them through this latest disruption.

As she headed for HQ, Sam put through a call to Gideon Lawson while navigating heavy Monday morning traffic.

When he answered, she said, "This is, um, Sam Cappuano."

"Mrs. Cappuano," Gideon said. "How lovely to hear from you."

"I can't help but wonder how long you'll be saying that."

Gideon laughed. "If I may say so, ma'am, I do love a good bit of snark. I suspect we'll be the best of friends in no time."

"Snark is my middle name. Sarcasm is my first name."

"A highly entertaining combination."

"I like you, Gideon, and others in my life will tell you how rare it is that I like anyone." In fact, she'd been liking a lot more people than usual lately, which was a rather revolting development.

"I'm pleased and delighted to have made the cut. What can I do for you today?"

"I talked it over with Nick, and I'm sorry, but I have to call him that."

"I understand," he said, chuckling.

"We'd like to accept your generous offer of staff to help with our move. We're both crazy busy—even crazier busy than usual, that is—and just have no time to devote to it. We understand, however, that the Secret Service wants to get it done as soon as possible."

"Say no more. We'll get right on it. Whom shall we contact to gain access?"

"Shelby Hill, our personal assistant." Sam gave him Shelby's phone number from memory. "I spoke with her last night about what furniture we'd like to bring. We're packing light since we'll be right across town if we need anything."

"Understood. We'll take care of everything for you. Mrs. Nelson plans to return to South Dakota for the local services on Thursday after the funeral service here in DC. We could move you in as soon as Friday, if that works for you and the president."

"Um, well, I guess that works. Is it okay to confess to my new best friend that I still can't believe this is happening?"

"I totally understand that the shock hasn't worn off yet. It might not for a while. We feel the same way here. A few days ago, we were working for a perfectly healthy President Nelson, and now he's gone. I've been here for twenty years, and this is the first time I've experienced the aftermath of a president dying in office. It's been rather jarring for everyone."

"Yes, and I'm well aware that it's not just about us."

"It's mostly about you and your husband. Our entire focus is on ensuring a seamless transition and helping to make your family comfortable in your new home."

"Thank you, Gideon. I mean that sincerely. I appreciate your help more than you'll ever know."

"I'm looking forward to working with you, ma'am. I'll be in touch if we have questions."

"I'll do my best to take your call."

"May I say..."

"Anything you want. Let's keep it real, shall we?"

"I like you too, ma'am, and I just want to say how amazing we all find it that you're intending to keep your police job while you're first lady. You have no idea how much that'll mean to so many women."

"That's so nice of you to say. I feel like half the world thinks I'm insane, but the job... The job is who I am."

"We'll do everything we can to support your efforts to be Superwoman."

Sam laughed. "If you could find me a cape and some superpowers, that'd be awesome."

"I'll dig around in the warehouse and see what I can find."

Yes, she liked this guy a lot. "There's a *warehouse*?"

"A gigantic one full of priceless treasures, in Maryland. We can take a field trip someday, if you'd like, to see if there's anything you want to use in your White House."

"That'd be awesome. I'd love to do that. Incidentally, I still have a storage unit from when I was between marriages. Finding out there's also a warehouse is a bit daunting."

"No need to be daunted by any of it. You have your own army of people here to make it easy for you."

"And I'm eternally grateful for that. I'll be in touch."

"I'll look forward to speaking to you again soon, ma'am."

Sam ended the call and realized she was smiling after talking to her new friend. After four of the most overwhelming days of her life, she took a deep breath and let it out, realizing she didn't have to do it all. She was surrounded by an incredible staff both at work and in her new home, and she would learn to delegate to those better equipped to take care of whatever challenges might arise.

She never had gotten a chance to speak to Celia about moving to the White House with them. Hopefully, she'd get to do that later.

As she took the final turn before arriving at HQ, she was astounded to see the largest-ever media presence outside the public safety building. The entire street was lined two deep with satellite trucks bearing the logos of every major network. *What the hell?* Did something happen she hadn't heard about? And then it occurred to her that they were there for her. *She* had happened.

She moaned. "For fuck's sake." Why did they still show up to stalk her at work when they knew they weren't going to get anywhere with her? Her colleagues must be incredibly annoyed by the disturbance, a thought that spiked her anxiety. Massive media presence outside HQ was the last thing she needed.

She drove around the building to the morgue entrance, hoping she could avoid having to deal with them. To her extreme dismay, a cadre of reporters was camped outside that door too. That was one of her worst nightmares come true. After parking, she glanced over at Vernon, who'd parked next to her.

He held up a finger, telling her to wait a minute.

Because she didn't ever feel like dealing with the media, especially now, she took the minute so he and Jimmy could clear the way, fuming all the while that the press was keeping her from getting to work. She fired off a text to Nick on the BlackBerry. *Holy media at HQ, Batman.*

She had no idea if she'd hear back from him, or if he'd even see the text right now.

When her phone chimed with a text, she smiled, knowing she shouldn't be surprised that even in his new job, he was still available to her.

Are Vernon and Jimmy dealing with it?

As much as they can. It's a mob scene.

I can ask about sending over more SS to clear the area if you want.

I hate to say it might be necessary. My colleagues already have enough reasons to hate my guts.

We can talk to them at the meeting today.

"Fucking hell." She'd forgotten all about that meeting. To Nick, she typed, *Remind me what time that meeting is...*

LOL, I knew you'd forget.

I didn't forget. I forgot the time.

Liar. Pants on fire.

That's not very presidential of you.

It's at two. Afterward, we can have an after-nooner in my study.

You have a study? Something to look forward to.

I can't wait. Love you. Be careful out there.

Always am. Love you too.

She'd no sooner sent the last text when Vernon knocked on her window, gesturing for her to come along.

Once inside, she stopped first at the morgue to see Lindsey McNamara.

"Good morning, Doc."

"There's the woman of the hour. How're you doing?"

"Just ducky. I've got the goddamned media stalking me even more than they used to, a detective in the hospital, a dead body on ice, a traumatized rape victim in the hospital and an unexpected move to coordinate this week. Other than that..."

Lindsey's green eyes twinkled with laughter. As usual while working, her long red hair was captured in a high ponytail. "I can't believe you're here like it's any other workday."

"It is any other workday, except this one will include a meeting at the White House about how the Secret Service will accommodate my desire to remain on the job."

"Is it okay to say as your friend and colleague that I'm so freaking proud of you for sticking to your guns and staying true to yourself?"

"It's okay to say, and thank you for that. Part of me wonders if I'm crazy to think I can pull this off."

"If anyone can, you can."

"I guess we'll see."

"How's Dominguez?"

"She's doing better physically. The emotional part is going to take a while. The boyfriend is undergoing a mental health eval at a hospital in Richmond."

"I'm glad she's on the mend. I heard you did an awesome job in Fairfax the other night."

"I'm just relieved it ended without anyone getting hurt. What've you got for me on Eduardo Carter?"

"Step into my office." She led Sam into the morgue, where Carter was on her table, the distinctive Y-shaped incision on his torso the sign of a recently completed autopsy. Lindsey pointed to the small but distinctive stab wound on his chest. "One fatal blow that severed his aorta. He was dead instantly. I noted bruising on his arms and chest as well as abrasions consistent with road rash."

"What about the tox screen?"

"Clean."

"Interesting. We have information that he's had addiction

issues in the past. He's estranged from his parents because he beat up his mother when she wouldn't give him money for drugs."

"What a nightmare. Those poor parents."

"I know."

"Are you really doing okay?"

"I'm just taking it a minute at a time. How about you? What's new with the wedding plans?"

"Nah, we're not doing that. It's all about you for the next little while around here."

"I'm sick of it being all about me. I really want to know how the wedding is coming along."

"Everything is great, thanks to Shelby, the miracle worker, who makes it so easy that all I have to do is point and say, 'That one.'"

"She really is the best."

"That party for the twins was *epic*. Thanks for including us."

"Of course we included you. You guys are family to us."

"Likewise, Sam. If I can do anything for you—anything at all—please ask. We're all so damned proud of you both and eager to help where we can."

Sam gave her a hug. "Thank you. Very much appreciated. I'll let you know. In the meantime, shoot me the report on Carter."

"Already done."

"See you later, Doc."

Sam left the morgue and was on her way to the pit when she nearly ran smack into Detective Ramsey, the person she least wished to see.

"Well, look who it is. Little Miss I'm Going to Keep My Job No Matter How Disruptive It Is for My Colleagues."

"Get the fuck out of my way, Ramsey."

Sam moved past him, but he kept talking.

"Everyone is talking about you today, Holland, how you ought to do the right thing for the rest of us and step aside to focus on your fancy new life at the White House. I've even heard the union is taking up the disruption of your continued presence here at the next meeting. You're not wanted, you selfish bitch."

She told herself he was full of shit, as usual, but that didn't take the sting out of the harsh words. "Consider the source," she muttered to herself as she stepped into the pit, where her detectives were hard at work.

"Bring me up to speed," Sam said, startling her team with her sudden presence. She loved when that happened.

"We have the five suspects involved in the rape and murder in custody," Freddie said. "Each of them is pointing the finger at the others on the murder. Hopefully, we'll get the DNA report today from the rape kit so we can start matching it to the samples we took last night."

"We've probably got enough to charge them all with felony murder and sexual assault," Sam said. "Let's get one of the AUSAs over here to lay it out."

"I'll make the call," Gonzo said, getting up to leave the room.

"Which one of them had the connection to Calvin Worthington?" Sam asked Freddie.

Freddie put a photo of a Hispanic man on the table and pushed it toward her. "Javier Lopez."

"What do we know about him?"

"Sealed juvie record, got snagged for an armed B and E nine years ago and did three years at Jessup. He was a year ahead of Calvin in high school."

"Did we ever talk to him about it?"

"Interestingly enough, we never talked to any of the classmates who were in trouble at the time."

Lieutenant Stahl had been the lead detective. His partner at the time, Detective Morse, left the department in the ensuing years.

"Let's track down Stahl's partner. I want some insight before I talk to Lopez."

"I'll work on that," Jeannie said.

"Captain, can you lean on the lab to get that rape kit processed?" Sam asked Captain Malone, who'd come in a minute after she did.

"I did this morning. They promised me something by noon."

"In the meantime, Cam and Matt, work on filling out the board with what we know about our five suspects," Sam said to Green and O'Brien, "and shoot me anything that pops. Let's get out and work the case."

As her detectives saw to her orders, she signaled for Malone to remain for a minute. She led him into her office, turned on the lights and gestured for him to close the door. "I had an interesting conversation with Hill yesterday." Sam went around her desk and faced the captain.

"About what?" Malone asked.

Sam forced herself to make eye contact with her mentor, boss and friend. "Hector Reese." She gave him a minute to think about how he knew that name and watched his eyes widen with recollection. "Hill asked me who else knows about what went down in the interrogation room. I dodged the question, but I wanted to give you a heads-up that he's on that scent."

"Probably helped along by someone with an agenda," Malone said bitterly.

"No doubt. If it comes out, I'll take the full blame. I did it. I shouldn't have. I knew it then, and I know it now. My only excuse is that I was running on emotion over finding the person who'd shot Freddie and the possibility of a break in my dad's case."

"I won't let you take the fall alone, Lieutenant. I knew what you were going to do, could've stopped it and didn't."

"Let's hope it doesn't come to a fall for either of us. Had a run-in with my BFF Ramsey just now. He says the union is going to take up the disruption of my continued presence here at its next meeting. Apparently, and I'm quoting him, I'm not wanted here."

"Which, of course, you know is complete bullshit."

"The media is a huge problem. I understand it's pissing people off. It's pissing *me* off. Nick said they can send more Secret Service over here to clear them out."

"The chief has Patrol on it too. Try not to worry. It'll die down when they realize they aren't getting anything from you."

"How can they still hope that's going to happen? I've never once given them anything about Nick. Why do they think I'm suddenly going to get chatty with them now that he's president?"

"Hope springs eternal."

"I could never do that job, stand around all day waiting for something that's not going to happen."

"Luckily, you have plenty to do in this job and don't need to change careers."

Sam wouldn't have thought she could laugh just then, but leave it to the captain. "What're we hearing about Dominguez? I tried to call her last night, but her voice mail picked up. I also left a message for Carlucci." It was odd that Carlucci hadn't called her back yet, which she should've realized before now.

"Apparently, Gigi was released from the hospital yesterday afternoon and went home to her mother's place to recuperate."

"Have you heard anything from Carlucci?" Sam asked.

"Not since yesterday."

"That's odd. Now that I think about it, I called her twice yesterday and didn't hear back."

"What're you thinking?"

"I don't know what to think. Ask Green to come in here, will you?"

Malone went to the door and summoned Detective Green into the office, closing the door when he was inside.

"What's up?" Green asked Sam.

"I promise I'm not trying to bust your balls, but I assume you saw Gigi yesterday?"

"Uh, yeah. I gave her a ride to her mother's place and hung out for a bit. Why?"

"Did you see Dani?"

"She was there when we first got Gigi home, but she had to leave for a birthday party for her niece. I haven't talked to her since then."

"What time was that?"

"Around three."

"I've left two messages for her since then. She hasn't returned either one."

Sam could tell Cam thought that was strange too. On their job, if your lieutenant called, you took the call or returned it right away. "Let's go to her place and do a welfare check. We need her address."

"I know where she lives," Cam said.

"Take backup," Malone said. "Just in case."

～

SAM HAD A SICK FEELING IN HER STOMACH AS SHE SIGNALED FOR Cruz to join her and Green as they headed for the morgue exit.

"I'm sure she's fine," Cam said.

"What's going on?" Freddie asked, donning a trench coat as he tried to keep up with her.

Cameron filled him in, saving Sam from having to repeat her concerns.

"Crap," Freddie said. "That's not like her."

"Cam, call Gigi," Sam said. "See if she's heard from Dani since yesterday."

Cameron put through the call. "Hey, it's me. How're you doing?" He listened for a second, said a few words and then asked, "Have you heard from Dani since she left yesterday?"

Sam watched him closely.

He shook his head as he continued to talk to Gigi.

Sam's stomach began to seriously hurt. What the hell was happening, and where in the hell was her detective?

CHAPTER TWENTY-SIX

"Where does she live?" Sam asked Cam when they were loaded into her car and headed out of the parking lot.

"Arlington."

"Shit, fuck, damn, hell. That means we have to notify Arlington PD to request backup. Make the call, Cam."

While he took care of that, Sam turned on her lights and siren and headed for the Memorial Bridge. She'd told Vernon they'd be moving fast. She hoped the Secret Service agents could keep up. On the ride across the Potomac into Northern Virginia, Sam tried not to think about the wide array of things that could've happened to Dani Carlucci.

"Are you scared?" Freddie asked in a low voice as Cam worked the phone in the back seat.

"Unsettled. Something has to be wrong for her to not return my calls. If I wasn't so caught up in my own shit right now, I would've realized it sooner."

"Don't blame yourself. You've had a crazy few days."

"It should never be so crazy that I don't notice when one of my detectives goes missing."

"You don't know she's missing. Anything could've happened."

"That's what I'm afraid of."

One thought niggled at her mind, sending a chill of fear to her bone marrow. What if some lunatic wanted to get at her, but couldn't get near her due to the Secret Service, so they struck at someone close to her? Sam's mouth went dry, and her pulse skyrocketed as anxiety gripped every cell in her body. Was Ramsey right? Was she selfish to think she could continue on like nothing had changed? Was she putting her team at risk simply by showing up to work the way she always did?

She'd felt queasy before, but now she felt downright nauseated.

That she could've put one of the detectives she loved like family in danger was unimaginable.

"You're spinning," Freddie said. "Don't do that until we know what's up."

"Hard not to. If this has something to do with me and Nick..."

"Sam. Stop. Take a breath."

"Arlington is sending backup," Cameron said.

They rode in tense silence for another twelve endless minutes before pulling into a townhouse complex that was less than a mile from where Nick had lived at the time of their first night together. Thinking about that was way better than considering what they might find at Dani's place.

"There's her car," Cam said, gesturing to a dark blue Honda Accord.

Knowing her car was there only made Sam more nervous. Did that mean they could rule out her taking off for some R and R and forgetting to check in? She wasn't due back to work until tonight, so she wasn't technically AWOL, but all of them knew they could be called in at any time. As Sam always told them, murder stopped for nothing and no one. Their plans were always being upended by the case of the moment, and Dani had never given her any reason to believe she didn't understand the expectations of the job.

Two Arlington cruisers were already in the lot when they arrived.

Sam went over to brief the officers on what was going on and asked them to be ready to provide backup if needed.

Cameron knocked on Dani's front door, which was painted a shiny black. The townhouse itself was white with black shutters that matched the door. "Dani, open up! It's Cam." He knocked some more, but there was no answer.

A shout from behind them had Sam reaching for her weapon and spinning around to see a tall, frantic-looking blonde woman practically dragging an older man behind her as they came across the parking lot.

"You're her lieutenant," the woman cried. "I can't reach my sister, and I asked the super to let me in! It's not like Dani to not answer her phone. Something's wrong. Is that why you're here?"

"We were concerned too," Sam said, realizing the presence of the sister and the super would move things along.

The woman, who Sam could now see bore a resemblance to Dani, began to cry. "I'm so afraid something terrible has happened."

She went to the woman, the way she'd want Dani to if her sisters were panicking about her. "Let's not jump to any conclusions."

"She thinks the world of you," the woman whispered.

"Likewise." To the super, Sam said, "Can you please let us in?" She flashed the gold badge that went a long way toward getting things done.

"Uh, yes, ma'am, Mrs. Cappuano," he said, clearly flustered to have the first lady in his presence.

"It's Lieutenant Holland, and could you please hurry it up? We're very concerned about Detective Carlucci."

"Yes, ma'am." He spooled through a huge ring of keys. "Pretty one, that detective."

Sam wanted to punch him in the face, but that wouldn't get them inside any quicker.

Freddie put a hand on her arm, probably to keep her from actually punching the guy.

Only because she was so tempted did she let him keep his hand there and not shake him off the way she normally would.

Finally, the guy found the key and had the door open a minute later.

"Stay here," she said to Dani's sister. "Let us check it out first."

"Please..."

"I know. Cam, stay with her."

Weapons drawn, Sam and Freddie went inside the townhouse. A sour smell greeted them. She couldn't immediately identify what it was, but at least it didn't smell like blood. For that much, she gave thanks. "Dani!"

No response.

They checked the first floor of the townhouse, which was decorated in a sleek, modern style that suited Dani, before venturing upstairs, where the smell was noticeably worse.

Sam nudged a door open and found what looked like a guest room. A second room was an office, and the third was a full bathroom. At the end of the hallway, she stepped into the largest bedroom, where a foul odor hit her in the face. "Dani?"

A low moan from an adjoining room had them moving quickly to get to her.

Dani lay on the floor of the bathroom in a war zone of vomit and other bodily fluids.

"Dani! Oh my God! What happened?"

"Food poisoning," she whispered. "I think."

"Call for a bus," Sam said to Freddie, who ran from the room.

The smell nearly made Sam vomit herself, but she found a towel on the counter, wet it and used it to bathe Dani's face.

"Sorry."

"Shh, don't be sorry. As long as you're okay, we are too."

∼

Twenty minutes later, with Dani and her sister on the way to the hospital in the ambulance, Sam eyed the Secret Service SUV. She handed her keys to Freddie. "I'm going home to change. Get back to HQ and pick it up with Lopez. I want everything you can find on him before I talk to him about Calvin."

"Yes, ma'am," Green said for both of them.

As she walked over to the SUV, she couldn't believe she was going to do this, but it would get her back to work faster than if she took Freddie and Cam to HQ and then went home. She cut through the next-door neighbor's lawn, using the grass to clean the puke off the bottoms of her shoes. Poor Carlucci had been so dreadfully ill. Sam hoped she was going to be okay.

Vernon lowered the window and raised an eyebrow. "May I help you, ma'am?"

"I could use a ride home to change."

He jumped out of the car and opened the back door for her.

"Sorry, I'm a little fragrant. My colleague has a bad case of food poisoning."

"Is she all right?"

"She will be." And thank God for that. As she got into the back of the SUV, Sam couldn't stop thinking about the possibility that she was putting her colleagues in danger by continuing to work. That hadn't occurred to her before now. It hadn't been an issue when she was second lady, but would her new, higher profile put her beloved colleagues in even more danger than they already faced on the job every day?

She couldn't bear to entertain that thought.

"Hey, Vernon," she said when they were on the way back to town.

He met her gaze in the rearview mirror. "Ma'am?"

"Could I ask you something?"

"Of course."

She hesitated for a second, reluctant to give voice to her fear. "Do you think I'm endangering my squad by staying on the job?"

"How so?"

"Does my higher profile make them targets too? The whole time we were driving out here, all I could think about was what if someone harmed her because of her proximity to me."

"I don't think the danger to them now is more than it was when you were second lady."

"Were there threats against them then?" Sam asked, horrified that she'd never thought to ask before.

"Not that I'm aware of, ma'am."

"And you'd know, right? Because you're assigned to me."

"Yes, ma'am."

"Well, that's a relief." After a long pause, Sam said, "Do you think I'm crazy to try to do this? To keep my job while I'm first lady?"

"I don't think you're crazy, ma'am. You've devoted your life to your career, and it means a lot to you—and many other people."

"Thank you," Sam said, strangely touched by the agent's kind words.

"You didn't ask me," Jimmy said, "but my wife and I think it's really cool you're keeping your job, ma'am."

"You're *married*? How's that possible? You're, like, twelve."

Jimmy laughed. "Actually, ma'am, I'm thirty, and I've been married for five years."

"Wow. Didn't see that coming."

"He has a baby face," Vernon said.

"Everyone tells me that," Jimmy added.

"Will you guys do me a big favor?"

"If we can, ma'am," Vernon said.

"If you ever hear of specific threats toward any member of my team, will you tell me?"

"We'll do whatever we can to help you keep them safe, ma'am."

With those words, Vernon had made a friend for life in Sam. She shouldn't be surprised that they'd understand her concerns as fellow law enforcement officers. "A big part of me is fairly certain I'm insane for trying to make this work."

"A big part of me is certain that if anyone can make it work, you can, ma'am," Vernon said.

Sam met his gaze in the mirror and saw respect, admiration and maybe a bit of affection. "Thank you, Vernon. Thank you both for what you do."

"It's an honor and a privilege, ma'am."

"You can stop calling me ma'am when it's just us. That makes me feel eighty."

"We'll try to remember that, ma'am."

"Ugh, try harder."

When they arrived at the Ninth Street checkpoint, she was shocked to see an even larger media presence than had been there earlier. The Secret Service had them contained behind metal fencing.

"I bet the neighbors can't wait to be rid of us," Sam said. "I'll be quick."

When she got out of the car, the roar of reporters shouting questions had her wanting to put her hands over her ears to drown out the noise. Nate was working the door and opened it for her.

Inside, Sam came to a dead stop at the sight of a room full of boxes and people. Shelby was in the middle of it, with Noah strapped to her chest as she barked out orders.

"What the hell, Tink?" Sam said.

"The White House doesn't mess around. They were here thirty minutes after Gideon called me."

"Wow." Standing in the midst of the packing frenzy, she had another reality check. They were *moving*. To the freaking *White House*. How was this her life?

"What're you doing here, and what's that smell?"

"I rescued one of my detectives from the horrors of food poisoning, so I came home to change."

Shelby wrinkled her little nose. "Bring your clothes down and put them right in the washer."

"Yes, Mom. Should you be carrying Noah and running around?"

"I'm fine. Don't worry."

"I will worry. I don't want you overdoing it."

"Yes, Mom."

Smiling, Sam said, "I'm going up to shower and change. Be right back."

"Hey, Sam?"

Sam turned to her. "Yes?"

"Were you serious about the social secretary thing?"

"Hello? Of course I was serious. Who else would I ask?"

"I just…" She blinked furiously as if trying not to cry. "I can't believe everything that's happened since the day you guys asked me to plan your wedding. The White House social secretary is the *pinnacle*, Sam. The absolute pinnacle, and as long as I can still be involved with my precious Scotty and the adorable Littles, I gratefully accept your kind offer."

"You do? Really?"

Shelby dabbed at her eyes as she nodded. "Avery and I talked about it, and we'll hire a part-time nanny to help with the kids and maybe make use of one of those rooms in the residence you mentioned so they can be close by while I'm at the White House."

"Whatever you need. Thanks, Tink. I couldn't do it without you."

"No, you really couldn't."

"Haha, and of course we want you to stay involved with the kids. None of us would have it any other way."

"You're going to need more help with them than I can provide if I'm the social secretary."

"I know, and I already have a plan."

"What's that?"

"Celia."

"Oh, yes. That's brilliant."

"I'm going to pop in to see her before I go back to work. Fingers crossed she'll want to do it."

"She will. She told me she's spinning her wheels alone in the house without Skip. She'll jump at the chance to shake things up."

"I hope so. Be right back." Since the day was getting away from her, Sam rushed through a shower and changed her clothes, bringing the soiled ones to the washer downstairs as directed by Tinker Bell. Thankfully, the moving team hadn't gotten to the second floor yet. After starting the wash, she found Shelby in the kitchen.

"Don't let them pack our beds and stuff. We need them for two more nights."

"I've got you covered. Don't worry."

"Thanks for everything, Tink. We love you."

"Love you too."

Sam left the house and signaled to Vernon that she needed a minute at her stepmother's home. She went up the ramp they no longer needed and gave a short knock on the door before she poked her head into Celia's house. That the house was no longer her dad's made her ache for him, as did walking into the familiar space he used to occupy. The pain of his loss was as fresh today as it had been the day of his sudden death.

"Celia? Are you home?"

"Up here, honey."

Sam followed the sound of her stepmother's voice to the second floor and found her in the room that'd been Skip's before he was shot. "What's up?" Sam asked, surprised to see piles of clothes on the bed and cardboard boxes on the floor.

"I'm starting to pack up your dad's clothes. He'd want me to donate them so someone can use them. I put a few things aside for you girls and the grandchildren." She gestured to a stack of shirts and sweatshirts. "Things I thought you might want."

"You... You don't have to do this by yourself, Celia."

"I don't mind. It gives me something to do. Your dad hated waste, and he'd want his things to go to someone in need."

"Yes, he would." Sam could barely swallow over the enormous lump that settled in her throat. "I can still catch a faint hint of the Polo cologne he used to wear."

"Me too. When we were first together, I had to tell him that half as much as he normally wore would do just fine."

Sam laughed and swiped at a tear that slid down her cheek. "We tried to tell him that for years."

"Thankfully, he listened to me, so I could continue to date him."

"We're all thankful for that."

"I miss him so much."

"I do too," Sam said, "especially this week. He'd be losing his shit over Nick becoming president."

"He would! He'd want to be the first to visit you at the White House."

"I'm so sad he can't be part of it."

"He's part of it, honey. I like to think he's close by, enjoying his new freedom from the limitations of his injury and hosting ragers in heaven for all his friends and family while keeping an eye on the goings-on around here."

"Is he dancing in this vision you have?"

"Like a bloody fool."

They shared a laugh and a tearful hug.

When she pulled back, Celia used her sleeve to wipe the tears from her face. "What's the latest?"

"We're moving to the White House on Friday."

"Oh, wow. That's just... Wow."

"I know, and I was wondering... Would you like to come with us? I could so use your help with the kids and with, well, everything."

Celia's pretty round face went flat with shock. "*What?*"

Sam nudged her. "You heard me. You need a change of scenery. I need the help since Shelby's agreed to be my social secretary.

Nick and I will have to travel occasionally, and the Littles are still adjusting to living with us. We're going to try so hard to keep things as normal as possible for them and Scotty. You'd have your own room and bathroom on the third floor, so you wouldn't have to be right on top of us and... Please say yes. I need you."

"You want me to *live with you* at the White House?"

"I want you to live with us at the White House."

"Oh my Lord, Sam."

"Is that a yes?"

"Of course that's a yes. I can't believe it. I've been thinking about getting a job to have something to do, but this..."

Sam put her arm around Celia. "This is so much better than a job, right?"

"So much better. I've been so sad about you guys not being down the street anymore and not seeing Scotty and the kids after school every day."

"Now you can. That's the number one thing I need—someone there for them when they get home from school."

"I would absolutely *love* to be that person."

They hugged again. "Thank you. You have no idea how much I need you."

"Right back at you, honey. Thank you so much for asking me to be part of this. I couldn't be more excited. Wait until I tell my sisters!"

"They can visit anytime they want. There's, like, twenty bedrooms. They can have their pick."

"They're going to *die*."

It was, Sam thought, the most animated and excited she'd seen her beloved stepmother since her father died. "I've gotta get back to work. Start packing! They're already working on our place."

"Do you want me to go over and help with that?"

"Would you?"

"I'd much rather do that than get rid of your father's things."

"Please feel free. Shelby is over there supervising, but I don't want her overdoing it. I'm sure she'd love to have your help."

"I'm on it. I'll finish this another day."

Sam picked up a red-and-blue-striped rugby shirt her dad had worn all the time when she was a kid, brought it to her face and took a deep breath, looking for some sign of him. But all she smelled was laundry detergent. "Will you put this one with my stuff? It's the shirt I most remember him wearing during my childhood."

"I sure will, honey."

"All right, I'm out. I'll ask my new best friend, Gideon, the chief usher at the White House, to get in touch with you about the details, okay?"

Celia fanned her face. "That'd be lovely. I'm still trying to believe this."

Sam kissed her stepmother's cheek. "We need you. You need us. It's perfect. See you later."

"Thanks again, Sam. You've given me something to be excited about, and I really needed that."

"Knowing you'll be there for my kids when I can't be is a huge relief." She blew a kiss and headed downstairs, thrilled Celia would be coming with them—and that she was so delighted to have been asked.

CHAPTER TWENTY-SEVEN

On the way back to HQ, Sam used the secure BlackBerry to call Nick, prepared to leave a message if he didn't answer. He surprised her by taking the call.

"Aren't you too busy dealing with world domination to talk to your wife?"

His low chuckle made her smile. "I'm never too busy for my lovely wife."

"That's not true, but I'm glad you picked up."

"You caught me between meetings. What's going on?"

"I made a couple of executive decisions for us that I figured I ought to tell you about, since you get bitchy when I keep things from you."

"Samantha, when do I ever get bitchy with you?"

"When I keep stuff from you. Anyway, Shelby is in to be our social secretary."

"That's fantastic. I can't imagine anyone else in that role."

"Me either. I also talked to Gideon, the chief usher, who's my new best friend, and he's sent people over to start packing us up. Tinker Bell is supervising that."

"You have a new best friend? You hate people."

"Focus, Nick. The third thing is I asked Celia to come live at the White House with us so she can be with the kids when we can't be."

"That's a brilliant idea, especially since Shelby won't be able to do both."

"Exactly. Shelby wants to still be involved with the kids, and of course we want that too, but even she can't do everything."

"Sounds like you've got it all figured out, babe."

"Not all of it, but I've made a good dent. I also asked Roni to be my communications director and spokesperson, and she's super excited. I haven't heard back from her about when she can start. I'll check with her tomorrow if I don't hear from her."

"I really appreciate everything you're doing to make this work. I know it's not what you want to be doing."

"I took you on for better or worse," she said in a teasing tone.

"Which is this?"

"Can I get back to you in a year or two?"

"Sure," he said, laughing. "It's important to me that you're happy in this new life of ours. I want you to tell me when it gets to be too much."

"I'm hanging in there and making new friends. I'll see you at two."

"Can't wait. Love you. Be careful out there."

"Always am. Love you too." She pressed three buttons before she managed to figure out how to end the call. As she stuffed the BlackBerry into her coat pocket, she yearned for the ease of her lovely flip phone. When you slapped it closed, the call was over. No stupid buttons to push.

When she got back to HQ, Jeannie was waiting for her in the pit with a slip of paper. "Morse's number."

"Thank you, Jeannie."

"No problem."

She gestured for Captain Malone to come into the office with her. After shedding her coat, she took a seat in the chair behind the desk and made an effort to shift back into police mode after spending some time in first lady mode. That was how it would be, she thought, constantly shifting back and forth to cover whatever demand most needed her attention at any given moment. She was exhausted just thinking about it, and it was only just beginning. "What do you know about Morse?"

"I was trying to remember him when he was mentioned

earlier. Haven't seen or thought about him in years. He made detective and quit shortly after without leaving much of an impression."

"Any objection to me reaching out to him about Calvin's case?"

"Not on my part. I can't imagine anyone would object. I'd be surprised if twenty people in the whole department remembered him."

Sam glanced at the paper Jeannie had given her. "Where is area code 305?"

"Miami area."

"You want to listen in?"

"Don't mind if I do."

She put the phone on speaker and dialed the number. It rang four times before a man answered, sounding out of breath.

"Is this Dan Morse?" Sam asked.

"Who wants to know?"

"Lieutenant Holland from the MPD in DC."

After a long pause, he said, "The president's wife?"

She rolled her eyes at Malone, who tried to hold back a laugh. "Yes."

"Well, this is a surprise. What can I do for you?"

"I'm here with Captain Jake Malone, and your name came up as one of the officers attached to a cold case we're taking a fresh look at."

"Hey, Jake."

"How goes it, Dan?" Malone asked.

"Can't complain. Which case?"

"Calvin Worthington, teenager murdered in his Southeast driveway fifteen years ago."

"Yeah, I remember that one. A tough case from the beginning. By all accounts, a really great kid."

"Yes, he was, and his mother has never stopped trying to get justice for him."

"I remember her too. You don't forget that kind of heartache."

"No, you don't. What can you tell me about the investigation and how it was run by then-Detective Stahl?"

He huffed out a laugh. "That guy... I've read about your issues with him."

"You mean how he wrapped me in razor wire and tried to set me on fire?"

"He's always been a sick son of a bitch. He's one of the reasons I left the department when I did. I saw the handwriting on the wall. He was going to be a commander before long, and I didn't want to work for someone like him."

"I know that feeling. But specific to the Worthington case, is there anything you can tell me about how he handled it?"

"He didn't handle it. What did he care about another dead Black kid?"

Sam sighed as she made eye contact with Malone. "I was afraid you might say that."

"I tried to get him to seriously investigate because there were a lot of oddities, but he refused to give the case more than a cursory glance, and since he outranked me, there wasn't much I could do to overrule him."

"I used to work for him. I know how that went. Can you shed any light on the oddities, as you referred to them?"

"For one thing, Calvin didn't hang with kids who were in trouble. You were more likely to see him at drama club or band practice than on the streets. His mom worked really hard to keep him away from trouble, and by all accounts, she'd succeeded at that."

"So there was never any talk of it being a gang hit?"

"No, not at all."

"Wrong place, wrong time? Mistaken identity?"

"Both were possibilities. He had a cousin who was the exact opposite of him. All in with the gangs, in and out of trouble, long juvie record."

"How old was the cousin?"

"I don't remember exactly, but a couple of years older than Calvin."

"Do you remember his name?"

"I don't, but Calvin's mother could tell you that."

"Does the name Javier Lopez mean anything to you?"

He thought about that for a second. "I can't say that it does. Why?"

"He was listed as a classmate of Calvin's, and his name has

come up in another investigation."

"I don't remember anyone by that name."

"Have you heard the FBI is investigating the MPD?"

"I read about that in the *Post*."

"Would you be willing to tell them what you told me about Stahl's reluctance to investigate Calvin's case?"

"Hell yes, I'd be willing. It always pissed me off that he got away with the shit he did, and even though he's already doing hard time, I'd be happy to tell the FBI how he behaved back in the day. He's the kind of cop that gave all of us a bad name."

"I'll pass along your name to Agent Hill, who's leading the investigation. One other thing I wanted to ask. What're your recollections of Paul Conklin?"

"I heard about his involvement in your dad's case and that of Skip's first partner, Steven Coyne. That was such a shock to me. I can't imagine how it must've been for you and everyone there."

"It was pretty horrible to know someone my dad considered a close friend had sat on that info for four long years."

"Your dad was a great guy. I was so sorry to hear he'd passed. As for Paul, he always struck me as a straight-up kind of dude. Had some trouble with booze way back when, but as far as I knew, he'd kicked it and gotten himself straightened out."

Thanks to my dad, Sam wanted to say, but didn't. "I very much appreciate your insights into all of this."

"I'm happy to help, and I'm so glad you're taking another look at the Worthington case. That one nagged at me for years, and I've always wished I'd had the stones to stand up to Stahl. But you probably remember what it was like to be a low man—or woman —in the department and how hard it is to bump up against more senior officers."

"I do remember." She'd have found a way to work around Stahl, the way she had for years when she was miserably under his command. Even before then, she'd raised hell about Calvin's case long before she had any standing to do so, but despite her best efforts, it hadn't gone anywhere. The case had gone cold, and fifteen years had passed without any new leads.

"I definitely think the cousin is worth a closer look. He was into all sorts of shit back in the day. Not sure about recent activity, but you'd be able to find that out."

"You've given me a thread I didn't have before, and I appreciate it."

"The cousin's name was D'Andre. It just came to me."

"That's great." Sam wrote down the name. "Give me a shout if you think of anything else that might be helpful."

"I will, and if I may... I'd just like to say that I'm an admirer of your husband's. I like the way he conducts himself. I'm wishing him—and you—all the best in your new roles."

"Thank you. We'll take all the good wishes we can get."

"You're staying on the job?"

"That's the plan."

"Good for you. I've admired your career too. You've got a lot of your old man in you."

"That's... That's the highest compliment you could pay me. Thank you again, Detective Morse."

"Happy to help."

Sam ended the call and looked to Malone. "I should've reopened this case the minute I took command of this squad."

"It's not like you've been sitting around twiddling your thumbs over the last two years, not to mention investigating your dad's case every spare second you had."

"Still, I knew how Stahl operated and should've done something before Lenore showed up to remind me of unfinished business." She took another minute to get her thoughts together before placing a call to Lenore Worthington. "This is Lieutenant Holland," she said when Lenore answered, sounding out of breath.

"Oh, hi. I wasn't sure if I'd hear from you again after everything that's happened."

"What happened?"

Lenore laughed. "Other than your husband becoming president?"

"Oh. That."

"Just another weekend, right?"

"That's how I'm trying to treat it."

"And how's that going for you?"

"Um, well..."

Lenore laughed again. "I'm glad you called. I wanted to thank you again for starting the grief group. I've already made some lovely friends from it, and we're all looking forward to the next meeting."

"That's great to hear. I'm so glad it's been helpful, and we're just getting started."

"It's a good thing you're doing for the people forever changed by murder."

"It feels good to me too. I'm hoping to make that effort part of my platform as first lady."

"That's an excellent idea."

"So the reason I called is I've been doing some work on Calvin's case, and I have a few questions for you. Would you mind if I stopped by in an hour or so?"

"My daughter and grandchildren are coming for lunch, but please feel free to join us."

"I don't want to interrupt your time with them."

"I've waited fifteen years for justice for my son, Lieutenant. Please come by. I'll even feed you lunch."

"Thank you. I'll see you soon." Sam wanted to see Lenore before she spoke with Javier Lopez. She grabbed her coat as well as the car keys Freddie had left on her desk and headed for the pit. "Where's Cruz?" she asked Green.

"Car trouble, apparently."

"I'll call him. Any word on Dani?"

"Nothing yet. I called Gigi to let her know what happened. She was relieved to hear Dani is sick and not something worse."

"As am I. I'm going to talk to Calvin Worthington's mother. I'll be back in an hour or two. Let me know if you hear anything from Dani."

"Will do."

Sam started to walk away but stopped herself since she rarely got a moment for a one-on-one with Green without others nearby. "What you said the other day about Gigi..."

He grimaced. "Moment of weakness, Lieutenant. Didn't mean to cross any lines."

"You didn't cross lines. You expressed your truth. Now I'm wondering what you're going to do about it."

"Because Gigi and I work together," he said, nodding. "I get that it's a problem—"

"Cameron. Stop. I'm not asking because you work together. I'm asking because the last I knew you had a girlfriend, and it seemed kind of serious. This is your personal business, so if I'm the one crossing lines, feel free to say so. It's just that I was there the other day in the hospital, and I know what I saw."

His cheek ticked with tension. "What did you see?"

"A man who cares deeply for a woman, even if he's not supposed to."

He blew out a deep breath, his shoulders hunching. "I'm crazy about her, even though I've told myself a million times not to be."

Sam leaned against Freddie's desk. "Why's that?"

"She was with Ezra, who'd been giving her a hard time for a while before he lost his shit and put her in the hospital. I've been with Jaycee for almost a year, and I know she thinks we're heading for happily ever after. Jaycee is great, and I like her so much, but..."

"You don't love her."

He shook his head.

"And you might love Gigi?"

"I think it's more than possible that I love Gigi."

"Do you want my advice?"

"God, yes. I have no idea what to do, and I've been tied up in knots over this for months, all the while knowing she was with a guy who so totally didn't deserve her."

"You didn't know me before I was married to Nick, but you were here when my ex-husband, Peter, was murdered, so you know I had an ex. I met Nick six years before we ended up together. I was living with Peter when I first met Nick. Peter was my platonic roommate, or so I thought. Turns out, though, he decided not to give me messages from Nick because he was interested in me himself. The whole time I was with Peter, I was thinking about that amazing guy I met that one night and wondering why I never heard from him. My greatest regret is that I didn't go to his house and ask him why he never called me. If I'd done that, I could've skipped the entire miserable four years I spent married to the wrong guy. Do you get why I'm telling you this?"

"I think I do."

"I married Peter knowing I was in love with someone else. I blame myself even more than him for the disaster our marriage was. There's absolutely nothing like being with the right one. You already know what you need to do as far as Jaycee is concerned. You don't need me to tell you that."

"No, I don't," he said with a sigh.

"If you were going to love her, Cam, you would by now."

He nodded. "You're right, and I really appreciate your advice. Do I need to worry about a conflict if something happens with Gigi?"

"We'll keep you on separate shifts. Should be fine."

"When I heard about Nick becoming president, you know what my first thought was?"

"What's that?"

"How sad I was at the possibility of you not being my boss anymore."

"Well, you're not getting rid of me yet."

"Very glad about that, LT. We all are."

"Let me know if I can help any more with the situation."

"I will. You've been a big help. You've given me a lot to think about."

"Follow your heart, Cameron. It won't steer you wrong. I'll be back." Sam walked out of the pit feeling like she'd genuinely helped someone who wasn't just a colleague but a friend. Green was one of the best detectives she'd ever worked with. He was always professional and gave a thousand percent to the job. She hoped he could resolve the issues that were weighing on him so he could find some peace of mind. Unfortunately, she knew all too well what it was like for personal concerns to get in the way of work.

Outside the morgue door, she signaled to Vernon, who was leaning against the SUV, that she was leaving. "Heading to Congress Heights in Southeast."

"By yourself?" Vernon asked, looking around her for Freddie.

"I'm seeing the mother of a murder victim from fifteen years ago. Nothing dangerous."

Vernon accepted her reply, but she could tell he wasn't happy about it as he and Jimmy got into the SUV to follow her.

Could she have gone with them and saved everyone some gas? Maybe, but she wanted to continue to drive herself on the job, and if she gave in now, she might eventually lose that ability. She recalled something her dad once told her when she was first on the job. *How you start is where you finish,* or something like that. In other words, don't do something today that you don't want to have to do in a year or two. At least that was how she chose to interpret Skip Holland's words of wisdom in this case.

Missing him had become a visceral part of her everyday life. So many times in the course of a shift, she wanted to call him to ask his opinion on something. Such as how to play what Morse had told her about Stahl and the Worthington case. The last freaking thing the chief or the department needed was more bad press, but there was no way she could sit on this info. Another of Skip's pearls of wisdom was to never withhold something her superior officers should know.

Malone would take care of briefing the chief on what Morse had told them, and she'd fill in any blanks when she had more info.

Her phone rang, and she took the call from Freddie on the Bluetooth. "Hey, what's up?"

"You won't believe it, but I think the Mustang finally died."

"Praise the Lord. It's finally out of my misery."

"That's not nice. She was my baby."

"I'm very sorry for your loss."

"No, you're not. Anyway, I'm waiting for the tow, and then I'll be back to work. Sorry for the snafu."

"No worries."

"What am I missing?" he asked.

"Besides a free lunch?"

"No way."

"Yep." His appetite was a thing of legends. "I'll eat your share."

"Where's this lunch taking place?"

"I'm going to see Lenore Worthington, and she offered to feed me."

"That's so not fair. No one ever offers to feed us when I'm with you, and if they did, you wouldn't let me anyway."

"I'm enjoying this far more than I should be."

"Should I meet you at Lenore's?"

"Not this time. I think I should do this myself, since she and I have formed a bond of sorts, going back to the first day when Calvin was shot, and I took the call. She may speak more freely to just me."

"All right. I'll see you back at the house."

"See you then. And, Freddie? I really am sorry about the Mustang."

"No, you're not, but thank you just the same."

Laughing, Sam ended the call and pressed the accelerator, eager to get to Southeast and back to talk to Lopez before the day got away from her. Then she remembered the meeting at two with the Secret Service director and was instantly pissed.

CHAPTER TWENTY-EIGHT

S am was almost to Lenore's when her phone rang with a call from Lilia.

"Hey, I'm on the fly. I've got five minutes."

"I took the liberty of contacting the designer you worked with for President Cappuano's fundraiser when he was a senator."

"Ah, yes, the champagne silk gown that Shelby said was pink when it absolutely wasn't."

"That's the one. I asked him about clothes for the visitation at the Capitol tomorrow and the funeral Thursday."

"What does it say about me that I hadn't given what to wear to either of those things a single thought?"

"It tells me you're busy, and it's my job to worry about those things."

"It's your job to dress me?"

"It's my job to make sure you shine, no matter what that entails."

"Did I ever tell you I was fully prepared to dislike you when we first met?"

She snorted with a very un-Lilia-like laugh. "I'm not at all surprised to hear that."

"I called you Lilly Von Noodle because I couldn't remember your real name."

"That is hilarious. You should see what people do with my

name. It was in the paper once when I made the Dean's List in college as Lillian Van Norseman. That's how I got the nickname Norseman in college."

"I love that. I'm glad it's not just me."

"It's not just you."

"The reason I'm telling you this is because you proved me wrong at every turn, and I absolutely adore you and appreciate everything you do to make me shine."

"I adore you right back, and it's my pleasure to make you shine. I'll have the designer send some things to the house for you to choose from."

"I want to let out a very un-cop-like girly squeal right now."

"Go ahead. I'll keep it between us."

"I'm doing it in my head. Thanks again, Lilia. You're the bomb dot com."

"Don't say the word 'bomb.' It'll trigger a federal response."

Shocked, Sam said, "Will it?"

"No, just kidding."

Sam laughed. "You got me—and that's not easy to do. Talk to you later."

"See you."

She'd really gone soft with all the new friends she'd made recently. That made her think of Roni, whom she still needed to check in with. Outside Lenore's tidy freestanding home, Sam signaled to Vernon that she was going inside. After a glance toward the driveway where Calvin's life had ended, Sam went up the stairs and knocked on the door, wondering how Lenore could stand to live in the place where her son had died.

Lenore answered with a welcoming smile for Sam. As she had been from the first time they met, Sam felt like a wannabe next to Lenore's effortless beauty. "Come in. Welcome."

"Thank you for seeing me."

"Always happy to see you, Lieutenant. Come back to the kitchen. You remember my daughter, Ayana, right?"

"Of course. Nice to see you again."

"You too. Congrats on the big promotion."

"I didn't actually get promoted. My husband did. I just got another full-time job."

Both women laughed.

"I think it's awesome you're planning to keep your job," Lenore said.

"I'm glad you think so. A few days in, and I'm already questioning my sanity in trying to do three jobs, if you count motherhood."

"That definitely counts," Lenore said. "These are my grandchildren, Calvin the second and Layla. Kids, say hi to my friend Lieutenant Holland. And can you believe she's our new first lady too?"

"Do you live at the White House?" Layla asked. She was about six, and her brother maybe eight.

"Not yet, but we're moving there on Friday. And you guys should call me Sam."

"Ms. Sam," Lenore said.

The children were at the table eating grilled cheese sandwiches and carrot sticks.

"Have a seat," Lenore said. "What can I get you to drink?"

"Water would be great."

Lenore returned with the drink and a tray containing a bowl of tomato soup and a stack of grilled cheese sandwiches. "We're all about the comfort food around here this time of year."

"It's perfect. Thank you for feeding me. My partner is jealous because no one ever feeds us when he's with me."

"He's welcome to join us," Lenore said. "Freddie, right? He's adorable. Is he single? My Ayana is back on the market."

"Mother! Stop."

Sam laughed. "No, he's very happily married and dealing with a broken-down car at the moment."

When the kids finished eating, they cleared their plates, loaded them into the dishwasher and then took off to play in an adjoining room that was visible from the kitchen.

"How do you get them to do that?" Sam asked, amazed by the dishwasher action.

"You make them do it every time," Lenore said. "That's how they grow up to not be useless."

"Good tip. I'll keep that in mind. This tomato soup is the best I've ever had."

"Mom is famous for it," Ayana said. "She makes it in huge batches."

"It's delicious." Sam pulled her notebook from her back pocket and put it on the table, flipping it open to the page she'd noted earlier. "I was wondering if we could talk about Calvin's cousin D'Andre."

Both women seemed alarmed at the mention of his name.

"What about him?" Lenore asked.

"His name came up when we were reviewing Calvin's case files, and when I spoke to former Detective Morse about Calvin's case, he mentioned D'Andre."

"Detective Morse wanted to do more, but they wouldn't let him," Lenore said. "He was good to us. I never forgot that."

"I don't know him personally, but he was very helpful when I talked to him."

"There was this blue wall of resistance when it came to dealing with dead Black kids back then. It's still there, in many cases. I could never get anyone who mattered to care about my son's case."

"I'm very sorry you had that experience."

"It wasn't just me. I know a lot of other people who did too. And others since then. We both know this is a much bigger topic than this one case."

"Yes," Sam said with a sigh. "It is."

"That's why I appreciate you so much. From the first minutes of this nightmare, when you responded after Calvin was shot, you've showed me your heart. I've never had any reason to think you're not exactly what you seem."

"Thank you, and I'm very sorry that Calvin's case wasn't given the attention it deserved from the beginning."

"I've read about what became of Detective Stahl and what he did to you. It was appalling."

"He's where he belongs, and I'm going to do my very best to help you get justice for Calvin. It may not happen right away. Hell, it might never happen after all this time. But I won't stop trying. I promise."

Lenore put her hand over Sam's. "You can't possibly know what it means to me to have someone of your caliber working on Calvin's case."

"Can we talk about D'Andre?" Sam asked, moved by Lenore's faith in her. "How is he related to you?"

"My late husband's nephew," Lenore said. "He was the sweetest boy you'd ever met until he was thirteen. That's when his father was shot in an armed robbery at a friend's house. He was in the wrong place at the wrong time, and D'Andre... He was just so bitter about losing his dad that way. My husband was equally distraught over the death of his baby brother. His heart stopped less than four months later, and I've always believed he died of a broken heart."

Sam took furious notes as Lenore told her story. "How old was Calvin when his uncle and father died?"

"He was eleven, two years younger than D'Andre, but they'd been very close until D'Andre's father was killed. After that, we didn't see much of D'Andre. It was like someone flipped a switch, and this very good boy became someone we barely recognized. He started hanging out with the wrong kids and doing everything he could to break his poor mother's heart. Then he started getting into trouble. Little things at first—shoplifting, underage drinking, speeding. It didn't take long for that to escalate into drug possession, assault. A girlfriend accused him of attacking her. He was in and out of juvie, and then, when he was twenty-one, he did two years at Jessup for possession of heroin."

"Where is he today?"

"That's where it gets interesting. While he was in Jessup, he found Jesus through a Bible study group there and completely turned his life around. He's the pastor at First Baptist on Capitol Hill."

"I drive by that church every day on my way to work. If you'd asked me to bet on what he was doing now, I wouldn't have guessed that."

Lenore laughed. "Right? He was a changed man after those two years in prison. It was like someone gave him a good shaking, and he remembered who he'd been before his daddy was killed. The sad part is his mama didn't live to see the change in him. She died of breast cancer while he was locked up."

"I'm so sorry to hear that."

"He's had us, and we've had him," Ayana said. "He's like a

brother to me. No one can take the place of my own brother, but D'Andre has been there for me, and vice versa. Our kids are growing up like siblings rather than third cousins. I was so afraid you were going to say he had something to do with Calvin's death, and neither of us wanted to hear that."

"I'm glad you've had each other." Sam hated to have to ask something that would upset them, but if she was going to get them answers, she had to ask the hard questions. "Is there any chance that Calvin's shooting was in some way tied to what D'Andre was up to at the time?"

Mother and daughter glanced at each other.

"Of course that's occurred to us," Lenore said. "But D'Andre has always said if it was related to him in some way, he would've known. He was as heartbroken by Calvin's death as anyone. He got even more remote and hostile after that."

"Do you have photos of both boys from around the time of Calvin's shooting?"

"I have school photos upstairs," Lenore said. "I'll be right back."

After she left the room, Ayana said, "She gets so, so excited whenever someone takes an interest in the case, and inevitably, it always ends up with her devastated again. Please don't do that to her. I don't think she'd survive it if you let her down too."

"I promise I won't let her down. I may not be able to solve the case, but I'll keep trying for as long as I wear the badge. You have my word on that."

"Thank you."

Lenore returned a few minutes later with two framed five-by-seven photos. "This is Calvin, and this is D'Andre. Sorry they're dusty."

Sam took the photos from her and studied the two young men, noting the family resemblance. "They look a lot alike."

"My husband and his brother were often mistaken for twins. The boys favored their fathers."

The further she dug into this case, the more she began to believe that Calvin might've been a victim of mistaken identity. The cousin who closely resembled him in age and looks had been in a lot of trouble. Had that trouble cost Calvin his life? After hearing what D'Andre had come to mean to these women, she hoped the case didn't go in that direction.

"Who else was close to Calvin in the year before he died who might be able to shed some light on things for me?"

"Clarissa," Ayana said. "She was his girlfriend from eighth grade on. I swear those two would've gotten married if he hadn't died. They were so crazy about each other."

"Where is she now?"

"Still in the neighborhood, married with three little ones." Lenore recited an address a few blocks away. "We still see her. She's remained very faithful to us and Calvin's memory."

"Will she mind if I stop by to see her?"

"I can't imagine she would. She wants justice for him as much as we do."

Sam glanced at the clock over the stove. "I have a stupid meeting at the stupid White House in thirty minutes." When she realized she'd said that out loud, she grinned. "Please don't tell anyone I said that."

"We never would," Lenore said, smiling.

"I'll stop to see Clarissa after the meeting. Would you mind telling her I'm going to stop by? But make sure she doesn't round up all her friends to meet the first lady or anything."

"We'll let her know," Lenore said as she stood to walk Sam out.

"Thank you for lunch and the information."

"It helps me to help you. Anytime you're in the area and hungry, my door's always open to you and your cute partner."

Sam gave her a quick hug. "I'll be in touch."

"I'll pray for you and your husband, and I'll pray for guidance for you to get us some answers."

"Thanks. I need all the help I can get on both fronts."

"You're going to be a wonderful first family. I have no doubt."

"I'm glad you don't," Sam said, leaving Lenore laughing.

Vernon and Jimmy were waiting by her car.

"To the White House." She grimaced at the realization that she'd have to drive by Clarissa's house on the way. Meetings were such a hideous waste of time, especially when they were with groups of men who thought they knew what was best for her.

"Ah, yes, the big meeting about keeping our new first lady safe," Vernon said with a smile.

"If you enjoy this too much, I'm going back to disliking you."

"I didn't know I'd graduated to you liking me."

"You're on the bubble. Could still go either way. Your performance in this meeting will make or break you."

He held her car door for her. "Good to know."

"You don't have to hold my door."

"Humor me."

"I already am! You're here, aren't you?"

He chuckled as he closed her door.

Sheesh! How accommodating was she supposed to be, anyway? On the way out of the neighborhood, she drove by Clarissa's home and groaned at what a waste of time it was to have this stupid meeting at the White House when she also needed to speak with D'Andre.

CHAPTER TWENTY-NINE

B y the time she arrived at her new home, Sam had worked up a steaming head of pissed off.

At the checkpoint, the young agent on duty did a double take when he realized the first lady was driving her own car. Or maybe it was the steam coming out of her ears that had the young man taking a step backward as he waved her through.

Lilia was waiting for her inside the door, looking prim and proper and put together, right down to the elegant strand of pearls and the leather portfolio she carried. She looked the way a first lady ought to, whereas Sam resembled something the cat had dragged through the mud.

They walked through the red-carpeted hallways from the East Wing to the West. Only the fact that she'd get to see Nick in the next few minutes kept her from completely losing her shit. "It's too bad we can't pass you off for me. You'd be much better at this than I'll ever be."

"Pardon me?"

"You heard me. What would it take for you to play the role of the first lady during the day around here? I'll handle the nighttime shift, so there'd be no sex involved for you. Just interviews and public appearances and freaking meetings. What do you say?"

"Uh, have you had a stroke or something?"

"No, but I'm about to. I've got threads to pull everywhere I look on a fifteen-year-old cold case, and where am I right now?"

Lilia glanced at her as if uncertain whether the question required a response.

"I'll tell you where I am. About to sit through a pointless meeting where a bunch of gray-haired dudes are gonna mansplain to me why I need a full detail and to be driven everywhere I go."

"Ah, I see now."

"What do you see?"

"You're irritated because of the meeting."

"Irritated," Sam said with a huff of laughter. "That's one way to put it. I agreed to let Vernon and Jimmy stalk me and to be accommodating as possible to them. What more do they want from me? Why do we need a freaking *meeting* in the middle of my workday? I have to take annual leave for this."

As they traversed the corridors, various staffers nodded to her with murmurs of "Afternoon, Mrs. Cappuano."

Sam was still getting used to the fact that everyone in the world knew who she was, which made her yearn for the anonymity she'd once taken for granted. What she wouldn't give... But that would mean not being with Nick, and since that wasn't an option she cared to entertain, she would suck it up and deal with the dreaded fame that came with being one-half of the most famous couple in the world. But she didn't have to like it.

Thankfully, Lilia knew the White House campus inside and out, because Sam would've taken a right when Lilia hooked a left and delivered her right to the Oval Office. She filed away the information for the next time she needed it.

To the woman working the desk outside the Oval Office, Lilia said, "Mrs. Cappuano is here to see the president."

"He said to send her right in," the woman said with a smile for Sam.

In a low voice, Sam said to Lilia, "I thought he had his vice presidential staff coming over here to work with him."

"Eventually. They're trying to find other jobs in government for Nelson's staff. Many were with him for more than twenty years."

"Ah, I see." It was another reminder that many lives had been upended by David Nelson's untimely death.

"Go ahead in and see your husband. I'll wait out here until the others arrive."

"Thanks for letting me vent. I'm sorry to be a miserable cow."

"You're not, and I get it. Most people have months to prepare for the possibility of this happening and then the reality of it. You had a matter of minutes. It's only natural you'd need some time to adjust."

"You're too kind, and I am a miserable cow. I promise not to take it out on you too often."

"I'm here for you, for whatever you need. I'm your girl."

"You're the best. Let me say in advance—thank you, and I'm sorry for whatever I do to drive you insane over the next three years."

"I'm made of sturdy stuff. I can take it."

"Oh, I hired a social secretary, and her name is Shelby Faircloth Hill."

"Fantastic choice. I'm looking forward to working with her. What about communications?"

"My friend Roni Connolly is on board for that, but I haven't heard when she can start. I'll figure that out soon."

"Let me know if there's anything I can do to help."

The door to the Oval Office swung open, and there he was, her love. Who also happened to be the president of the United States. Dear God. How in the world had this happened? Before she could fall into that rabbit hole full of what-the-fuck, he held out a hand to her.

When she joined her hand with his, the storm inside her subsided just that quickly.

"Come in."

Sam swore she heard the woman working the reception desk sigh as he led Sam into the most important office in the world, closing the door behind them.

"What's the matter?" he asked, smoothly removing her coat, tossing it over a chair and putting his arms around her, all in a matter of seconds.

Sam relaxed into his embrace, inhaled the potent scent of home and had to resist the urge to purr like a contented kitten.

"Nothing. Now." She slid her arms around his waist and held on tight. "Like always, you make everything better."

"What was wrong before?"

"It'll make you mad if I tell you. This is the loveliest minute of my day so far, and I'd hate to ruin it."

"Tell me anyway."

He ran his fingers through the hair she'd never put up in the usual workday clip and caressed her back. "I was raging to Lilia about this stupid-ass Secret Service meeting interrupting my day. I came in pretty hot, actually. I've got leads galore on a fifteen-year-old cold case, and all I want to do is—"

"Pound the pavement. Am I right?"

"You're so right."

He pulled back to look down at her with the potent eyes that were her kryptonite. "Those leads will still be there when we finish here, won't they?"

"Don't do that."

His eyes twinkled with the start of laughter. "Don't do what?"

"Don't use reason to talk me out of a good mad. That's annoying."

"Will they or won't they still be there after the meeting?"

"They will, but that doesn't make the meeting any less stupid."

"In my opinion, it's the most important meeting I've had since I took office."

"How is that possible? You nearly went to war with Iran to get back your secretary of State."

"My ex-secretary of State, and alas, my adorable, cantankerous, sexy, exasperating wife is more important to me than that. But shhhh, don't tell anyone I said that, or we'll be in for a world of abuse from the media."

Sam batted her eyelashes at him. "I'm more important than an international incident?"

"My love, you're more important to me than anything, and the whole world knows that, which is what makes you so exquisitely vulnerable. And that's what makes this the most important meeting I'll ever have as president."

She scowled at him. "You think you're so smooth."

"How's that?" he asked, laughing as he towed her along with him to sit on one of the two sofas.

"You think if you wow me with the most romantic words ever that I'll just turn to putty in your hands and let you surround me with an armada of Secret Service."

"First of all, an armada is a fleet of warships—"

Her elbow connected with his ribs, which led to a swift exhale of breath and another laugh from him.

"You know what I mean."

"Second of all, the idea of you being putty in anyone's hands is the funniest thing I've ever heard."

"I'm putty in your hands, and you know it. So don't take advantage of that in this meeting. You hear me?"

"I hear you. Third of all, I love you, and I appreciate you interrupting your day and your cold case to come in for this stupid-ass, most-important meeting ever."

"Whatever." She crossed her arms and gave him her best mulish look, even though she was nowhere near as mulish as she'd been a few minutes ago. His superpower was dealing with her, and he was very, very good at it.

"Want to make out until the others get here?"

"How much time do we have?"

He checked the watch that had been her father's. "Twelve minutes."

"There's a lot we can get done in twelve minutes."

"Hold that thought until after the meeting and kiss me."

Since Sam couldn't think of anything she liked to do more than kiss him, she wrapped her arms around his neck and went for it. They were still kissing like teenagers five minutes later when something dropping on the floor outside the door had them pulling apart like they'd just been caught by their parents.

Nick glanced in the direction of the noise at one of the doors that led outside. "If I'm in the Oval, there's a Marine positioned at that door. That's how you can tell I'm here."

Sam tipped her neck to give him access. "That's good info to have."

"You can come here anytime you want. I don't care what's going on, you're always welcome here." As he cupped her breast through her sweater and ran his thumb over her nipple, he said, "I'm going to *love* working from home."

Sam laughed and turned her head to kiss him again, noting that his cheeks were flushed with color, the way they got when he was aroused. "We'd better quit this now, or everyone will know we've been fooling around in here."

"I don't care if they know."

Sam pulled back, but not because she wanted to. "Time out. For now. To be continued."

He groaned and sat back against the sofa.

"It's your own fault for scheduling stupid-ass meetings."

"My entire life is stupid-ass meetings these days. But I guess that's what I signed on for."

"I couldn't do it. I'd go insane being stuck in meetings all day."

"Well, they do have a purpose."

"Still." She glanced down at his lap. "You might want to do something about... *that*... before you get caught with a boner in the Oval Office."

Blowing out a deep breath, he got up and went into an adjoining room. "Come check this out."

"Is that code for 'come finish me off'?"

Laughing, he said, "Not this time, but we'll play that game after the meeting."

Sam got up to see what he wanted to show her. Through the door, she found a sitting room and bathroom. "This is so cool. You've got your own place to hide out."

He came out of the bathroom, having splashed cold water on his face. He'd also combed the hair she'd messed up during their make-out session. "They can always find me," he said, gesturing to the official-looking phone on a table.

She went to one of the fancy upholstered chairs and ran a hand along the back of it. "This one doesn't have arms."

"I see that."

"You know what that's good for?"

"Maybe you can show me after the meeting."

She went to him and dragged a finger straight down the middle of his tie, hooking it in the waistband of his pants. "If I have time. The faster the meeting ends, the more time I'll have."

"Keep that up, and my problem will be back."

A knock sounded on the door to the Oval Office.

He kissed her and lingered for an extra second. "Let's get this taken care of so we can get back to this conversation ASAP."

"ASAP is one of my favorite acronyms." She let him lead her back into the office. "As in, get rid of these people ASAP. As in, get me back to work ASAP."

Smiling at her, he said, "Come in."

As expected, a group of somber older men in suits came marching in.

Sam was pleased to see one stern-looking woman in a black suit, her hair pulled back into a tight twist that looked painful. She recognized the Secret Service director, Ambrose Pierce, whom she'd met before, and was introduced to each of the others, though she forgot their names as soon as she heard them.

Vernon and Jimmy were among the group that sat in the chairs and sofas around a coffee table where someone had put beverages and snacks.

She had to give props to the White House staff. Their food and beverage game was spot-on. Since this was technically her house, she helped herself to a glass of water and a sprig of grapes. She'd rather have the cheese and crackers, but she needed to watch what she ate if she was going to have twenty-four-hour food service.

"Sam?" Nick's voice interrupted her private musings.

She looked up to find all eyes on her. "Yes?"

Nick's eyes danced with amusement, probably because he could tell she'd zoned right out of the room. "Director Pierce was asking how things are going with your detail so far."

"Oh. Sorry. So far, everything has been fine. Vernon and Jimmy are very good about allowing me to do my thing while they do theirs."

"They've reported that, so far, things are going smoothly, and the three of you are working out a system," Pierce said. "They're scheduled to be with you Monday through Friday from eight a.m. to six p.m. to cover your work hours."

Sam wanted to laugh in the director's face. "Those are my technical hours. I often start much earlier and end much later, and I work a lot of weekends as well."

"We'll provide additional coverages as needed," Pierce said.

That was better than him telling her she had to work within those hours and those hours only. Fortunately, he didn't say that.

"We're planning to assign two additional agents to your workday detail," Pierce said.

Sam gave him a blank look. "Why?"

"We believe the threat level is high enough to warrant additional coverage."

"I don't think that's necessary. In the course of my work, I'm usually accompanied by at least one other Metro PD officer, if not more."

Pierce consulted his notes. "Earlier today, you were alone when you went to do an interview in the Southeast neighborhood of Congress Heights." He glanced at her with sharp eyes that reminded her of Skip and how he'd seen right through her even when she'd tried to lie to his face. "Is that correct?"

She couldn't believe Vernon had ratted her out, even if he was probably just following agency rules. "That's correct, but I was going to see a woman who's become a friend in the fifteen years since her son was murdered. We recently reopened his cold case. His mother invited me for lunch and to go over the list of questions I had. At no time was I in any danger."

"That you know of."

She cast a glance at Vernon, who stood behind the sofa with Jimmy and Brant. "What does that even mean?"

"It means the threats may not be visible to you or your team," Pierce said.

"If you know about them, all you have to do is tell us so we'll be extra aware. We don't have to go overboard. We can simply share information and react accordingly. There's really no need for overkill."

Pierce looked to Nick for his input.

"I think Sam makes a good point. If you share information with her, she and her team can be more vigilant."

Sam wanted to kiss him on the lips but held back that urge until they were alone, when he would be richly rewarded for having her back.

"Very well," Pierce said, visibly displeased to have his

recommendation shot down. "We'll go with two agents for now and reassess as needed."

"I want to say something." While Sam took a second to collect her thoughts, she reached for Nick's hand. "I have a lot to live for." She smiled at Nick, who looked at her with love and admiration. "I finally have the family I've always wanted and a husband I adore. I'm always careful and vigilant on the job. Yes, things happen. Sometimes crazy, unexpected things happen, but I'm very well trained to handle those situations. I know you'd all prefer for me to be a traditional first lady, but I'm just not that person. I'll do everything I can to support my husband in this new role and to be extra careful on the job going forward.

"I know what can happen. I understand your job is to protect our family, and we *so* appreciate what the agents do for us every day. My goal is not to make your jobs harder. My goal is to continue doing my job while you do yours. If the day comes when that's truly not possible, we'll revisit this arrangement. But until then, you've fulfilled your due diligence by making me aware of your concerns. I take full responsibility for the decision to keep my detail limited to two agents and to continue to drive myself on the job. I only ask that the agents be on standby for worst-case scenarios and refrain from involving themselves in any police action."

"We appreciate your cooperation and will do what we can to make it possible for you to remain on the job while serving as first lady," Pierce said. "I want you to know that as fellow LEOs, we admire your determination to continue working."

"Even if it complicates things for you all?" Sam asked, smiling.

"Even if. We'll do everything we can for you."

"Thank you."

"Mr. President, you've requested to keep Agent Brantley as your lead agent."

"Yes," Nick said. "He's done an excellent job, and we're all very comfortable with him."

"I've approved his appointment to continue heading up your detail."

"That's wonderful." Nick looked at the young agent who'd

become such a big part of their lives since he became vice president. "Congratulations, Brant."

"Thank you, sir, for your faith in me. I'm honored to continue working with you and your family."

They spent the next fifteen minutes reviewing arrangements for each of the children, including Elijah, who was now under the protection of a detail at Princeton.

"We had a few challenges working out logistics for him on short notice, but we were able to secure off-campus housing for his detail and made arrangements in conjunction with Princeton's campus police," Pierce said. "We expect there to be a moment of adjustment for a college junior who isn't accustomed to being surrounded by security. But so far, he's cooperating and understands the need."

"If that changes, please let me know," Nick said. "I'll take care of it."

"Yes, sir, Mr. President."

The meeting ended a few minutes later with the others filing out of the Oval Office.

Sam expelled a deep breath full of relief. "That went pretty well."

"You were *so* sexy when you were telling Ambrose how it was gonna be."

"Stop it. I was not."

"Were too, and every guy in the room thought it was hot as fuck."

"You're insane."

"I'm insanely hot for you." He somehow managed to lift her onto his lap and into his arms in one very smooth move. "Hi," he said, smiling down at her.

"What've I told you about handling me like I'm a side of beef?"

He kissed her forehead, nose and lips. "Can't remember."

She placed her hand on his face to encourage him to keep up the kissing. "Funny, I can't either." Even though she had threads to pull and more to do than she could get done in a year, she gave herself ten more minutes to be held and kissed by him. "I gotta go."

"I know." He made no move to release her. "Thanks for doing

this, for putting up with it all, for bending over backward to make it work even when you're freaking out all over the place, for not leaving me. All of it."

Sam pulled back so she could see his face. "*Leave you?* Where in the hell would I go when the only thing I want is to be with you?"

"Even here?" he asked, his gaze taking in the room.

"Anywhere. If you're there, I'm good."

"That's all it takes?"

"That's all it takes, and you know it. Don't add to your stress by worrying about me freaking out all over the place or leaving you. I'm handling it, and I'm not going anywhere. The kids are handling it. It's going to be great. I keep thinking about the awesome house parties we can have with everyone we love sleeping over, watching movies, bowling, swimming. And we haven't even talked about Camp David yet."

"That does sound fun."

"Right? We'll make it fun. We'll bring back the glamour, the entertainment, the celebrities and the music."

"That sounds perfect, babe."

"If we have to be here, we may as well enjoy the hell out of it, right?"

"I guess so. You know that all I need to be happy is for you to be happy."

"I'm good. Much better after this meeting and knowing there's not going to be pushback about my job. And I'm fully aware that I have you to thank for making sure Ambrose knew that trying to talk me out of keeping the job was a nonstarter."

"We did have a preliminary conversation ahead of the meeting."

"I had a feeling." She kissed him again, making it a good one to hold them over until later. "You're the best, and I love you. If you want to talk sexy, seeing you in this room as the leader of the free world..." She fanned her face. "*That* is hot as fuck."

"If you say so."

"I say so, and we'll discuss this further later. Right now, I need to get back to work."

Nick got up to walk her to the door. "What Ambrose said about threats you can't see... Keep that in mind, okay? There're so many ways they can come for you, babe. It's the stuff of nightmares."

She rested her hand on his chest, feeling the rapid beat of his heart under her palm. "Don't do that. Don't go to worst-case. I was fine as second lady, and I'll be fine as first lady. I promise."

"I'm going to hold you to that."

"Please do."

He kissed her one more time before he let her go.

As she walked toward the reception area, a strikingly beautiful dark-haired woman wearing a red power suit and matching three-inch heels came in from the hallway. Sam took one look at her and hated her for no good reason. Her reaction was immediate and visceral.

"Oh, Sam," Nick said. "This is Gretchen Henderson. Gretchen, my wife, Sam."

She wanted to ask Nick who this woman was and why she was here, but she held her barbed tongue and shook the woman's hand.

"Such a pleasure to meet you," Gretchen said. "I'm a huge admirer."

"Thank you," Sam said. To Nick, she added, "I'll see you later."

"Yes, you will."

Sam felt his eyes on her until she turned the corner.

CHAPTER THIRTY

"Come in, Gretchen." Since Terry and Derek would be joining them, Nick left the door open as he led her into the Oval Office. "Thanks for making the time."

She laughed. "When the president calls, you make the time."

"Have a seat."

Nick was relieved when Terry and Derek came in to join them. Something about her put him on edge, but he couldn't say what it was. One of the butlers followed the staffers with coffee and cookies. "Please," he said, gesturing to the refreshments. "Help yourself." To make her feel more at ease, he took one of the chocolate chip cookies and took a bite. Damn, that was good.

Gretchen poured herself a cup of coffee and stirred in some cream. "I'll confess to being uncertain as to why I'm here, Mr. President."

"We're meeting with potential vice president candidates."

Her face slackened with shock. "Seriously?"

"Very seriously. Your name is on our short list."

"I, uh, well..." She made a visible effort to recover her composure. "I'm honored to be considered, Mr. President."

He knew she was forty-three, the mother of two and a graduate of Harvard and Oxford. She was a rising star the party wanted to groom for bigger things, which was how she'd ended up on his short list for vice president.

"Before we go any further, I need to ask if you'd actually be interested in the position. As the most recent holder of the office, I feel compelled to share the downsides. Chief among them is suddenly being surrounded by Secret Service, which totally changes your life as well as the lives of your family. I know you have children..."

"Yes, sir. I have a daughter who's twelve, and my son is fourteen."

"They would have Secret Service details trailing them at school, when they're with friends, at their activities. It's a huge adjustment, especially for kids entering their high school years. I'm not trying to talk you out of it so much as make you aware that it's one thing to consider Secret Service in the abstract. It's another thing altogether to be under their protection."

"I understand, sir, and I appreciate you sharing your personal experience."

"I'm looking for a vice president who can be a partner to me in governing, someone I can rely on to have my back and to handle some of the travel demands for me. My preference is to spend most of my time here, and I'm looking for someone who can travel if need be."

"I can do that. My mother lives with us and is available to help with my kids as needed. Their father lives three miles from us and is also present for them."

"I'm sorry I have to ask about this, but the vetting process uncovered restraining orders on both sides during your second divorce."

The question seemed to surprise her. "I'm not proud of how either of us behaved during that difficult time, but we're in a much better place now and are able to put our kids first, which is what matters."

"That information would be available to the media if we were to announce you as our choice. I'm not interested in this first important decision turning into a circus, so I'd like to know what other details will come out when the media digs deeper."

"He accused me of hitting him, but I never did." Her face flushed with embarrassment. "He's an alcoholic, and while he was in rehab, he was also diagnosed with bipolar disorder. That's a potent combination, to say the least, and we struggled for a number of years to hold our marriage together. In the end, it was impossible. He's worked hard on his sobriety and his mental health, and he's doing very well now. I'm thankful for that, because my children love him very much."

"I'm glad to hear he's doing better. I'm sorry that I have to ask if there's anything else we need to be aware of, any potential land mines that might detonate if we put you forward as our nominee."

"Nothing that I can think of."

"Then I'll ask whether you're interested in the job."

"Yes, Mr. President. I'd be honored to be your vice president as well as your partner in governing."

Nick stood to indicate the meeting was finished. He shook her hand. "Thank you so much for coming in. We'll be in touch."

"Thank you, Mr. President."

Terry walked her out and then returned, closing the door behind him as he came back into the room. "Impressions?"

"I liked her, and I appreciated her candor about the difficulties with her ex-husband. But we need to dig deeper and make sure we have the full story."

"I've already done some additional digging," Derek said, "and from what I was able to learn, her story adds up. The husband has been very public on his social media about his struggles, his regrets, his recovery. He owns the demise of their marriage and speaks of her respectfully and with admiration."

"Well, that's good, I guess," Nick said. "Do we like her for VP?"

Terry hesitated for a second before he said, "I like her, and she certainly has the political and policy chops to step into the role. I just liked Sanford more."

Hearing her name triggered the memory of Chanel No. 5 and his predictable reaction to the scent his mother had worn all her life.

"What I don't understand," Terry said, his tone measured, "is why you're not enthusiastic about her."

"It's the dumbest thing," Nick said, mortified to have to say the words out loud.

"What is?" Terry asked.

Nick took a deep breath and let it out. "She wears the same

perfume as my mother. My associations with it are... negative, to say the least. Like I said... It's dumb."

"No," Derek said firmly. "It isn't. After watching your mother put you through the wringer for as long as I've known you, I completely understand."

"Sam says we just ask her not to wear it around me, but I can't imagine actually asking that of her."

"We'll ask it of her," Terry said. "If you want her to be your vice president, we'll tell her the truth about the perfume and ask if it'd be a problem for her not to wear it. She'll say of course not. Problem solved."

That something so complex to him could actually be so simple...

"You tell us what you want or need, Mr. President, and we'll make it happen," Terry said. "Even things that seem dumb to you."

"Thank you, Terry. Thank you both for having my back in this."

"Always, Mr. President," Terry said as he and Derek stood to leave. "When you decide on who you want, let us know, and we'll get that ball rolling."

"Will do. Thanks again."

They left him alone to think about the biggest decision he'd had to make in a long time. After spending half an hour reviewing the two finalists, their vetting documents and reviewing his personal impressions of each, Nick was no closer to a decision. So he did what he always did when he needed outside counsel. He called Graham O'Connor.

"Mr. President," Graham said, his tone jubilant. "To what do I owe the honor?"

Nick smiled, delighted by the older man as usual. "I'm in need of some counsel from one of my senior advisers."

"What can I do for you?"

"I'm down to two candidates for vice president."

"Sanford and Henderson, right?"

"That's right."

"What's your gut telling you?"

"Sanford is the more experienced DC insider, the conventional choice, but Henderson has her finger on the pulse of young people, which has been an area of interest for me, as you know."

"Let's dig into each one and figure this out."

Nick sat back, put his feet up on the Resolute desk and got comfortable. If anyone could help him make the best possible decision, Graham could.

~

Upon leaving the White House, Sam went right back to Congress Heights, eager to speak to Calvin's girlfriend Clarissa. In the rearview mirror, she noted Vernon and Jimmy following her in the black SUV that would be a constant presence in her life going forward. She told herself it was a small price to pay to give Nick peace of mind and herself some added security, but it rankled nonetheless.

She prided herself on her ability to take care of herself, but after the meeting, she had to acknowledge that even after chasing murderers for years, her imagination probably wasn't vivid enough to conjure up all the scenarios the Secret Service dealt with every day. It was probably better for her mental health and anxiety level not to know that stuff.

Outside of Clarissa's house, she spotted an open space and parallel parked. She felt giddy with excitement at the possibility of closing this case once and for all, even as she reminded herself it was never as easy as one, two, three, done. But they were further along than they'd ever been, and that was something.

She knocked on Clarissa's door and heard children talking inside.

The door swung open to reveal a young Black woman with long braids and a child on her hip. Through the storm door, she gestured for Sam to come in.

"Sorry about the chaos and the mess," she said.

"No worries. I have kids too. I get it." Once upon a time, she'd wondered if she'd ever be able to say those words, and now she had three kids and a college student she'd come to love like a son. She followed Clarissa into a cozy but messy space where kids and toys were the focus, just the way they should be.

Clarissa put the little one down to play with her siblings. "I made coffee. Would you like some?"

"That'd be great. Thanks for taking the time to see me."

"When Lenore called to tell me you'd be coming by to talk about Calvin's case..." She sighed deeply. "I have to admit, I cried a little. We've waited so long for answers. So, so long."

Sam sat with her at the kitchen table. "Too long."

Clarissa took the seat that had a direct view into the family room where the children were playing and watching TV.

"Mostly what I'm looking for are any thoughts or impressions you had from around that time. We've found that with cases that have gone cold like this one, the smallest recollection can blow the whole thing wide open."

"I wish you knew how often I've thought of Calvin and that night over the years. Even after I married my husband, who I love very much, my heart still yearns for Cal. We were the very best of friends long before we started dating in eighth grade. And by dating, I mean running around with groups of kids, going to the movies and the park and the arcade. Typical kid stuff. But my feelings for him—and his for me—weren't typical thirteen-year-old feelings. We were very much in love."

Sam's heart broke for her. "I'm so sorry you lost him and that it happened the way it did."

"It was the worst day of my life. I'll never forget that call from Ayana." She wiped away tears and made an effort to pull herself together. When her little one toddled into the room, she scooped him up and held him on her lap.

"What do you remember about the days and weeks leading up to the day Calvin died?"

"For the first time since his dad and uncle died, he was really happy. He'd decided to pursue chemical engineering in college and had picked classes for his junior year with that in mind. It was nice to see him excited again. It'd been really tough for him after his dad died." She subtly wiped away more tears. "He was *so* smart. He would've been so successful in whatever he did."

"He was well liked among his peers?"

"Very much so. It was impossible not to like him. His death messed up a lot of lives. Many of us were never the same after."

"What do you remember about his cousin D'Andre around the time Calvin died?"

"We tried to stay far away from him and his scumbag friends."

"Calvin stayed away from him too?"

She hesitated only slightly, but Sam noticed. "He was so torn. He knew what D'Andre was up to, but they'd been raised like brothers by two very close brothers who died within months of each other. Cal and D'Andre shared a bond, even if they were as different as two boys could be."

"So Calvin saw him?"

"Once in a while. It certainly wasn't like it'd been when they were younger and were together every day. They were on two very different paths. Calvin never gave up on trying to get D'Andre to see that he was going nowhere fast with his crap, but D'Andre didn't listen until he went to prison and found Jesus."

Sam took copious notes. "Lenore showed me photos of both boys from around that time, and I couldn't help but note their resemblance to each other."

Clarissa nodded. "People thought they were twins when they were younger. No one could believe they were first cousins and not brothers. Calvin used to say they were brothers from another mother."

"Do you think it's possible that Calvin was mistaken for D'Andre the day he was killed?"

"I've thought of that. Of course I have. But the one thing I can't get past was that D'Andre hadn't shown his face around Lenore's for a long time by then. He knew she didn't approve of his lifestyle, and he went out of his way to avoid her for that reason. Anyone who was watching him would have to know that was the last place he'd ever be."

"Is it possible that someone was looking to send a message to D'Andre by killing his cousin?"

"That's far more likely than someone mistaking Calvin for D'Andre at Calvin's house. Do you think Calvin was killed because of D'Andre?"

"Part of me thinks it's too simple to say his cousin was in trouble, so of course it's related. I've been doing this long enough to know to look beyond the obvious. Which is why I'm wondering if there was anything else from around that time that stands out to you. Even the smallest thing can make a difference."

"The only thing that stands out is that Cal was in a fight for the first time in his life two weeks before."

Sam felt a tingle in her backbone, which was always a good sign that she was on to something. Her tingles rarely steered her wrong. "What was that about?"

"There was this girl at school who people liked to pick on. We never knew what it was about her that made her a target. She was a really nice girl. This one guy, he decided to play like he was interested in her. He asked her out, made her feel special, treated her nice, and then she found out it was all a big joke. He and his friends were making fun of her the whole time. Calvin was so mad. So, so mad. I told him to stay out of it, but one day at lunch, he was in line behind the guy, and he told him he was a douchebag for treating her that way."

"What did he say to that?"

"That Calvin needed to watch his mouth. Calvin told him he needed to get some manners, and it escalated from there. Next thing we knew, they were on the floor punching each other. Two teachers pulled them apart. Calvin got suspended for two days for fighting. It was the first time he'd ever been in any kind of trouble. The other kid got expelled because it was, like, his sixth offense that year."

"Did it escalate beyond that?"

"Lots of chirping, but that was it as far as I knew."

"Would Calvin have told you if it went beyond that?"

She thought about that for a second. "Maybe not. I was pissed with him for fighting in the first place. I was worried about him doing anything to mess up his chances to go to college. That was all he talked about—when he got to college."

"Do you remember the name of the guy he fought?"

"Javier Lopez."

Sam felt like she'd been hit by a taser. No way was this a coincidence. Besides, she didn't believe in coincidences. "This has been incredibly helpful. Thank you for taking the time."

"I should be thanking you. We've been hoping someone would take another look at Cal's case for years."

"I'm sorry again that it took so long. That never should've happened. I'll let you know what I find out."

"I'd appreciate it."

"You have a lovely home and family, Clarissa. I'd have to believe that Calvin would be proud of you."

"I hope so," she said softly.

"I'll be in touch."

As Sam got back in her car, she noticed Clarissa standing in the doorway, holding her littlest one. Her heart ached for the people who'd loved Calvin and suffered over his death for so long without the answers they deserved.

CHAPTER THIRTY-ONE

After pulling away from Clarissa's house, Sam called Captain Malone.

"Hey," he said. "What's up?"

"So, Calvin Worthington..."

"What about him?"

"Cap..." Sam was seized by regret and anger and sadness all at the same time. "I think I might have an idea of what happened. It's not solid yet, but Stahl... He totally dropped the ball and left these people twisting in the wind all this time. When that gets out..."

"I know," he said with a sigh. "More bad press for the department."

"Right. Which is the last thing we need with Feds up in our grill. I've spent a half day on it, and I think I know what went down. A *half day*. I'm so fucking furious right now that these lovely people were forced to wait this long for answers."

"I'm right there with you. I'm ashamed to say I barely remember the case."

"I remember it vividly. I was in Patrol and took the initial call. I've never forgotten Lenore or her terrible grief, and I'm pissed at myself that I didn't circle back to this one the first second I was in command."

"I get why you feel that way, but like I said before, the last two years have been insane for you professionally and personally."

"I feel sick about this." She took a winding path to Capitol Hill, dodging the worst of the midday traffic.

"We all do the best we can."

"No, we don't all do the best we can. Most of us do, but the few who don't make us all look like shit. Stahl barely bothered with the most rudimentary investigation. I want to take another look at all his cases from the time he first became a detective. If there're others like this one, I want to know."

"That'd be a monumental task."

"That absolutely has to be done. I don't care what it takes or how long, but we're going to look at every one of his case files. We probably ought to do Conklin's too."

"Jesus, Sam."

"I'm so pissed with myself. I knew full well that Stahl didn't do everything he could with the Worthington case. That was the first time I tangled with him, when I sought him out to see what was being done, because I couldn't forget Lenore's awful grief. He told me to stay in my lane and mind my own business. What was I supposed to do with that? I was a Patrol officer, and he was a detective on his way to sergeant."

"You couldn't do anything."

"No, that's actually not true. I could've gone to my dad and asked him to look into it."

"And what kind of trouble would that have caused you?"

"All the trouble," Sam said, sighing. She hadn't gone to her dad because she'd known exactly what kind of shit storm that would've created for her—and her dad. "I'm really spun up about this, on multiple levels."

"I can tell, and with good reason. Let's sit down and figure out a plan after things calm down for you."

"We're doing this. I don't care if I have to do it on my own time. We're doing a full review of all their cases, and we're going to own the results."

"You'll need to loop the chief in on this plan of yours."

"I will." Sam had no doubt her beloved uncle Joe would feel the same way she did. There was nothing good cops hated more than bad cops. "It probably goes far beyond the two of them."

"Maybe so, but in the grand scheme of things, I think it's a small percentage."

"That's cold comfort to someone like Lenore Worthington, who's had to wait fifteen years to find out what happened to her son."

"Yeah, you're right."

"We can't move on from this like we don't know it's a huge problem, Cap. Please tell me you agree with me."

"I do, but we have to find a way to do this without making things worse for the chief and the rest of us. We can't go at it like bulls in a china shop."

"I guess I'm the bull in this scenario."

"You said that, not me."

Sam laughed. "I hear you. And I appreciate what you're saying. It's just so upsetting to realize how many corners have been cut in places where they shouldn't have been."

"I wish we had a full team of cops who approached the job like you do, but the fact is we're a massive department full of flawed human beings. Some more so than others. We'll fix what we can and find a way to live with what we can't do anything about."

"I guess I can do that."

"I'll talk to the chief, and we'll sit down about this after you get done moving into the White House."

"You just had to say that, didn't you?"

He sputtered with laughter. "Are you or are you not about to move into the White House?"

"Don't remind me."

"You know who'd totally love this so much?"

"I was thinking that earlier. He'd be busting his buttons." She blinked furiously to contain the sudden rush of tears. "I'm so sad he won't be able to visit us there."

"He'll be there. He'll be right in the middle of it. You know that."

"Yeah, I do. All right, I need to go talk to a former criminal who found Jesus in prison and is now a pastor at a Baptist church."

"That's a mouthful. Is he tied to Worthington?"

"His look-alike cousin, who was in all the trouble at the time Calvin was killed."

"Are you thinking mistaken identity?"

"I was until Calvin's girlfriend gave me another thread to pull. Javier Lopez, who's in our custody with the Carter murder?"

"What about him?"

"He had fisticuffs with Calvin two weeks before he died, and it apparently escalated. Of course, none of this was in Stahl's reports because he never bothered to talk to the girlfriend or the cousin."

"I hate that son of a bitch for so many reasons, but if this turns out to be the tip of an iceberg with his cases..."

"I'd bet my badge on the iceberg."

His deep sigh said it all. "I'll talk to the chief. I'll let you know."

"Just a reminder that I'm leaving at four on Wednesday to do the viewing at the Capitol, and I'm out all day Thursday for the funeral and flight to South fucking Dakota. I guess I'm moving on Friday. I'm already in a pissed-off mood about this week, and it's just getting started."

"Are you flying on *Air Force One*?"

"I guess."

"That's *so* freaking cool."

"You wanna go in my place?"

"I'd do it in a minute. I've always wanted to ride on *Air Force One*."

"We'll see what we can do to make that happen."

"That'd be amazing. I guess I'll see you when I see you, and when I see you, I'll steer clear."

"Good idea. Later."

Sam's stomach ached after the conversation about icebergs. It made her sick to think about cops cutting corners and victims of violent crime suffering as a result. She parked in the lot outside the church, approached the attached office and stepped inside to encounter one of her favorite things—a receptionist. This one was an older woman with a sweet, accommodating face. As she showed her badge, Sam hoped she was actually accommodating.

The woman's face went flat with shock. "You... You're... *Oh my heavens!*"

"Hi there, I'm Lieutenant Holland with the Metro PD, looking for D'Andre Worthington. Is he available?"

"He... I... You're the first lady!"

For fuck's sake. "I am. Is Pastor Worthington available?"

"He..." She stood so quickly she managed to upend her office chair, which crashed to the floor with a loud bang that brought the man Sam was looking for from an adjoining office to see what'd happened. D'Andre wore a dark suit with a white dress shirt and no tie. Even years later, Sam could see his startling resemblance to his late cousin.

"Are you all right?" He tended to his receptionist before he noticed Sam standing there. Then he did a double take when he too recognized her.

She introduced herself to him and asked for a minute of his time.

D'Andre hesitated, for only a second, but he hesitated, nonetheless. "Sure. Come on back." He led her into his office, where the walls were lined with books and the desk stacked with papers. "Pardon the mess. Happens when I'm writing my sermons."

"Not to worry. My office is always a disaster."

"You'll have to pardon me for being somewhat stunned to have the first lady drop by to see me."

"I'm not here as the first lady. I'm here as the commander of the MPD's Homicide division."

"You're here about Calvin."

"That's right."

"Why now after all this time?"

"Because Lenore reminded me recently that we had unfinished business when it came to your cousin."

"The MPD never took much interest in what happened to my cousin," he said with an edge of bitterness to his tone that she could certainly understand.

"You're absolutely right, and I apologize for that. I was the Patrol officer who responded the night Calvin was killed. I've never forgotten Lenore or him."

"So what can I do for you, other than confirm that yes, I was in a lot of trouble around that time, but I certainly didn't kill the cousin I loved like a brother."

"Did people think you'd killed him?"

"There were rumors that I'd had something to do with it, or that it was related to me in some way, but I've never heard anything solid that would tie it back to me or my friends at the time. I loved him. I would've thrown myself in front of that bullet to save him."

"Did you know Javier Lopez?"

D'Andre's eyes went wide. "What about him?"

"I'm asking if you knew him."

"I went to school with him. Cal and I both did. He was in the grade between Cal and me."

"What was your impression of him?"

"He was an asshole bully, always picking on people who couldn't defend themselves. You know the type. No one liked him, but everyone was afraid of him." He chuckled softly. "Except Cal, of course. He got right up in Javier's face and told him he was a douche for what he'd done to this girl—her name was Maisy—by acting like he was into her when he was just making fun of her."

"So you knew about their fight?"

"Everyone knew about it. People thought Cal was a badass for confronting him."

"What did Javier think?"

"I don't really know. I stayed away from him. I was no choirboy and made a lot of mistakes that I genuinely regret, but that guy was seriously bad news. From the time he was a little kid, he was just a nasty son of a bitch, and I don't say those words lightly in this house of God. It's the truth."

"Did you ever consider that he was behind Cal's murder?"

"I think most people figured he had something to do with it."

Sam couldn't bear to hear that. *Most people* thought Javier was probably involved, but somehow the police had never even talked to him about the case. She handed D'Andre her card. "If there's anything else you think might be relevant, please give me a call."

"I really hope you can get some answers for Lenore and Ayana. They've waited long enough."

"I couldn't agree more. Thanks for your time."

In the car, she used the Bluetooth to call Freddie.

"Hey," he said. "Where are you?"

"On the way back to HQ. You?"

"I'm there after learning my baby has a blown head gasket, and there's no point to getting her fixed."

"I'm very sorry for your loss."

"Yeah, yeah, I'm sure you are."

"I'm truly sorry you're sad about it."

"Thank you."

"I won't, however, miss the backfiring that made me feel like I was under attack."

"There it is," he said, laughing.

"Do me a favor and ask one of the Millers to meet me at HQ in twenty minutes, if possible. Get Javier Lopez into an interview room and ask Green to get me a list of Lopez's known associates from fifteen years ago. I just need two or three names."

"Will do. What's going on?"

"I think I've got the Worthington case put together."

"Seriously? Already?"

"Yes, and it was revoltingly easy, actually. Our good friend Stahl didn't do even the most rudimentary investigation. If he had, Lenore and her family wouldn't have had to wait fifteen years for justice for Calvin."

"That's disgusting."

"Truly. I told Malone I'm going back to look at every one Stahl's open cases to find out what other corners he cut. But first, I want to wrap this up for Lenore."

His deep sigh said it all. "We'll be ready when you get here."

She ended the call and pushed the accelerator, eager to get to HQ and get this case sewn up for Lenore and Calvin. Sam couldn't change the past, but she could correct a terrible wrong by making an arrest in Calvin's case. Now she just had to figure out how she was going to play it with Javier.

That's why she needed to talk to one of the identical blonde triplets who served the District as Assistant U.S. Attorneys. Sam arrived at HQ a few minutes later to discover a much larger Secret Service presence had effectively moved the media mob out of the way. "Huh, well, look at them being useful." She parked in her usual spot outside the morgue and went inside, stopping first to check in with Lindsey. "Have we got DNA back from the rape kit on Shanice Williams?"

"Just now." Lindsey handed her a printout of the report. "All five suspects matched."

"Vile."

"Extremely."

"That poor girl." After so many years on the job, Sam had become almost immune to the horrors she experienced on a daily basis. But some were worse than others. "I've possibly tied one of them to a cold-case murder from fifteen years ago."

"Wow."

"I'm trying to figure out how I'm going to play it with him. Maybe let him think I'm going to deal on the murder and assault of Carter in exchange for info on Worthington."

"Good luck with it. I hope you can get some answers for the Worthingtons."

"Me too."

"So, um, Terry invited me to go along on the trip to South Dakota on *Air Force One*."

"If you squeal like a girl, I'm gonna stab you."

Lindsey cracked up laughing. "It's *Air Force One*, Sam."

"Go to work, Lindsey."

Sam left her laughing as she exited the morgue and headed for her pit. She'd always be more at home there than on *Air Force One* or at the White House. This was her world, and it was where she thrived. Maybe there was something missing in her that she didn't feel the need to squeal like a girl over the trappings of the presidency. But then again, she'd never been a typical girl or gotten excited about things other women did. Sure, she loved shoes and clothes as much as the next gal, but she drew the line at squealing.

Freddie was waiting for her when she came in. "Faith will be here in ten, Lopez is in interview one, and Dr. Trulo is waiting for you in your office."

"Great, thanks. Has the lab reported back about the prints on the knife that killed Carter?"

Freddie checked his computer. "I just got the report. There

were two sets of prints—one belongs to Shanice Williams and the other to Fernando Toppa, one of our five suspects."

"Excellent." It worked out perfectly for her plan that Lopez wasn't the one who actually stabbed Eduardo Carter. "Send Faith in when she gets here, and ask Captain Malone to sit in too."

"Will do."

CHAPTER THIRTY-TWO

Sam went into her office, where Dr. Trulo was in her visitor chair, scrolling through his phone while he waited for her. "You're like a teenager with that thing," she said with a teasing smile. After initially resisting the need for shrinking, Sam had come around to adoring the department psychiatrist who'd been so good to her during some of the rougher moments in her career —and her life.

"My daughters say the same thing. They say I'm addicted."

Sam was ashamed to realize she hadn't known he had daughters. "How old are they?"

"Twenty-nine, twenty-seven and twenty-three, and so far, they've given me four grandchildren, two of each."

"Ah, that's lovely." She sat behind her desk and put her hair up in a clip to keep it out of her way. "What's going on?"

"I wanted to check in to see how you're holding up with everything that's going on."

Sam gave him her best blank look. "What's going on?"

He busted up laughing. "You're such a piece of work."

"So I'm told," she said, amused by him. "I'm fine. I'm coping. I'm doing my thing while he does his. It's all good. For now, anyway."

"I'm glad to hear you're holding up well. My first thought upon hearing the news of President Nelson's tragic death was for you, actually."

"Why me?"

"Well, I'd like to think we've become friends over the years, and as such, I was worried about how my friend and colleague would cope with this rather major change in her life and her family's life."

"Thank you for thinking of me, but I'm quite determined to keep things as normal as possible for myself and the kids, and so far, that's what I've been doing."

"Good for you. It'll mean so much to other women to see you continuing to do your job while taking care of your kids and supporting your husband. The country is lucky to have you both."

"I'm glad you think so. Not everyone does."

"I suppose that's to be expected."

"The only thing that truly freaks me out is someone trying to harm Nick simply because of the office he holds."

"A logical concern, but he's surrounded by the best security in the world, as you certainly know from his tenure as VP."

"I do know, but still, I worry."

"I'm here if I can help with that."

"If it gets to be too much, you'll be the first to know."

"My door is always open to you, Lieutenant. The other reason I came by was to tell you I received a call from a producer with the *Today* show. They'd like to interview us about our grief group in the next couple of weeks."

"For real?"

"Yep. Remember how we talked about you using your platform to make this a national project? Here's our opportunity to make that happen. If you're game, that is. Of course, they only want me if you're there too."

Sam scowled at that. "You'd be fine without me."

"Perhaps, but you bring the star power, my dear."

"Ugh. Whatever."

Chuckling, he said, "I'd love to do it if I can convince you to appear with me. If nothing else, my girls will be impressed to see me on *Today*, and they're a tough crowd. I need all the help I can get to look cool with them."

"If it'll make you look cool to them, I'll be happy to do it—but only if we can do it from here. I'm not going to New York for this. Too much else going on right now."

He stood to leave. "I'll see what we can work out and let you know."

"You should probably clear it with the chief too."

"Already did. He's all for it."

"Of course he is."

"The department could use the good press."

"That's for sure."

Faith Miller appeared at her door, dressed to the nines as always.

"I'll let you get back to work," Trulo said, nodding to Faith as he left.

"Come in," Sam said. "Cruz! Where's the captain?"

"Right here," Malone said as he came in.

"Close the door."

When all the players were in the room, Sam said, "I've spent the day on the Worthington case, and I think I know who killed Calvin."

"You already know that?" Faith asked. "Didn't you just reopen that case?"

"Yes, and I found that Detective Stahl failed to do even the most basic investigation while reporting that he could find no leads to pursue."

Faith grimaced and blew out a breath. "Damn it." She shook her head and met Sam's gaze with the fiery determination that made her so good at her job. "What've you got?"

Sam laid out the details of the case she'd put together over the course of that day.

"So you're saying that Javier Lopez killed Calvin after he embarrassed him at school," Faith said.

"That's my theory."

"How do you plan to get him to cop to that?"

"I want to offer him a deal on the Carter murder in exchange for information about what happened to Calvin."

"Why would he suddenly confess to a fifteen-year-old murder?"

"I was thinking I might try to convince him that I've spoken to associates of his who are willing to testify that he's the one who killed Calvin."

"It's a risk. If he calls your bluff and doesn't give you anything on Calvin, he's off the hook on Carter's murder."

"No info on Calvin, no deal on Carter. We'll still charge him with participating in the gang rape of Shanice Williams, and we've got him nailed with DNA there, so there's no chance of him walking away. We've got four other defendants facing felony murder for Carter, so there's justice for him as well."

"I think it's the best chance we have to get Lopez for the Worthington murder," Malone said. "I like the lieutenant's plan to let him think others have rolled on him. Do we have a list of his known associates from the time of the Worthington murder?"

"Green is working on that."

Malone opened the door and called for Detective Green. "What've you got on Lopez from fifteen years ago?"

"Hang on." Green returned to his cubicle and came back with a file folder. "I was able to access his high school yearbook and found several photos of him with three other boys." He handed the list to Sam. "I couldn't access his sealed juvenile record, but I was able to confirm that all three of the others also have sealed juvenile records."

Sam scanned the list. "Good work, Green. This is exactly what I need."

"No problem," Cam said as he left the room.

Malone closed the door behind him.

"I could take the time to interview each of these men, but the chance of them actually rolling on him is probably slim, especially since they might've been involved. Do we agree with the strategy to let him think we talked to them and they gave him up?"

"I think it's worth a try," Faith said, "as long as he knows he'll be charged with the sexual assault of Shanice Williams and no info on Worthington means the murder charge for Carter sticks. That's nonnegotiable."

"Agreed." Sam gathered her notes and the file folder Green had given her. "Let's get this done." As she walked the corridors that led to the interview rooms, her spine tingled with the feeling she got anytime she was about to nail a murdering scumbag. And from everything she'd seen and heard about Lopez, not to mention what he'd done to Shanice, he was scummier than most. Nailing him to the wall for Shanice, Calvin and Lenore would bring her pleasure. Getting justice for people like them and taking dangerous criminals off the street was the most satisfying part of an otherwise shitty job.

After Faith and Malone went to observe, Sam burst into the interrogation room, startling the two men who were waiting there. She took tremendous satisfaction in that. Lopez had light brown skin, dark hair and eyes and tattoos on his neck and face.

His lip curled into a sneer. "They didn't tell me I'd be getting VIP treatment."

"Shut up, Javier," the lawyer said.

"They sent in the president's piece."

"Shut *up*," the lawyer said through gritted teeth.

Sam turned on the recorder and noted who was in the room before sitting in a chair across from them. "Oh, please, Mr. Kincaid. Let your client say whatever is on his mind."

"He's got nothing to say."

"Well, good thing I do, or this might've been a rather awkward meeting." Sam opened the file, shuffled some papers and appeared to be checking her notes when, in fact, she didn't need notes for this. "You're aware of the charges you're facing, Mr. Lopez?"

"I didn't do nothing to those people."

"We hear that a lot. It wasn't me. I didn't do it. But you know what's funny about that? You can lie to my face, but the DNA doesn't lie. It always tells the truth, and your DNA was found in Shanice Williams's vagina and on her skin."

Lopez cast a nervous glance at his lawyer, who ignored him.

"Are you also aware that simply being present when Mr. Carter was murdered makes you an accessory, even if you weren't the one who stabbed him?"

"I wasn't the one!"

"Doesn't matter. You were there, committing felony assault and kidnapping when the murder went down, which makes you as guilty as the one who plunged that knife into his chest."

"That ain't fair. I didn't touch him."

"No, but you did more than touch her, didn't you?"

He had nothing to say to that.

"I'm willing to cut you a deal on the murder charge."

Both men perked up at that.

"What kind of deal?" Kincaid asked.

"We'll drop the murder charge."

"In exchange for what?"

Sam buzzed with an adrenaline high as the pieces fell into place. "Information on another case."

Lopez glanced at his attorney. "What other case?"

"Calvin Worthington."

In a single second, Sam saw the truth in Javier's eyes before he seemed to catch himself and school his expression. That second was all she needed to be certain she was right about what'd happened to Calvin. "Ring a bell?"

"I don't know anyone by that name."

"Now that's just a bald-faced lie, Javier. I know for a fact that you went to high school with him, got into a fight with him, got expelled because that was your sixth fight that year, and had a major beef with him after he told you off in front of your friends."

"You don't know shit."

"Really? So what part of what I just described was untrue? Did you go to high school with Calvin Worthington?"

He shrugged.

Sam rifled through papers to find the one she wanted, which was actually the DNA report on the gang rape. He didn't need to know that. "I have here a statement from Ballou High School that puts you and Calvin one year apart in school. Do you still want to deny that you went to school with him?"

"I don't remember him."

"You don't remember him calling you a douchebag in the lunchroom after you were unkind to a friend of his, a girl named Maisy? You don't remember punching him in the face after he said that or him tackling you and both of you getting in trouble for the incident? Seems to me that something like that might stand out in my memories of high school, but I heard you got suspended so many times, you probably can't remember them all. One last chance... Did you know Calvin?"

MARIE FORCE

"Answer the question, Javier," Kincaid said. "Did you know the kid?"

"What if I did?"

"Must've made you mad to have him call you out that way in front of everyone at school."

Javier shrugged as if it had been no big deal, but the set of his shoulders and the tension in his jaw told her how he really felt.

"I talked to some of your homies." She read the names from the list that Green had given her. "They said you were pretty spun up about it. 'Enraged' was the word one of them used."

"That's bullshit," he said, sounding less nonchalant after hearing the names of his friends. "They'd never say shit about that to you."

"Why's that? Were they there maybe when you decided to do something about the kid who embarrassed you in front of your friends?"

"I didn't do anything. I didn't care about him."

"That's not what your friends said. According to them, you cared very much about him disrespecting you that way, especially over a girl like her."

"She was a fucking loser. Everyone knew it."

"Not everyone. Calvin liked her, considered her a friend. He didn't like how you treated her, and he told you so, didn't he? That must've made you really mad. A kid like him, calling you out, sticking his nose where it didn't belong." Sam kept it up while Javier silently seethed. "What business was it of his to talk to you that way?"

"It was *none* of his business." The words fairly exploded out of Javier.

"Something like that... I mean, I imagine it's a point of honor. You can't let him get away with disrespecting you like that in front of people. What would they say about you if you let him do that? You had to do something about him, right? You didn't have any choice." Sam kept tightening the screws. All the while, the blood zinged through her veins. These were the moments she lived for. *Come on, Javier. Give it up.* "You couldn't let a pussy like him say something like that about you and continue living. Isn't that right, Javier?"

She let him stew in that for a second, starting to fear that she wasn't going to break him. "Your friend Monty... He said he'd never seen you so pissed off than you were after Calvin mouthed off. He said you were out to kill. Were you out to kill, Javier?"

"Don't answer that, Javier," Kincaid said.

"You're fucking right I was!" Javier exploded. "That motherfucker had no idea who he was fucking with when he got in my face."

"Javier—"

"Shut the fuck up," he said to the lawyer. "You got no clue." Rage infected every cell in Javier's body and rolled off him in palpable waves.

"What happened, Javier? What did you do to Calvin?"

His jaw set in a mulish expression. "I don't gotta tell you shit."

"No, you don't, but I have enough to charge you with Eduardo Carter's murder, whether you tell me shit or not about Calvin Worthington." She gathered her paperwork and put it in the file folder and stood to leave the room.

"What about my deal?" Javier shouted after her.

Sam turned back to face him. "There's no deal unless you tell me what happened to Calvin."

With his arms folded, he gave her a hateful look. "Calvin was a *pussy*."

"That doesn't mean he deserved to die."

"Yes, he did."

"So what're you saying?"

"If I tell you what happened to Calvin, you won't charge me on Carter? I didn't touch him."

"That's right."

"Javier, you need to stop talking right now," Kincaid said.

"I want my fucking deal. I shot at Calvin, but I didn't go there to kill him. I just wanted to scare him."

"So you shot him by accident."

Javier shrugged. "I guess."

It wasn't a full confession, but it was enough to charge him. "You're under the arrest for the murder of Calvin Worthington."

Javier sat up straighter. "What about my deal?"

"I won't charge you for Carter's murder."

"That ain't no deal if I'm still in here."

"It's not my fault that you murdered Calvin fifteen years ago and participated in the gang rape of a woman. Nothing I can do about either of those things, so you might want to get comfortable, Javier. You're going to be here awhile."

"You fucking cunt cop bitch."

"Awww, are you upset, Javier? Imagine how upset Calvin's mother has been for fifteen years with her son buried in the ground while you were out living your life?"

When he had nothing to say to that, Sam decided the interview was over. He hadn't fully copped to the murder, but he'd given her enough to proceed with charges. She left the room and met up with Faith and Malone in the hallway.

"Well done, Lieutenant," Malone said.

"I'll take care of filing the capital murder charge for Calvin Worthington," Faith said.

"I was hoping it was enough."

"It was enough, but I want you to interview the friends after the fact and see if you can get anyone on record as a witness, and I want a warrant to search Javier's house. Maybe he still has the gun he used to kill Calvin. We want to make sure we've got it sewn up for trial."

"I'll have my team take care of that tomorrow."

"I assume you'll let Mrs. Worthington know we've made an arrest in her son's case?" Malone asked.

"I'll do it on the way home." As she returned to the pit, her elation from closing the case was tempered by despair that the answers Lenore had craved had been right there all along. It had only taken someone asking the questions.

"How'd it go?" Freddie asked.

"We charged him with Calvin Worthington's murder."

"That's awesome, Lieutenant. Congratulations."

"It was a team effort. Thank you all for the help. Starting tomorrow, we're going to review every one of Detective Stahl's unsolved cases to find out what other corners he cut. You all can get busy pulling the files while I go tell Lenore that we solved Calvin's case in one afternoon. I'm not sure whether to be elated or mortified."

"It's okay to be a little of both, LT," Green said. "At the end of the day, you got her the answers she's needed for a long time, even if it should've happened so much sooner."

Sam nodded, appreciating the support of her colleagues even as her heart ached for Lenore, Ayana, Clarissa, D'Andre and all the people who'd loved and lost Calvin over something so pointless. Suddenly, she wanted out of there. She wanted to go home and see her kids and Nick and cleanse her soul of these two painful cases. "I'm going to talk to Lenore and then head home. I'll see you all in the morning."

"Have a good night, Lieutenant," Green said for all of them.

"You too."

CHAPTER THIRTY-THREE

Since Lindsey wasn't in her office when she went by the morgue, Sam kept walking until she was outside. Lindsey and everyone else would hear soon enough that they'd arrested Javier for Calvin's murder. In the car, she called Lenore.

"Hi there," Lenore said. "I didn't expect to hear from you again so soon."

"We've had a break in the case."

"*Already?*"

"Yes. Is Ayana still there with you?"

"No, she took the kids to a friend's house."

"Would you ask her to come back without the kids?"

"Sam..."

"Please, Lenore? I'll be there in fifteen minutes."

"I'll call her."

"I'm on my way."

Sam forced herself to pay attention, to drive the car, to do what needed to be done even as she ached with regrets and recriminations that had nothing to do with Stahl. She should've reopened this case the minute she took command of Homicide. An emotional tsunami wanted to overtake her, but she fought it off so she could meet with Lenore. There'd be time for emotion after the job was done.

Naturally, traffic was a bear, which only drew out the agony that much longer. As Sam pulled up to Lenore's house, Ayana was getting out of a car across the street. Sam met up with her on the sidewalk, noting that Vernon and Jimmy had parked behind her and were watching.

"What's going on?" Ayana asked, clearly on guard.

"Let's go in, and I'll update you and your mom."

Ayana led the way up the stairs and into the house. Lenore was seated at the kitchen table, her hands wrapped around a mug of tea.

"Can I get you anything?" she asked.

"No, thank you." Sam sat with them at the table. While they looked at her expectantly, Sam said, "We've made an arrest in Calvin's case."

Lenore gasped and covered her mouth as tears filled her eyes and spilled down her cheeks.

"Before I say anything else, I want to extend my personal apology that you were forced to wait this long for answers. That never should've happened, and I hold myself and others responsible for dropping balls that never should've been dropped." She took a moment to collect her thoughts before continuing. "We've arrested a man named Javier Lopez, who was a year ahead of Calvin at Ballou."

"Why do I recognize that name?" Lenore asked her daughter.

"He was the one Cal had the fight with when he got suspended."

"That's right." Sam took them through the series of events, from Calvin calling out Javier for his treatment of Maisy, to the fight that led to Calvin's suspension and Javier's expulsion, to Javier's rage at Calvin disrespecting him in front of his friends. "Javier admitted he shot at Calvin. He said he didn't intend to kill him but just wanted to scare him. He said enough for us to charge him, and he said what he did in front of the Assistant U.S. Attorney who'll prosecute him. We believe we have a very good case against him that'll hold up in court. We're going to do everything we can to make sure he spends the rest of his life in jail for what he did to Calvin and for his role in the gang rape of a young woman earlier this week."

Lenore broke down into sobs.

Ayana put her arms around her mother and held on tight.

"It's all so pointless," Lenore said sometime later, after she'd recovered the ability to speak.

"You can be proud of the way he stood up for his friend and called out a bully."

"Even if that cost him his life?" Lenore asked.

"You raised a very good boy who would've become a very fine man. I never knew him, but I'm proud of what he did."

"Thank you," she said softly.

"Please don't thank me. This case should've been closed years ago. We're going to be reopening every one of Detective Stahl's unsolved cases and taking another look at them. Because of you and because of Calvin, other families might get long-overdue justice as well. But I don't put all the blame on that detective. I could've done something about this two years ago when I took command of Homicide, and I'll always be sorry I didn't."

"I don't blame you. I blame him. He was the one who could've solved this case in an afternoon, the way you did."

"Still... I should've revisited it before now."

"What matters to me is that you gave me something I've wanted for fifteen years—answers. I needed to know *why*, and now I do. It doesn't bring Calvin back, but it does bring a measure of peace I haven't had before now."

Sam nodded, taking comfort in Lenore's words. "I want you to know that we're going to learn from this. I swear to you, we're going to do better in memory of Calvin."

"Thank you for caring. It means the world to me."

Lenore and Ayana walked Sam to the door. She hugged them both. "I'll keep you apprised as the case proceeds."

"I'd appreciate that. I plan to attend every hearing."

Sam started out the door, but turned back to Lenore. "I hope if I'm ever faced with such a devastating loss that I'd handle myself with the same class and dignity you've shown from the beginning. I admire you more than I could ever tell you."

"Being admired by someone like you is an honor, Lieutenant."

"Thank you." Sam left the house feeling as if she'd done her job but hollowed out on the inside over the many ways she and the department had let this family down. In the days ahead, she would do what she could to root out other cases like Calvin's. Knowing Leonard Stahl the way she did, Sam had no doubt there would be more.

"Enough," she said as she drove home to Capitol Hill. "That's enough for today."

∼

THEY SPENT MOST OF WEDNESDAY HUNTING DOWN HIGH SCHOOL friends of Javier's. By midafternoon, they had two who were willing to testify to Javier's rage at Calvin after the incident at school. They'd also talked to the ex-girlfriend of one of Javier's friends who was willing to testify that being expelled for fighting with Calvin had only added to Javier's rage, which strengthened the motive in their growing case. Apparently, he'd never expected the school to actually kick him out.

And when they sent Crime Scene detectives into Javier's home, they uncovered a nine-millimeter handgun, which was the gun they believed was used to kill Calvin.

Sam hoped the lab would be able to tie the bullet that killed Calvin to Javier's gun. They had enough without it, but connecting the gun would seal the deal.

At four o'clock, she left her team with a long to-do list for the next two days and went home to change for the Nelson viewing at the Capitol. While she'd rather be at work than attending a funeral and moving to the White House over the next few days, at least she got to spend those days with her husband.

"I won't make you late," was the first thing she said to Nick when she landed in the bedroom they shared to find him straightening his tie in the mirror. Like the entire downstairs, the room was full of packing boxes.

He smiled at her in the mirror. "It never occurred to me that you would."

"Don't stand there and lie to my face."

"Wouldn't dream of it."

She ran for the shower, put her hair in an elegant twist and applied enough makeup to make herself presentable, giving extra attention to covering the still-colorful bruise on her face. Out of deference to the agents all over the house, she put on a robe and headed for the closet across the hall, where almost everything had been packed except for a gorgeous black suit with a ruffle lapel that had her squealing like a girl.

Until she remembered admonishing Lindsey for the same thing. Badass cops didn't squeal, except over gorgeous silk suits. The designer had left notes and underwear to go with the two outfits. For tomorrow, she had a black dress made of the same fabric. As she got dressed, she tried not to be too excited about the clothes, since she was preparing for a funeral, after all.

When she was dressed, she put on her black Louboutins, donned her engagement ring and diamond key necklace, spritzed on perfume and headed downstairs carrying the black-and-white plaid coat the designer had sent to complete her ensemble. Tomorrow's coat was all black for the funeral. It was so nice to have someone taking the guesswork out of things like this for her.

Downstairs, she found Nick and Scotty dressed for the viewing and gave Nick a curious look.

"He wanted to come. I don't see a problem with it."

"I knew him a little," Scotty said. "I want to pay my respects."

"Of course you should come. I was just wondering whose idea it was. Now I know."

Nick held her coat for her. "You look gorgeous, babe."

"No kissing," Scotty said. "It's not respectful to the deceased."

Sam laughed. "Whatever you say, buster. Where are my Littles?"

"At the park with Shelby and Noah," Nick said. "I told them we'd be home in time to have dinner with them. The Secret Service told me this is an in-and-out thing for us."

With Scotty having already headed for the door and out of earshot, Sam said, "That's our favorite kind of thing."

Nick's laughter followed her out of the house and into The Beast. There were at least twenty other vehicles in the motorcade, which Sam thought was overkill, but no one had asked her opinion.

"I gotta say that there are some benefits to being driven places," Sam said as she snuggled up to Nick.

He put his arm around her and held her close. "Yes, there sure are."

Sitting across from them, Scotty rolled his eyes. "So what happens at this thing, anyway?"

Sam detected a note of uncertainty in his voice that she found endearing.

"The president is lying in state at the Capitol, which is an honor given to very few people," Nick said.

"What does it mean to lie in state?"

"He's being honored in the seat of the United States government, and after the VIPs come through, the Capitol will be opened to the public so they can pay their respects. After the funeral, we'll fly him home on *Air Force One*, and he'll lie in state in the South Dakota State Capitol before he's buried in Pierre. Here's a piece of interesting presidential trivia for you. When we get to the Capitol, the coffin will be situated in the Great Rotunda under the dome. It'll be placed on top of what's called a catafalque, which is a fancy word for a stand. It's the same catafalque that was used for Presidents Lincoln and Kennedy when they died in office."

"That's really cool," Scotty said. "How do you know this stuff?"

"It was in the briefing documents I received about the funeral."

"Oh good. For a minute there, I was afraid you learned that in school a hundred years ago and actually remembered it."

Both his parents got a good laugh out of that.

"Nope. I heard about that earlier today."

"That's a relief. I knew you were crazy smart, but that'd be too damned much."

"I agree, Scotty," Sam said, earning her a playful glare from her husband.

"When we get to the Capitol, we'll be the first to greet the Nelson family," Nick said. "After us will come past presidents, members of Congress, the Supreme Court justices, President Nelson's staff and cabinet as well as visiting dignitaries from other countries. I'm hosting a breakfast reception for the VIPs and the Nelson family at the White House tomorrow before the funeral."

"Thankfully, you don't have to do the cooking," Sam said.

"You said it, babe. We just have to show up, shake some hands and eat."

"I'm really worried about getting used to White House-level service," Sam said. "How will we ever go back to taking care of ourselves after that?"

"It won't be easy," Nick said. "I've read about how past presidents miss the residence staff more than any of the other perks when they leave office."

"We don't even officially live there yet, and I believe it."

At the Capitol, they were taken inside with the sort of efficiency the Secret Service specialized in.

Gloria hugged them all and introduced them to her family, each of whom shook hands with them and made them feel welcome.

Sam wondered how they felt about their brother Christopher, who was in prison for killing Sam's ex-husband, among other crimes. After they greeted the family and expressed their condolences, Sam, Nick and Scotty stood before the flag-draped coffin while photographers took pictures that would be online in a matter of minutes and on the front page of every paper in the world tomorrow. Those photos were part of the imagery that signified the peaceful transition of power.

Since she didn't want to think about being in papers around the world, she reflected on her encounters with David Nelson, beginning at John O'Connor's funeral and continuing throughout Nick's tenure as Nelson's second vice president. Despite the differences she'd had with him, Sam was sad that his life had ended prematurely.

Nick gave her healing hand a gentle squeeze, which brought her right back to the man who was her present and her future. He put his other hand on Scotty's back to guide him toward the exit where Brant waited to lead them back to the car. In all, they'd been there about twenty minutes. Not too bad.

As they left the Capitol, Nick drew their attention to the long lines of people waiting to pay their respects to their late president. Even though they couldn't be seen inside The Beast, people waved to them as they went by.

"That was cool," Scotty said. "Thanks for letting me go."

"You're witnessing history," Nick said. "You're welcome to attend the funeral tomorrow if you'd like to."

Scotty thought about that for a minute. "As much as I love any excuse to miss school, if it's okay with you, I think I'll pass on that. It's kinda soon after Gramps and everything."

"You're right, buddy," Nick said. "It is."

"Will you be okay, Mom?"

How blessed they were to have such a sweet, sensitive son. "I'll be fine, pal. Don't worry. But thanks for asking."

At home, they had dinner with the twins and played Candy Land with them until they couldn't stay awake any longer. Sam and Nick each carried one of them up the stairs to bed and tucked them in. They were so tired, they didn't even ask for a story.

"Shelby will be here with you and Scotty in the morning," Nick reminded them.

"And we might not be back until after you're asleep tomorrow night, but we'll sneak in and give you kisses while you sleep," Sam said. "Scotty will be here, and Celia is coming too. We'll call you after school to see how your day was, okay?"

Aubrey nodded. "Okay." She turned on her side and snuggled up to her brother.

"I hate to miss a whole day with them," Sam said after they left the room.

"Me too. But we have to do this."

"I know, but we don't have to like it. What time do I need to be presentable tomorrow?"

"We leave here at seven thirty."

"Oh nice, I get to sleep in."

She crawled into bed with Nick a short time later and was asleep almost the minute her head hit the pillow.

CHAPTER THIRTY-FOUR

T he next thing Sam knew, Nick's alarm was going off. "Holy crap, I slept like a dead woman."

"You sure did. I was talking to you and realized you were asleep."

"Sorry. I'll make it up to you tonight."

"I'll look forward to that all day. You must've needed the sleep."

"Eh, not really. Nothing much went on this week."

Nick laughed as he followed her into the shower.

They left the house thirty minutes later for the breakfast reception in the East Room at the White House. Sam met a staggering number of dignitaries, including the prime ministers of England and Canada, the German chancellor, the presidents of Mexico and France, as well as the Supreme Court justices.

In a poignant moment, the White House residence staff presented Mrs. Nelson with shadow boxes made from wood preserved from past White House renovations. The shadow boxes contained the flags that flew over the White House on President Nelson's first and last days in office. Gloria hugged each member of the staff before she departed the White House for the last time.

Everyone wanted a moment with Nick, and he barely got to eat before they were ushered into the motorcade that would leave from the White House and travel to the Capitol. A military unit would carry the casket to a horse-drawn carriage for the trip to the

National Cathedral for the funeral service. The streets of the District were lined with people watching the procession.

Every other member of the Metro PD was on duty that day, providing security and traffic control to ensure a smooth event. It made her uncomfortable to be exempted from an all-hands-on-duty situation. While she was where she needed to be, her heart was also with her brothers and sisters in blue.

"I feel guilty," Sam said, the words popping out before she had time to consider whether she should say them.

"They understand why you can't be with them today."

"Do they? Or do they just think it's another special privilege for a special snowflake?"

"You're the most special of snowflakes, my love."

"I hope you know... Nothing they say or do matters to me as much as supporting you does. I don't care what they think or what they say. I only care about you and our family and doing my very best on the job. That's it."

"I know that, babe. And I so appreciate everything you're doing to make it a smooth transition for all of us. It was an inspired idea to ask Celia to move with us. That'll give us such peace of mind when we can't be with the kids, and it'll give her all-new purpose."

"I hope so."

He put his arm around her and kissed her temple. "No husband in the history of husbands has ever asked more of his wife than I have this week, and you've stepped up to the occasion so beautifully and with such grace."

"Really?" she asked, moved by his kind words. "I feel like a red-hot mess fumbling my way through it."

"Not at all. You're doing great. And in the midst of the greatest upheaval in the history of our lives, you also managed to solve a murder, a gang rape and a fifteen-year-old cold case, not to mention successfully ending a hostage situation. You're my Wonder Woman."

"You're very good for a fledgling first lady's ego, my friend."

"Your ego should be very, very healthy. After today and tomorrow, hopefully things will calm down a bit, and we can try to find a new normal in all of this."

Sam laughed—hard. "We've been waiting for things to 'calm down' for two years now. How's that going for ya?"

He joined her laughter, which was a good reminder that as much as things had changed, the most important thing never would.

"What're you hearing from Dani and Gigi?"

"Dani is much better after receiving IV fluids. She's set to go home today, and Gigi is on the mend. She should be back to work in about three weeks."

"That's good news."

"Have you picked a vice president yet?"

"I'm afraid to risk losing a seat in the Senate, so I think I'm going with Henderson."

"Oh. Well, that's good."

"What're you not saying?"

"Huh? Nothing."

"Samantha, try that with someone who doesn't know you as well as I do. What is it you really want to say?"

"I just... I don't know. I got a weird vibe from her."

"What kind of weird vibe?"

"I can't explain it. It was just... weird."

"I didn't have the best feeling about her either, and I've learned to trust that gut of yours. I guess I'll ask Jessica Sanford then."

"Seriously? Just because I picked up a vibe?"

"Yep."

"Nick, you can't decide on a vice president based on my weird vibes."

"The last thing I need is to make a bad choice in this first important decision I'll make as president. I trust your gut, and it's giving you a vibe, so I'll ask Sanford and take my chances with the Senate."

"What about the perfume?"

"Terry will tell her the truth and ask her not to wear it."

"Perfect, but I still can't believe you're making a decision based on my gut."

"Believe it. It's the best gut I know. Anytime you get one of your feelings while I'm in office, please share it with me. You're my most trusted adviser."

"I'm happy to share my gut checks with you." She looked out at the crowds that lined the streets for the late president. "Did Gloria ask you to speak at this?"

"No, and I'm glad she didn't. It would've been weird after everything that happened between Nelson and us."

"For sure."

"Hanigan is doing the eulogy along with Nelson's daughter and granddaughter."

They arrived at the National Cathedral and were ushered into the pomp and circumstance of a presidential funeral. Before John O'Connor's funeral, Sam had never been in the National Cathedral, and it was odd to recall meeting the Nelsons for the first time that day. As she sat through the service and listened to the touching memories shared by Tom Hanigan, Amanda Nelson and her daughter, she realized Scotty had been right about it being too soon after Skip's funeral to be attending another one.

Her emotions were all over the place, which she hadn't expected in connection to David Nelson. He'd played a minor role in her life at best.

Nick held her hand throughout the service and as they departed the cathedral for Joint Base Andrews to fly the Nelsons home.

During the ride to Andrews, Sam placed a call to Roni Connolly and reached her voice mail.

"Hey, Roni, it's Sam. Just calling to check in. I'm traveling with the Nelsons to South Dakota today, but you can give me a call tomorrow if you have a chance, or shoot me a text. Hope to catch up soon."

Sam ended the call and decided to text Darren Tabor, Roni's colleague at the *Washington Star*. *Hey, it's Sam. Just wondering if you've talked to Roni in the last few days. Let me know.*

He wrote back a few minutes later. *Madam First Lady, how nice to hear from you. I haven't talked to Roni this week. She took some leave, and when I texted her, she didn't reply. I'll check on her after work and let you know when I see her. You looked good on TV today. How's AF One?*

Sam smiled as she responded. *On our way there now. I'm sure it's super cool, but still an airplane, which makes it my least favorite place to be. Thanks for checking on Roni. Do let me know when you catch up with her.*

Will do. Safe travels, and keep your old pal in mind for any exclusives you might wish to share, or if you ever need someone to hold your hand on AF One.

Sam laughed and responded with three laughing emojis.

"What's so funny?" Nick asked.

"Darren making himself available for all exclusives and rides on *Air Force One*."

"We'll bring him sometime. Remind me to make that happen."

"He'll die."

When they arrived at Andrews a short time later, they stood on the tarmac while Nelson's casket was loaded onto *Air Force One*, and then they led the Nelson family up the stairs to board the plane. Sam and Nick stood with Gloria as she turned to wave to the gathered crowd and media who'd come to see them off.

Sam had chills as she witnessed the former first lady's dignity during a time of great sorrow.

The moment they stepped foot inside the plane, Sam's usual preflight panic kicked in with cold sweats and the urgent need to pee. It was the weirdest reaction that happened every single time she was on an airplane. She was shown to a restroom that was unlike any airplane bathroom she'd ever seen. The entire plane was pure luxury, from the sitting room to the president's bedroom to Nick's office, which made it easy to forget where she was, until the plane bobbed or hit a bump and reminded her of exactly why she hated flying so much.

With the entire Nelson family and much of the late president's staff on board for the three-hour trip to South Dakota, there were plenty of people to keep her mind off the fact that she was on an airplane. Sam didn't get much time alone with Nick, who spent most of the flight in his office with Terry and other aides.

"This is so cool," Lindsey whispered to Sam as they were served roast beef, baby potatoes, steamed spinach and delicious chocolate cake for lunch. "Well worth taking a day off, even if it's for a funeral."

"I can't believe you volunteered to spend six hours on a plane today. This is the last place I'd be if I didn't have to."

"Sam, it's *Air Force One*."

"Lindsey, it's a fucking *airplane*."

Her friend cracked up laughing. "Just think, you might get to join the Mile High Club at some point. That'd take your mind off the fact that you're on a plane."

"Very true. In other news, I'm going to be as big as a house living at the White House with my own pastry chefs. I'm powerless against the pastry, not to mention all the other chefs who'll be working to fatten me up."

"Enjoy every minute of it. You'll have plenty of time to lose the weight after Nick leaves office."

Sam took another bite of mouthwatering chocolate cake. "Also very true."

Terry came into the cabin, smiled at Lindsey and said to Sam, "Mrs. Nelson is asking for a private moment with you and the president before we land."

"Duty calls," Sam said to Lindsey as she wiped her face with a white cloth napkin. "Did I get all the chocolate off my face?"

Lindsey gave her a close once-over. "You look perfect."

"How are you liking the flight, Linds?" Terry asked his fiancée.

"Eh, just another day."

He laughed and bent to kiss her. "I'll be right back." Terry led Sam to Nick's office. "Mrs. Nelson will be right in." Terry left the room and closed the door.

"What's this about?" Sam asked Nick, who came around the desk to her.

"Not sure, but I guess we'll find out."

A soft knock sounded on the door before Terry showed Gloria in.

"So sorry to disturb you, Mr. President, Sam," Gloria said.

"You're not disturbing us," Nick said. "Please, have a seat." He held the back of the chair for her.

When she was settled, Gloria said, "I wanted to tell you myself that after the autopsy determined David died from a pulmonary embolism, I spoke to the White House physician, who confirmed David hadn't mentioned any sort of chest pain or other symptoms. That leads us to believe it came on somewhat suddenly. When he was younger, he had a blood clot in his leg, but he'd not had any other problems like that in decades. I guess we'll never know if he felt unwell beforehand." She looked down at her folded hands. "Maybe if I'd been there..."

"You did what was best for you, Gloria," Sam said, "and for what it's worth, I would've done the same thing."

She offered a small smile and dabbed at her eyes with a tissue. "It was the first Thanksgiving we'd spent apart in forty-three years. I think maybe his heart actually broke when I left him. He didn't expect me to do that. Ah, well, I suppose it's all part of God's plan. I may never understand why it had to be this way."

"We hope you're able to find some peace," Nick said.

"It'll take a while, but I'll get there. I just wanted you to hear the other details about what happened from me."

"We appreciate the courtesy," Nick said.

"I'd better get back to my grandchildren before they eat all the ice cream on board."

Nick walked her to the door. "If there's anything we can do for you or your family, you know how to reach us."

"Likewise." Gloria looked up at him. "You're one of the good ones, Mr. President. Make me proud."

"Thank you, ma'am. I'll do my best."

"She's right," Sam said when they were alone. "You *are* one of the good ones."

He put his arms around her and held on tight. "As long as you think so. That's all that matters."

"I definitely think so."

When they landed in Pierre, Sam and Nick disembarked along with the Nelson family and stood with them on the tarmac as members from each branch of the military carried the late president's casket off the plane.

After the casket was loaded into a hearse, Gloria turned to Nick. "Thank you for everything, Mr. President. I'll pray for you and your family. I wish you all the best. Enjoy every minute. It goes by so fast."

Nick hugged her. "Thank you again for your graciousness to us during this difficult time for your family."

Gloria hugged Sam. "I'm a phone call away if I can be of any assistance to you at any time."

"Thank you for sharing your wisdom and advice with me. It's very much appreciated."

Gloria stood back and reached out her hands to them while photographers and TV cameras captured the moment. "Take good care of each other. Don't let the job swallow you whole. Trust me when I tell you it's not worth the sacrifice. God bless you both." She dropped their hands and walked away to join her family in the car that would follow the hearse to the South Dakota State Capitol.

Nick shook hands with Tom Hanigan, the South Dakota governor and the state's two senators, all of whom had ridden home on *Air Force One* and would attend the local services for Nelson.

All told, they were on the ground in Pierre for an hour before they were on their way back to Washington to face whatever came next.

When they'd reached cruising altitude, Sam went looking for Nick and found him in the president's bedroom, staring out the window. She slipped her arms around him from behind. "What're you thinking about?"

"That I'm president of everything as far as my eye can see and way beyond what's visible."

"That's a rather daunting thought."

"It's a rather daunting reality."

"You're going to be a wonderful president. I have no doubt about that."

He turned and put his arms around her, holding on tight for a long time. "Tonight's our last night at Ninth Street for a while. I asked them to pack the loft last so we can spend some time together before the move."

"That sounds perfect. We may even get home in time to see the kids before bed."

"I hope so." He kissed her neck and then her lips. "What Gloria said about holding on to what's important... You're the most important thing. You and the kids. Stay close these next few years, okay?"

"I'm planning to stay close for the next fifty or sixty years."

"That won't be long enough, but it's a good start."

Smiling, Sam burrowed into his embrace, determined to do everything she could to give him comfort during their White House years and to love him long after those years were a distant memory.

EPILOGUE

The move to the White House was carried off with the same kind of precision Sam had come to expect from the Secret Service. With Gideon and Shelby supervising, Sam barely had to do anything more than unpack a few boxes and help the kids get settled in their new rooms. With a goal of getting the twins into their own rooms eventually, she'd assigned them each a bedroom, but they'd chosen to sleep together for a while longer. Whatever brought them comfort was fine with her and Nick.

His surprise of the playground equipment on the South Lawn was a huge hit, with the kids playing for hours until the cold drove them inside.

As Scotty predicted, the movie theater, bowling alley and pool made the transition much more exciting for the Littles than it would've been otherwise. They wanted to do and see everything the first day, until Scotty told them they had to save something for the next day.

At bedtime the first night, they FaceTimed with Elijah to show him their new rooms and to tell him everything about life at the White House so far. Their excitement was such that Sam feared they'd never sleep that night. Sam had kept the three kids at their end of the hallway, so they could be as close as possible, and after they tucked them all in, Sam and Nick went into their room and closed the door.

"See how it's the same as it was at home?" Sam asked. "We put our kids to bed and run off and hide from the world by ourselves. Only here, if we want midnight snacks, we only have to make a call. That doesn't suck."

"The staff is amazing. The food is amazing. The movie theater, the bowling alley... All of it."

"The kids are so excited, I was afraid they wouldn't be able to sleep."

"Haven't heard a peep out of them," he said, gesturing to the monitor on the bedside table.

"That's good." Sam stretched and then pulled her sweater over her head and dropped it on the floor. "Moving is so exhausting, even when I didn't have to do anything."

"Come here and let me rub all your sore muscles from watching other people move us."

"I love how you get me. Hold that thought for one minute." She went into the adjoining bathroom, where her toothbrush had been laid out on a silver tray. The staff took care of every detail, right down to her favorite shampoo and the lavender-and-vanilla-scented lotion she preferred. Despite her significant reservations about being first lady, she could definitely get used to the lifestyle that went with it.

"Sam, our interview is on," Nick said from the bedroom.

She donned a robe with the White House crest that she'd found in the larger-than-expected closet and went to join him. "Jeez," she said after a quick glance at the TV. "I look like a deer caught in headlights."

"We both do. The shock was still fresh then."

"It's still fresh now."

They shared a laugh as she cuddled up to him in bed to watch themselves on national TV, something that would never become routine, or so she hoped.

"I sound so stupid," she said.

"No, you don't."

"You look hot."

"Shut up."

"What? You do."

"Shut up."

"Shut me up."

"With pleasure." He rolled toward her, wrapped his arms around her and kissed her until she shut up.

"I bet White House sex is extra hot. You want to find out?"

He nuzzled her neck and left a trail of kisses. "Uh-huh."

"You think this old bed creaks when it gets a good workout?"

"Probably."

"Wanna find out?"

"You're supposed to be shutting up."

"See?" She smiled up at him as he gazed down at her with those incredible eyes of his. "Same marriage, different house."

"Thank God for that. Now what do you say we get busy christening this place?"

"I say fill her, buster."

Laughing, he kissed her, and as he made love to her, they found out the old bed did, in fact, creak when it got a good workout.

~

THE NEXT DAY, NICK AND SAM WERE WAITING WITH SCOTTY AT THE door to the South Portico when the Secret Service delivered the twins from school. They shot out of the car and into the arms of Sam and Nick, while the White House photographer captured the moment for posterity.

"Dad has another surprise for us, but he wouldn't tell me what it is until you guys got home," Scotty told the twins. He looked up at his father. "*Now* can you tell us?"

"Almost," Nick said with a mysterious smile. "Everyone in The Beast for a quick ride if you want to find out what the surprise is."

Groaning, Scotty led the way down the steps and into the car. He had the twins belted into booster seats in the time it took Sam and Nick to join them. Scotty would turn fourteen that weekend and was having his classmates over for a pool-and-bowling party at the White House. He was playing it down as no big deal, but they knew how excited he was to share his new home with his friends.

The kids were giddy with excitement on the short ride toward a prearranged meeting. They'd gone round and round with the shelter until they finally settled on a Lab mix-breed puppy, who'd been found wandering the streets a few weeks earlier. She'd been malnourished and filthy when she was found, but the shelter had nursed her back to full health and was delighted that the president's family wanted to adopt her.

They'd discussed going to the shelter versus having the dog delivered to the White House, but they'd wanted Scotty to have the full experience of going to the shelter and signing the paperwork that made the puppy his.

A small contingent of press and the ever-present White House photographer were accompanying them.

Sam looked over at Nick, who was almost as excited as the kids were. He'd wanted this for Scotty almost as much as Scotty wanted it for himself.

They were almost to their destination when Sam got a text from Darren that made her heart sink.

Hearing that Roni took a leave of absence from work. No one has talked to her, but she sent me a cryptic reply that she's "taking some time away." Not really sure what that means, but that's all I know.

Thanks for the update. I hope she's okay.

Me too.

Sam sent a message to Roni. *Heard you're taking some time away. I hope you're okay and wanted you to know two things—I can wait for you to start the job until you are ready, and if you need anything, please call me. I'm here.*

Poor Roni had been through such an ordeal since her husband, Patrick, had been killed in a random shooting. Sam hoped Roni was doing something that brought her comfort.

The car rolled to a stop outside the shelter.

When Scotty saw where they were, he let out a shout of excitement that drew Sam's attention away from her phone and her worries about her new friend.

"We're at the pound! Oh my God, it's *happening*!"

Sam had never seen him happier about anything.

"What's a pound?" Alden asked.

"It's a place where they take dogs and cats who have no homes and help them find families." Scotty freed the twins from their car seats and bent to look outside to see what was happening with the Secret Service. "Can they hurry up already? Don't they know I've waited all my life for this?"

Sam smiled at Nick, who was equally delighted with Scotty's reaction to their big surprise.

"Before I forget to say thank you for this..." He looked at them with his heart in his eyes. "Thank you *so* much."

"Anything for you, pal," Nick said.

"Well, not *anything*," Sam said.

"Just about," Nick said as he fist-bumped his son.

"Have we had a complete role reversal here or something?" Sam asked.

"He's the president," Scotty said. "He can do whatever he wants."

"Um, no, I actually can't."

"Just about," Scotty said with a cheeky grin that was so similar to Nick's that you'd never believe they weren't biological father and son. They were father and son in every way that mattered.

Scotty was about to spontaneously combust by the time the doors opened and the Secret Service escorted them inside, where the staff was giddy with excitement as they greeted the first family. Sam enjoyed watching Scotty make an effort to be polite when he really wanted to tell them to get on with it. In that way, he was very much her son.

"Come on in," the director said, leading them into a private room that had been arranged in advance.

When they were safely inside the room, another door opened, and a staffer came in carrying the little yellow furball that Sam had first spotted online. She'd immediately requested the puppy be put on hold for Scotty. She'd been watching the local shelters for a while by the time the little yellow doll came available, and she'd had one of her gut feelings. This was the dog for them.

The staffer put the dog in Scotty's arms, as they'd been asked to do, and he fell to his knees, laughing with unbridled delight as the dog climbed all over him and laid wet, sloppy kisses on his face. "Oh my God, she's *adorable*!" Looking up at his parents, he said, "She's really mine?"

"All yours as long as you promise to take very good care of her."

"I will. Of course I will."

And he would, Sam thought, because he knew what it was like to be alone in the world and in need of someone to take care of him. She dabbed at tears and saw Nick doing the same.

"What'll we name her?" Nick asked.

"Skippy," Scotty said without hesitation. "Her name is Skippy."

"My heart," Sam said, her hand on her chest.

"Do you think Gramps would approve?" Scotty asked her as he tried to contain the exuberant puppy.

"Oh yeah, buddy. He'd be thrilled—and honored."

"I miss him so much. I wish he could see her."

"He's here, he's watching and he loves that you're so happy."

Skippy was so excited to meet her new family that she peed on Scotty, which made him laugh as hard as Sam had ever seen him laugh.

The three kids chased the puppy around the big room, screaming with delight as the puppy took them on a merry chase.

Brant approached them, phone pressed to his ear. "Mr. President, we received a call from Elijah's detail in New Jersey."

Sam's stomach fell to the floor. "What's wrong?"

Brant handed the phone to Nick. "Elijah needs to speak to you."

Nick's entire body had gone rigid with tension. "Eli? What's up?"

He held the phone so Sam could hear too.

"Oh my God, Nick. Cleo's parents had me served with papers. They're suing for custody of the twins."

∾

AHHH, YES, I'M REALLY GOING TO LEAVE YOU THERE UNTIL WE PICK UP Sam and Nick's story in the next book, *State of Grace*, which will detail the Cappuano family's first Christmas in the White House. I don't want you to stress out too much about the fate of the Littles. This is still romance, and things almost always work out the way we want them to. That doesn't mean it'll be easy, but I promise not to break your hearts—or Sam's and Nick's.

Preorder *State of Grace* at *marieforce.com* to read on December 21, 2021, and if you want to know what's up with Roni, check out my brand-new Wild Widows Series, beginning with Roni's story in *Someone Like You*, out in October. Preorder *Someone Like You* at *marieforce.com.*

Thank you so much for all the enthusiasm about Sam and Nick's new adventure as the first couple. I've never experienced anything quite like the response to *Fatal Fraud* and the pivot to the new First Family Series. Your excitement fueled mine as I wrote this book.

I've had so much fun diving into White House and presidential history to set the stage for the Cappuano administration in *State of Affairs.* I had a similar experience writing this book as I did while writing *Fatal Affair*, when I quickly realized I could never do justice to the massive scope of the Metropolitan Police Department. So I created my own world within the MPD that made sense for the story I wanted to tell.

The same is true with the White House and the presidency. I purposely chose not to give every member of the administration a name, sometimes referring to them only by their titles to enhance readability and not overwhelm you with new people and names. I've included a cheat sheet at the end of this note to remind you of some of the new characters we met in this book.

The following resources were helpful to me as I put together Sam and Nick's new world within the White House:

The Residence by Kate Andersen Brower

Upstairs at the White House: My Life with the First Ladies by J.B. West

Becoming by Michelle Obama, particularly the section on the White House years, which provided the most recent details available on contemporary first family life in the White House

First Families: The Impact of the White House on Their Lives by Bonnie Angelo

Inside Camp David: The Private World of the Presidential Retreat by Rear Admiral Michael Giorgione, CEC, USN (Ret.)

The Triumph and Tragedy of Lyndon Johnson: The White House Years, A Personal Memoir by President Johnson's Top Domestic Adviser

by Joseph A. Califano, Jr., particularly the details surrounding the assassination of President John F. Kennedy and the transition to the Johnson administration.

I've taken a few liberties with history with fictional presidents representing the last few and skipped Nick ahead to number forty-seven, which keeps our divisive modern politics mostly out of this series. I think we all get more than enough of that in real life!

A huge shout-out to photographer Regina Wamba and models Robert John and Ellie Dulac, who star as Nick and Sam on the covers of the new First Family Series. We had so much fun putting together a couple that we felt accurately captured the characters we've come to love so much, and I appreciate Regina's hard work in making my vision a reality and Kristina Brinton for the beautiful cover of *State of Affairs*. If you haven't yet seen the dazzling trailer video created by my colleague Tia Kelly that introduces the new series and this first book, I encourage you to check it out at *https://youtu.be/gykioen-_OA*.

Join the Fatal Series/First Family Reader Group at facebook.com/groups/fatalseries to be among the first to see new covers and receive updates on future books. Talk about *State of Affairs* with spoilers allowed and encouraged at facebook.com/groups/stateofaffairs1.

As always, thank you to the amazing team that supports me every day: Julie Cupp, Lisa Cafferty, Nikki Haley, Tia Kelly, Jean Mello and Ashley Lopez. It takes a village to produce these books, and I'm so thankful to my editors, Joyce Lamb and Linda Ingmanson, my beta readers Anne Woodall, Kara Conrad, Tia Kelly and Tracey Suppo, as well as the Fatal Series/First Family beta readers: Karina, Gwen, Jenny, Sarah, Mona, Irene, Jennifer, Marianne, Isabel, Kelley, Juliane, Sheri, Ellen, Tiffany, Marti, Viki, Elizabeth, Heidi, Phuong and Gina.

A special thanks to retired Capt. Russell Hayes of the Newport, RI, Police Department for reading each book and checking me on the police details. I so appreciate his help with seventeen books so far, with much more to come!

And to the faithful readers who've supported Sam and Nick's journey for eleven years, I'm incredibly thankful to you. Your enthusiasm for each new book has helped me prove that you *can* write a romance series that features the same couple in every book. Sam and Nick's story is just getting started, and I can't wait for what's next.

xoxo

Marie

~

New First Family Series Characters
Teresa Howard, National Security Advisor
Martin Ruskin, Secretary of State
Tobias Jennings, Secretary of Defense
Reginald Cox, Attorney General
LeRoy Chastain, White House butler
Lieutenant Commander Juan Rodriguez, USN, military aide, nuclear football
Vernon, Secret Service Agent on Sam's detail
Jimmy, Secret Service Agent on Sam's detail
Jessica Sanford, Vice Presidential candidate
Gretchen Henderson, Vice Presidential candidate
Anthony Jones, White House butler
Army General Michael Wilson, chairman of the Joint Chiefs of Staff
Roland Daniels, White House butler
Cornelia, the Nelson's social secretary
Gideon Lawson, White House chief usher
Davida, White House hair stylist
Kendra, White House nail technician
Ginger, White House makeup artist

ALSO BY MARIE FORCE

Romantic Suspense Novels Available from Marie Force

The Fatal Series

One Night With You, *A Fatal Series Prequel Novella*

Book 1: Fatal Affair

Book 2: Fatal Justice

Book 3: Fatal Consequences

Book 3.5: Fatal Destiny, *the Wedding Novella*

Book 4: Fatal Flaw

Book 5: Fatal Deception

Book 6: Fatal Mistake

Book 7: Fatal Jeopardy

Book 8: Fatal Scandal

Book 9: Fatal Frenzy

Book 10: Fatal Identity

Book 11: Fatal Threat

Book 12: Fatal Chaos

Book 13: Fatal Invasion

Book 14: Fatal Reckoning

Book 15: Fatal Accusation

Book 16: Fatal Fraud

The First Family Series

Book 1: State of Affairs

Book 2: State of Grace

Contemporary Romances Available from Marie Force

The Wild Widows Series

Book 1: Someone Like You

The Gansett Island Series

Book 1: Maid for Love *(Mac & Maddie)*

Book 2: Fool for Love *(Joe & Janey)*

Book 3: Ready for Love *(Luke & Sydney)*

Book 4: Falling for Love *(Grant & Stephanie)*

Book 5: Hoping for Love *(Evan & Grace)*

Book 6: Season for Love *(Owen & Laura)*

Book 7: Longing for Love *(Blaine & Tiffany)*

Book 8: Waiting for Love *(Adam & Abby)*

Book 9: Time for Love *(David & Daisy)*

Book 10: Meant for Love *(Jenny & Alex)*

Book 10.5: Chance for Love, *A Gansett Island Novella (Jared & Lizzie)*

Book 11: Gansett After Dark *(Owen & Laura)*

Book 12: Kisses After Dark *(Shane & Katie)*

Book 13: Love After Dark *(Paul & Hope)*

Book 14: Celebration After Dark *(Big Mac & Linda)*

Book 15: Desire After Dark *(Slim & Erin)*

Book 16: Light After Dark *(Mallory & Quinn)*

Book 17: Victoria & Shannon (Episode 1)

Book 18: Kevin & Chelsea (Episode 2)

A Gansett Island Christmas Novella

Book 19: Mine After Dark *(Riley & Nikki)*

Book 20: Yours After Dark *(Finn & Chloe)*

Book 21: Trouble After Dark *(Deacon & Julia)*

Book 22: Rescue After Dark *(Mason & Jordan)*

Book 23: Blackout After Dark *(full cast)*

Book 24: Temptation After Dark *(Gigi & Cooper) Coming Soon*

The Green Mountain Series

Book 1: All You Need Is Love *(Will & Cameron)*

Book 2: I Want to Hold Your Hand *(Nolan & Hannah)*

Book 3: I Saw Her Standing There *(Colton & Lucy)*

Book 4: And I Love Her *(Hunter & Megan)*

Novella: You'll Be Mine *(Will & Cam's Wedding)*

Book 5: It's Only Love *(Gavin & Ella)*

Book 6: Ain't She Sweet *(Tyler & Charlotte)*

The Butler, Vermont Series

(Continuation of Green Mountain)

Book 1: Every Little Thing *(Grayson & Emma)*

Book 2: Can't Buy Me Love *(Mary & Patrick)*

Book 3: Here Comes the Sun *(Wade & Mia)*

Book 4: Till There Was You *(Lucas & Dani)*

Book 5: All My Loving *(Landon & Amanda)*

Book 6: Let It Be *(Lincoln & Molly)*

Book 7: Come Together *(Noah & Brianna)*

The Treading Water Series

Book 1: Treading Water

Book 2: Marking Time

Book 3: Starting Over

Book 4: Coming Home

Book 5: Finding Forever

The Miami Nights Series

Book 1: How Much I Feel *(Carmen & Jason)*

Book 2: How Much I Care *(Maria & Austin)*

Book 3: How Much I Love *(Dee & Wyatt)*

The Quantum Series

Book 1: Virtuous *(Flynn & Natalie)*

Book 2: Valorous *(Flynn & Natalie)*

Book 3: Victorious *(Flynn & Natalie)*

Book 4: Rapturous *(Addie & Hayden)*

Book 5: Ravenous *(Jasper & Ellie)*

Book 6: Delirious *(Kristian & Aileen)*

Book 7: Outrageous *(Emmett & Leah)*

Book 8: Famous *(Marlowe & Sebastian)*

Single Titles

Five Years Gone

One Year Home

Sex Machine

Sex God

Georgia on My Mind

True North

The Fall

The Wreck

Love at First Flight

Everyone Loves a Hero

Line of Scrimmage

Historical Romance Available from Marie Force

The Gilded Series

Book 1: Duchess by Deception

Book 2: Deceived by Desire

ABOUT THE AUTHOR

Marie Force is the *New York Times* bestselling author of contemporary romance, romantic suspense and erotic romance. Her series include Gansett Island, Fatal, Treading Water, Butler Vermont, Quantum and Miami Nights.

Her books have sold more than 10 million copies worldwide, have been translated into more than a dozen languages and have appeared on the *New York Times* bestseller more than 30 times. She is also a *USA Today* and *Wall Street Journal* bestseller, as well as a Speigel bestseller in Germany.

Her goals in life are simple—to finish raising two happy, healthy, productive young adults, to keep writing books for as long as she possibly can and to never be on a flight that makes the news.

Join Marie's mailing list on her website at *marieforce.com* for news about new books and upcoming appearances in your area. Follow her on Facebook at *www.Facebook.com/MarieForceAuthor* and on Instagram at *www.instagram.com/marieforceauthor/*. Contact Marie at *marie@marieforce.com*.

Made in the USA
Las Vegas, NV
01 May 2021